# The
# winter oak

James A. Hetley

**ACE BOOKS, NEW YORK**

**THE BERKLEY PUBLISHING GROUP**
**Published by the Penguin Group**
**Penguin Group (USA) Inc.**
**375 Hudson Street, New York, New York 10014, USA**
Penguin Group (Canada), 90 Eglinton Avenue East, Suite 700, Toronto, Ontario M4P 2Y3, Canada
(a division of Pearson Penguin Canada Inc.)
Penguin Books Ltd., 80 Strand, London WC2R 0RL, England
Penguin Group Ireland, 25 St. Stephen's Green, Dublin 2, Ireland (a division of Penguin Books Ltd.)
Penguin Group (Australia), 250 Camberwell Road, Camberwell, Victoria 3124, Australia
(a division of Pearson Australia Group Pty. Ltd.)
Penguin Books India Pvt. Ltd., 11 Community Centre, Panchsheel Park, New Delhi—110 017, India
Penguin Group (NZ), Cnr. Airborne and Rosedale Roads, Albany, Auckland 1310, New Zealand
(a division of Pearson New Zealand Ltd.)
Penguin Books (South Africa) (Pty.) Ltd., 24 Sturdee Avenue, Rosebank, Johannesburg 2196,
South Africa

Penguin Books Ltd., Registered Offices: 80 Strand, London WC2R 0RL, England

This is a work of fiction. Names, characters, places, and incidents either are the product of the author's imagination or are used fictitiously, and any resemblance to actual persons, living or dead, business establishments, events, or locales is entirely coincidental. The publisher does not have any control over and does not assume any responsibility for author or third-party websites or their content.

THE WINTER OAK

An Ace Book / published by arrangement with the author

PRINTING HISTORY
Ace trade paperback edition / November 2004
Ace mass market edition / November 2005

Copyright © 2004 by James A. Hetley.
Cover art by Lori Earley.
Cover design by Rita Frangie.
Interior text design by Kristin del Rosario.

ISBN: 0-441-01255-8

ACE
Ace Books are published by The Berkley Publishing Group,
a division of Penguin Group (USA) Inc.,
375 Hudson Street, New York, New York 10014.
ACE and the "A" design are trademarks belonging to Penguin Group (USA) Inc.

PRINTED IN THE UNITED STATES OF AMERICA

10  9  8  7  6  5  4  3  2  1

*Ace Books by James A. Hetley*

THE SUMMER COUNTRY
THE WINTER OAK
DRAGON'S EYE

"After reading *The Winter Oak*, I was stunned by the depth of the continuing story started in *The Summer Country*. The dark, twisted, urban fantasy only expanded to another level while allowing us readers to enjoy the ride . . . The realism further validates James Hetley as not your average fantasy author. While most fantasy books rely on the fantastic to convey interesting stories, Hetley relies on the underbelly of what we all have come to believe in as real . . . *The Winter Oak* is earthy, dark, and yet redeeming all at once." —*SF Site*

"Fans of urban fantasy in the style of Charles de Lint and Tanya Huff should enjoy [*The Winter Oak*]." —*Library Journal*

"Very well written. The words flow smoothly and freely. The characters and the settings are cleanly and carefully drawn. Each setting, from luxurious castle to stone dungeon to sterile hospital to dreary nursing home to open forest, is perfectly described; not too sparse and not overly emphasizing the detail. His characters are distinct and interesting, especially the dragon." —*SFRevu*

"Hetley still has the power to knock convention off its blocks." —*Locus*

"[Hetley is a] talented writer . . . This is adult literature at its finest . . . the dragons in these novels are very, very cool. And none that you've encountered elsewhere . . . I am looking forward to more books in the series . . . *The Winter Oak* is that rarity of sequels, one that perfectly builds off the previous novel. James Hetley can be very proud of the story he has created—it's that good." —*Green Man Review*

"Readers tired of stereotypical fantasy fairylands will find [*The Winter Oak*] rather refreshing. This enchanted land is as dark and gritty as any urban landscape, which should appeal to fans of Tanya Huff and Laurell K. Hamilton." —*Romantic Times*

*continued . . .*

# one

—◆—

DAVID GRITTED HIS teeth and followed Jo's hand through the darkness. He assumed the rest of her was still attached. Damp, clammy nothings brushed past his face and hissed in his ears. Phantoms teased the corners of his eyes, shapes black against black, yellow against yellow, flowing through the ghost images his brain played to give substance to emptiness.

The touches, sounds, and shapes plucked at his fear like virtuosi on overtaut harp strings. The air smelled of sodden graveyards, thick and rank in his nose and against his skin as if he had to swim through it.

*Under the Sidhe hill,* he thought. *Three steps between magic and reality.* Magic with teeth and claws as long as his forearm, magic that Jo carried in her genes.

He felt cold sweat between his shoulder blades and trickling down his sides under his arms. This was taking *far* too long. When Brian had brought him to the Summer Country, it had been step, step, step, and they were there, sunshine and green grass and warm sweet breezes contrasting with the icy mess of winter in Maine. David hadn't even had time to be scared. That had happened later.

Jo's hand gripped his, tight enough that his bones creaked. It tugged, and he took another step and another. The darkness held firm. Hot breath chuckled in his left ear, and feathery fingers brushed across his eyes like someone testing ripe fruit in the market. He flinched.

Jo scared him, but not enough to give her up. The *other* Old Ones, Dougal and Sean and Fiona, they were a different can of worms. No wonder Irish tales painted the Sidhe as lacking heart and soul. Anything they *could* do, they *would* do.

Tunnels seemed to open to one side or the other in the black, wet air, felt or heard in receding echoes rather than seen. Despair flooded over him. They were lost.

And then orange light flickered in the corner of his eye, a rectangle barred by darkness. He blinked, his brain whirled and reset, and he recognized the window in Jo's living room. Venetian blinds, half open, with the sodium streetlight beyond.

Night, not the perpetual velvet blackness of the space between the worlds.

Home.

He sagged with relief, hugging the small woman who had just dragged him headlong through the nothingness. She shivered in his arms.

"Jo, you may be the sexiest woman alive, but sometimes you scare the shit out of me. I swear you'd teach a kid to swim by throwing him off the dock."

She stepped back half a pace in his arms, enough room to wipe her sleeve across her forehead. "No. But I never *did* have training wheels on my bike."

"What took so long?"

He felt her head shake in the gloom. "So long? It was three steps, just like Brian said."

"Next time, try shorter steps. I feel like I just chased you for half a mile." He paused and took a deep breath, calming his heart. "Cancel that. Ain't gonna *be* any 'next time.' I'll take the rest of my fairy tales out of books."

She seemed to be looking at him funny, as if she was having second thoughts about getting tied up with a pureblood human coward. But he'd never claimed to be anything else. He wasn't a natural warrior like Brian, handling weapons like they'd been forged to fit his hands, running ten miles around the walls of Maureen's castle each morning without breaking a sweat. Guitar players don't need that kind of training.

She shook her head, sniffed, and started looking around. The Old Blood had sensitive noses.

"Oh, *shit*. The garbage." And dishes petrified in the sink, milk curdled in the fridge, last night's lasagna two or three weeks gone and furry. He'd walked over to Maureen's place to check with Brian, because Jo hadn't come home that night. And they'd stepped out of the world without coming back here. God only knew what mutated life-forms now lurked in the potato salad.

Jo groped for the light switch and flipped it on. David blinked like an owl at the sudden glare, catching flashes of the room as his eyes adjusted. Something didn't look right, but he couldn't pin it down.

Dishes waited in the drainer, clean. The garbage pail was empty, with a fresh liner. Jo stepped over to the refrigerator and swung it open. No milk, no meat, no fresh vegetables or cheese, just a few unopened cans of soda and the like. Jo shut the door and stood staring at the answering machine. The lid was up and the tape cassette gone. She pulled out the drawer underneath the phone, fumbled for her emergency cash envelope, and checked it. It looked full.

"Damnedest burglars I've ever seen, washing dishes and leaving the money."

She stared at the phone for a moment and stood like a statue, plotting her next move. That girl could be ice when she wanted to, just like the Sidhe, no reaction or a flip comment where a sane person would dash around in panic. David headed for the apartment door, to check with the Mendozas and use their phone.

Yellow plastic streamers barred the door, POLICE LINE in reversed letters in the hall light. "Jo . . ."

He felt her behind his shoulder, tallying up the evidence. "How long *have* we been gone?"

*Brigadoon. Rip Van Winkle. Spend a night in Faerie and find a lifetime has passed when you return.*

David clenched his fist and gnawed on a knuckle, staring at the door. A glued paper seal had joined the frame to the metal door, someone's signature now split by a rip through the middle. Proof the door had been opened, tampering with evidence. Jo studied it, calmly adding another tickmark to her checklist.

*She's inhuman.* He shuddered, realizing that the phrase meant just what it said.

"Okay, we need some excuse for opening the door, some way to toss off a few weeks without a story," she said decisively.

She glanced up. The stairwell light flashed blue and went dark, filament burned out. She flipped the kitchen light off, plunging them back into night. Enough light filtered up from the second floor so that David could see her climbing through the tape, leaving it in place. He followed her, numb, and pulled the door closed behind him.

She ticked off one finger on her right hand. "First thing we do, we buy a pint of booze and split it. We're drunk. Dark hall, drunk, we didn't notice the tape and seal in time. No criminal intent, no crime."

Second finger. "We've been drunk or stoned for weeks, no idea how long. Off on a trip with Brian and Mo, celebrating. They're engaged, we're engaged, big party, got crazy and took it on the road—out West, down South, Canada, don't have a clue where and when, you and I tell different stories, no problem."

Third finger. "They've just dropped us off, Brian drove away, no idea where they're going. I've got to get back to my job, you've got gigs to play. Gonna be a hell of a hangover."

THE CHAIRS HURT. David couldn't recall anyone mentioning that in the detective movies. And they weren't even "under interrogation," just sitting in a cluttered detective's office across the government-issue gray steel desk from a polite cop. Everyone had been polite, and he and Jo were still together rather than split apart to see if their stories matched. He wondered how long that would last.

He blinked and forced his eyes to focus. "Hey, what's this about, anyway?"

The man in blue wrinkled his nose with disgust. The collar tabs called him a sergeant, square body with a bit of a donut belly and buzz-cut brown hair and medium-dark skin, maybe Naskeag or black genes in there somewhere.

David blinked again and focused on the name tag, working his way through half a pint of vodka. Getchell, that was the name. Sergeant Getchell. No ethnic clues there.

"Family tried to call you, urgent. No answer for weeks, so they asked us to check. We went in with a key from your landlord."

Jo squirmed in her chair, glancing across at David. "Weeks? *Weeks?* We've only been gone a week or two!"

The cop frowned. He looked like he was giving a blood alcohol test by eye and nose. "Ms. Pierce, our records show that your last day at work was February fifteenth. Same for your sister. Last time anyone saw any of you was the next morning. Today's date is April thirteenth. I think your people had a right to be concerned."

"Shit."

Jo looked pale, worse than her normal fair skin. Scared. Now the freckles stood out like a rash. But that date explained the shrunken snowbanks along the road that had graced their walk to the cop shop. Mud Season, Maine's least lovely face.

The silence stretched out until David felt compelled to fill it. "Why the crime scene tape? We were out celebrating. What's wrong with that?"

"Food rotting, mail piling up, looked suspicious. So we called in a lab team. The forensics guys came up with blood between the kitchen tiles. A lot of blood, looked like, then somebody had scrubbed it up. Maybe murder. We secured the scene in case the DA wanted more tests."

Oh. Brian's blood, from when Fiona had set a street gang on him, trying to capture him. He'd staggered back to Maureen for help. But they didn't want to talk about that . . .

"Brian cut himself, bad. Kitchen knife. You go into their apartment, as well? Find the old bandages, same blood type?"

The cop nodded, reluctantly. "Yeah. Forensics says there's not much doubt, blood type is rare as hell. But we still want to talk to this 'Brian Albion' of yours. Some street rats got beat up in an alley. One died. They identified him, *by name.* Kids like those, we wouldn't take their word for what day it was. Myself, even if the story's true, I think he's done us a favor. But we still need to talk to him, to close the file."

*Right,* thought David. *And you think I'm drunk enough to believe that. Then you'll sell me some prime Florida swampland.*

The sergeant consulted his notes. "You say you spent last night in Toronto. Can you give me a name for the motel?"

David glanced at Jo and shook his head. She waved it off. "Wrong. Last night was Syracuse. Toronto was last week.

Brian had to return a car to this friend of his. Apartment, not motel."

He burped and tasted recycled vodka. Damn good thing there wasn't any law against *walking* under the influence. "No. Car was in *Detroit. Toronto* was that big blue crew-cab pickup."

The cop was getting pissed. "Look, my notes say that you claim to have rented a blue pickup in Kentucky. Is that the same vehicle?"

Jo blinked and stared at David. "We were in *Kentucky?*"

David nodded and then shook his head, trying to clear it. "Fort Knox. Brian wanted to see the old tanks and stuff at the Armor Museum." He flopped a hand at the police sergeant. "Brian was in the British Army for years. Officer, Gurkha Scouts, SAS, all that macho stuff."

The cop's frown deepened. "British Consul says those records are . . . confused. There seem to have been three or four different 'Captain Brian Albions' at different times, going back to the Second World War. Some embassy people would like a word or two with him after we get through. You *sure* you don't know where to find him?"

David thought he smelled the smoke of burning bridges. "Look, are we charged with anything? Do we need a lawyer?"

He almost *saw* thoughts chasing across the sergeant's forehead: *They've asked for a lawyer. They're drunk and incompetent. There are so many contradictions in this statement, it would be laughed out of court. Whole frigging thing stinks.*

The cop shuffled papers in their file. "You've got a citation here, 'Possession of a usable amount of marijuana.' Civil fine. That's it."

Hell. Two joints in his guitar case. Three, and they might have tried to stretch it to "Intent to distribute," a felony. Anyway, another hundred bucks shot to hell.

The cop's chair groaned as he leaned back, his face a study in disgust. "Time was, I could toss both of you into cells for the night, let you sober up. Can't do that anymore. Bleeding hearts." He made the phrase sound like cussing. "But it's a slow night, and I don't have anything better to do. We all can just sit here and talk until you decide to tell this numb old cop something *close* to the truth."

His eyes narrowed, and he squinted first at David and then at Jo. "Now let's start in from the top. What kind of car is Albion driving?"

Jo swayed in her chair, face shiny with sweat. "I don't feel good." She lurched forward and vomited across the desk, drenching papers and the sergeant's lap. He jumped up and swore, inventively and at length, while he rescued their file. The reek of puked alcohol filled the room, and David's stomach churned in sympathy.

The cop stood behind the desk and shook his head, jaw clenched. "I come on duty at three o'clock tomorrow. I want your butts in those chairs when I walk through that door. Clean, sober, and ready to talk. And I want a story we can *check*. Understand?"

David nodded. The sergeant pulled out a small manila envelope and tossed it to David. "Answering machine tape. Get her out of here. Call her family."

"Can we use the apartment?"

"Hell, go ahead. Just get out of my office!"

The air outside was cold and damp and raw, threatening rain or sleet, stinking of four months of winter filth finally surfacing again. It didn't help him any in fighting back the queasy vodka that surged at his throat. But Jo's timing had been too damn perfect, and she had seemed to aim. Even stone drunk, the Old Blood ruled her.

Shadows lurked away from the streetlights, hiding furtive things with fangs. He shivered, remembering the fear of stepping between the worlds.

Jo lifted her head and glanced around. She grinned up at him. "Did I get anything on you? Those notes he took aren't going to be worth a hell of a lot, once he gets them cleaned up."

She seemed to be cold sober. He wondered just how much she had . . . *witched* . . . that cop.

SOMETHING SHOOK HIM hard enough to rattle his brain. It hurt. His eyelids seemed to be stuck shut, and his hands missed their target when he tried to knuckle the glue away.

"Wake *up,* damn you!" The voice echoed from one ear to the other, across a cavern full of pain.

He pried one eye open. Jo. She had a pitcher of water in her hand, aimed at his face. He ducked, and the sudden move made the room spin around him. He grabbed the sofa to make the cushion hold still. His stomach heaved.

"Never again. No more booze. Done."

"Screw that. We've got problems."

He tried thinking for a moment. It didn't work. "Who cleaned the place up?"

"Maria Mendoza, you idiot. The cops let her come in after they did their thing. Just kept an eye on her while she cleaned."

The neighbor woman. Self-defense, probably could smell the garbage through the walls.

David concentrated on breathing slowly, not rushing his nose and throat and lungs. Jo looked like she'd just walked out of a beauty parlor, bright eyes and every strand of hair in place, damn her.

She waved the pitcher again. It rattled. She'd dumped *ice cubes* in the water.

He struggled to sit up, holding his head in his hands. He felt like he'd just been on a month-long bender, just like they'd told the cops. She backed off a step.

"Problems? That citation? For the grass? No worse than a parking ticket. And Brian doesn't give a damn about the cops."

"I played that tape from the answering machine."

David forced his eyes to focus. She looked mad. Mad and grim, with a touch of grief. "What's wrong?"

"Mom fell, she's in the hospital. That's why Dad was trying to find us. Fucking fifty years old, and she had a stroke and fell down the stairs. Can't talk, can't move her left arm or leg."

"Shit."

"And I've been fired. No job."

"Shit."

"And Dé hAoine has a new guitar man. They've played four gigs without you."

David staggered to his feet, took the pitcher of ice water from her, and finger-danced along a wall to find the bathroom. He stood in the tub, clothes and all, and dumped the water on his head. An ice cube slithered down the back of his shirt and hung up against his spine. It almost helped.

Of course, if he *really* wanted to sober up, all he had to do was think about that dragon. It haunted him.

# two

—⁓—

KHE'SHA BROODED OVER the skull of his mate. He coiled his body around the nest mound, a living wall of obsidian scales looming taller than a man above the murky water and deep marsh grass.

Sha'khe was dead, her song cut short between one word and the next. He flicked out his tongue and caressed the sharp ridges of her crest, stroking up the long slope of her muzzle from her nose. She'd always enjoyed that, stretching flat in the sun with a rumbling sigh while he groomed her scales. He remembered how she'd relax, the membrane rising slowly across her great yellow eye as she drowsed.

Now she was gone, murdered, her bones scattered in a long cold drift through the forest where she had fallen. Her kin should have carried ribs and thighbones and the great links of her spine to the hidden bone-cave and sung her deeds each step of the way in a strong deep-noted poem that distilled her life into its essence, but her nest-mates lived in another land; her clan lived in another land. Her bones should lie with her ancestors in another land.

Her kind, his kind, did not belong in this land. He hated it. He hated the humans and Old Ones who had brought them here and forced them to guard a grim, gray castle instead of the bright crimson Temples of the Moon.

<I will kill them,> he mind-spoke to her empty skull. <I will rend their flesh and feed it to our young. I will tear at their keep until the stones lie scattered like autumn leaves and their bones gleam cold and white under the moon. They all will die. No one will sing their deeds and deaths. They will have never been.>

He tested the mound's warmth with his tongue, thrusting gently at both the sun side and the shade, and then rested his sensitive throat across the surface to judge the heat that flowed from deep around the eggs. He pawed dry marsh-grass over the shaded side to hold in the heat of the leaves that rotted there, warming the clutch. He studied the sky, afraid of rain—the long, soaking rains that could flood the marsh until dark water swallowed the nest and killed the tiny dragonets inside their eggs.

Dragons grew slowly, and the seasons turned slowly. The season for nesting had finally come. Now Khe'sha guarded the end of Sha'khe's song. Twelve of the mottled brown eggs lay buried, near the time of hatching. Twelve dragons alone, far from their ancestors, far from the Celestial Temple and the Sages. Perhaps six or eight or ten would live to taste air and see the sky. Then what?

The strongest *might* survive to breed. With luck. But who would they join their souls to, in this land of puny apes? Who would teach them the songs, the long sonorous history of clan and bloodline, the deep thoughts and resplendent deeds that echoed through the hills and valleys and grew with each generation? They would live alone, and die alone, as he would die alone.

Only the nest remained, his life and heart. He would never take another mate. The dragon bond tied a pair for centuries, their bodies and thoughts mirrored like their hatchling half-names were mirrored around the deep booming sound in the gut those clothed monkeys couldn't make. A dragon pair grew together through the ages until one could not live without the other. Only the nest kept Khe'sha alive, now that Sha'khe was dead.

*I will see the hatchlings leave the nest and hunt. I will teach them the songs I know. I will have revenge.*

His belly rumbled. A huge body needed huge quantities of food. Khe'sha uncoiled himself from the nest mound. He slithered through the black water of the marsh, over muck deeper than a man, through thorn tangles that scratched harmlessly back across his scales but that would claw bare flesh to ribbons, twisting and backtracking on his own trail to create a maze of traps and blind but deadly alleys. A beast of his bulk left a mark anyone could see. He made sure that trying to follow it would be foolish and dangerous.

He came to open water, cool after the sun on his black scales, cooler still in the depths. He sank lower, swimming slow and sinuous like a snake, controlling his breath to hold his eyes and nostrils just awash. The surface barely rippled with his passage.

Something moved in the water at the marsh's edge, head dipping and rising, a plant-eater pulling up roots and leaves, chewing, wading on, dipping, rising, shaking loose a spray of water, chewing. It was large enough to make a meal, large enough to be worth the hunt, slow and stupid and unafraid. Khe'sha lined up his body on his prey, exhaled, and sank beneath the water. He floated through the darkness, a shadow within the shadows, touched bottom, crouched low and slithered on across the muck until he felt air touch his crest, and threw his bulk forward.

His teeth slashed into meat, hot and salty and sweet, and he clamped the weight of it in his jaws and rolled. Bones cracked. His prey struggled for an instant, shuddered, and fell limp. Khe'sha whipped his neck once more to be sure, snapping more bones, tearing at the bottom of the marsh and flinging muck and blood-tinged water in wide sheets.

He rose out of the water and examined his kill. It was new to him, a body the size of the "cattle" the Master used to bring but with longer legs, suited for wading. It would fill his belly for days. He hoped more of them would come.

His teeth sheared through meat and bone, and he swallowed. Meat, bone, hide, hooves—his belly didn't care. He swallowed again, and again, and again. The beast vanished. Khe'sha licked the blood-soaked marsh grass, savoring the bitterness of leaves under the salt of the blood. His belly swelled and quieted. He rumbled contentment.

"You have enjoyed my gift?"

Khe'sha spun in his tracks, water boiling around his tail. A dark woman stood above him on a low rise of land, just slightly out of reach—olive skin, black hair, her clothing dark smoke gray. He tested the air again with his tongue. No, not human. She was an Old One, one of those who came before the humans. No matter. He eased himself onto land.

<Gift?>

He slid farther up the slope. Humans or Old Ones—the only difference was that Old Ones could draw on the Power of this land. Both were his enemies; both were his prey.

She smiled at him, faintly mocking. "Don't waste your effort, love. I can move even faster than you. And we aren't enemies. Do enemies bring food? Was that moose the gift of an enemy?"

So that prey was called "moose." No wonder he'd never tasted its blood before. Someone had brought it here, to the edge of his marsh. He studied the dark witch. She claimed to have brought the "moose" as a gift, but his kind knew how to read truth. This Old One tasted slippery and evasive. She kept many secrets.

She smiled again, as if she read his thoughts. "There is a

saying in many lands: 'The enemy of my enemy is my friend.'
I hear vengeance in your thoughts."

&lt;Then you hear well. There is another saying in the Celestial Temple: "The friend of my enemy is my enemy." I
smell your kinship with those I hate. Why should I not eat
you, along with them?&gt;

She laughed. "Because you can't, love." And then her face
turned grim, and he sensed truth in her thoughts. "I also
seek revenge. I had a brother, a twin, as close to me as a
dragon's mate. His bones lie near to your mate's in the forest. His killers also live in that stone house that crowns the
hill. Kinship or not, they owe me blood and pain. For that
and other things."

He eased back, letting his full belly float in the shallows.
He felt the inner warmth that made him lazy for days after
feeding, that called him to bask in the sun and drowse until
hunger woke him again to hunt.

&lt;You, too, seek revenge?&gt;

"We think much alike, your kind and mine. Not surpris-
ing, since our dreams built these lands of legend and filled
them with our thoughts. Your kind and mine have walked
together since long before the humans drove us from the
earth. The Sages of the Celestial Temple are my cousins."

Once again, her words walked the edge between truth
and lie. Khe'sha remembered the Sages. They spoke with
less malice and more calm. Their words danced in the sunlight while hers wore darkness like a cloak.

&lt;What help can you offer? I have smelled the new rulers.
They smell of trees and the ways of dangerous men; they
smell of old songs and the ecstasies of breeding. I taste nothing of the Master's Power that bound us to his bidding.
They are weak. I do not need your help for my revenge.&gt;

"Ah, but they killed your mate, for all that taste of weakness. They killed the Master, and my brother. Don't think
them weak. They have strength in ways you can't imagine,

ways I can fight if we make alliance. We'll need subtlety as well as strength, if we're to taste their blood."

Khe'sha heard more than she said. He tasted the memory of traps that turned on the ones who set them, of plots twisted to ruin and power hidden and weakness destroying strength. This dark witch breathed out the smell of treachery. Such allies were dangerous.

But Sha'khe was dead. The new rulers of the keep had murdered her. And he did not care if he lived past his revenge. Khe'sha dipped his head and narrowed his eyes in the mode of watchful distrust.

<The enemy of my enemy is my friend.>

He could eat this one afterward.

Her smile also tasted of wariness. "I'll need time to cast my nets around them. We'll need other allies, you and I. We'll need to divide them, bard and warrior and redheaded witch-sisters, set them each by themselves with their backs bared to knife and fang. You have great strength, but you'd attack a castle the same way you took that moose. Trust me for guile, love. Trust me for guile."

*That* carried the flavor of truth. Khe'sha slithered backward until he floated free of the marsh muck. The nest called to him, and the slow drowse of a full belly in the sun. Dragons were the most patient race in all the lands. Their plots spanned centuries. The songs told of revenge passed down through generations and finally brought to hatching when even the names of the first enemies were no more than echoes.

# three

———⚡———

FIONA CLOSED HER eyes and breathed deep through her nose, savoring the blended aromas of dew on the meadow grass, of clover and hedgerow flowers and the hidden traps she'd set. Her fields pleased her, neat and smoothly rolling and laid out like an artist's dream of farm country. No ragged stubble after harvest or bare soil newly planted, no manure piles or stinking farting cattle and bleating sheep. Neat and sweet-smelling and totally controlled.

So much cleaner than the carrion reek of that dragon, a meat-eater who'd never heard of flossing. So much cleaner than the swamp where the beast laired, foul and tangled and sulfurous with rotting muck.

The other dragon hadn't stunk like that, the one Brian and the human killed. She remembered a damp whiff of vinegar the one time she'd talked to it, no more. But Dougal had liked to keep his guards hungry, keep them sharp. He'd fed short rations to his falcons and hunting cats and hounds, and none of his slaves were fat.

The female dragon probably hadn't eaten in weeks,

maybe months if they had metabolisms like a snake's. Fiona's mind poked at this intellectual puzzle, planning some research as a diversion while she waited for her revenge to mature and bear fruit.

Perhaps the dragons secreted some enzymes in their saliva? Or maybe they harbored a strain of that "flesh-eating bacteria" that humans splashed across their tabloid covers—something that digested the scraps of meat between those serrated dagger fangs? She could work with that, do some genetic engineering on the hawthorns and roses of her hedge. They already held venom, but this gave the possibility of an exquisite refinement.

She smiled at the thought of a trespasser brushing up against a thorn and then suffering as the scratch festered into stinking necrosis that spread and rotted his living flesh until he died after weeks of agony. Other Old Ones feared her cottage, feared her lands and her defenses. They had reason.

Or they *had* feared her. She'd lost a battle, lost to Maureen. News spread with the wind in the Summer Country. Fiona shook her head. Appearance meant more than reality in this land. Now she *appeared* weak. She had to prove her Power again, crush Maureen and the rest, spread fear close on the heels of the news of that defeat. In the Summer Country, the second-place trophy was a grave.

Then she smiled. She'd thought of the dragon as a tool—planned to destroy that nest in a way that fanned his hatred of the old keep on the hill. Now she needed to twist her plan into collecting a specimen or two from the hatchlings. But she'd still have to lay the blame at Maureen's gate. That would be a challenge, almost entertaining. A successful plot could be a work of art.

The witch considered the grass under her boots. Hatred seethed back at her. A stem searched up toward her ankle, touched the smooth gray leather, and crumbled into dust.

She walked on, leaving a blackened footprint where her field had attempted to rebel.

Really, she ought to thank little Maureen. The Summer Country had grown boring in the past few decades—no challenges, no enemies worth noticing. Dougal had been beneath contempt. Now that redheaded bitch had made life interesting again. Fiona had almost forgotten the joys of plotting, planning, slyly seeking allies and pawns for a Byzantine revenge.

The grass turned away from pain and sought its own targets elsewhere. She'd woven enough intelligence into all her plants so that they served as guardians. Now their vibrations told her of other footfalls sneaking across the fields and into the hedge maze surrounding her cottage. Fiona smiled again, her eyes slitting like a cat drowsing with dreams of mice. Someone was making a *big* mistake.

Maureen had set the hedge free and turned it against its owner. Now Fiona held a tighter leash and the hawthorns and roses whimpered while they did exactly what she told them. That intruder would never reach her garden.

She walked on, feeling the pulse of her fields through the soles of her boots, beating the boundaries of her land. Dougal had been so predictable, sending his wildwood to push against the ancient dry-stone wall that separated his forest from her domain, sending his marsh to spread dark water across the lowland grasses.

He'd dealt in blunt force, wielding a mace in their battles. Maureen used a rapier, thrusting skillfully. She seduced plants like she'd seduced Brian from Fiona's binding spell. Expect the unexpected, Fiona had learned. Look for the trap. Fiona had studied her enemy's past and present, after first misjudging her. Maureen's damaged sexuality had been her weakest point. Who would have thought she'd turn to it for a weapon?

Fiona ran her fingers over the rough bark of a pasture oak, thick-trunked and tall and glossy green over grass studded with shamrocks, a landmark within a stone's throw of the no-man's-land and Maureen's forest. Fiona had never truly owned the tree, never bent it to her will. It had dominated this corner field for centuries before she claimed the cottage as her own, and its taproot bored deep beyond her reach into the water and Power of the land. But she'd controlled it, limited its influence.

Now acorns sprouted in the turf, far beyond the spread of its branches as if it had flung them wide to free them from a struggle with long-established roots, doubled leaves and doubled again as the wildwood leaped the stone wall to extend its Power. They'd crammed years of growth into the space of the few days since she'd last walked this line.

Fiona rubbed her belly, over the baby growing there. She used the same twists of time, making days do the work of weeks while her Power swelled as the child swelled within her. Even if Maureen learned what pregnancy meant to the Old Blood, she would never dream that danger rushed on her so fast.

But those tiny oaks had to go. Fiona squatted down in the grass and ran her fingers through the cool dampness of its weave. She summoned her Power and gathered the plants to her will. The turf heaved as if snakes wrestled underneath, and the seedling trees toppled. Leaves withered and crumbled before her eyes, their slow death compressed into seconds by the same sort of magic that had sped them from the seed. Again Fiona smiled, breathing in the bitter oak tannin of their rotting, letting the wildwood see her teeth.

She searched her deadly spiderweb for the touch of her hedge, found the fierce glee of hounds that had brought the fox to bay. The trap had closed, walling her enemy into a tightening noose of green. No, *enemies*. The brambles told of two pockets, two knots of sweat and fear and hatred. The thorns had drawn blood. She asked the grasses under her hand, and they told her the guests tasted of Old Blood instead of human. Her enemies grew bold and foolish.

Mostly foolish. Of all the Old Ones walking the green grass of the Summer Country, only Maureen and her sex-mad sister had the strength to break through that hedge and live. And the hedge would have remembered *their* distinctive taste. Maureen had used her own blood in the unbinding spell.

Fiona stood and stretched, a calculated pose smooth and supple like a cat rising, loosening and testing every single bone and muscle and tendon from whiskers to tail-tip, making sure her claws were sharp for the hunt. Her guests could wait. The hedge wouldn't kill them yet. And she might have a use for living bodies bound to her will. It depended on just who had underestimated her.

But they'd suffer, suffer in a way that would spread fear and rumor through the land. She had to dream up some form of exquisite, public humiliation that went beyond mere death. Otherwise there'd be twenty or thirty more following in their steps, today, tomorrow, next week. Just like the ravens feeding at the carcass of the fallen dragon.

Fiona strolled on, relaxed, her eyes measuring the dry-stone wall that separated her fields from the wildwood. Even the moss and lichen belonged to her. It formed the frame of her picture, her composition in green and brown and gray. One stone lay on the sod, pushed loose by the branches of a massive holly just within Maureen's lands.

That was wrong. The holly shouldn't be taking sides. He was an ancient force, almost a god ruling this corner of the forest. He'd never belonged to Dougal, just as the pasture oak had never belonged to Fiona.

She replaced the stone and wove a binding on it, using

moss and lichen as her threads. She stood for a moment and studied the holly, her eyes narrowed and a frown-line creasing her forehead.

No, she would never underestimate her enemy again.

THE HEDGE BARRED her way, thorn and branch and root, sullen, resentful after once tasting freedom. It remembered her defeat, just as the prisoners it held had thought they would find weakness replacing her former strength. She slid her mind into the tangle of thorns and pinched a bud here, a rootlet there, tightening the vascular structure of the stems until leaves knew the thirst of drought. She'd given the plants mind enough to feel fear.

The nearest rose nodded in surrender, spokes-flower for the whole. Gnarled hawthorns bent and shuffled aside, pulling greenbriar and blackthorn and bramble with them and opening a grassy path where none had existed a moment earlier.

The path cut through her maze, straight to a dense knot of green. As she strolled along, she felt quivering tension on each side, anticipation like a zoo at feeding time. She kept these plants starved for nitrogen and phosphorous, just as Dougal had kept his dragons hungry. Her hedge craved flesh and blood and bone. Maureen had been too soft to kill an enemy, but Fiona knew that the price of weakness was pain and slavery and death.

Leaves parted. They revealed a face, broad and brown and feral with wide eyes showing terror. They parted further and showed her a short body, stocky and lumpy with muscles, arms and legs wrapped in the hungry tangling vines that held the gnome-shape tight and waited for her will.

Fiona smiled. "So. 'Tis little Fergus that's come calling. Welcome to my cottage, love. Too bad you weren't invited."

Vines trembled as the gnome's muscles bunched and

relaxed and twisted. His strength and magic broke two of the greenbriar strands, but four new bindings whipped across and took their places. Two more spiraled around his throat and tightened. His eyes bulged and he fought for breath.

Again Fiona dipped her thoughts into the hedge. She found the other knot of vines and sent a summons. Screams answered it, and the rattle of thrashing branches as the plants lifted her second enemy from the ground and passed the body along new tunnels through the maze. She cocked her head at the sounds.

"A friend of yours, love? Sounds female, and too sweet-voiced to match your ugliness." Fiona relaxed the thorns and let him breathe again. Blood trickled down from deep scratches on his throat.

The hedge rustled as it lifted him, bringing him to eye-level so that she could talk more comfortably. "And what brings you courting death, and why shouldn't I be giving it to you and to your sweetheart?"

The gnome cursed and spat. "No *sweetheart*. Saw Cáitlin snooping around when I first walked through your fields. One of *your* kind, not mine." He struggled again, but the thorns gripped firm and he weakened steadily as she held him free of the earth that gave him strength.

"*Cáitlin?* Oh, that *would* be a pairing. I should bind you together with claws free and watch the flying fur, drop the both of you into a bull-pit and charge admission. But I've asked you a question, *love,* and you didn't answer. What brings you to your death?" She asked the vines to twitch around his neck, and they supplied the proper emphasis.

He calmed, saving his powers for a better chance. "You still owe me for the stones. Hearth and threshold, corner-stone and keystone to the arch, bound to your will and the harmony of your house. I spoke to them and carved them and set the spells, and you never paid. May their virtue turn against you as a thief!"

She laughed. "Virtue? Hearth and threshold lie cracked in two pieces, love, and the untrained child who broke them stepped through your spells and never felt the warding. *You* owe *me* for that failure, and you're a fool and worse to come asking for your pay."

"We had a bargain. 'Tis nae my fault you weren't strong enough to hold what others crafted."

She'd started to turn away from him, bored with the doomed gnome and this game of words. Then a thought crossed her mind and connected with memories and she turned back, measuring his face and build with her eyes. The match would do. Yes, she could *make* it do. "Strong enough? Bargain? In this land, you hold what you are strong enough to keep. I'm still alive. You're a failure, and your life belongs to me. Think hard on how much living's worth to you."

Leaves rustled and parted, and her other enemy surfaced through the high walls of the hedge. Fiona hung the woman upside down, elven face beside dwarf face, and studied olive skin drawn over high cheekbones, dark eyes, straight black hair tangled with leaves and matted by sweat. The body, too, slim and boyish, bound by vines and thorny briar. Yes, indeed, the match would do. Sometimes a limited gene-pool *could* be useful.

"Ah, the lovely Cáit has come to join our party. And what is it that *you'd* be wanting of me, love? I don't recall asking you to tea."

Cáitlin hung there on the hedge, head down and feet to the sky, dark face quiet but her eyes narrowed in hatred. Breezes touched the highest branches and then swirled down in a whirlwind as she summoned her own peculiar Powers. The thorn and bramble simply bent and spilled the attack in a wave of hissing leaves.

She frowned and shook her head in wry acceptance, up-side down. "You betrayed me. I should have known better than to trust *you* to hold an oath sworn by the Tree and by the Well."

Fiona stared at the woman for a moment, mind spinning down the branches of choice. Then she let a smile twitch the corners of her mouth. She'd play Cáitlin's game for long enough to learn its nature. "Remember the *exact* words, love. I said I'd help to bind sweet Kevin, and that I did. I never said I'd help you *keep* him. He made me a better offer."

Fiona stepped back from her enemies, and the hedge rustled as it created space for her. Thin tendrils wrapped around Cáitlin's neck and pressed tightly on the arteries, then matched that touch on Fergus, cutting off blood flow to each brain. Fiona held the plants' hunger in check; she didn't want her captives dead. Not yet.

She told the plants to relax a fraction, waited until thought returned to the glazed eyes, and smiled. "So you heard that I'd lost a battle, and came to pick the bones. Vultures circling over dead meat, you thought, the two of you. What should I be doing with you? Should I hang your rotting heads from my gateposts like Dougal would, a warning to all that come?"

Her eyes lost focus as she considered. It was strange, how well human science explained their race. Hybrids that lived were rare between the species, and fertile ones still rarer. Ten thousand years of mixing human and Old Blood brought forth those breeds that looked so much alike, the gnomes of earth and fair folk and dark elves. Those were the genes that lived. So Fergus looked much like Dougal, and Cáitlin looked much like Fiona or her dead twin. So Maureen looked like a twin to her older sister or to the young face her mother had long forgotten. Fiona shook her head, then nodded.

"So, loves, think deep. Do you live or do you die? Dying's such a simple thing. Living may cost more. Give me your blood in binding, your will to mine, your lives to mine, and you'll go on breathing the sweet air. Refuse and you'll feed the hunger of my maze. Think deep."

Fergus made a wry face, hanging there on her hedge like some shrike's prey impaled on a thorn. "Small choice you give us. 'Tis much like death, living as your slave. I've seen what it means. Yet I'll trade death later for death now. Maybe you'll lose."

Cáitlin nodded. "I'll cast my bet with his, hoping that this war of yours will end with your black heart silent and all your slaves set free. Think on that before you sleep and when you wake. She broke your hold once, half dead as she was. I'd not lay good money against her blood now that she's healthy."

Fiona wondered if Cáitlin was acting, or voicing her true thoughts for a change. Aer witches *were* notorious liars . . .

A quiet smile tugged at Fiona's lips. She couldn't resist taunting them, adding more acid to despair. "Ah, but you don't know all the changes to the balance. I have a large and scaly friend who also hungers for that blood. And then there's the tale told by my belly. I'm pregnant, love, with all that means for the Powers of our kind."

Both Cáitlin and Fergus blenched. Then the woman took a deep breath and swallowed. Her chin stiffened, and a grim defiance settled into her eyes. "Make good use of it while you have it, *love.* Soon enough that babe will be draining your Power rather than adding to it. Once it starts to breathe air and suck, you'll weaken to less than you ever were before. That's the price you pay for giving birth."

Fiona's smile broadened. "Maybe, love, maybe. Or maybe I'll swap the wee bairn into some human's cradle like a cuckoo and let *her* pay the price of motherhood. Then I'll go back and fetch my changeling when she's old enough to be worth the bother."

She reached out to run a finger along Cáitlin's cheek. "So make your choice, love—your will to mine, your heart to mine, your flesh and blood and bone to mine, sworn on that selfsame blood. Or die. It's your own free choice I'm offering to you, but you don't want me to get bored with waiting for your word. I might start thinking of other games to play."

Cáitlin squinched her eyes shut, took a deep breath, and nodded. Beside her, Fergus growled "choice" in a fashion that made it sound like cursing. Then he also nodded, with a bitter twist to his mouth as if he were chewing wormwood.

Fiona nodded back at her captives, smiling like a cat with a broken-winged bird trapped between her paws. "So. Say the words. You know the ritual as well as any."

She reached out a finger and gathered a drop of blood from Cáitlin's scratched cheek. The salty sweetness burned on her tongue as the Power of the binding flowed through it. A second touch brought the blood of Fergus with its faint tinge of earth and stone. Fiona cocked an eyebrow at her new slaves, willing them to speak the ritual even though the fetters were already woven.

In unison, hoarse-voiced, they whispered, "In return for the gift of my life, I pledge my thoughts, my deeds, my will, my flesh and blood and bone to Fiona of the Maze, whenever she requires them. I give my blood as token of my body, in bondage until she frees me or until death."

Then Fiona reached out again, both hands, taking Cáitlin's face between her palms and kneading flesh and bone as if they were clay and she the sculptor. The woman screamed and screamed and screamed again, her body and face molding into Sean's remembered image, a slim and androgynous twin mirror of Fiona's dark beauty. Pain-sweat sheened the new-formed mask when she was done, and tears tracked lines down Cáitlin's face.

Fiona smiled, and turned to Fergus. Her fingers traced scars into his body, white shiny welts and purple furrows of claw or fang trailing her fingers to show the beast-master's history and trade. His body flowed in subtle ways until

Dougal hung before her, trembling and weeping with terror at what she'd done. His shrieks of pain still echoed back from the hills. Perhaps Maureen would hear them from her tower and wonder at the meaning.

The dark witch stepped back and admired her handiwork. The warmth of creation washed over her, and she relaxed into it. Flesh *could* be clay, in the hands of a skilled witch. Doomed clay, but molding it could hold the same fascination as the more lasting sculpture that was her garden realm.

"I'll add one more touch," she said, "and that's the easy part. When people look at you, they'll see what they expect to see. It's easy, because that's what people mostly do.

"Fergus, love, they'll not just see our late lamented Dougal. Maureen will see the Dougal she left behind her, brought back to life as her memories would make him rise from his funeral pyre. And Cáitlin, dear Cáitlin, they'll see what my dear Sean looked like after the forest got through with him."

She waved dismissal. "Go now, Fergus, and haunt the halls and towers where you died. Serve as my eyes and ears, serve as my hands and feet, bring news to me and send messages of fear to my enemies."

The brambles unwound from his body and Fiona's newminted slave moved, uncertain in his changed form. He turned and the hedge opened before him, recognizing his blood now and allowing it to pass.

Fiona turned her back on him and studied Cáitlin where she still hung on the hedge's thorns. She stepped closer, close enough to smell the fear-sweat and the bitter sap from broken hawthorn. "So, love, what's it really now? I never swear help to another, twisting words or no. What would you be hiding from our little Fergus? What brings you into my hedge, looking for your death?"

"I've come asking a favor for a favor. There's a question

someone wanted asked of you, someone both you and I might find useful to have in our debt. Your plants let me past before."

"Ah, but I've had to make a change or two. Surely your winds have told you that. I've learned I was too trusting."

Cáitlin's nose wrinkled, as if that last sentence tainted the air around them. "You and I aren't rivals, *love*. We each stick to our own realms. Now will you let me down and break the binding?"

Fiona tilted her head to one side and studied her captive. "I think not, cousin. You shouldn't have come sneaking like a thief. Now what's this question, and who might it be that's asking?"

"The question? Why are you looking to destroy a certain castle beyond the one that's closest by? The humans mean nothing to you. As far as 'who,' there's a Welshman who takes an interest in the Christians."

Fiona studied that statement from all sides. "Naming no names, love, for the trees to hear—I wonder if this Welshman might bear a gold banner with a red dragon blazoned on it?"

"He might."

Fiona shook her head. "Your Welshman should see Dougal behind that war, not me. Free humans offended him. They turned into an obsession. He had more than one obsession, some of them unwise. Some even fatal."

Cáitlin studied one of the briars that bound her wrist, and then spoke as if to it. "Some of the Welshman's friends seem to think you've taken up the cause. They seem to feel they have reason to watch and listen around your new neighbors."

" 'Tis no business of theirs. The Pendragons simply guard the border between the lands. If they start meddling inside the Summer Country, the rules will change. And not to their advantage."

Fiona smiled, baring her teeth. "But *if* I were to carry on Dougal's war, there'd be a simple reason. Strategy, love, an answer that your military Welshman ought to understand. Before I open battle, I make sure my enemy has no allies who can attack my back or flanks. Even ones she doesn't know are there. You can pass that word across the winds."

She turned away, and then turned back. "*And* you can tell the Welshman that if he wants to act so holy, he can explain some of the innocents that go missing when they touch the border or meet up with the Pendragons' claws. Either that, or admit that the worlds haven't changed since Merlin's day, and my rules are the only ones that I need follow."

Then her mind spoke to the briars, loosing Cáitlin. Fiona waved her captive toward Maureen's forest. "Haunt the place of Sean's dying, love, listen to your winds whispering past branch and leaf. Tell me and your Welshman what they say. Serve my revenge well, and I might set you free."

Fiona dropped her puppet strings for the moment, turned, and stepped through another gap in the maze, into sunshine and the gardens close on her cottage. It waited for her, white-washed stone and thatch, curiously dead to the eye like the bare-limbed skeleton of the house rowan standing by the kitchen door. She crossed the broken threshold into air cooler than the true temperature, with the clammy touch of a cellar or a grave. Maureen's curse still hung here, the Power holding strong between ridge-pole and foundation.

The red-haired bitch would die for it.

# four

MAUREEN LOWERED THE binoculars and stared into her memories. She couldn't see any point where she could have done otherwise.

She ought to love this place—the clean sweet air, the castle's wealth, the magic, a gentle, loving man who understood just who and what she was and still cared for her, the trees . . . the trees, ancient gray-bearded wise trees she'd only dreamed about in forestry school, trees that talked to her and guarded her and wrapped her in miles of wild green beauty. She *ought* to love this place. So why did the castle still feel like a trap closing in around her?

And the dragon hated her.

The dragon swam out like some kind of nuclear attack submarine, black and sleek and swift and deadly, one of the most wonderful animals she'd ever seen. It came back wallowing like an overloaded supertanker with engine trouble, almost too fat to clear the channel into port. She couldn't see what happened in between, but she could guess. She'd never thought of dragons as amphibians, but it made a lot of sense.

The dragon laired down in the swamp, vibrant and beautiful and brave, a living wonder, and it wanted to eat her. Maureen tested each step in her memories. Dougal had bound the dragons to defend his keep, sent Liam to kidnap Maureen, trapped Jo in a sinkhole. David had killed the female dragon when he and Brian had come to Dougal's forest in their doomed attempt at rescuing Maureen and Jo.

Maureen stared down at her hand squeezing the binoculars. She set Brian's Leicas on the gray stone of the windowsill and flexed her fingers.

That column of smoke still smudged the sky, far beyond her forest. Brian didn't know what it meant—probably some feud or other brought to the burning point. Power ruled the Summer Country.

She still didn't understand the soul of this place, what it would accept and what it would reject. Apparently the moose had fit within the rules. God knows, Maine was up to its ass in moose, more than the range could bear. Some years, more people died in car-moose collisions than were murdered. She could kidnap a moose a week to feed the dragon and nobody would notice.

"And that one had brainworm," she whispered to herself. "A *lot* worse than getting chomped by a dragon."

And she thought there might be advantages to getting the dragon used to looking in Fiona's direction for its next meal.

Test the limits, find out the rules, make a map and get the names down right. Did the dragon have a name? That could be important. Just like there probably was a proper castle term for this narrow slit in a stone bay sticking out from the castle wall, not a window but an arrow slit or a quillon or something.

Brian would know. He was the frigging soldier, fifty years in the British Army with a sideline for the Pendragons, defending humanity against the Old Ones out of Celtic legend. Fifty years with the Gurkhas and the SAS, diddling the records God knows how, over seventy years old, and he still looked like thirty. Just like she looked sixteen, Jo looked eighteen, when their true ages sat to either side of thirty.

Her hand looked like a human hand, looked like it always had, almost a child's hand. She'd had only a couple of weeks to get used to the fact that it wasn't human. Brian wasn't human, she wasn't human, Jo wasn't human. The Old Blood ran in their veins, the race the humans had kicked out of Europe back during the last ice age. It didn't seem real.

The Old Blood had brought her here, to this land out of Grandfather O'Brian's tales of Irish myth. It gave her the power to work magic. She really *could* talk to trees and discuss the balance of ecosystems with an articulate fox. Magic had made sense out of the voices that had seemed like symptoms of paranoid schizophrenia. She felt the needs of the forest, touched the *heart* of the forest like she never had in forestry school. The Old Blood . . .

Such small hands, to have killed a man. Crushed Dougal's throat, clawed his eyes out of their sockets, hacked him to pieces with a Gurkha *kukri*. Burned his body to ashes in his own bed, burned his tower and all the blood-soaked bedding in which she'd slept the night. She'd been crazy then, straight from a dungeon cell and living in the disjointed nightmares of sleep deprivation. Now she was sane.

Maybe.

A breath of air whispered behind her, and something feather-touched her arm. She whirled, claws out, and raked her nails across flesh. Power gathered, using her, ready to kill again.

Brian stood there, just stood there patiently waiting for her claws and Power to tear him to shreds. Blood welled up across his cheek, flowing just beneath one blue eye and beside that broad nose his genes had stolen from a Neanderthal.

The rage flowed out of her. She sagged against the cold

stone wall, as limp as if the Power had dissolved her bones. "Oh, *God!* I'm sorry . . ."

The bleeding stopped, even as she forced herself to stand again. Fresh skin spread across his gouged flesh, and the blood dried and flaked away. Magic.

He shook his head. "My fault. Bloody hell, I should know better than to surprise you. Used to have to wake the troopers by nudging them with a boot and stepping back."

"But Dougal's dead. I'm not crazy anymore."

"Dougal may be dead. But the rest that happened to you, when you were a child . . . Buddy Johnson is alive and well and living in the back of your skull. Your . . . rapist has been there for eighteen years. It'll take more than a few days to kick him out."

Maureen closed her eyes. Goddamn fucking Buddy Johnson.

She started to shake all over. "You didn't even defend yourself. Twice my size, trained fighter, you didn't even try to *duck,* goddamn it! I could have *killed* you!"

He reached for her, tentative, and stopped when she flinched away. "If I'd blocked you, grabbed you, then you *would* have tried to kill me. I'd just as soon not find out how. You had to see that I was harmless."

"You're too damned quiet."

"Kept me alive a score of times. I'll wear a bloody jester's dingle hat, all points and bells and motley, if that'll help."

Maureen stepped back out of the window into the tapestry-draped room of Dougal's castle. *Her* castle, what was left of it. The corner towers and most of the central keep had survived the fire. So had the kitchens and the cellars and the outbuildings within the walls. Plenty to live in.

Enough for her and Brian, enough for Jo and David if they'd wanted to stay, enough for Dougal's former slaves to live in safety in this fucking land that said that human blood meant the same thing as black skin on an Old South plantation. Even the fairest legends could turn ugly when you started poking around under the rocks.

She grabbed a bottle at random from the sideboard, poured a double shot of booze, and tossed it back. The fire burned down her throat and out into her veins, calming the shakes.

"That stuff will kill you if you don't watch out."

She glared at Brian. "Fuck off. Sometimes I *need* a drink."

He winced away from her eyes and shook his head. "If you don't want to quit, nobody can make you. All I can say is, a bottle of rum used to make the nightmares worse."

She knew Brian had his own share of horrors, earned in places like the Malay jungles and Aden and the Falklands. He'd killed and bled, come within a hair of dying, and held good friends as they died. Sometimes that shared experience helped.

Maureen poured herself another double. Whiskey, she noticed, Scotch. Glenraven Special Reserve, smooth and smoky like the nectar of the gods, she'd never even heard of it before. Label looked like it was printed on gold leaf. Bottle probably cost twice what she'd used to earn in a week. Not that Dougal would have paid for it. His kind *took* what they wanted, like he'd taken her.

Brian didn't touch her unless she wanted to be touched. Problem was, no matter how good it felt afterward, she had to . . . become someone else, in order to let a man touch her. Even a man she loved. Buddy Johnson could burn in hell forever. She just might send him there, if she got the chance.

"What's the name of that place, the window I was using?"

Brian's right eyebrow lifted at the change of subject, but he looked relieved. "Balistraria. That little part that sticks out from the wall is called a bartizan. Not all that common for a Scots or Irish castle, but it helps you shoot at anyone who gets close in to the wall. Dougal messed with the design a little when he rebuilt the place. That, and the indoor plumbing and the photocell panels on the roof."

"*Re*built?"

"Yeah. Everyone has an image in the Summer Country. Everyone's an actor in his own play—Fiona with her cloak of shadow and her witch's cottage, Dougal the Highland laird with his hawks and slaves and hunting beasts. He wanted something more impressive than a crumbling stone tower and a ring of thatched-roof huts. This place was designed to stand against King Edward and those mucking big trebuchets."

"Fat lot of good it did him."

"Most feudal lords had more sense than to sleep with their worst enemy."

Maureen winced and poured another drink. Killing Dougal had served as some kind of catharsis, but it had also created new nightmares. She'd gone to bed with him, and in the morning she'd killed him. Fucking schizoid black widow spider. And Brian was still willing to sleep with her. Either a brave man, or a fool. Maybe both.

The whiskey was finally starting to work. She reached out and caressed his cheek, the smooth fresh skin where she'd scratched him. He smelled good, as always, that feral woodland smell that told her that he was the right species. A faint tickle of desire stirred in her belly. Maybe it was time to invoke Jo, the inner whore.

He took her hand, kissed it, and shook his head. "We can't. You asked me not to, unless you're sober."

The kiss sent shivers down her spine. "Don't be a goddamn saint. Takes more booze than that to get me drunk."

"Matter of opinion. You've dumped at least four ounces of fine single-malt into a body that weighs less than ninety pounds. You still haven't regained all the weight you lost."

They'd starved her in that dungeon, too. And apparently doing magic burned fat out of her body. If she didn't *have* any fat, like after she'd escaped, then the magic burned muscle instead. She'd recovered some, but she'd still have a hard time wrestling with a kitten.

Maybe she wasn't drunk. Her legs *did* seem a touch shaky, though. Either that, or the stone floor was turning into marshmallows. She found a chair and flopped into it, staring at the depths of her glass.

"A billion men in the world," she muttered, "and I have to fall in love with the fucking *one* who believes that no means *no.* Even when I say yes."

"That was the Scotch saying yes, not Maureen. And I ain't bein' noble. I'm trying to stay alive."

He grinned, as if he was making some kind of joke. She remembered blood dripping off her hands, splashed in teardrop arcs across the walls, slimy under her thighs as she straddled Dougal's body and hacked his head loose from his neck. The sexy warmth died.

She swallowed more whiskey. "Okay. Jo and David have left. I've fed the pets. You don't want to play with me. What's next on the checklist?"

Brian glared at her glass again and shrugged. "Probably you should go out and plan defense with the trees. Fiona's going to come calling, one of these days, and we'd be wise to be ready for her. In case you've forgotten, she uses plant-magic, too."

"Meaning I ought to talk to Father Oak about a few traps of our own." She set the glass down on the floor and sagged back into her chair. "Okay. Later. Right now, I'm so damned tired I'd probably fall flat on my face before I got as far as the front gate."

"Rest. Eat. Rest some more, eat some more. Quit drinking. And the land will give you strength if you need it. Remember, the trees *like* you."

Maureen felt the rage building in her. "Lay off about the fucking *booze,* okay? I want a drink, I'll take it." She fought with her anger. She didn't have the strength for it. "Yeah. I can do resting. I'm up to that. What's on *your* schedule?"

"Back to poking around in the cellars, I guess."

Maureen forced her eyes to focus. "What're you looking for, down there? Magic rings? The Horn of Roland? Rodents of Unusual Size?"

He looked like he understood her references. Must have read some of the same books. "No. I'm looking for the back door. You don't build a place like this without an emergency exit."

"Would somebody like *Dougal* worry about that kind of shit? He thought he was fucking invincible."

Brian winced at her language. "The Castle Perilous is a *lot* older than Dougal. There's been some kind of hold or keep guarding this hill since the earliest memories of the Summer Country. It sits on one of the strongest flows of Power in the land."

"Well, if you find Excalibur down there, let me know. We could use it."

Brian jerked as if he'd just touched a live wire. He hated her references to Camelot. For all that he was christened Arthur Pendragon, he didn't have much use for sappy legends. Brian Arthur Pendragon Albion, her Knight of the Table Round. She wanted to feel his arms around her, his warrior skills protecting her, his body between her and this world of teeth and claws and scheming witches, but she didn't have enough strength to climb out of the chair. Later.

And *that* connection brought up a question that had been nagging at her. "Are the Pendragons just going to let you walk?"

"Bugger if I know. Nobody's ever tried. We all talk about it, but that's just like the old sergeant sayin' 'e plans to use 'is pension and buy a farm in Wessex. An' then 'e cops it takin' th' next 'ill. It's just soldier-talk, probably goes back to Caesar's Legions or the spear-carriers walking the walls of Babylon."

He'd switched into Kipling Cockney and then out of it as smoothly as any actor. For all his Welsh ancestry, he rarely sounded British. From bits and pieces he'd let slip, she guessed he'd spent years undercover at times, military intelligence.

He sighed. "Besides, I'd've probably been fired before I could resign. I got this message . . ." He paused, looking like he tasted something foul. "I think the coding garbled it. Ordered me to leave Liam alone. It didn't make sense, so I ignored it. But I've been wondering, ever since. The Pendragons don't take kindly to that sort of thing."

"I'm glad you disobeyed."

She sagged farther back into the chair, feeling as if she were going to dribble out between the leather seat and the back. At that, she'd lasted longer today than yesterday, and longer yesterday than the day before. The land *was* giving her strength, but snatching that moose had taken a lot out of her.

She waved him off in the direction of the dungeon stairs. "Let me know if you find Arthur's sword down there. We'll give it to the Pendragons as the price of leaving you alone."

"Look, just bugger Good King Arthur and Merlin and Camelot . . ." He stopped in midrant and shook his head. "If Dougal had Caliburn, he'd have hung it on the wall with the rest of his trophies. They're all ash and rusty scrap down in the bottom of the tower. Don't count on legends to save us. Or whiskey."

He closed the door behind his last words—probably didn't slam it only because you couldn't slam three inches of oak cross-ply planks. Too heavy to get it moving fast. Barrier against battle-axes. Or drunken witches.

*At least he's still here.*

*Yeah. A sane man would be a thousand miles away. One of*

*these days, he's going to figure that out. Then where will you be?*

Her internal critic was back. She'd used to think that was the voice of schizophrenia. Normal people don't hold debates with themselves. Then Brian had pointed out that post-traumatic stress disorder explained everything except the Powers of the Blood. All the shrinks had misdiagnosed her case because she'd lied to them. Telling about Buddy would have let Jo in for a dose of Dad's black leather belt, probably would have beaten her to death.

*Hell,* Maureen remembered, *you even lied to yourself.* She'd taken a minor in psych in college, knew all the PTSD stuff about trauma and nightmares and waking flashbacks and startle reflexes, but that hadn't applied to *her.* Buddy Johnson didn't exist.

But she didn't have to hide him now. Brian knew. Even Jo had figured out what Buddy did, how he'd poisoned Maureen's mind for nearly twenty years. God, *that* had been a scene. No wonder Jo didn't want to stay.

Plus, David was a human. A bard, maybe, but still a *human* bard, a more valuable brand of slave. Jo didn't care, but this freaky place ranked humans as a trainable class of monkey. After all, he couldn't do magic, work with Power.

So they'd gone home, leaving green grass and sunshine and summer to go back to fucking Maine in the middle of fucking winter.

She stared into the bottom of her glass and wished that somebody had bothered to explain the concept of Happily Ever After to the scriptwriter of this play. She ought to follow Brian, help him, learn more about the history and secrets of this land. But that cell waited down there, stone walls closing in from all four sides, stone ceiling so heavy over her head . . .

*I could be bounded in a nutshell, were it not that I have bad dreams. Yet who would have thought the old man to have had so much blood in him?*

The room blurred, and tears scalded her cheeks again.

# five

―⌇―

BRIAN STUDIED THE walls of the narrow corridor, holding his flashlight close and running fingertips over cold dry stone. The left side showed raw sandstone ledge, rough-dressed and still bearing gouges from the picks and drills that carved these cellars out of the hilltop. Right side was dry-stone masonry as tight-fitted as those Inca walls he'd seen in Cuzco. He couldn't slide a fingernail between the blocks. A masonry arch formed the ceiling, age-blackened from the smoke of torches and ribbed with enough reinforcing that he could be under the keep walls.

He knelt down and pulled a brush from his back pocket, cleaning thick dust from the floor. The cleared spot showed smooth stone paving here, patterned in red and green slate, a diamond tessellation with small square insets of gray at the corners. Excellent craftsmanship. Some areas had mosaics, looked like Greek or Roman work. He wondered just *who* had first lived on this site and drawn on the Power that flowed up from the earth. So far, the underground layout seemed more like a Roman villa than a Celtic keep—a rich villa deliberately buried and hidden beneath rude huts and a plain stone tower.

The Old Blood loved hidden things and secrets, like Fiona with her "cottage." The Pendragons showed their ancestry in that, as paranoid and ruthless as the KGB when their secrets were in danger. Agents disappeared, and no one ever asked because people who asked too many questions also disappeared.

Like these passages and the feet that had walked them had disappeared, centuries ago. But the keep was thoroughly Irish now. For probably the twentieth time, Brian considered inviting a clúrichán to haunt these musty cellars and drain every drop of alcohol in the keep. Maybe then Maureen could throw away the crutch that kept her from knowing her true strength.

But she wouldn't thank him. Besides, it wouldn't work. She had to face her own devils and best them, two falls out of three. *And* if she wanted a drink, she could summon enough booze to drown the thirstiest Irish elf. That was how the Summer Country worked, for one with the Old Blood strong in her veins.

She still didn't understand the power of her wishes. If she fancied baked ham for dinner, there was a smoked and sugar-cured specimen of Smithfield's finest in the larder, waiting for the cooks. That was the taste she imagined, so some warehouse in Virginia came up short on inventory.

She wondered why Dougal's slaves were anxious to stay and work, once she'd freed them? She fed them. She was spending energy every day, just maintaining the keep and everyone who lived there. She wanted them to be happy, so she fed them better than Dougal ever had, not even knowing what she did, and they weren't about to walk away from easy labor without a whip to drive it. They knew the choices a human could expect, in this land.

Brian, however, had choices. He turned his flashlight

back to the stone wall of the corridor, wryly comparing it to this new woman in his life. She had about as much give in her as that sandstone. She was as abrasive, and as brittle, and usually as cold. All in all, *not* a comfortable person to find on the other side of your bed when you woke up in the morning.

And dangerous. Life with her was walking through a minefield. Oh, he knew *why* she showed the world nothing but detonators and foul language. The things she'd been through would have killed a lesser woman, or driven her insane. That didn't drop the tension to a level he could bear.

Her drinking could, for a little while. But when she sobered up, she was more dangerous than before. So he mostly tried to get out of her way, be someplace quiet and relatively safe like this dusty dark rabbit-warren of ancient tunnels and rooms that twisted around under the hilltop and keep like Fiona's green maze. It made a good excuse.

It would be so easy to be someplace else. Someplace far away. Someplace calmer and a hell of a lot safer.

But she'd asked him if he would stay, and he'd said yes. The first night they'd met, she had touched something deep inside him, something that had grown powerful in the strange weeks that followed. And he'd told her that he loved her, after he'd known damn well what the whole package meant. He'd lived before with Death resting a skeletal hand on his shoulder for months and years on end, with less reason.

If he left her now, odds were that the betrayal would push her over the edge into madness. She skirted it close enough as it was. So he had to weigh that, as well.

*Buggering psychological blackmail, like threatening suicide if she doesn't get her way. No. Be honest. She hasn't said anything like that. You've just thought it.*

Brian grimaced, sighed, and shook his head. He'd been gnawing at the problem for days now, without an answer.

Mapping the cellars was simpler and more straightforward. At least the corridors and rooms stayed in one place, didn't move around impossibly like Fiona's hedge. Or at least he *thought* they didn't. Judging by the feel of creeping finger-tips on the back of his neck, the corridors might change if they thought it necessary.

He'd told Maureen he was looking for the back door. That was half of it, the part she'd understand. He searched for something else as well, something less defined. This keep felt *wrong.* The stones resented people—humans, Old Ones, men, women, impartial. The hilltop held a grudge deep in its heart, old and festering. And it resisted prying. Coming down here took an act of will.

Judging by the finishes, the cellars had been important once. Judging by the undisturbed dust and stale air, nobody had entered them in centuries—long before Dougal's time, anyway. Why did people avoid these tunnels?

Some of the rooms had held supplies, old bins of wheat and barley long gnawed to scattered hulls by mice, kegs of wine evaporated to red vinegar stains in the wood. Rooms full of weapons, short javelins with age-split shafts and rust-eaten heads, bundles of warped arrows with shreds of fletching, longbows that shattered when he tried to string them. He'd found racks of swords, short Celtic swords with straight heavy blades, but none of them showed any sign of magic. So much for finding Excalibur.

Siege stores, anyway. Some ancient castellan had ex-pected to have to hold this tower against an army, without the option of escaping through the walk between the worlds. That logic troubled Brian.

Or was he wrong? Did the prospect of siege mean some-thing lurked down here that was worth defending? Some-thing that shouldn't, or couldn't, be carried away? Something forgotten, even in legend? Something that *wanted* to stay hid-den? So he kept searching.

Another doorway loomed ahead, dark in the shadows from his flashlight, age-blackened wood in a carved stone frame. He ran his fingers over the worn jamb and lintel, trying to trace out a design. This doorway opened to the left, into the raw native stone. His skin prickled in the peculiar fashion that had stopped him half an inch from putting his hand on a lump of rock while tracking Yemeni guerrillas up the eroded yellow sides of a wadi. He'd stepped back that time, studied the trail, and only then noticed the clean gravel scattered over dust. Tripwire. Antipersonnel mine.

He shuddered at the memory. And stepped away again, careful with his feet, just as he had that time before, because sometimes the buggers hid another booby trap close by, where you'd trigger it while avoiding the first.

Undisturbed dust covered the floor, the only marks his own footprints. He pulled out the brush again and uncovered the stone pavers, as gently as he had probed for that deadly little mine. The floor's pattern flowed continuously along, the grout all matching and gray with time, without gaps or cracks that could mean a pit trap or tampering. Nothing different or suspicious on the walls, either.

He studied the doorway again, the jambs and header of carved stone set into the natural rock. Old. Worn by centuries of hands bracing against the drag of the door, smoothed by centuries of bodies brushing through. He held the flashlight so its beam just grazed the surface, bringing out carved forms. The remains of a faint line skipped and dotted down the center of each side, a vertical stem with horizontal or slanting branches extending to either side in varied lengths—Ogham runes, the tree alphabet of the ancient Celts.

His fingers brushed the latch, nervous, as if he expected it to bite. He rested his hand on the hilt of his *kukri,* the Gurkha knife he wore as unconsciously as the belt on which it hung. He gnawed at his lip.

*Hell, you'd think I wanted to live forever.*

He shrugged with a wry grin, reached out again and tripped the latch, and shoved the door open with his foot. It swung away, jerky and groaning with rust on the hinges. Blackness waited behind it, and nothing came flying out at him to cut or bite or burn. He aimed his flashlight into shadows.

Firewood. Ranks and ranks of firewood marched away into the gloom, ends hewn rather than sawed, stacked wall to wall and within a hand-span of the ceiling higher than he could reach. Brian shook his head.

He eased into the room, sliding each foot in a curve ahead of him before he trusted his weight to it, still wary of traps. Whoever had stacked the wood, centuries ago, had left space to work next to the door. Brian studied the piles of wood again. Just wood, bark and grain looked like oak, nothing remarkable about it except that it was about as well seasoned as firewood could ever get.

He turned to the door behind him, eased it nearly shut, and examined the latch and hinges with his flashlight. Iron latch and lever and hook, iron hinges, nothing remarkable. Sockets for a heavy wooden bar to block the door from the inside, which *did* seem strange, as if the man who'd designed and built this long ago had intended the room as a last retreat against invaders. Brian wondered if he'd finally tracked down that missing back door.

And that, and the siege stores, nagged at him. What of the walk between the worlds? Not just escape, but attack as well. Stepping into an unknown space was dangerous as hell, but so was assaulting a castle. If your enemy hated you deeply enough to risk his own life, he could just walk through nothing into your bedroom and kill you as you slept. Damned few Old Ones were willing to take such a risk. Most preferred to kill their enemies in safer ways. This whole picture, though . . .

Did something ward this keep against trespass? Jo and David had stepped *out* of the keep, but that was a different thing, with no one trying to stop them or track them through the void. Another puzzle.

He liked puzzles, as long as they didn't bite.

He flashed his light across the exposed stone wall, dusting with the brush, searching for any other inscription, Ogham or otherwise. Nothing showed, but the surface on the hinge side seemed darker. Darker, he noticed, from hip to shoulder height, as if hands or bodies had brushed up against it for countless years and left a thin smear of oil and sweat behind. He probed the woodpile with his flashlight beam. Close along the wall, the light found black hollows instead of log after log, bark face after split face after bark face.

Brian smiled and started stacking firewood, shifting sticks from one side to the other. Now he knew why they'd left as much empty space as they had around the door. He sneezed, and blinked, and sneezed again, stirring up centuries of dust. And he opened up a hole and a passage along the side wall that slipped away into darkness.

The way was narrow, a single body wide, and he moved cautiously. This sort of thing was *made* for traps, where you could force an enemy to place his foot on a single particular stone. Ten paces, then a turn to the right. His flashlight beam picked out motes of dust and bored on into darkness, past still more ranks of wood.

A shadow along the wall turned into a niche and then into another door set into the thick uncut stone. If he hadn't gotten confused by the twists and turns, it led under the oldest tower of all, the simple stonework that predated any of Dougal's changes. The chill of Power flowed over Brian's skin, raising hairs on the back of his neck.

He licked his lips. Damnfool thing, doing this alone. He ought to go back, find Maureen and a couple of those smithy boys whose biceps were bigger than their brains, and figure out just what he was getting into before he got into it. Call for backup before poking his nose into an IRA arms cache.

But he liked puzzles.

What the hell. He shrugged. He'd been doing that a lot, lately. Sharing a bed with Maureen must be giving him a new perspective on the relative risks of life. Anyway, he reached out and touched the latch with the back of his hand. Nothing bit him.

He tripped the latch and pushed. Hinges groaned again, and the door shuddered away from him. The air that flowed out of the darkness seemed warmer and somewhat fresher, with a tang of forest and something odd, almost brine and seaweed. Brian could feel Power beating on his skin like sunshine. Whatever had drawn people to this hill through the ages, star-stone or sacred circle or magic well, lived in that darkness. And it was angry.

His flashlight beam probed here and there. It lit a smooth stone wall, then poked to right and left to draw form out of the gloom. A large room, circular and maybe forty feet across, centering on a stone pillar as an axis. A crucifix hanging on the pillar, crude work but powerful, old and dusty, and some long-dead hand had chiseled a flat for it. That was the only evidence of finishing on the rough-shaped stone, and Brian had seen its like in Wales and Ireland and Brittany. Menhir. This room had once been open to the sun and stars.

As in so many places, the Christians had worshipped in a space already sacred to the old Powers of the land. He circled the room, feeling that Power swell and ebb. It seemed strongest just in front of the crucifix, and he didn't think that was coincidence. With this much Power flowing from the land, even humans could have felt the presence of their God.

He stopped and closed his eyes, *feeling* the air around him. The anger still throbbed, low and slow and with the patience of a thousand years. Dies Irae, the Day of Wrath and an angry God casting the damned into hell. That atmosphere would have suited the old brimstone Christians. But the sense of hiding had faded, had left him at one door or the other. Two separate puzzles?

And now that he thought about it and separated it out, the hiding had a flavor he'd tasted more than once before, the same dark tingle as the oldest wardings on the secrets of the Pendragons. Those dated back to Merlin.

Brian shuddered at the thought. He'd never much cared for Merlin. To hell with the pretty legends—that man had been a dangerous paranoid. His spells had *teeth*.

Brian looked the room over with fresh eyes. His footprints had stirred the dust, uncovering a design on the floor. It seemed irregular, perhaps part of a single larger figure rather than repeated patterns. Odd. He knelt down and cleared more of it.

This paving looked *old*, buff stone of a slightly paler color set into smoothed native ledge. He traced the design, a single hand-span wide as it led in twists to right and left across the floor. A maze. No, a *labyrinth*, a single winding line without false turns or dead-end passages. Medieval Christians had set these into their cathedral floors, a reminder of the one true path to God and an aid to meditation.

But this was older than the Christians, older than Merlin, and it led to the center of Power just in front of the menhir. A starburst of white quartz filled the spot; he couldn't tell if it was natural or set into the stone by a master craftsman. He settled back on his haunches and stared at it. He'd never seen, or felt, anything like this before. When he ran his fingers over the quartz, it hummed at him, low and soothing.

Meditation. Comfortable. Inviting.

Almost the opposite of Maureen.

And the opposite of the menhir. Now that he could sort out the conflicting Powers in this room, he knew that the menhir held the anger. It remembered ancient injury and hated anything on two legs. *It* held the malice that darkened Castle Perilous.

Meanwhile, Brian decided he could use some soothing. He stood up and found the entry to the labyrinth. He set his right foot on the narrow line and then his left, letting the room fall away from him as he concentrated on each step, each twist, each shift in the feel of the Power warm and electric against his body as he approached the quartz focus and receded and circled it from right to left and back again.

Maureen just needed time. The land would heal her. The forest would heal her. But could he last that long? He knew, from the inside, the deep dark secret of the drunk. *A drunk won't give up the bottle unless he has no other choice.* He'd been there. He'd managed to come out the other side, to the rare balance where he could take that demon rum or leave it—and actually *could* stop at just one drink. But he didn't dare take a second.

Maureen wouldn't stop until the cost of drink stood up and punched her in the nose. Until she hit bottom, as they called it in the programs. And she needed him. He grimaced. She needed *him,* in a way that went far beyond sex and into magic. She'd bound her heart to him with the same seduction spell that broke Fiona's hold on his mind and body. With Buddy Johnson lurking in her memory, that was the only way she could force herself into sex. Brian shook his head. What would she do if he left her?

*Tell her. One more week. Quit the drinking, or I'm gone. I'll stand by her while she fights it, but she* has *to fight.*

With that decision, Brian felt tension flow out of his shoulders as he walked the pattern, eyes on the buff stone set against the yellow.

The path straightened out in front of him and broadened, until he walked easily. It felt like the way a Zen archer finds the target growing in his mind until it is so large and clear and close that missing is impossible. He loosed himself as an arrow and found the quartz starburst as his target.

Brian opened his eyes, blinking, amazed that he had walked the last steps blind. The pattern had drawn him in and taken his will. But he was left . . . hungry? Left with a sense of powerful magic somehow incomplete. A sense that something should have happened.

He stared at the menhir right in front of him and the crude flat chiseled on one face. Now it radiated pain as well as simmering rage.

# SIX

—⌇—

A GUST OF wind and cold rain chased Jo under a portico. She stood there, dripping and shaking wet hair out of her eyes and swearing under her breath, biting her tongue out of ingrained deference to the funeral home behind her and the long solemn black cars waiting for their next load.

A funeral home, for crissakes, with the hospital only a block away and in plain sight. It seemed a little tacky. At least the florist's shop on the next corner held out the promise of birth and spring and "Get Well" cards in their display window, keeping the funeral wreaths tucked discreetly away in the back cooler.

She'd never noticed those things before, but then she was noticing a lot that had just been common background to her life. Part of it was contrast with the magical forest she'd just left; part almost reached into paranoia as she kept an eye out for the perennial cop cruiser. They were following her around, a constant reminder that Sergeant Getchell didn't believe her story.

Oh, she could make them go away. Just like she could

make Sergeant Getchell wrinkle his nose in irritation and let them walk out past the buzzing electronic locks of the police station every time they went in to tell their muddled and inconsistent stories about where two months of their lives had vanished and what had happened to Brian and Maureen.

But then she'd look over her shoulder and see a cruiser again, just like she'd pick up the phone to hear the sergeant's gravelly voice "suggesting" that he'd like to talk to them again. She'd always been . . . ambivalent . . . about policemen, but she had to admire their tenacity. Bulldogs, never letting go once they sank teeth into their prey. Sort of like a Maine winter. If only they'd been like that with Daddy . . .

Jo shuddered away from her memories and returned to the current problem. Sooner or later, she was going to have to step across into Maureen's world. Ask her and Brian to come back to this mess and prove that they were still alive.

Cars splashed past, throwing up muddy spray from the gutters as four months' worth of road sand worked its way toward the storm sewers. Jo's goal frowned at her, blurry through the rain. Wet stains darkened the concrete jumble of boxy slabs and see-through corridors and elevator towers, turning the medical center into some kind of grim futuristic Bastille, poking a line of battlements and angles and narrow windows against gray skies. *All hope abandon, ye who enter here.*

Jo shrugged herself deeper into her jacket and stood under cover, waiting out the burst of rain and glowering back at the ugly mess of additions that spread out from the old brick cube of Naskeag General Hospital. She did not want to go in there. She'd rather stand out here and flirt with hypothermia, given the choice.

Her experience was, people died in hospitals. Grannie, Grandfather O'Brian after his wreck, Nan Langlais back in high school . . . Hospitals meant pain and sickness and bad smells, all glossed over with the fake promise of healing. Oh, sure, some people came out better than they went in. The damned places didn't kill *everybody*. Go in with a nice simple broken arm and you might get out alive. Or you might die of the drug-resistant pneumococcus you picked up in the emergency room while sitting for three hours in a crowded stinking waiting area. That was what killed Grannie.

But they weren't going to cure Mom. "Therapy." "Rehab." "Adaptive equipment." "Support from visiting nurses." "Respite care." Those were the weasel-words for "She ain't gonna get better." Modern medicine offered damned few miracles for a brain damaged by a stroke.

The best Jo could hope for was she wouldn't open the door to Mom's room to be greeted by a respirator wheezing and beeping next to the bed, holding death at arm's length and recording the battle on a paper chart. The best she could hope for was her mother might know her own name, might blink twice in code as if she recognized Jo as one or the other of her interchangeable daughters. Or maybe the best she could hope for was an empty bed waiting for its next victim. Death.

Jo thought she'd rather die than end up where Mom was now. The first time, just seeing her had been a punch in the gut. As if *that* wasn't bad enough, Dad was in there. Dad, putting on the loving, "worried husband" look in between squint-eyed drooling stares at the nurse's butt and legs as she bent over the bed, adjusting pillows and the tubing of the IV drip. Head nurse had complained that he'd even groped her once when she squeezed past him to check the catheter bag.

Dad. That cheerful word carried some heavy chunks of psychological baggage Jo hadn't cleared away, between her and Maureen. The little twit had probably wiped it from her memory, burned it to ash and buried it under Buddy and then buried *him* under a rock the size of Mount Katahdin.

Jo ran her fingertips over the lumpy spot on her left side, the place where a couple of broken ribs had healed crooked. David had asked her about that once, making love. She'd told him it happened playing soccer. Like she'd ever played soccer in her life. She shook her head. *We get so used to hiding, it's a reflex.*

The rain and wind moved on to bedevil some other dumb pedestrian, leaving cold damp drizzle behind. Jo pulled the hood of her jacket back over her hair, gritted her teeth, and forced her feet toward the waiting morgue. Hospital. Whatever.

She trudged unwilling past the acres of cars—clapped-out rust-buckets like Maureen's old Toyota and dented, mud-splashed, backwoods pickups parked cheek by jowl with yuppie Beemers and SAABs wearing the wash of road grime like a barely tolerated insult. Naskeag Falls might be a backwoods hick village with delusions of grandeur, but it was still the closest thing to a city for a hundred miles in any direction. Rich or poor, you wanted medical services, you came here. Same for the airport and the shopping malls.

Security cameras recorded her face as she walked up to the entry. Rent-a-cops opened doors for her while meditating on her psychological balance and morals. She had to sign in at the reception desk and show picture ID. She was mildly surprised that they didn't run her through a metal detector.

Jo followed echoing tiled hallways, passing banks of elevators that either led to the wrong wing or were marked STAFF ONLY, turning corners marked by cryptic initials, and moving through three different room-numbering systems before she reached the proper wing and the proper set of elevators.

She wondered how long it took the staff to learn just

what led where and how you got from one ward to another without going outside and starting in again from the beginning. She knew that she wouldn't have a clue which way to run if they had a fire while she was there.

And then she faced the almost-shut door of her mother's room and her brain couldn't dodge anymore. She swallowed and pushed through. Dad was there.

She felt herself cringing, automatically. But again he was smaller than her memories, not much larger than she was, and somewhere he'd lost that sense of dominance. Maybe it was the touch of the Summer Country, and her living through other battles fought and won. He looked thinner, almost scrawny, with bony hands and big ears and brown hair rucked up into a blue jay's crest where he'd run his fingers through it, almost comical.

Then she met his eyes, and the clown image died. His eyes weighed her and squinted into a frown. Ice cubes touched her spine. She remembered that frown. It meant pain.

She stiffened and slipped to the other side of the hospital bed. She'd learned very young that she was safer with Mom between them. Mom had shrunken as well, small and frail and suddenly *old,* lying there with her pale thin immobile face and eyes unfocused in the general direction of the ceiling. Wrinkles spiderwebbed the corners of her eyes and mouth. More gray in the hair and the stubble covering the shaved patch on one side of her head, gray hair streaked with red now rather than the other way around.

Mom's hand felt cold. Her fingernails were blue-tinged, almost like a corpse. The nurse had said there was nothing wrong with her heart and lungs, but that sometimes the body just started to shut down when things went seriously wrong. Mom still lived somewhere down underneath that husk. Maybe she'd just decided to quit. Prayed to her God to take her home.

Jo wondered if faith helped when you ended up like this.

If *she'd* still believed in God, she would have been pissed off at the old bastard. Hospitals sure made you question the concept of a loving deity.

Hospitals and men like Dad. He was staring at her again, and she had to fight the automatic cringe he was expecting. He *wanted* evidence of her fear. She could feel the hunger in him, could see it in his eyes. Some of Maureen's problems had roots far older than Buddy Johnson.

Jo shuddered. She'd learned a few things in her visit to the Summer Country. If Dad tried anything, he'd find out that the rules had changed.

But she'd learned other uses for her Power, bright gifts of the Old Blood as well as dark. She closed her eyes and let her mind settle into the calm pool of her breathing, relaxing, slowing her own heartbeat and cutting loose from the world. Cutting loose from the ugliness of hospital and unemployment and Dad.

She let the room fall away from her, silencing the intercom and the gurneys in the hall, washing the disinfectant and vomit and bedpans from the air, pulling on the clear warmth and crystal air of the Summer Country, flowing the yellow glow of her thoughts down her arms and through her hands into the cold hand of her mother. She let her glow beat with the pulse she found there, weak and reluctant, and spread the warmth of her light through blood and veins flowing back to the heart and lungs and brain.

<I'm here, Mom.>

Something stirred. It slid away from her, confused and fearful. It refused to trust her.

<It's Jo, Mom. I might be able to help you.>

The reluctance strengthened. <Evil.> It turned from her. <Hail Mary, full of grace . . .>

Jo pushed herself against the wall of prayer. It resisted and then retreated rather than breaking. Jo backed off, afraid of chasing this timid strength, afraid of frightening it rather than soothing it. It puzzled her for a moment, and then she remembered something Brian had told her. Power was inherited. The Old Blood was inherited. Mom knew about witches. And feared them.

She reached out again, offering a vision of herself holding a cool damp cloth on Mom's head, vision of herself taking Mom's hand, vision of herself lifting Mom to stand beside the hospital bed and then walk and dress and leave the hospital smiling and healthy.

<Witch blood! Demon blood! Get thee behind me, Satan!> The Mom-figure turned away, fingering a rosary so hard Jo expected to see smoke curling up from the beads. <Our Father, Who art in heaven . . .>

Jo blinked and stared at the Mom in the hospital bed. It showed no change. Then, slowly, jerkily, the head turned toward Jo and away from Dad. Sweat beaded its face. The eyes focused. The lips trembled on the right side, tongue licked, stuttering consonants and vowels tumbled over each other, vainly trying to give meaning. The brow furrowed in frustration.

Mom's right hand twitched, and Jo took it gently in hers. The fingers pressed against hers, warmer than they had been, and Jo closed her eyes and let her soul flow down her arm again to seek her mother and give healing.

<Demon-spawn!>

A vision exploded in Jo's face, flashing views of a goat-man standing on his hind legs, penis rampant, with Dad's face crowned by the classic devil's horns. The choking reek of brimstone filled the air. She staggered back, shielding her eyes.

*Shit.* So this was what you got when you mixed a rigid Catholic upbringing with the Old Blood, and then topped it off with Dad. The girls finally grew up and escaped, but Mom wouldn't find refuge short of the grave. No divorce. Jo swallowed bitterness and took a deep breath.

Back into her center, back into the calm. *Send gentle waves of hope and love through the bond of touch between them. Think warm, think peace, think healing. Ride the pale yellow flow up past the walls and into Mom's inner sanctuary, gently, gently, through onion-layer after onion-layer of defenses and evasions.*

Aftermath of blood clot and swelling. Dead tissue. Marks of surgery. *Spread soothing. Touch the thoughts cowering deep inside the bunker.*

Dad's face, red with rage, breath reeking of whiskey. Shouted words. A woman's face, painted and streetwise. The fist. Sudden red pain, and falling, and terror, and blessed darkness.

Jo staggered back, shoved away by the force of her mother's will slamming the door on this intrusion. She leaned against the wall of the hospital room, panting, sickened by what she'd found in her vain attempt at healing. It hadn't been a stroke. Mom's brain had been damaged, yes, but not by stroke or fall. She didn't *want* to come out and face the world. Not *that* world.

She caught her breath and straightened up. Dad's rat-face stared at her from across the bed, crafty, nervous, too aware of what had happened. *Old Blood.* Brian had said they must have inherited it from both sides.

*So that was how he controlled us.*

Jo took another breath, deep and slow, feeling the Power building within her like a lightning charge. Hair rose on her head like that time she'd drawn on the magic of the Summer Country and her blood to blast two slugs from a pistol that defied the laws of faery. Guns weren't supposed to work, under the rules of that land. She'd *made* one work, and damn near killed that slimy fucker Sean in the process.

Her father caught the rage on her face. He seemed to shrink as her anger swelled to fill the room, and he slid furtively toward the door.

"You *bastard*!" Space twisted around them, shoving her

into the doorway and leaving him cornered. Her shout echoed between hard plaster walls, but she knew the sound was trapped in here with them. Whatever happened between them, no stranger could hear.

"You did this." Her rage narrowed and turned quiet, hissing like a welding torch adjusted to pure blue flame for burning straight through steel. "You've hit her a hundred times, a thousand times. Never again. You'll never hit *any* of us again."

He cringed away, deeper into the farthest corner of the tiny room. "Sh-sh-she fell," he stammered. "Sh-sh-she hit her head. It was an ac-ac-accident."

"Bull*shit*!"

She stared down at him, huddled there like a child trying to escape a beating, like *her* trying to escape *him*. Contemptible. She'd lived in fear of *that*?

"She found out about another one of your ten-buck syphilitic street-crawler whores. What was that, the hundredth time? You were drunk, like you've been drunk six days out of seven of your life. You hit her. You hurt her, without thought or care like you've lived your whole life without thought or care for others. You'll never hit her again."

The magic took her then, flashing up through her legs and spine to the back of her skull to send shivers down her arms. She raised her right hand and pointed dead between his eyes as if she were carrying out an execution.

"If you ever touch another woman, may your manhood fail you. If you take strong drink, may it twist your guts into knots and leave you puking sober. If you raise your hand against her or any woman, may your own hand turn against you and be your death. I lay this curse upon you by the blood tie between us. I call on the stones and trees and waters to witness it, I call on the winds to spread it wide, I call on the sun and moon and stars to guard it. If you break this doom, may you be called to judgment before the altar where you swore faith to God and to that woman lying wounded by your blows."

Then the Power released her, and she nearly staggered with the sudden weakness that washed over her. Where had those words come from? Where had they come from, in the Summer Country, when she'd been taken by the magic and shaken and wrung dry?

She stepped to one side, allowing him to scuttle past sideways like a retreating crab. "Don't let the door hit you in the ass on your way out."

The plaster wall felt cool against her forehead, gritty, reassuring in its strength and hardness. She leaned against it, trying to draw that cool soothing in to quench her headache. The room seemed to pulse around her in time with her pounding heart.

Jo turned and leaned back against the wall, staring at the rainbow auras that lined the hospital bed and side stand and IV pole. *Gods above and below, I thought I'd escaped from that. I killed a man. I strangled him with the twisting vines of Maureen's forest and enjoyed every twitch that he made dying, and I ran away because of what I'd found in my own heart. And it's followed me here, like a wolf I made the mistake of feeding.*

Her mother had turned slightly, to stare across the bed at her. Her right hand stirred. Jo felt her purpose through their shared blood, the bond of the Old Blood flowing in their veins. Her mother was trying to cross herself.

Trying to guard her soul against the demon that had left the room and the more dangerous demon that had scared him away.

# seven

—m—

"YOU HAVE THE right to remain silent. Anything you say can and will be used against you in a court of law. You have the right to speak to an attorney, and to have an attorney present during any questioning. If you cannot afford a lawyer, one will be provided for you at government expense."

Was that the third time they'd read the Miranda card at him, or the fourth? At least they hadn't read it in Spanish or Ukrainian, to make sure they'd stopped up all the mouse-holes. Brian shook his head. The cop across the table looked so young and neatly crewcut and earnest and upright, the whole scene was bloody pathetic.

*Under arrest? I could stare into your eyes, snap my fingers, and you'd escort me out through that locked door with a smile on your face. Or I could just lean across the table and kill you with one strike, then step through the edge of the world into Maureen's forest.*

Cop procedures weren't designed to deal with the Old Blood. For that matter, cop procedures and cop stations and county jails weren't designed to deal with SAS commandos. Brian let his mind float, ticking off the worn scratched gray metal doors with their electric locks, the laminated glass judas windows smoke dark so that you saw only anonymous shadows of the watchers on the other side, the concrete block walls with their dingy off-green paint designed to calm the inmates. He mapped the halls and cameras and checkpoints and the total lack of weapons inside the jail. They even had weapons lockers for beat cops coming in with a prisoner.

*Three men, five minutes, I could take this place apart and be back out through the wire with my choice of prisoners.*

He focused back on the cop in front of him, sheriff's deputy, really, corporal by the collar tabs. The man looked a bit twitchy now, with squint-wrinkles next to his eyes as if some of Brian's thoughts had leaked through to his face.

"And the charge would be . . . ?"

"Possession of forged documents, violations of the Immigration and Naturalization laws, and weapons violations. Those are enough for the hearing."

Brian relaxed a touch. They were all bail offenses. No murder charges or planted drugs. Spend a night or two in jail, hand them some fairy gold—or more accurately, a fairy check that would evaporate in midtransfer—and walk away. He'd eaten prison food before. No worse than field rations and a hell of a lot better than gnawing on cold mutton in a Falkland Islands trench. The place was even warm and dry.

The corporal guided him through a maze of corridors and rooms, booking and mug shot and fingerprints, change into an orange jumpsuit and inventory of prisoner's possessions with signed receipt. Doors clicked and banged and echoed. He wrinkled his nose as they passed a trusty hosing down the holding cell and the drunk inside it, sour with puke, battered from a fight or the arrest, still screaming abuse at some distant bint named Carla. He mapped it all and rated it, compared with other prisons he'd seen in Burma and Turkey and Mexico and England. *About a seven,* he thought, *on a scale of ten. I've stayed in worse hotels.*

And he didn't kill anybody. After all, he was here to take pressure off Jo and David, not add to it. The cops had demanded to see first Maureen and then him, proof that they were still alive and kicking. Otherwise, they would just keep on sitting in their cruisers outside of Jo's apartment and idling, calling them in for questioning every day or so, tapping phones and presenting search warrants at odd hours, tracking bank transactions. Cops had a million ways to make themselves obnoxious, all within the law.

A final buzz-click and hollow clang behind him, and he stood inside a dormitory cell. A thick stale mix of male bodies and disinfectant washed over him. Six metal bunks, two of them didn't match the other four. Over the design capacity, your tax dollars at work. A metal table, bolted down to floor and wall, with some sort of card game going on, five pairs of cold cynical eyes measuring him and then looking away as they decided they were *not* going to shake down the fresh meat. Wise choice.

He ignored them, didn't try to reset or even read the cell's pecking order, and sat down on the single unused bunk. He let his aura expand, testing the walls, and decided they didn't have enough iron reinforcing in them to be any problem at all. Cold iron. Only prison that had ever slowed him down was that cockroach cesspit in eastern Turkey, an iron cage. That one, he'd had to control one of the guards to escape. Amazing, the places that Queen and Country sent a man. Or the Pendragons, for that matter.

Meanwhile, he had some thinking left to do. Jails were good for that, nearly as good as a monastery or a hermit's cave. The charges stank. "Forged papers?" "Immigration laws?" Those meant some serious balls-up in the works. He'd handed the cops a *good* passport, true government issue with his own name and photo and real seals. Only way that could have broken down was with a three- or four-layer search, not just consul records but back to the Home Office and even field checks at the Cornwall address he'd claimed. *That* meant trouble for the Pendragons' inside man. Or trouble *with* the inside man, one or the other. Either meant a can of Grade A worms. He needed to get a report back to Duncan, soonest.

The weapons charge might be even worse. The Bobbies weren't talking about Maureen's toy .38—she had a license for that, concealed-carry and all. But he'd had his selector-fire FAL and a couple of suppressed machine pistols hidden in the flat, without the paper to cover them.

Thing was, the way he'd hidden them, the cops could have taken the bloody building apart down to the subcellar and never found the bleeding abditory. He'd wrapped it in some damned strong spells, and the weapons sat at about ninety degrees to human "reality."

That meant somebody with the Old Blood was involved. Fiona would be the logical suspect there. It smelled just like her kind of trick. And she might have been mucking about at the embassy as well. It should have been impossible to link up all his military records. Sometimes his sister could be a right royal pain.

The weapons and papers really didn't mean much, all things considered. It wouldn't be the first time that he'd made things vanish from an evidence locker. The Bobbies tended to get very quiet when things like that happened.

The door buzzed and clanged again, noise echoing off the bare concrete walls, and another deputy stuck his head through the opening. "Hey, Albion! Don't bother getting comfy—you've got bail." The jailer glanced across at the card players, and a nasty grin spread across his face. "Eat your hearts out, jailbirds. None of you losers has a broad that's willing to pay hard cash to get her hands on your smelly bod." Then he waggled his tongue salaciously while his hands sketched big bumps in front of his own chest.

That was fast. Brian shrugged at the other prisoners,

flipped one hand in a "Nice to meet you" gesture, and turned toward the door. Should he tell Maureen about that little byplay? He never could tell about her and sex—she might find it amusing. Or bite his head off. But her *own* description for her figure was "skinny and flat-chested," not the voluptuous curves that deputy had mimed. Brian found her beautiful, but she wasn't top-heavy by any measure.

Brian continued chewing on his puzzles while the deputy marched him back out through the process. Change clothes. Check inventory and sign again. Log the prisoner out. Buzz-click-clang of another door, a different one next to the command room with all the CCTV monitors and control switches for those doors, and he added a few more twists and turns to his mental map. And then he stepped into a corridor and faced a woman. Brian stopped short.

*Not* Maureen.

A stranger, dark-haired and dark-skinned, with big breasts and wide hips offset by a waist that would have done credit to a wasp—a shape guaranteed to make most males forget the face above it. She smiled at him, sardonic, with the lazy narrowed eyes of a cat studying a trapped mouse, and the smile rang alarm bells all up and down his spine. His nose flared in reflex, sniffing the stale prison air.

Fiona.

She'd disguised her face and body, but hadn't bothered with either her smile or the dangerous whiff of pregnant Old One. For whatever twisty reason, she wanted him and *only* him to know just who she was.

He guessed that they still had two locked doors between them and whatever other surprises she had waiting. His brain chased down the branches of her chess moves, operating in overdrive. She wanted to spook him, make him jump in some particular way. She knew how to follow him between the worlds, a nasty trick of hers that he'd never figured out.

The pasture oak was rooted in her lands and the keep might be shielded.

The Pendragons, then. And if she followed, he knew another step to safety. His old partner Claire had blurted it to him one time together in a dead run from some Sidhe that had seemed likely to cut them both to bits and burn the bits.

He stepped and felt the jail fade around him and stepped again and stepped again, quick through the darkness and the clammy air. And then he stepped into the parlor of a Georgian town house in Chelsea Court, furniture draped in yellowed dust-cloths and wallpaper peeling from the age and damp. No changes allowed—they'd never even pulled the old gas lamps from the walls.

*"If they follow us, remember. Any safe-house transit room, there'll be a circle somewhere on the walls or floor. Round mirror, round rug, a scrawl of graffiti. Walk right through it, holding a red circle in your head. You'll end up in a place with friendly guards."*

That had been Claire's message, trimmed of gasps for breath and breaks as she spun behind cover and bore her weapon on their back-trail while he sprinted and dodged ahead to find a place where he could cover her. Then they'd reached a place where they could dare to drop their guards and take a world-walk.

Those Sidhe hadn't followed, either through lack of skill or lack of caring. Fiona had—he felt it along his spine from the base of his skull clear down to his ass, and he'd learned long since to trust that feeling. And she wasn't in any hurry, either.

He scanned the walls, the floor, even the ceiling. The whole bloody place was rectilinear, wide solid furniture and heavy dusty picture frames and a square shallow hearth with a long clouded mirror mantelpiece above. He felt his sister behind him, getting closer, taking her own sweet time and savoring every step of it. She liked to play with the mice she caught.

A shadow negative on his right, the wallpaper, ghost of a picture or mirror *removed* and the old fresh paper exposed, a circle where centuries of sun and grime and smoke had never made their marks. He stared at it, making the edges red in his mind. He stepped to it and into it and through it. His sister flickered in the corner of his eye.

Then she vanished. The room vanished. He stepped into a stone room, gray and bare and square, lit by flickering oil lamps, with one open doorway to the right and a faux arch in the masonry facing him. The place looked old, smelled old, like the cellars under Maureen's keep. Just clean instead of dusty. Raised smooth stone formed a disk in the middle of the archway. He assumed that was his next gate. He could walk right through.

Except for the guards flanking the arch. Two guards, in ruffled purple velvet that put him in mind of Oscar Wilde, balloon pants and tunics and floppy poofter hats like over-grown berets straight out of Renaissance Italy. The men looked like they should be hoisting halberds at shoulder arms, instead of those 9mm SMGs. SMGs bearing on his chest, and fingers inside the trigger guards. Brian lifted his hands slowly over his head. He reminded himself that men could dress like drag queens and still be dangerous. Witness the Vatican's Swiss Guards.

They stared at him, eyes narrowed, waiting for something. Safeties clicked. Off, he presumed.

"Brian Albion, House Emris, access code Alpha Nancy Niner Fiver Seven Charlie." And if they wanted a bloody password, he was buggered.

Well, he'd reached some kind of refuge, anyway. No sign of Fiona, no sense of danger behind him. But he didn't dare relax. He'd never seen uniforms like those. And the Pendragons guarded their secrets like, well, dragons. The guards stood maybe ten feet apart, corners of the facing wall. Too far for him to take both down, and too alert. He could get one, but that wasn't good enough.

"Captain of the watch to the gatehouse!" The shout echoed back through that right-hand door into a tunnel, doubtless with a murder-hole overhead and a portcullis beyond. The place gave that same feel of a castle's outer gate. Defense-in-depth, against expected siege.

Brian thought he recognized the men, higher-ranking Pendragons he'd never actually met, didn't know their names. Field ops weren't *supposed* to know most of the roster. What you don't know, you can't tell under torture.

They kept their weapons ready, held relaxed rather than tense, but it looked like the relaxed readiness of a judo master waiting for a false move, rather than carelessness. He focused back and forth between the fingers hovering above triggers, moving in unison, slowly settling into contact and tightening on the slack. He could take one of them, but the other wouldn't miss. They'd had the same training he had. He held his ground and didn't move.

And then the captain strode out of the shadowed door, another purple poofter outfit but with gold slashes on the sleeves and a sword at his belt. Brian felt the tension easing from his shoulders. Duncan. One of his field commanders.

Duncan stopped, looking as startled as the guards had been. "Brian Albion, by all that's holy! When did *you* join the Circle?" He turned to the guards and waved them back. They snapped to attention, presenting the SMGs as a salute, boot-heels ringing on the stone. Bloody Coldstream Guards.

Then the captain scowled, staring first at Brian and then the guards. "Forgot the password again? This isn't the SAS, laddie. Every man in the unit doesn't know you and wave you through on the strength of your pretty face. But I'm glad to see you made the grade. I'll walk you through the next Circle." And he turned and stepped toward the archway with the disk.

Brian felt the tension return. "Circle," again. He grunted noncommittal agreement. Following Duncan sounded like a bad idea. The guards would let him move now, and he'd lost Fiona for the moment . . . he set his thoughts on the pasture oak and stepped forward. *Circle? What have I walked into? And can I walk out again?*

Instead of sunshine and green fields and the fieldstone border fence, he stepped into another dark heavy space lit by oil lamps. That "gatehouse" must be shielded, with a one-way ticket out. And then pieces of the scene fit together in his head—this room made a twin to the one in Maureen's cellar, complete with central menhir. He glanced down. Yes, it had the same stone flooring, the same labyrinth pattern leading to the twin of her quartz star. But this space was clean and lit and occupied, and the brooding atmosphere of old injury and hate was gone. Whatever the labyrinths were designed to do, this one would work.

Another purple body stood dead ahead, next to Duncan, arms akimbo, staring. The stance and angular body canceled any faint hint of femininity. *Oh, shit. Dierdre.*

He could have gotten on just fine without adding her to his day. She taught the order's survival classes, the meanest drill-sergeant he had ever met. As far as he could tell, she didn't want her students to live through the course. Some of them didn't.

And she did interrogations when the Pendragons *really* wanted to learn whatever a prisoner happened to know.

"What the fuck's he doing here?"

She stalked over to glare in Brian's face. No, she hadn't mellowed any since he'd last seen her.

Duncan smiled. But then, he outranked her. "Brian's come into the Circle. Nobody ever tells me anything."

"Congratulations!" She reached out to shake his hand,

her grip stronger than you'd believe from a woman of her build, and suddenly jerked him forward. She spun, pulling his hand and arm up until she tucked in under his armpit while slamming her left elbow into his gut. He sagged around the pain, and she carried him over her hip into a throw. Brian tucked and started to roll out of it, but came up against her knee in his throat. Two fingers hung an inch in front of his eyes.

He fought for breath, his head ringing. He heard dim noises. Duncan? Questioning?

"The *hell* he is," Dierdre growled in answer. "I'm on the Board. I'd know. And he's been AWOL since he offed Liam. I'm taking him through to Corbin. Summon the captain-general."

# eight

—⁂—

HE LEFT ME.

The rain poured down, matching her mood. Maureen sat under a tree, a European copper beech to be fucking specific, and let the cold water soak her jeans and blouse and run dripping down her forehead and into her eyes. Raindrops, not tears. She saved her magic for protecting the bottle. No way was she adding water to the precious *uisce beatha*.

Maureen raised her bottle in a toast to the lightning that danced around her tower, wishing it health and happiness. *Somebody* fucking deserved a little happiness.

White fire burned a jagged line across her eyes, leaving a purple glow in its wake. The snap of thunder followed so close that she didn't have time to blink. It came back as rumbling booms that echoed across emptiness.

*He left me.*

*Well, you tried to claw his eyes out.* The critic had come back to fight another round. *Getting to be kind of a habit, isn't it? Only with Dougal, you succeeded.*

The keep was empty. Sure, there were maybe twenty or

thirty humans in there, former slaves huddling away from her wrath. But Brian had left. The heart of it had left. She'd felt him leave, as she'd walked toward the Sunrise County Courthouse to post his bail. One moment there in Naskeag Falls, the next moment gone. And he hadn't come back. He hadn't bothered to leave a goddamn note or even yell at her.

Left with some brunette with big tits, the duty sergeant had made it plain. One of so many ways in which Maureen couldn't compete to hold a man.

*And what would he come back for? A kick in the balls, next time? Or would you just carve his heart out of his chest with your fingernails and eat it for a morning snack?*

She'd tried to follow his path down into the cellars, see if he'd left some clues down there. Down into the dungeons, to be more exact, and the damp sour musty reek and darkness had closed in around her and sucked her back to Dougal and Padric and weeks of beatings, weeks without sleep, weeks of hunger and cold and the slow dive into madness as she stared at the stone walls of her cell. Part of her soul was still locked behind cold iron.

Her hand shook with the memories, and she drained another swallow from the bottle. Maybe she would just drink herself to death and save Fiona or the dragon the trouble of killing her.

<And here we'd thought we could let the suicide watch stand down.>

Stand down. That was a Brian phrase, military-speak. But it was the fox. Her brain conjured up a red fox vixen whenever she deluded herself into thinking she could talk to the forest. The vixen sat in front of Maureen, prim and catlike on her haunches, dry in spite of the raging storm and with every hair and whisker perfect like she'd just come from the groomer's bench at some goddamn poodle salon.

<*Poodle?* For that, I should just let you drown yourself in your yellow poison.>

"Get the fuck out of my brain. I've got enough problems without having to take shit from a sarcastic hallucination."

<And who started with the insults, already? Delusions? Hallucinations? A perfectly innocent numenon for the magic wildwood, and you compare me to a *poodle?*>

"I don't need this crap."

The fox stood up, stretching fore and aft like a cat making sure that her spine was the correct length, and stepped daintily over wet rocks and roots and leaves until she stood by Maureen's right hand. She brought her sphere of dry air with her through the pounding rain. Delusion or not, Maureen smelled the faint skunky fox-musk of her, felt her warmth close enough to touch.

<I'll tell you what you don't need. You don't need that bottle. The FDA has never approved ethanol for the treatment of clinical depression or paranoid schizophrenia or any other psychosis. Besides which, you aren't crazy. You're just lazy. Get off your butt and quit whining. You've got work to do.>

Then the fox turned her head slightly, snapped, and pain lanced through Maureen's wrist. She stared at the blood welling up where the vixen's teeth had slashed the skin. The bottle lay next to her foot, glugging quietly to itself as the sharp fumes of Black Bush spread through the wet furry earthiness of the forest.

Maureen was too shocked to rescue her booze. She just crouched there staring at the blood twisting into thin ribbons mingling with the rain, too shocked even to stop the bleeding and bring her Power to heal the punctures.

"You bit me."

<Damn straight. Hey, if you weren't sitting on it, I'd do the same number on your ass.>

"You *bit* me!"

<I work with what I've got. If I had hands, I'd try to slap some sense into your pointy little head.>

"Get fucked! Who appointed *you* God for the day?"

<You did. You bound yourself to the good of the forest. You gave us your memories and speech when you smeared your blood on the tree and threatened to burn this land bare of life if we didn't let your sister go. I'm just doing the job you gave me.>

"Jesus Christ, now I've got a four-legged shrink nagging me into AA! As if Brian wasn't enough." And then she stopped and swallowed. Brian . . .

<Exactly.> The vixen wrinkled her nose at the reek of whiskey, stepped daintily around the polluted earth, and walked away. Bone dry. She looked back over her shoulder. <And you might spend some time thinking about whose storm this was, and just where all the lightning struck.>

The storm had subsided into thin rain while they talked, with only a few rumbled memories high in the clouds. Maureen's clothing and hair were dry again, her magical subconscious handling little details like fending off hypothermia while she was busy elsewhere. Where *had* the lightning struck? She'd been outside for the entire storm, shivering with the claustrophobia of the dungeons, the stone walls closing in around her and the cold burn of iron binding her neck and wrists and ankles.

Most of the fireworks had flashed from cloud to cloud, as usual. She turned to the beech and laid her palm against its smooth bark, sending her thoughts into the forest, asking. Nothing had struck the trees. No list of killed or wounded from her tantrum.

She played back the *Frankenstein* memory of dark sky and black castle ruins on a high hill, strobed by lightning flashes. All the ground strokes had hit her keep. Hit the burned stones of Dougal's tower. Sure, it was the highest point for miles around, but that was carrying things a little far.

*Jeezum.* She hadn't realized how much she loathed that pile of stone and all the pain that oozed from it. Only Brian and whiskey had made it bearable. And now *he* had left.

Brian had taken it for granted that they'd move into the castle and live there. She owned the place, right? Feudal *fort main* shit, right? And he thought of walls as defenses, a way to keep threats outside and at arm's length.

She guessed that he'd never been a prisoner. Sometimes people built walls to keep things *in*.

The bottle of Irish ambrosia still lay at her feet, nearly half full. Or half empty. She bent down and picked it up. The smooth sharp tang of its golden liquid pulled at her. She lifted it to the paling sky and dissipating clouds, toasting whatever gods ruled this land.

Then she tilted the bottle and poured the whiskey out in a slow deliberate stream that gave her hand plenty of chance to argue with her head. Her body shuddered with longing as each drop splattered and sank into the deep forest duff at her feet.

She started to heave the empty bottle against a rock, sort of like christening her ship of tentative sobriety, but her environmental conscience intervened. She set it down unbroken against the tree trunk, stared at it for a moment, and then inverted it. *Sort of like flying a flag upside down.*

And that was that. She turned her back on the keep. *I'd rather drink muddy water, and sleep in a hollowed-out log . . .* She wondered what song that line came from. David would know. David, back in Naskeag Falls with Jo and with a normal life to live.

She looked at her wrist. The vixen's bite had healed, leaving faint pale scars on top and bottom where fangs had torn her skin. *Thanks for the memories.* Memories of the sweet oblivion of booze.

Alcohol. Alcoholic. A shudder ran down her spine. Sobriety looked like a black gap as wide as the Grand Canyon. Never take another drink? Where the *hell* had *that* notion come from?

The forest wanted her sober.

That bite grabbed her attention more than Brian's quiet protests ever had. He'd been too polite to say what needed saying. He'd stayed with her far too long. Trust Mother Nature for "tough love," personified by a true bitch goddess.

The air still reeked of whiskey. She eyed the bottle, sitting upside down against the trunk of the old beech. Right side up, there'd be a trickle of nectar gathering in the bottom by now, the film from the glass walls sliding down. You could get a few more drops that way . . .

*Jesus, what a lush!*

How do you stay sober? Classic AA question. She'd been to the meetings. You stay sober one drink at a time. *The next one. That's all. Turning down* one *drink isn't hard. You've done that a thousand times before.*

She knew the rules. Whatever "hitting bottom" meant, she thought she qualified. Admit that you're an alcoholic. One day at a time. She didn't know about that "higher power" shit. Her image of God was too mixed up with Daddy, not a good concept for positive reinforcement. Maybe she should hand her problem to the forest, instead. She believed in *it*.

What did the forest want of her? She stopped next to an oak, rough-barked and thick and ancient but not the patriarch of the forest. Not the Summer Country's incarnation of Father Oak. Her hands explored the trunk, tasting the bitterness of oak-tannin through her palms, feeling deep into the xylem and phloem, the lignin and cellulose in rings of summer and winter wood even here in the unchanging Summer Country.

It welcomed the rain. It wanted more. Dougal had held tight control on *everything* that way, just like he'd starved her to control her and weaken her magic.

Maureen relaxed into the land, the currents of water beneath it and the flow of air above and the life between the two. She summoned clouds again, but gentle this time. The rain pattered down around her, rustling the leaves and soaking slowly into the ground and raising the damp, healthy mold-rot incense from the soil. No storms, not another toad-strangler with lightning stabbing down to mirror her rage. A gentle spring rain.

Deep into the heart of the forest, she asked how much and how long before the roots and surface sponge could take no more. An inch seemed to be the answer, spread over a day or maybe two. That wouldn't cause the swamp to rise, not with the natural capacity of an old-growth forest to retard runoff. That wouldn't bring danger to the dragon's nest. The oak would like more, to recharge aquifers and the deep sub-soil that its taproot touched, but she voted for a balance. The dragon hated her, but she didn't hate the dragon.

That was the other thing. She remembered that her forest wasn't just wood and leaf and stone and small crawling decomposers. It defended her, and she had enemies. It saw and smelled and felt what passed within it. God knows, it could stop trespassers and kill them if it wished. Just ask Jo and David.

Or Sean. His skeleton lay somewhere close by, slowly adding calcium to the soil as the leafy acid loam dissolved it. Best use he'd ever had.

Maureen shuddered. Sometimes she thought this land was one long booze-induced DT session as her pickled brain-cells tried to detox in a drunk ward of Naskeag General's Kelly Four. Or maybe she was spaced out on one of those psycho-drugs the shrinks had tried.

<It isn't paranoia if they really *are* out to get you.>

Now the fox was quoting Maureen's flip clichés back at her. She wished the forest had picked up a little less of Jo's personality from their bonding.

But it was a good point. She let her thoughts slip into the tree again, and through the tree into the net of rootlets and mycelium that intertwined for miles around and bound the entire wildwood into one living unit. If she had defenses, she ought to use them. If she had ears, she damned well ought to listen.

Or use her million eyes. A slim shadow slipped through the woods, short dark hair and olive skin, androgynous. It wore gray rags, torn by thorns and briars.

Sick memory settled in Maureen's belly. Fiona's twin, that was, the treacherous bastard who'd bewitched her into Dougal's hands. Sean's etched crumbling skeleton brought back to life. How much could healing magic do?

Or necromancy? But the forest still touched his bones, still wrapped them in briars and rootlets and fungi hungry for the minerals he bore. He was dead. The forest told her that, for true.

Then what walked her lands?

What, not who. Celtic myth told many tales of ghosts. The ones she remembered did not call them good omens.

*It could be worse. It could be Dougal, back to gnaw at your soul and sanity.*

As if the thought had given him form, the forest showed her another scene. A small gnarled man watched the keep's open gate through the rain. Old scars curled around his arms and seamed his body. Dark empty pits replaced his eyes, even though he acted as if he had full sight, and a raw line of red crossed the joining of his neck to his body.

Maureen broke her bond with the tree. Her knees buckled, and she collapsed into a shivering huddle among the roots.

Dougal. She stared at her hands, seeing blood fresh and dripping, feeling the warm slick stickiness of it. She smelled smoke, not the clean sharp aromatic smoke of the kitchen cookstoves or a campfire stoked with well-dried yellow birch but the acrid reek of a burning building with charred meat in it.

No. She didn't have to take this. She didn't have to stay here. There were rules for hauntings. Those tales bound their ghosts to certain places. She could escape.

Not toward the dragon. Her forest stretched westward, away from the marsh and from Fiona's cottage. She could walk for miles that way and still hold her vow to preserve the land. She staggered to her feet, unsteady with the shock and with the whiskey still flowing through her veins. Drunk. That was it, not ghosts but whiskey. Another form of seeing spirits.

She didn't touch the oak, though, didn't sink her own spirit into the forest's intricate weave. She didn't feel the need for any more closed-circuit TV images from Tir na Nog. Instead, she shuffled through her pockets and her automatic Great North Woods checklist—the Bic lighter that Jo always laughed at because neither of them smoked, the combination whistle, match-safe and compass, the Swiss Army Knife, and ten yards of parachute cord—all the gear she'd carried since her first Girl Scout overnight.

And then there was that damned Gurkha knife hanging from her belt, so heavy it felt like it dragged her sideways. Brian told her to always carry the ugly *kukri,* even in the keep. He seemed completely blind to the memories it brought.

Or maybe he thought it was important enough to be worth the cost.

She turned her back on the keep and all the booze she could ever dream of drinking. She concentrated on placing one foot in front of the other, walking away. One step at a time. One day at a time.

The rain fell, not touching her, steady and slow, no faster than the soil could absorb it. As it soaked in, it released the forest's perfume. She drank it straight, the mingled rot and growth of an incredibly complex living thing, deep into her lungs, and felt the clean air and time and exercise wash the whiskey from her blood. She walked until the clouds turned dark above her, and twice she caught glimpses of the fox trotting through the woods beside her. Even glimpses were a gift.

As the light faded, she picked out another oak and touched it, gently, not going deep but renewing her bond and her vision of the land close by. She blinked at what she found, and her hand caressed the hilt of the *kukri* as she thought about it. Not a ghost this time, but she might decide to make it one . . .

She asked the forest for a hollow tree and a pair of rabbits, fat and female, too old to bear another litter of tiny fuzzball bunnies. She walked about fifty yards through the forest and found them in a small open glade. She thanked the rabbits for their gift before she lopped their heads off with the *kukri*.

A dead limb offered firewood, dry but sound from the core, and she kindled a fire in front of a Maureen-sized hollow in the trunk of a lime tree large enough that she couldn't span the bole with her outstretched arms. While the fire burned to coals, she cleaned and skinned and spitted the rabbits on green maple saplings. The forest watched and waited, guarding her, listening to a frightened heartbeat in the shadows.

The smell of roast meat filled the clearing. She turned the spits every few minutes, watching the fat boil up and sizzle down into the coals, thinking, remembering.

She looked beyond the red glow of her fire, into the darkness under the far trees. "The second rabbit is for you. If I don't decide to kill you first."

One of the shadows detached itself from its tree and stepped forward, becoming a man. She felt his fear. He came closer in spite of it. Maureen clenched her fists, digging fingernails into the pain of her own flesh, as his face took form in the fire's glow. The dungeon walls closed in around her.

Padric. Dougal MacKenzie's master falconer and huntsman, jailer, torturer, slave.

# nine

—✹—

THUNDER RUMBLED IN the distance, faint but menacing. Khe'sha shivered. The sun faded, bringing an icy touch to the waters of the marsh, and gusts of wind roiled the surface. They whipped the sawgrass flat in flashing whorls and pulled pine-smell down from the forest. A storm was brewing. But he couldn't leave the nest mound. The time of hatching had come.

> <All life was an egg, a black egg in darkness,
> Black inside, black outside, all was the egg.
> The earth was inside, the earth lay in darkness,
> The sun was inside, giving no light.
> Pan'gu was inside, both mother and father,
> Pan'gu who had laid the dark egg was inside it.>

He chanted the ancient story in mind-speech, binding tradition to the new lives in the nest, tying them to clan and blood across the ages and the edges of the world. Sha'khe should have joined him, repeating the words as they took turns and turns again as the eggs trembled on the edge of hatching, but Sha'khe was dead. Khe'sha had to stay and guard and chant for both of them.

Thunder boomed again over the hilltops, much nearer, and he ducked his head close to the water. Black clouds billowed on the horizon. The rain he feared was coming, coming in a sudden fierce storm that could chill or drown his hatchlings just as they broke forth from their shells. The songs said that he should let such chances happen, praising them as he praised the warmth of the sun. The songs said that luck was as important to a hatchling as strength.

Luck? He glared up at the dark tower on the hilltop. In this land, *luck* didn't bring storms down upon your head or cause them to pass safely by. The weather was *her* mood, *her* whim. The red witch. Someday soon, he would taste her blood.

But now he must stand guard and sing. He told the tiny lives of that first hatching: of Pan'gu breaking out of the egg he/she had laid, of Pan'gu igniting the sun and casting it into the heavens and following it with the moon and the stars, of she/he forming the oceans and the dry lands and all that lived within them.

Chanting the slow deep lines, he told of how the tribes and clans grew, of the long lineages father to son, mother to daughter, through ages and ages to Khe'sha and Sha'khe and the nest mound in this swamp of exile. Of how the bloodlines would flow on and on until the end of time and the coming of Pan'gu yet again, to lay the final egg of the world and slip inside it for rebirth.

Beginning and end, and yet endless as the telling should be endless until the last egg lay as empty fragments of shell. Even the form of the telling was ancient, the *Kunja* form used only for the hatching song.

A white flash dazzled him for an instant, lightning against the darkness boiling over the crest of the hill. Rain hissed across the sky in dark slanting lines against the blazing outlines of the backlit thunderclouds. But their main fury missed the swamp. Witch winds battled overhead, holding the storm at bay and deflecting it into the forest to soak the moss and dry duff among the roots. The lightning and the driving rain set his nerves tingling, as if he felt the charge of those clouds gathering on his crest to draw fire from the sky. His kind feared lightning, one of the few things they *did* fear.

The shiver turned into that prickly feeling of hostile eyes. Someone watched, out there in the rain. Khe'sha squinted against the raindrops, looking up toward the keep and his enemy. Clouds shrouded the hilltop now, veiling everything in formless gray.

He lifted his head, nervous from the storm, and looked around. The edge of the marsh lay gray and faint under low clouds. The mists parted. A figure stood on a nearby point, untouched by the rain and wind, watching him, watching the nest, watching the hatching. Dark cloth covered the form's head and shadowed its face.

He couldn't see the color of its hair.

CÁITLIN SHIVERED. SHE *hated* being cold and wet. And she'd never had to put up with it before. Though her cottage stood exposed on a lonely tor surrounded by bog and rolling moorland, the breeze always caressed her cheek with a warm and gentle touch and the peat fire burned clean and clear. And anytime she wished, she could walk the warm coral sands of Bora Bora and listen to the gossip the trade winds whispered in her ears.

Spiteful downdrafts chasing smoke back into the kitchen to sting your eyes, bitter searching winter winds, the clammy creep of fog that chilled you to the bone and left you wandering lost through mires that spelled death to the unwary—those had always been for others. Being an aer witch had its benefits.

Her nod of agreement and the blood gift had ended that. Fiona had swallowed Cáitlin's blood and swallowed Cáitlin's will with it in a rite as binding as Communion. Things once connected remained connected. Cáitlin could still command the winds, but only in Fiona's service.

Or when the dark witch focused her attention elsewhere. Even then, Cáitlin didn't try to work the winds in *this* forest. She wasn't sure she could. Few Old Ones cared to waste their power in extravagant displays like a thunderstorm. Dougal's killer wrote her rage across the sky and underlined it with a lightning bolt. If Cáitlin touched her fingers to the weaving of the aer, this forest would know it in an instant and pass word to its new mistress. So Cáitlin bit her tongue and lived with the cold.

Cold, and wet, and her bones ached. Walking *hurt,* jabbing knives into her joints and tendons. Even standing left her with a dull red throb like arthritis or fever where her hips and shoulders grew used to the changes Fiona had wrought in molding this body to a semblance of a man. Cáitlin felt awkward every time she moved, a stranger in her own skin. She could never forget.

*I have made a mistake.* That was supposed to be one of the deepest expressions of shame in the Japanese language. The phrase should be followed by a formal apology in exquisite calligraphy, and suicide. Well, the Old Blood often treated mistakes as ritual suicide.

*Her* mistake lay in thinking that Fiona wanted allies in her war, that the old custom of trading favor for favor still ruled the land. However, Fiona seemed to think her Power met her needs. She certainly hadn't needed any help to reduce that rebel keep to smoking rubble. Slaves and pawns had done the job quite thoroughly.

Pawns could wear many forms. Cáitlin turned and studied a black shadow sprawled along one limb of a massive oak, sheltering from the rain. The shadow blinked lazily back at her and then licked its paw, its pink tongue framed by white fangs longer than her fingers. The winds said that it was one of Dougal's pets, a mutated leopard trained to guard the keep and kill trespassers. It scrubbed behind one ear with the damp paw, a housecat magnified a hundredfold. But it watched her through the entire move. Apparently it wasn't hungry. Yet. Death walked this forest in a dozen different bodies.

Or none at all. Cáitlin's shiver turned into a shudder of distaste. She stared down at the moldering skeleton that now served as the center of her life. Brambles still bound the form like a Druid's sacrifice wrapped in wicker, and rootlets fuzzed across each bone and flowed acid into the porous calcium to etch it into dust. That had been a living man a few days past. Now it looked as if it had lain on the forest floor for centuries. No, she did *not* want to attract the redhead's attention.

Instead of talking to the winds, she listened, hearing words the branches creaked when they flexed and shed the storm's raindrops, words the leaves whispered as the air brushed past. The forest told her where the redhead walked, and Cáitlin slipped quietly away in the opposite direction, moving with the gentle flow of a breeze, moving like a ghost reluctant to show itself to living eyes. For her, stealth came easy. No one ever saw the wind. Fiona's command meshed perfectly with Cáitlin's tattered remnants of self-preservation.

That command bound Cáitlin to a hundred double paces in any direction through the woods, a soft-edged circle with the skeleton as its focus. Fiona had commanded her to haunt the place of Sean's dying. When Cáitlin neared the limit, each further step became a battle until she gasped with the effort of another inch. That was as far as Fiona thought her ghost should roam without direct command.

Cáitlin roamed to her limit, then, the safer limit farthest from Maureen's aura, and her winds carried what she saw to Fiona's cottage and to Llewes, the Welshman she'd spoken of, wherever the Pendragons' master wove his webs. The dark wet stones of Dougal's keep loomed through the trees, and she wondered why Maureen would stray so far away from home and comfort and safety. That witch had a lot of faith in her Powers.

No wonder Fiona hated her.

And a deep shielded part of Cáitlin's mind followed a wisp of thought. *Let my enemy think I hide in fear. She wants a spy. If I hide from danger, I hide from the very sights she wants to see. If she wants a puppet, then that is all she'll get. The precise wording of the vow, just as she would give. ". . . whenever she requires them." She's looking elsewhere now.*

*What I don't know, I can't report.*

Cáitlin reached out with her thoughts, gently caressing the flow of Power through the forest. The trees and rocks around here brimmed with magic—the wildwood rejoicing in its new freedom and the stewardship of a mistress who loved trees. If Cáitlin used the merest drop of that exuberance, her touch would fall no heavier than a leaf fluttering to the forest floor. The red witch walked far away and found distraction. She shouldn't notice.

Cáitlin fetched scones and cheese and a skin of wine, local food she could pull from the table and shelves of her own small hut. That would least disturb the currents of the land, least attract attention.

Her feet stirred without her will. The puppet's mistress had returned, sending her captive eyes deeper into the tangled woods. The feet retraced their steps, past the skeleton and its rags of rain-matted moldering cloth, under the oak's spread and the long shadow whose yellow-slitted lazy eyes almost let you forget jaws that could rip your throat out at a whim, across a moss-slick stream chattering from the thunderstorm. Day slid into dusk under the clouds, and the rain turned gentle.

Cáitlin felt Maureen's presence strengthening in the breeze that brushed her cheek, the leaves that rustled damply under her feet. Fiona loosened the anchor chain, and her puppet crept beyond that ghostly limit. As quiet as an evening breeze, Cáitlin sought her enemy's enemy.

Faint wood-smoke twisted through the forest and orange light twinkled between tree-trunks, a campfire immune to rain. The savor of roasting meat drifted downwind. Cáitlin smelled a tinge of puzzlement wafting back from Fiona.

What kind of trick was this, leaving hearth and home for a woods camp in the storm?

FERGUS TOUCHED THE stone wall again, feeling its grain alive under his fingertips, old stonework even as the Summer Country reckoned time. The new work? He sneered at that. But the old . . . It was good work, work by hands that knew stone and mortar and gravity, firm foundations and the strength of compression. This wall knew its roots.

He cared little for the swings of power in the Summer Country, the balance between one witch and another, the question of Maureen's strength or Fiona's. Stone, now, and the minerals and flows of the earth's blood found there—those warmed his heart and soul. Not just gold, as some fools had typified his kind. A geode of clear purple amethyst spoke as much truth and beauty as a diamond.

So he'd made a mistake, entering Fiona's maze? No need to weep over it like that fool Cáitlin. That mistake had brought him here, where he had never been.

His hand tingled with the residue of a lightning stroke.

That was design and love of good stone again—the bolt had burned into the highest point of the tallest tower, far from where Fergus sheltered. All that power had spread throughout the stonework until each carved block had carried part, well within its strength. Walls, towers, lintels and arches and buttresses all worked together like the cells of plant or animal.

Fergus liked this keep. It spoke to him.

And it was *empty*. That puzzled him, and Fiona through him. Power laired here, deep beneath the ground, and human slaves cowered in their stinking hovels, but the Old Blood had left.

When Fiona had learned that, she had turned her eyes elsewhere. Stone held no interest to her. She thought it was lifeless, without soul and without a will she could command. That was a blindness in her.

And this stone was more alive than most. He let his fingers slide into it, molecules between molecules, and felt the heartbeat of it. It welcomed him. Given time and no guard watching, he could walk straight through the thickest masonry of these walls, sink down into the foundations. But it was easier to use doors.

He turned and looked across the rain-streaked courtyard at one. A human stood in the doorway there, frozen, eyes wide. She paled as his glance fell on her, and she crossed herself with trembling fingers before she slammed the door. He heard the thump as a bar dropped across the wooden slab and settled into sockets.

Apparently he made an effective ghost. He wondered what the woman had seen. Old scars, yes, everyone who knew Dougal would know those. Those had to match. His new scars itched like true healing wounds, wrist and neck and belly. No way of knowing how Fiona chose that pattern, whether she drew memories out of the redhead's blood scattered through the hedge maze or had just guessed at the death-cuts.

According to rumor, only Maureen would know what

she'd left behind to wait for the flames. No one else had seen Dougal's corpse. But gossip about his death spread on the winds of magic and flowed through the waters beneath the land, just as the news of Fiona's defeat had followed close behind. The land knew many things.

He wondered what the tower would say. Even within the Old Blood, Fergus knew that his skills were rare. Few believed that stone could see and hear and speak. He knew otherwise. You just had to ask the right questions and have the Power to listen.

Stones as old as these would have seen a lot of blood. They wouldn't think in terms of days or weeks or even years. Centuries, yes, rain and wind eating the walls grain by patient grain—that they'd notice. They would remember Dougal's coming and the changes that he'd made. They would remember a thing as rare as fire.

Fergus trailed his hand along the wall, listening, walking slowly through the rain. Old, older, younger, older, the stones told him how they'd stood and the fleeting lives they'd framed.

And the Power that flowed through them.

Fiona had lost interest in him. She wanted news of her half-brother and this new witch. If they went elsewhere, her mind went elsewhere, following them. Fiona was riding Cáitlin now.

Fiona didn't care about stone, about the craft and art and magic of working it, about the ways to draw it up and pile it high and delve it deep and frame air and light with it and stand it strong against the ages. Above all, she didn't understand the Power in it. He felt that Power. He felt that life. He felt pain and long-simmering anger, deep down beneath, and a flicker of hope that he could be the healing touch it needed.

He followed that sense, to older stone and yet older, deeper into the heart of the keep. He felt the fear around him, peeking from between the slats of shuttered windows. Dougal's ghost walked his cobbled courtyard, and the humans listened to the rumbles of departing thunder and heard death in them. He could go where he willed, take whatever time was necessary. No one dared to face him.

Old oak waited for him, set strong in old stone and bound about with old iron and old spells. The door was locked. He closed his eyes and set his hand on the pull-ring. Iron. Only one like Fergus could do this, talking to the cold hard crystals that sucked magic into themselves and gave back pain to the Old Blood. He felt the icy fire burning the palm of his hand, but as the metal drew Power from him, he used it to align crystal with crystal, stress with stress, until the lock answered him and opened.

The way led downward, to anger that had darkened these stones for centuries.

FIONA CHEWED ON her lip. She studied the branching diagram on her laptop screen, typed in a few words, added another branch, and frowned.

Something like genetics, this was, a decision tree that broadened with every step. When she charted genealogy, each level narrowed from past to present. She found that more pleasing. She liked to narrow people's choices until nothing remained but the path she set for them.

She pushed her chair back from the computer and rested her eyes. Shadows formed out of the darkness beyond the pool of lamplight—Cáitlin squatting inelegantly on her haunches, wincing with pain and wishing herself closer to a fire, Fergus stirring soaked ash inside a burned-out tower. Nothing interesting. She left them to their boredom.

The orange lamplight glinted off stainless steel, gray and green enamel, the curve of Dewar flask and petri dish and test tube. These instruments gave her facts, but more importantly they fed her image as a *scientific* witch.

None of this uncertainty. Who would have predicted that Maureen would leave her castle to eat scorched rabbit and sleep in a hollow tree? Who would have predicted that Brian would simply disappear before her eyes?

It had been such an *elegant* plot. And it *had* separated him from his darling Maureen. But she'd really rather know exactly where he was, or better, have him back under her control. She'd tried to trace him through the mists of the layered worlds, drawing on the blood ties between them and the tissue samples she'd stored in liquid nitrogen. She'd come up empty.

Oh, she'd lost him before, once and then again, smelling out the faint traces as he stepped through this gate or that, but she'd always known whether he was alive or dead. Even dead meat would carry their shared DNA. She'd know a vector even if she lacked the distance to place him on the map. But now he had walked behind some wall and vanished totally.

She frowned again and added another "what if" to the branching flow chart. "What if" he hadn't left at all, but had simply learned to hide from her the same way that she hid from him? She didn't like that one. It implied he was turning from brute force to finesse, from his lifelong study of weapons and the fighting arts to the heritage of his blood. That he was starting to use his *brain*, a disused tool in his kit. Then he'd have both.

Then he would have to die.

That was a pity. He was a beautiful boy, and he carried such interesting genes. She wanted a son to mate with the daughter that she carried. Still, she had his sperm stored for breeding.

Fiona stood up, leaving the flow chart active on the screen. It sat there as a puzzle unfinished, glowing blue against the orange-white light of the mantle lamp hanging overhead. She caressed her microscope and centrifuge, the cold unambiguous enamel and steel of science and the thoroughly modern touch she brought to magic. She used human tools when they suited her task, just as Brian used human firearms when he walked lands where they would work.

And the Summer Country had no rules against electricity. She had electric lights to use when a flame would be dangerous in the lab. Still, she mostly used kerosene for light and wood for heat and cooking, because she could summon them at need. As far as she knew, no Old One yet had figured out how to summon electrons from the human power grid. So she relied on solar panels on the roof and batteries in a shed out back where the sulfur stink wouldn't wrinkle her nose and brow.

The orange-tinged kerosene light felt warmer, though, more natural, fighting against the chill of Maureen's curse. She frowned. The bitch shouldn't have been able to do that. Obviously, Fergus had cheated on his promise. He'd given the feeling of protection while not spending time and effort on the true warding.

Then her face relaxed into the mocking drooped-eyelid smirk she'd practiced in a mirror. Fergus was a problem solved. And his treachery also meant that Maureen thought herself stronger than she was. If the bitch thought she could walk safely through Fiona's gate and hedge and door a second time . . .

The smile broadened as it became real. But whether her smile was "real" or "false" meant very little. She was an actress, yes. This lab formed one of her many stages, a threat of a kind of Power no one else in the Summer Country could wield. Fully half of her strength lay in convincing her enemies to fear her. If she could do it with a calculated sneer or a piece of lab equipment she rarely used instead of a spell, that craft saved her true Power for when she needed it.

But if the sneer wasn't enough . . .

Fiona rubbed her belly, feeling the Power growing there.

The baby kicked and turned. She felt her mother's touch, the magic flowing between them as the child grew. Already they recognized each other.

She let her mind sink into that touch, testing, measuring. She'd been right in her calculations—the baby would be fertile. The mutation that both mother and father carried would breed true. Her children and her children's children would rule both the Summer Country and the humans' world.

With a casual flick of thought, Fiona adjusted the lamp overhead, turning its wick down to a blue glow and withdrawing her gift of fire from the flame. A second touch from her mind, and the computer started its complex shutdown dance. The door opened behind her, answering her whim, and she stepped out of the lab. The door closed again, obedient, and locked itself. She glanced over the tangled spells that would kill any stranger who set hand to the lock. They stood firm.

She climbed the spiral stair to her kitchen, slowly, making sure of each step and keeping one hand on the smooth oak rail because her swelling belly did strange things to her balance. Why did pregnancy have to be so inelegant? The whole process seemed poorly designed. And then there was birth at the end of it, all sweat and blood and pain and mess. Some women even died.

The kitchen waited, cold and cheerless in spite of a fire in the stove. Smoke pricked her eyes, the curse again, choking the draft of her chimney flue.

Her stairway vanished behind her, becoming a closet even to Fiona's own eyes. That spell also held. Maureen had never guessed.

Illusion and acting, the basis of that toy humans called "magic." Smoke and mirrors. And then, hiding behind that veil, the iron claw of true power. It all made life worth living.

# ten

—※—

MAUREEN STUDIED THE curved blade of her *kukri*, red with blood and the flickering light of her campfire, glowing with the dull shine of decades of use and honing. How many men had died on this blade? She'd killed Dougal with it, and Brian said he'd carried it in Malaysia and the Falklands. Used it on night raids. And now she balanced its weight in her fingers and weighed the shadow across her cooking fire.

Padric.

Dougal's huntsman and jailer. He'd tortured her. He'd starved her and broken her sleep into shattered moments and beaten her bloody and staged a rape scene to push her into Dougal's arms. And after all of that, she'd let him live. She'd freed him, just like he'd cut the jesses and thrown that deadly peregrine into the sky to fly free after she'd killed Dougal.

Now the peregrine had returned. She stared across the fire. He squatted there, tearing at a roasted haunch as if he hadn't eaten since he left the keep. Tall and thin, long blond hair pulled back into a ponytail, worn leather jacket and forester's green twill pants wet from the rain. He had some kind of coarse scarf wound around his neck.

"Any reason I shouldn't just kill you?"

He looked up from the carcass, face shiny with grease and blood. Feral. He chewed and swallowed, not *totally* lost to manners. "None, lady. Please let me speak before you do it." And his teeth tore another chunk from the rabbit.

Maureen cleaned the blade and dried it on a scrap of fur. Brian would skin *her* if she let it rust, or sheathed it bloody. Brian was . . . particular about his weapons. His professional tools.

The rain pattered down through the trees, thickening as if calling in reinforcements to wash away more blood. It didn't touch her, though, or the fire. She slid the blade into its leather sheath and shuddered.

She needed a drink.

Instead, she grabbed her rabbit from the fire, juggling hot grease on the green wooden spit until she found a spot that was both cooked and cool enough to eat. Tough, gamy, unsalted, and no herbs, she chewed and criticized her cooking. And her mind listed bay and sorrel and sage that she'd seen, and bushes of rosemary, that's for remembrance, and sweet maple sap and apples and a salt lick—running off on culinary tangents to escape the twin questions of Padric and blood. Her back-brain saw him and saw Dougal behind him and sent her hand twitching for the knife.

She could live out here without the keep. The forest welcomed and protected her. Something heavy nudged her elbow, and she looked down into deep yellow pools of eyes set in ebony fur. The black leopard settled under her arm, purring in an earthquake rumble and staring across the fire at his former master. Padric and the cat studied each other, quiet and appraising, as if their eyes renegotiated their old relationship of one slave to another. The cat yawned. Padric took another bite, and chewed.

Slave. Dougal had been a beast-master, able to force the cat and the dragons to obey his will, owning Padric's soul. For Dougal, even Maureen had been just another dangerous animal to tame. That was why she'd let Padric walk away. But it would be so fucking *easy* to gut him like one of those suicidal bunnies. Part of her wanted that so much she quivered with the tension.

Maureen lowered one end of her spit, letting the rabbit slide off under the leopard's nose. He sniffed at it, looked back at her with a faint quizzical tilt to his whiskers that seemed to ask why she'd cooked all the goodness out of it if she wasn't going to eat it, and then licked his chops.

"Not hungry." If she ate now, she'd probably just puke the meat back up when she butchered Padric. If.

The rabbit vanished in one gulp. Padric's stare followed the carcass down the cat's throat as if he was tempted to dive in after it. He looked *hungry.*

But he nodded. "More than one way to tame a cat."

"Apparently he comes with the castle." The whole scene shimmered with surrealism, something by Kafka or Dali. Maureen wondered if she'd *ever* break free of the dissociation and depersonalization that was *almost,* but not quite, schizophrenia. PTSD.

And she was about to commit another act of trauma. *Getting good at it, aren't we? Practice makes perfect? Pretty soon you'll turn into Fiona, so hardened that nothing outside yourself has any meaning.*

She rested her hand on the *kukri,* caressing its solid reliable coldness.

"What the hell you want?"

He wiped his mouth on the sleeve of his jacket and then his hands on his pants. So much for manners. But then, she hadn't provided napkins or finger bowls.

Then he reached up and unwound the scarf from his neck. It turned into a rope. Fresh shiny hemp, ending in a hangman's noose. "I've come to ask for help, with my life as the price."

You had to give him points for drama. Maureen's stomach twisted in her belly, and she dropped her hand from the knife. The cat shoved his head under her fingers, and she scratched his ears and forehead reflexively. He purred again. She felt the vibration in her teeth.

"What kind of help? For who?"

"Long story. The short answer is, for slaves."

Well, he knew the hot buttons. "Okay, you've bought the time for the long version."

He eyed the knife and the cat. Did he prefer them to the rope? Faster? Maureen didn't know if she had the guts to hang a man. That took premeditation, and she wasn't strong on malice aforethought. Offering her the rope was a good choice. Psychology.

He looked like he was picking words. "Slaves run away. Some of them even survive. There is a keep . . . *was* a keep, where they were welcome. A couple of Old Ones who treated humans like people. Like they say you do." He shrugged.

"About three hundred of them, men, women, children. I got there just after it happened. A few of the neighboring lords and ladies decided we were powerful enough to be a threat. End of keep. End of village. End of a couple of hundred lives."

He paused and shuddered, as if unable to talk for a moment. "Dougal had been part of the plot, another one of his games. That's how I knew about it, how I knew where to find them. Men burned to the bone but still walking, holding dead children but not knowing they were dead because smoke and fire had destroyed sight and their own pain kept them from feeling the cold seeping through the body. Women with empty faces and skirts soaked in blood. A child bound to a post by his own guts and left alive for the ravens."

Silence hung between them, and the images he'd

invoked, and lasted long. Maureen had read enough about ancient warfare that she could *see* it. Crude stuff, almost Biblical, and she'd bet that the Old Ones didn't pretty it up any.

The shadows had darkened as the small fire died down to red coals shrouded in ash. Now Padric's face glowed faintly in the night, and the rope around his neck glistened like fresh blood. *Screw the symbolism.* "What the fuck you want *me* to do about it? Think I'm the Second Coming of Jesus, here to raise the dead?"

He crossed himself. She remembered him crossing himself when he'd met her with Dougal's falcon on his wrist and her with the knife bare in her hand. But all he'd asked for was the time to release all the birds before he died. Freedom for them, nothing for himself. Instead, she'd set *him* free.

*Must be damned hard to hold your faith in God in a place like this.*

"Some survived. Some got away and others faked dead. Even one of the Old Ones made it out. She's a water witch. She would have stayed and fought the fires, but the magic took over and moved her."

"And?" Although Maureen could see it coming.

"And we need a place to hide. *They* need a place to hide." He picked up the charred rabbit and gnawed away with apparent relish, as if he hadn't just described scenes that would leave most men puking.

She frowned. "They sent *you* to ask?"

He shook his head, swallowed, and wiped his mouth again. "I volunteered. I doubt if anyone else could have gotten past Shadow or your other pets."

"And why wouldn't your enemies just follow you here?"

He glanced at the black leopard warming her ankles like a house cat. "Because they're afraid of you." The cat blinked lazy eyes and continued to purr, as if he'd understood every word.

Maureen flowed to her feet and the cat suddenly tensed, heavy against her knee as if her slightest wish would launch him across the fire at Padric's throat. *That could become a problem. But then, so's the magic. Learn to keep your temper, girl.*

"Screw it. Bring them in. You can *have* the fucking dump."

Padric stood, slowly, cautious, eyeing the cat. "Something you need to know. Fiona was there. So were some Fair Folk we've always connected to the Pendragons. Conservatives, people who really like the status quo." He paused, still staring at Shadow.

"You bring change." Then he vanished into the darkness, as if he were a leopard himself.

*Probably doesn't want to give you time to change your mind.*

She needed a drink to wash away the stench of his story. But she'd sworn off that stuff. And now she had to walk back into temptation. She had to walk under the keystone of the arch back into Dougal's lair, before a bunch of strangers crowded in and muddled every trail.

The trail to Brian. Those cellars might give a clue as to where he went. He'd found someplace where her bond didn't reach.

Thunder rumbled again, closer. She turned until she felt the keep in front of her and strode off into the dark between the trees. The cat padded along beside her, a moving pool of black among black shadows and against black rocks and trunks. Fresh rain drowned the dying campfire behind her, and she didn't worry about coals eating down into dead roots and duff and surfacing again in flames twenty feet and five weeks away. This forest could take care of itself. She'd made sure of *that.*

Shadow froze and then inched forward paw by careful paw, glaring up into the blackness of a tree, tail-tip twitching, and Maureen touched the trunk. Smooth bark, beech, rejoicing in the rain washing its leaves and soaking down to its roots. Sean's ghost perched on an upper limb, cold and afraid. Maureen shrugged. Any ghost that was afraid of a leopard was no concern of hers. She waved the cat on.

*Why does he follow me? I don't command the beasts like Dougal did.* Maybe he'd gotten so used to people that it was habit. *Or maybe he senses a fellow killer and is looking to clean up the scraps.*

And then they were on the edge of the forest, with the keep's stone walls and jagged towers outlined against forked purple lightning. Frankenstein's castle, and the monster was coming home. Rain poured down out of the thunder, around her but not on her. She gritted her teeth and stalked across open rock and grass to the open gate. The cat waited behind, under the shelter of the forest and away from her personal thundercloud.

Through the empty courtyard until lightning strobed off the top of the burned tower right in front of her and she felt the tingle in her feet, into the empty kitchen and down into the empty cellars, grabbing a flashlight from the shelf behind the door. Doors, servants hiding behind locked doors.

*Evil things walk the storm winds. The Mistress is angry. Yea, though I walk through the valley·of the shadow of death, I will fear no evil. For I am the evilest son-of-a-bitch in the whole fucking valley.*

Her heart started to race again, and her palms turned slick. She stalked on, moving fast to get *something* done before she ran screaming from the weight of stone crushing down on her shoulders. Down past the cell door with its melted hinges. Stupid waste of energy, should have just had the smith chisel the damn thing off for scrap. But she felt better with it behind her. Down through the ironbound oak doors that marked the end of the spaces that were used and into dust and must and darkness. The stones glowed faintly in the beam of her flashlight.

Footprints in the dust. One pair led on, close-spaced as if

they were walking slowly and checking everything for traps as they went along, farther apart as they returned through passages they'd cleared already. She could see Brian and decades of soldiering in the methodical way of them, into and out of connecting doors. She checked empty rooms and cellars choked with ancient trash, finding nothing that gave a clue as to where he'd gone.

Another pair of feet, smaller, came out of one wall and went into another. Hidden passages? She thumped on one wall and then the other and got a bruised hand for her trouble. Pixies?

Brian's footprints led into a doorway to the left, into bare living stone. She pushed against the door and it creaked on its hinges, not barred or locked or even latched. She pushed through into the wood-yard at Great Northern Paper's pulp mill, cords of wood as far as her flashlight beam could reach, stacked solid under a stone ceiling.

Except along one wall. The footprints led on. She followed them. She trailed one hand along the wood, identifying bark, drawing strength from the dried-up corpses of old friends. Make a project, work out dendrochronology from the rings and find out how long ago this fuel was cut. Oak. Oak. Beech. Maple. Oak. *Walnut?* Some brainless fool was cutting up *walnut* for firewood? Even if the tree had been storm-killed, they should have made boards and furniture out of it.

And then she faced another door, also a hand's-breadth ajar, and pushed through it. Her flashlight picked out a crucifix under stone vaulting, and she dropped to one knee out of habit, crossing herself before she entered. A chapel, hidden for centuries.

Brian's footprints led on, through the dust, circling the room as he scouted it and coming to rest at a pattern on the floor. Smears showed where he'd knelt and studied the thing, then shuffled along on hands and knees to brush the dust away and show the extent of it. Some kind of maze, set into the stone flooring. He'd followed it; she could see the traces in the thin film of dust his cleaning had left behind. And then his footsteps turned and headed back. No clue.

She squatted on her heels, eyes blurry. *He left me. He came down here to get as far away from me as possible and finally worked up enough mad thinking about what kind of bitch I am and then he found a better choice and left me.*

She felt the tons of stone overhead, the vaulted roof and the cubic yards of fill and the castle towers. The walls inched closer. Something rustled behind her, a rat or ghost or magic guardian, and she turned and Dougal stood just inside the door, livid scar across his throat from the blade of her *kukri* where she'd hacked his head from off his shoulders.

The blade flashed between them, spinning hilt for tip and whacking point-first into the wooden door. The thump echoed away through empty corridors before her hand and arm even *thought* about drawing the knife and whipping it across the room and the ghost vanishing the instant cold steel entered its space.

She stared at her hand. Yes, she could do that again—you held the knife *so* and whipped your wrist *so* and the knife made exactly *this* many turns in *that* many feet and she could choose to strike with point or edge or pommel if she wanted. Her hand and the knife loved each other.

The walls inched closer. The ceiling sagged above her. She backed away from the altar, crossed herself again, wrenched the *kukri* from the door where it had buried itself two inches deep in solid oak, and whimpered. Small footprints led straight into the wall.

*What kind of ghost leaves footprints?*

Brian had told her of the Old Ones' powers to heal themselves. She hadn't actually *seen* Dougal's body burn. She *had* seen Brian chop Liam's body into pieces in that alley in Naskeag Falls, and seen a hand finger-walking across slush trying to find its wrist and rejoin it.

Cold terror ran down her spine. She pushed back through the door and the tunnel beside the firewood and the narrow, narrow spaces under low ceilings and the crushing weight of stone. Sweat greased her hands around the tube of the flashlight and the grip of the *kukri*. She heard her own screams and curses echoing from the cell.

And then she stood in the wine cellar, corkscrew at her feet, with the astringent ambrosia of fine burgundy in her throat. She took another swallow, long throat-pulsing chug-a-lug really, and let the fire spread through her body from her belly out to the rigid muscles of her shoulders and the tips of her cramped fingers.

She slid the *kukri* back into its sheath, picked up the corkscrew and another bottle, and climbed the cold stairway back to the kitchen. She found people there, strangers with white faces drawn with pain and memories, strangers with eyes that probably matched her own for madness. They moved like mannequins and showed about as much awareness of the world around them.

She handed her bottle to a woman and started to open another. Padric's face loomed across the room, the only familiar one, and the wine loosened her tongue and brain.

"Hey, Torquemada!" He turned, puzzled. "Yeah, *you*, fuckwad! Find out where Mairéad is hiding and drag her ass out of her bomb shelter. We need food and bandages and a bunch of beds and crap." He nodded and vanished.

Maureen took another gulp of Château DeFeat, giving the finger to wine-lovers everywhere because she wanted the alcohol, not the sublime blend of French sunshine and rain and soil. Who the fuck needed sobriety? She didn't have anyone to stay sober *for*. Not like Jo and David.

# eleven

—⁓—

DAVID FLEXED HIS aching fingers and stared at them as if they'd betrayed him. Actually, he knew it was the other way around. He hadn't touched his guitar for a couple of weeks—months, if you went by the calendar they used in Naskeag Falls—and any little problems he had with chording and finger-picking were his own damn fault.

But his fingertips felt like they'd ballooned to twice their legal size, been sandpapered raw, and then spliced to red-hot wires for tendons. Playing a good riff depended on muscle memory, notes heard in the brain and expressed through the strings without an intervening thought. His hands refused to do that.

He set the worn Gibson on the sofa beside him, wincing as his shoulders joined the chorus of complaints. He'd been playing tense, hunched over the axe as if somebody stood behind him with a whip. That was the real problem. He had to get a gig somewhere, connect with a group and earn some eating money. Either that, or ask Jo to swipe some fairy gold from a leprechaun's hoard.

The way things had been going, it would just vanish when it touched cold iron. His bank account had shrunk to the point where he'd need a microscope to find the balance, and Jo wasn't any better off. They'd been fine when there was money coming in each Friday. They'd neatly balanced income and outgo, blissfully ignoring that strange concept known as "savings."

Catching up on two months' rent and midwinter utilities had been the killer. At that, they were damned lucky the landlord hadn't just dumped their stuff on the sidewalk while they were gone.

He stood up, trying to stretch the kinks out of his back, and walked to the window. Of course, the scene out there just matched his depression, all mud and filthy snow and rusty cars. It was raining again, a nasty spitting half-sleet. To hell with the calendar—winter just wouldn't let go.

This part of Naskeag Falls was a dump at the best of times, peeling paint and empty storefronts and old warehouses with the roofs caving in. Mud season made it worse, hard as that might seem, nothing but dark potholed streets robbed by ice storms and Dutch elm disease of even the slight softening touch of bare winter trees.

But any time he started longing for the fresh green magic of Maureen's fantasies, he remembered dragon teeth and claws. He remembered strangling briars that sank rootlets into his flesh and drank his blood. He remembered cold-eyed heartless soulless Old Ones who would torture or kill him on a moment's whim.

David squeezed his eyes shut against the memories. That didn't help, of course. The images were inside his head, not out that window.

*And they all lived happily ever after. The End.*

Well, at least Maureen had her prince and her castle and her household full of servants. She got something out of the fairy tale. All he had to show for it were the persistent nightmares.

And the professional attention of the cops. That was a weird scene, however you looked at it. Maureen and then Brian had shown up and gone to the cops like good little girls and boys. They'd arrested Brian. Maureen had gone to bail him out. Now the cops seemed more interested in talking to both of them than before, and both of them had vanished.

He wrinkled his nose and scanned along the street in both directions. No light-bars or two-way radio whips showing, no idling black-and-white cruisers from the city or tan specials from the county sheriff, no unmarked Crown Victorias or Caprices that looked out of place in the neighborhood because they didn't sport rust-eaten fenders and cracked windshields. Must be time for a donut run.

Or they were following Jo, not bothering to hide, giving her a gentle reminder that they *still* wanted answers. Answers no cop would believe even if David or Jo had felt inclined to give them. "Yes, we know where Maureen and Brian are. No, you can't call up the local police to question them. Not even Interpol. The Sidhe don't use telephones, and the feds don't have an extradition treaty with Camelot."

He didn't want to think about *that* scene. Instead, he wondered where Jo had gone. "Errands," she'd said. After a breakfast-table "discussion" about finances. "Fight" would be more accurate. David wondered what percentage of divorces hid "discussions" over money. Empty cupboards and refrigerator sure added to the tension factor. And Jo wasn't stuck with him, wasn't even married to him. Any time she wanted, she could just take three steps and be warm and dry and rich.

A key scratched in the lock, and Jo walked in. He glanced out the window. Yep, black-and-white cruiser idling to a stop right next to the NO PARKING THIS SIDE OF STREET sign.

Didn't they have anything *better* to do with their time, like hand out summonses for littering? Looked like Barnes behind the wheel. David made a habit of asking all of them for identification. Politely.

Jo dumped a fistful of mail on the kitchen table, ads and bills most likely, tossed her soaked jacket over the coat rack, and slumped into a chair. She looked tired and bedraggled, and David noticed the knife-edge crease between her lowered eyebrows that meant she had turned into a ticking bomb. Whatever she'd been doing all morning, it sure hadn't turned out well.

"I stopped by Dom's on the way back from the nursing home. Start tomorrow, breakfast shift."

David blinked and then stared at her. "*Dom's?* Doing what?"

She glared back at him and then shrugged. "Waiting tables."

Dom's. *Dominic's Café.* "God, the health inspector let them open up again? Hey, nobody but winos and day labor eats there. Breakfast shift, your high-rollers are going to tip a quarter."

Jo shrugged again. "Hey back at you. Right now, I've got twenty-three dollars and seventy-six cents to my name. Just counted it to make sure. Supper tonight is stone soup. What're you tossing into the pot?"

"Jo, you won't even *eat* at Dom's. Isn't there anything else?"

"Haven't you heard, we've got a fucking recession on. Fifteen restaurants and gin joints and greasy spoons in two hours, working downwards. Fourteen places ain't hiring. At least four of *them* are thinking of letting people go. Three guesses who was at the bottom of the list, and the first two don't count."

"But . . . *Dom's?*"

"Look, babe, I'll do lap dances down at *The London*

*Derriere* if that's what it takes to stay warm and fed. What are *you* planning to do?"

Now the corners of her lips had turned white with tension. David felt the hairs standing up on his forearms and the crown of his skull, the static charge of a thunderstorm right overhead. He reminded himself of what this woman was, what she could do. He needed to defuse the bomb before that timer hit zero. "They're closed, remember? Burned out?"

"Moved over two blocks and reopened. Can't keep a good strip-joint down. Essential civic service."

Jeezum. She'd checked. He'd been joking. She wasn't.

"What about the CAD jobs? You've got the certificate, you've got the experience . . ." He stopped. That knife-edge on her forehead was getting deeper, and her eyes had narrowed to slits.

"Screwed. They check with Rob. He just tells them the truth. I didn't show up. I didn't call. He had a deadline, and I didn't even answer the frigging *phone*. Two expletive-deleted months, and our *official* tale is, I was off on a drunk. Would *you* hire me, with that word out on the street?"

"Do you have to tell them about your last job? Can't you just go in with your certificate—"

Her right hand chopped air. "Small town. You know every musician in this pissant burg, right? Played gigs with most of them, one time or another? Same thing with the architects and engineers. It's a frigging club. Everybody knows everybody else. I've been blackballed. For cause."

Then she turned deadly calm. "What are you doing about a job? Or are you pulling a Maureen on me?" He could cut himself on her voice.

Maureen. Maureen used to live in this apartment—eating half the food, drinking nine-tenths of the booze, sucking out about five times what she put in. Certified crazy, fit only for a part-time job at minimum wage. Dumping her in the

Summer Country had solved a major problem for Jo. Kid even seemed happy there.

And now Jo saw *him* the same way?

"I've got cards up at all the music shops and clubs, spread word around that I'm available again. Give it a few weeks, I'll find some gigs."

"Available. *Available?* Fucking a-*vail*-a-ble?" Now she was shouting. "Mother of God, you think you're Adam fucking *Lester*? I'm slinging hash browns to hung-over drunks at five A.M. in fucking *Dom's* so you can sit home and wait for the fucking music fairy to tap you on the shoulder with her fucking magic *wand*?"

Normal conditions, Jo cussed maybe a tenth as much as Maureen. Profanity served as a psychic barometer with her, and right now the needle pointed at "Hurricane." David found himself backing away.

"Look . . . here . . . mister . . . man." She bit each word off, stabbing her forefinger at him. He expected blue flame to shoot from it. "Get yourself a fucking *job*. There's probably twenty guitarists in this hick town looking for work. Ten of them are better than you. You wait for the fucking music fairy, the Red Sox will win the World Series first. I like eating at least once a week."

Her hand scrabbled around on the table, as if searching for something to throw at him, some way to discharge the lightning she'd been building. "*Fuck* this!" She closed her eyes, gritted her teeth, and stood up. She grabbed her coat, wrenched the door open, and turned back. "Get a fucking *job*, already!" And the door slammed shut, with her on the far side of it.

*God. Almighty. Damn.* David squashed his impulse to throw the deadbolt and chain the door behind her. She'd just blow it open, anyway, if she wanted in to get a clear shot at frying his ass. He dropped into a chair, hands shaking, sweat chilling on his back. That woman could kill him.

She didn't even have to be mad at him. PMS or a bad day at the office, anything in the neighborhood could get scorched. He'd known that, back before the world twisted around him and dumped him into magic. But now her temper came with built-in tactical nukes.

His hands started the mechanical process of sorting the mail she'd dumped. Wet, cold, floppy mail. Any of it he didn't drop directly into the trash bucket would need a spell on the radiator to dry out. Well over a hundred years and the damned postal service still hadn't figured out that mail satchels needed rain covers.

Ads. Ads. Bill, electrical service. David winced at that one; time to check into the winter shut-off laws. Credit card application, "transfer your balance," brought a wry snort. As if they needed *that* particular quicksand pit added to their swamp. Ads. Envelope with a PO Box return address, Naskeag Falls, no other info. Probably an offer of investment advice. David almost tossed it unopened, then noticed the Elvis stamp and figured a stockbroker who pasted Elvis on his mail might at least be amusing.

Letterhead, Adam Lester Productions. Offer to buy nonexclusive rights to perform certain original songs, royalty schedule attached, with further offer that the principals would like the chance to review any future work with right of first refusal on an exclusive basis. Performances to be by Adam Lester and Ayisha Powell, with selected local musicians backing up.

What the *fuck*? David stopped, blinked his eyes, and read the letter through again. Songs? David had never written any songs. He wrote poems, when they forced themselves into his head, and he tended to keep them mostly to himself. Some members of *Dé hAoine* might have copies from when he'd lived with the band before he met Jo . . .

A handwritten note scrawled across the bottom of the page, "Call me when you get a chance—Adam." A phone number followed, looked like a cell phone from the code.

He shook his head and frowned. Adam and Ish were Names, capital "N," big-money performers. *Wicked* good. They made a true musical fairy tale, guitar wizard and princess royal of the blues who had climbed out of the grungy Naskeag Falls bar scene and onto a world stage. The best set *Dé hAoine* had ever played was the time Adam had borrowed David's guitar, leaving him to sit and watch and tap his feet. That reel had been magic, true enough, but *he* hadn't played a note of it.

But Jo's blood warped the world around her. What she *really* wanted, happened. Like she'd said, Naskeag Falls was a small town and the music scene a tiny fraction of it. If you owned an instrument, you were family. Family gossip, family feuds, family ties you could lean on when life turned shitty. And once or twice a lifetime, family connections that opened doors . . .

Adam had lived on the grimy end of it all for years, an army vet blinded by a head injury in the Gulf War. He'd worked the same bars, starved on the same piss-poor gigs, paid the same dues, dreamed the same dreams. Only, for him they'd come true.

And there was Ayisha Powell, short and wide and black. Ish hadn't even been a performer two years ago. She'd been a heavy machinist at the local GE plant, carving turbine shafts out of steel billets on the day shift and hauling Adam to gigs at night. She still had the muscles to show for it, used to win her drinks for the night from suckers who tried to arm-wrestle her. You didn't want to get her mad.

Then she'd filled in for a missing singer when Adam cut a demo record. Fairy tale . . .

David picked up the phone, hoping against the odds to hear a dial tone rather than the dead hollow of a disconnected line. Luck still held. He punched in the number. He listened to the ring on the other end, holding his breath.

Two rings. Three. Four. A click, and David expected to hear an answering machine.

"Yo."

"Adam?"

"Himself in person. What's it to you?"

Yep, that was Adam "This is David, David Marx. I just got your letter."

David heard a crackling pause on the line, as if Adam had to shift mental gears—or was thinking of a way to crawfish out of his offer.

"Yeah. David. Been trying to get in touch with you. Heard about *Dé hAoine*, heard about Jo's job, heard about her mother. Bad scene all around."

Family gossip. "Yeah. We haven't been sleeping too well."

"Look, how's it going with her mother?"

Ugh. "They moved her out of the hospital a couple of days ago, nothing more they could do for her there. Nursing home, long-term care. Different window, same view." And not a pretty one.

"Man, that sucks. Look, I just stepped out of a meeting, so we'll have to catch up later. What I wrote you about was, these damn fools want another album from Ish, hit the market quick while she's still hot. We're talking fusion stuff this time, not blues. 'World Music' and 'Cross-over' are big. We were thinking maybe like some of the stuff *Dé hAoine* backed on that disk I cut. Ish really likes that flavor."

David winced again. "*Dé hAoine* dumped me. I thought you'd heard."

"Yeah, we'd heard. *Macht nichts.* That's not what we're after. What we want, what *Ish* wants, is to throw a couple of your songs into the mix and maybe make one of them the title cut."

"*Songs?* Hey, man, I'm a musician. Not a songwriter."

"Songs. She's thinking of 'Derry' and 'Grania' and maybe

'Naskeag Mollie.' 'Derry' might be the title cut. Depends on what fits in with the rest of the stuff."

"But . . ." David sat there for a moment, lost and vaguely stunned. "Those aren't songs, they're just poems."

"Hey, man, songs *are* poems. And those three just about rip your guts out and dance on 'em. 'Derry' and those poor kids caught up in all the hate . . . anyway, I've started in on settings for them, worked out the melody and some of the harmony. Celtic flavor, of course, and we think it'll be more electric than acoustic. 'Derry' is too hard and modern and nasty for a traditional treatment, and we think that will set the theme for the entire album. Give 'em a different side of Ish."

Silence hung between them. David hadn't thought of those poems as songs, never even crossed his mind. And he sure hadn't tried to market them—somebody in *Dé hAoine* must have passed his photocopy along, as a kind of penance for booting him out of the band.

"You want my *songs?*" David struggled to wrap his mind around the concept. He'd always thought you needed to write words to a tune, not the other way around.

David could almost *hear* Adam shaking his head in amusement. "Hey, man, if you think we're trying to screw you, don't worry. Ish isn't big on getting rich—she always says she can only ride one Harley at a time. Check that schedule with whoever you like. We pay good royalties."

David swallowed, his mouth suddenly gone dry. "Uh, the answer is yes. *Hell,* yes! I'm just taking a while to get used to the idea."

"Get used to it. Look, man, I gotta go. The meter's running. I'll have our agent get a contract and advance check over to you." The phone clicked in his ear, and he hung it up and stared at it.

Royalties. *Money,* by damn, money for *words,* words he'd already *written.* He jerked the door open and bounced down the stairs, two and three at a time, and shot out onto the front steps of the tenement. If he could catch Jo . . .

The cop cruiser had left. The only figure in sight was a scrawny stubble-faced man with a garbage bag at his feet, pawing through the trash in search of bottles and cans.

David checked the parking lot. Jo had taken Maureen's car, *real* safe, driving in the mood she was in. But that meant he couldn't find her just by walking around the block.

He climbed back up the stairs, imagining. *That* voice, Ish's powerful voice, evoking all the gut-wringing emotion that she brought to the blues. Singing his poems. With Adam crafting the tune.

*And the Catholic child,*
*And the Protestant child,*
*Scream their hate 'cross the barbed wire border.*
*And each finds a rock,*
*But he can't throw it far,*
*And he swears he'll be back when he's older.*

# twelve

—◆◆◆—

JO STARED AT her knuckles, white with strain from squeezing the steering wheel. Maureen's steering wheel, the damned rust-bucket Toyota that had spent two months of a Maine winter frozen into a snow-bank but still started bang-off because Brian had once laid hands on it like a televangelist at a faith-healing.

She was turning into her sister.

Unemployed, hearing "voices," boozing, believing that the world was out to get her. Jeeze Louise.

Flying into rages and lashing out at those closest to her. And now, driving over to Carlysle Woods to seek wisdom and healing from the trees. Driving *drunk,* for Chrissakes, just like Grandfather O'Brian. But she'd walked out of that goddamned nursing home and right into the bar down the street. Good marketing move, that was, putting your whiskey shop within walking distance of a reliable source of depressed people.

She'd ordered three quick shots of bar Scotch as a sedative, stared into the bottom of the second, and froze with it halfway to her lips. Her sister was a drunk. Her father was a drunk. Her grandfather had *died* from drink, and there'd been others. Odds were, if she went on and drank that second and third shot, she'd follow her family down the neck of a whiskey bottle and drown there.

Heredity or environment, nature or nurture, she was screwed either way. Hand shaking, she'd set the shot glass down on the bar and backed away from it, then climbed into Maureen's car.

That didn't erase the reason *why* she'd wanted a drink. Three cheers for modern medicine. Bastards couldn't even tell the difference between a stroke or faint followed by a fall down the front stairs, and good old-fashioned wife-beating. They couldn't *do* anything about the results, either way, so let's clear the bed out and move the empty husk off to a warehouse for long-term storage.

And Dad wouldn't pay the extra for a private room that his insurance wouldn't cover. So now Mom was in a double with a fat blind diabetic Indian who could really have used a roommate she could talk to.

She relaxed her hands, took a deep breath, and shut off the engine. She climbed out, slammed the car door because if you didn't slam it hard enough to shake rust loose from the body, it wouldn't latch, and locked it before she sobered up. Or sanity intervened. Or something.

The city plowed out this parking lot, chewing up the gravel surface and piling mud in the corners, but did nothing about the paths winding through the woods. Jo climbed over the heaps of old snow and followed snowshoe tracks that led between two birches, her boots sinking ankle-deep into the gray surface of Maine "spring." Snow rarely hung on so late, but this year looked like a record.

Maureen had dragged her out here a few times, sharing her world and trying to explain the differences between this tree and that. Birches were easy, the white papery bark peeling and curling loose to show pale orange underneath. Jo had also figured out the smooth-trunked gray beeches and could tell an oak if it dropped an acorn on her head, but that was about it. All the evergreens were pines to her.

The old snow was filthy, heavy, wet, shifting almost like loose gravel under her feet. Tracks had turned into grotesque negatives with the thaw so that the hard-packed trail was actually higher than the sides, with reversed ski and snowshoe prints made of ice that resisted the sun and rain. She closed her eyes, matching up the trail turns and branches with her memory. There was a certain tree that Maureen loved above all others; she called it Father Oak. She'd claimed it talked to her. She'd claimed it gave her strength.

Well, Jo had always been the strong one, protecting her little sister. Maybe it was time to tap into Maureen's support network for a refill.

Jo's memories led her down trails to the right and then left, until she found an old beech by the beaten path. A hole showed dark against the gray; Maureen said it was the daytime roost of some kind of owl. Jo couldn't tell, but she remembered that shape and smooth bark and the hole about twenty feet above the ground. Except that it was lower now, with something like five feet of drifted snow paring down the height.

Okay. Now it got tricky, moving off the trail and into unmarked snow. Second step, she sank up to her knees, above her boot-tops, and the wet cold washed right through her jeans. Bad choice for clothing, but she hadn't *planned* to go for a hike in the woods when she'd dressed that morning. She ignored the chill and pushed on.

She barely remembered the way to Father Oak. Maureen had brought her out in summer, with leaves all over and bugs whining in her ears. Winter gave the woods a very different look. Did she want to go right, now, or left, climb that rise or go downhill? There'd been a small creek, but it

must lie buried underneath the ice and the winter's accumu-
lated litter of small twigs and drifted grit. So maybe she
wanted to go down and *then* up again.

At least she couldn't get lost. Her tracks made sure of
that, leaving a trail like a moose floundering through the
woods. She wiped sweat off her forehead and unzipped her
jacket. Hiking through deep snow was perilously close to
*work*. She waded on, once or twice almost swimming through
the endless waves of sodden off-white crap.

Jo stopped and stood still, panting, up to her waist in a
thawing snowdrift with ice-water running into her boots.
Another hundred yards through the drifts and she might
not be able to get back to the car, even if she wasn't lost.

And the chilled sweat on her back reminded her of that
panicked afternoon in Dougal's forest when she'd acciden-
tally followed Maureen into the Summer Country.

Panic fear. Maureen always said *that* was the most dangerous animal in the woods. Forget about the lions and
tigers and bears, oh my—if you gave in to panic, you were
dead. All the other stuff, ranging from poison ivy up to
running flat out off a cliff, was just choosing the way you
died.

And Jo had already tried that last route once. It sucked.
She took a deep breath. She closed her eyes. Maureen had
said you could *feel* the power of her sacred tree. That was
how she'd found it.

<Come.>

The hair rose on her arms and on the back of her neck.
The dragon had talked like that, a voice that reached inside
her skull and echoed without the bother of touching her ears
on the way. She'd come out here to try to find some calm.
Those memories didn't help one bit.

However, something to her left felt soothing, like a fire
crackling warm and yellow and fragrant on the hearth. She
followed it, uphill, and the snow grew both harder and

shallower as she climbed. Soon she was only ankle deep again, and her breathing calmed.

She saw him. No mistaking that huge old tree with the lightning scar spiraling down from its highest branches to the earth. He stood on the crown of a small hill, and the sun and wind had opened bare ground at his roots. Jo brushed the lingering ice from her jeans.

Father Oak. She'd just shaken her head at Maureen for years, the voices of schizophrenia and her claim that God lived in everything. That even trees had souls, and voices that could speak if you just sat still enough and listened.

She clumped up to the tree, leaned on it while she pulled off her left boot and emptied it of melting slush, then did the same thing for her right. Then she squatted down on a gnarled root that somebody's butt had worn smooth through years of contact. Maureen's most likely, although other people might have worshipped at the same shrine.

The trunk felt warm against her back, warm and strong and thick-barked against troubles. The sun warmed her face, as well, and she left her jacket open to the gentle breeze. Maine weather, you could sometimes change seasons just by walking fifty yards.

"Bless me, Father, for I have sinned. It has been twenty years since my last confession."

Silence answered her.

"You're supposed to ask for my confession."

Father Oak waited.

"Right. You're a Druid, if you're anything. Not a Catholic priest."

Jo chewed on her guilt. "Well, I'm going to dump it on you anyway. I'm a bitch. The world hurt me, so I hurt David. I *wanted* to hurt him. It felt good. Then it felt shitty."

She stared off into the trees. "And I'm going to do it again. I don't have an off-switch on my temper. Just like that stupid popcorn maker we bought—plug it in, and it's on. I tried to unplug by leaving Maureen's forest, and that didn't work."

<Come unto me, all ye that labor and are heavy laden, and I will give you rest.>

She couldn't tell if that was the tree speaking, or her memories of Sunday school. How did those gentle words turn into dogma that justified the rack and the stake? And why would Father Oak trigger memories of old gray smile-wrinkled Sister Anne sitting in a basement classroom of Saint John's?

Jo pulled out the crucifix she wore around her neck, ran her fingers over the body tortured there, and wondered. It meant so many different things to so many different people. She wore it mainly because it had been a gift from Grandfather O'Brian—he'd given one just like it to Maureen. It obviously hadn't meant the same thing to him that it did to Mom.

He'd found warmth and strength and friendship in his religion and his God, not fear. But then, the old man hadn't paid much attention to Saint Paul or the Apocalypse. Grandpa's religion centered more on the Christ who had made sure that a wedding party didn't run out of wine and that everyone at his sermons got enough to eat.

Grandfather O'Brian and his daughter, such a contrast. Grannie hadn't been that hard-shelled, either, what Jo could remember of her. So something else had happened to Mom. Now Jo had a glimmer of just what *that* was. Something had scared the shit out of Mom, once upon a time, and she'd fallen into the same power that grabbed Jo when she was scared or angry and turned her into some kind of avenging Fury. And *that* had frightened Mom even more. She'd chained it with her rosary and walled it off inside a barred iron cell of denial and damnation.

And then there was Dad. If you're already in Hell, it's pretty easy to believe in the place.

Jo closed her eyes and relaxed, soaking up the peace and warmth and strength that surrounded Maureen's oak. She fingered the crucifix again, transported back to Sister Anne's class and acceptance. "Our Father, who—"

A drip splashed on her nose, intruding. She blinked, and then blinked again. The forest lay shadowed around her, late evening, and a gentle rain pattered down through green leaves.

Green leaves.

"What the *fuck!*"

She staggered to her feet, stiff from sitting, seeing the whole world at a tilt. She grabbed the tree behind her to find her balance, and her hands fell on a scarred welt of bark healing a wound. The lightning strike. This was the same tree, in a different forest.

<My roots drink the waters of many worlds. God wears many faces. Look behind the mask to find out if what you see is God, or something else.>

Things moved between the trees in front of her, a gray shadow and a black, and then she stood in Carlysle Woods again, leaning on the old oak and shaking. She pressed her forehead against the rough bark, welcoming the way its edges bit into her skin. It felt solid. It felt *real*.

The magic was growing, transforming like some insect larva inside her that would split its husk and emerge as something different. *Goddamn Maureen's naturalist images; it'd be a help to know if this was a butterfly or some kind of parasitic wasp.*

Jo was sure that glimpse had shown her Maureen's forest. She'd felt her sister somewhere near—nearby and in a dangerous temper. Jo had booted her back to the Summer Country—nothing the kid could do to help Mom. And she had enough troubles of her own.

The boundaries wore thin. Now Jo could move from real to fantasy while sitting still. How long before she couldn't tell the difference?

But the sun was warm on her back and the tree felt strong against her chest like David holding her. The quiet forest soaked into her, and she found the calm that had touched her earlier. Maureen could wait. Mom wasn't going anywhere, wasn't dying, nothing urgent there. Even Dad could wait. He couldn't touch Jo anymore. She'd broken his power. David was the urgent one.

"I should ask David to forgive me, right? That's my penance? And go and sin no more? But I'm no good at that. I've never had to learn, never found a man I couldn't stand to lose. Maybe I'd better learn?"

She hugged the oak, or rather pressed against it because it was far too thick to wrap her arms around. Then she turned and wrinkled her nose at the thought of wading back to the car. Not a fun way to travel.

But . . .

She stepped to the edge of the snow and set one boot on the surface. *Okay, babe, you* will *support me.* She visualized a hundred tiny snowmen under the sole, raising their stick arms over their heads and lifting. She thought of dandelion fluff drifting from her breath and of soap bubbles blown iridescent from a plastic ring. And then she moved her other foot and danced out onto the snow. It held her.

It held her all the way back to the car. Anyone who followed her tracks, expecting firm footing, was going to get a bit of a surprise.

The nursing home sat a block or so off the route back to her apartment. Maybe she could bring some of that serenity and understanding back to Mom, pass some of it in to her where she hid inside that shell.

Jo pulled into the parking lot and stared at the place, reluctant to move, to get out of the car, to do that hospital thing again. Long and low, wood-shingled walls, with broad eaves and wide windows, it did its best to look like a home rather than a warehouse for discarded people. And it was new, with bright colors inside and carpet instead of tile on the floor, and smelled clean, and the nurses seemed to smile a lot. Mom could have ended up in a lot worse places. Too bad it didn't really matter.

But the shift nurses recognized Jo and waved at her. They seemed to care. That meant as much to the families as it did to the patients.

Then she stood at Mom's door again, with the same gut-wrenching scene waiting on the other side. Jo found that there were limits to her newfound serenity.

She swallowed and pushed through the door as quietly as possible. Mom's roommate had been asleep, seemed to be asleep every time Jo visited. And the doors were new and silent. But the old Naskeag was sitting up in one of the chairs, seamed brown face and sightless eyes turned toward the door. Mary Thomas, her name was on the door, knitting away with strong gnarled hands crisscrossed by tiny scars. Jo wondered if she had been a basket maker—those were the cuts and scratches and scrapes of a lifetime's craft. Apparently the old woman didn't need to see in order to knit.

"I swear, Alice Haskell *again.* Don't you have better things to do than to visit an old lady two days in a row?"

Jo stopped short. "I'm sorry, I should have knocked."

"Oh, mercy. You're that nice girl comes in to visit her mother. I thought you were a friend of mine. Can't see too good no more."

"If you're expecting a visitor, I'll leave. Mom won't know if I'm here, anyway."

"She knows, child. She knows." The old lady kept knitting, needles clicking along like quiet castanets. Jo noticed that she was making a scarf, two colors of yarn in a complex pattern. Must be counting stitches and have a hell of a memory.

"No, you stay. Don't worry 'bout me." The old woman shook her head, waving toward the chair across from Mom's bed. "Lordy, I'm not expecting nobody. Felt you coming down the hall, child, that's all. That's why I got confused. You felt like Alice."

"*Felt* me?" Peculiar choice of words.

"You *glow,* child. Aunt Alice, she's our witch. What's that whitefolk word she uses, sha-man? We just say witch. You got witch power falling off you like summer rain."

She cocked her head and stared at Jo, as if she could see Jo's face and feel the shock of her words. "Nothing to be ashamed of, child. Nothing bad. Just how you use it, that's all that matters."

*She talks about it like she was discussing whether anchovies were good or bad on pizza.*

"I'm just a crazy old Indian, girl. Don't mind me. I've got scarves to knit. Ten grandchildren with cold necks, and their mommas all want different patterns so's they can tell the little scamps apart without unwrapping 'em. You go and try to help your mommy."

Jo felt like a cartoon lightbulb had lit up in her head. "You've been awake, those times I came in before?"

"Child, any fool could see you needed to be alone with her. Best thing I could do was close my eyes. Now do what you need to do." She made a shooing motion and then ran her fingers along the full needle, counting stitches and tracing each thread of yarn back to its skein. The old woman nodded to herself and started another row.

Jo did as she was told. The Naskeag woman seemed to bring a feeling of solid Maine granite into the room, rooting it in life and generations and the comfort of an old house.

She knew where she stood in the world and knew it was a good place to stand. Jo envied her family.

And then Dad was there, oozing around the door like the slime he was, and the feeling vanished. He looked startled for an instant, glanced at the old woman, and shrugged. His smile turned mean.

# thirteen

—❦—

JO FOUND HERSELF on the far side of the hospital bed, backing into the corner behind the bathroom door, instinct again putting Mom between her and the pain. Even if Mom wasn't really there, her bed and silent body still made a wall between Jo and Dad.

When Daddy smiled like that, he was thinking of ways to hurt. Sometimes it meant his belt across her back or bare butt, sometimes the fists pounding her body—never her face where some stranger could see the bruises.

But she didn't have to be afraid anymore. She'd summoned the Power of her blood, of the blood she bore from *both* her parents, and bound him with a curse out of the Summer Country. She was stronger now than he was.

"Now *that's* a piece of luck." Good luck or bad luck, he didn't specify. "Finding *you* here saves me an extra trip."

He closed the door behind him, setting the lock, putting another barrier between them and any help from people out in the halls of the nursing home. The nurses could open it, of course. No dead bolts, and they had a passkey for emergencies. But locks gave the residents privacy from each other.

Jo shook the distractions out of her head. *Pay attention to Dad. He's dangerous.* Power of the Old Blood or no, he *still* was dangerous.

He was here. She'd hoped the curse would keep him away. She glanced at the nurse-call button, wondering if she could reach it before he did.

He was here, and he was smiling. "I'd planned to find you first, before coming to deal with your mother. But every time I called, I just got that pothead boyfriend of yours. Is he your pimp, too, you little whore? Is that how you pay the rent, since you can't hold a *real* job?"

"You don't sound like a good man." It was the Naskeag woman, with her half-knitted scarf lying abandoned in her lap and a single long bare needle shining in one hand like a dagger. Jo had forgotten about her, staring at Dad's sadist smile and listening to his words as casually brutal as his fists.

"I don't think you sound like the kind of man who could be such a good girl's father. She comes here every day to talk to her momma, not like you. I think she's some other man's daughter. Some nicer man, who cared about her mother and his children."

The old Indian stared with her blind eyes, face aimed at a point just over Dad's shoulder. Jo wondered what she saw. A woman that old, living on the reservation, she'd have seen plenty of evil. Men like Dad. Poverty and drink and hopelessness brought out the worst in people.

"Shut up, old woman. Shut up and stay alive. This is family business."

He had a gun.

It appeared as if by magic, suddenly there. It sat small and shiny and blue in his hand but seemed to fill the room.

Time froze around Jo. The steel blue sights and black hole pointed straight at her heart. She could see shadows in the other chambers, lead gray with copper rings and black centers, hollow-pointed slugs. Killer slugs.

"You put the curse on me, witch. You and your witch-Irish mother. Bad blood, Old Blood from under the hill. But I know how to break it. A curse dies with the witch who spoke it."

The old Naskeag moved, standing up big and round and bulky like a wave humping up to break on the shore, flowing forward with her knitting needle extended. It had become a knife in her hand, held low, with her other arm above it in a guard. The move looked like something she'd done a hundred times before. What kind of a life had she survived?

"The child put no curse on you, mister man. You wrote it on your own forehead. The child just read the words out loud. No woman ever dared do that before. Now you finally ran up against one strong enough."

His hand jerked away from Jo, the gun seeking closer danger and then flashing blue light streaked with orange, and the room echoed. The roar of the shot squeezed Jo's head. He turned back, snapping a shot point-blank into the helpless form on the bed, and her ears didn't register the sound. The muzzle rose back to her and found her and the hammer flashed again and she saw the red of burning powder blaze around a black shadow as it flew out of that short bore.

Jo shrank back hard against the wall. Plaster stung her cheek, blasted out of a sudden crater next to her left shoulder. He'd missed. Somehow he'd missed, at ten feet or less across the bed. No *way* he could miss twice at that range.

The hammer lifted again as he squeezed the trigger, aiming this time instead of a snap shot, taking no chances. His hand trembled and the hammer froze at half-cock. The muzzle turned away from Jo's heart, wavering, uncertain, traversing the empty wall above Mom's bed where blood pooled red and wet across white sheets.

Jo's ears still rang. She couldn't believe how *loud* a pistol was, in a small hard-walled room like this. And she couldn't believe she'd noticed that, when her father still held a loaded pistol and tried to aim it at her heart. But she'd moved beyond fear into that space of quiet rage she'd found when she called the curse down on her father.

Words formed in the shattered gun-smoke air, not Jo's voice this time. "You wrote the curse, little man." The Naskeag woman stood, a breaking wave frozen above the granite ledge, apparently unharmed. Her age and blind eyes gave her the aura of a priestess, untouchable unswerving voice of the gods.

"And since you wrote it in your own blood, you found that it was true. Tried to take another woman, did you? Planting Woman heard the words, and made your balls shrivel into prunes. You couldn't get it up. And then you tried drink and couldn't keep it down. You come through the door stinking of puked whiskey."

The gun turned inward, seeking, groping, hunting for its target. Dad's arm trembled with muscle fighting muscle, nerve wrestling with nerve. He brought up his other hand to grab the gun and force it away, but the muzzle still turned toward him.

"And now you've harmed a woman, lifted your hand against your wife and daughter and an old blind stranger. You remember the last of the curse, mister man? The words you wrote on your forehead like Cain's own mark for all the world to see? May your own hand turn against you and be your death!"

His hand turned the gun. Veins stood out on his forehead, streaked with sweat under the cold fluorescents on the ceiling. Strangled noises forced their way past gritted teeth. Jo could stop him with a word. She knew it. She saw her mother's blood dark on the white linen, felt again the shock of the bullet tearing into the wall instead of her own heart.

*I will not say it.* Her nails bit into her palms where she clenched her fists. *No. Die and burn, you bastard.*

Her eyes wouldn't close. That was part of the magic. She had to watch it through, or it wouldn't work. The gun's muzzle touched his head, pressed into his temple, then skidded sideways on sweat-drenched hair. She saw the hammer inch back on the Smith, shudder for an instant's pause, and then blur forward.

The shot seemed muffled, as if sound had changed into the explosion of blood. His hand flew back and chunks of something spattered the wall where the pistol bounced free. He stood for a moment and then fell sideways, rigid, like a tree.

Jo stared at the empty space where he had been. She couldn't move. She couldn't blink. Her back pressed against the plaster wall, cold and hard, gritty with shards blown out of the hole by her left shoulder. She slid down the wall, bit by bit, until she sat huddled in the corner and her eyes sank below the level of the bed. That broke the spell's hold, and she could blink the searing memories out of her eyes. Red seeped over the edge of the mattress, spreading, dripping. *Plastic sheet under the linen,* she thought, *liquids can't soak in. Need it in a nursing home.*

Something dark covered her eyes, a searching hand gentle across her face. Warmth and softness enveloped her, rocking her head in comfort. "It's over, child. It's over. Your momma's free. The Lord knows *why* it happened, and He understands."

Tension and shock leaked out of her as tears. She heard noises in the distance, the crash of the door flung open and then screams and then the more precise shouts of professionals who saw crisis and death on a weekly basis and knew what to do about them. Someone tucked Jo's head down between her knees and wrapped a blanket around her. Someone lifted her into a chair and then it moved, rolling, turning, rolling, bumping and scraping along a wall as it skirted something on the floor. Warm comfort held her hand, rested on her arm, spoke quiet words of care and safety and love. The warmth smelled of mothballs and wool and old woman, not starch and medicine.

"But you weren't there," Jo whispered. "You *can't* have heard the curse."

"Planting Woman told me, child. She heard you call the Powers of the earth and sky. That was her voice that spoke, not mine."

"He shot you," she whispered.

Breath touched her cheek, warm, slightly spicy of chewed spruce gum. "Lordy, no, child. Your magic wouldn't let him. You think I was being *brave?*"

It was quiet and warm and safe and dark, like talking to Mother Mary under the protection of her blankets. "I let him shoot Momma."

Arms enfolded her again, soft arms with hard old muscles underneath a padding of old fat. "Your momma let him shoot your momma, child. She wanted to die. I could feel it, come midnights. I felt her spirit beating at the walls like a trapped bird. Now she's free."

Free at last.

Sirens whined and homed in on the nursing home. Feet squeaked by at a run and then returned at a walking pace when they found . . . what they found. Hands touched her, medical hands smelling of medical care. She didn't need them and shook them off. More feet arrived, black shoes instead of white, attached to blue legs. She followed the legs up to uniforms and badges.

"I killed him."

Dark bulk pushed between her and the uniforms. "You

leave her be. Child just saw her daddy kill her mommy. You got questions, you ask Mary. I was there."

"I *killed* him."

"Hush, child. How could she kill him, from the far side of the bed? Look for the bullet holes, po-lice man. Child has plaster dust all over her, from the bullet hole by the bathroom door. Mary can't see good, but I sure can hear. I can feel the dust. Mary heard where she was, where he was. He shot his wife, tried to shoot both of us, shot himself. Four shots. Man gone crazy, grief."

Jo stood, shaky, leaning on one arm of the wheelchair and then inching around it to take the pusher grips and force herself upright, letting the blanket's protection fall to the floor. "She's blind. I could have stopped him from shooting Mom. I let him do it, and then I took the gun and killed him. He deserved to die."

The old Indian kept her bulk between Jo and the uniforms. "The child's off her head. Look at the room, look at the bullet holes, check the fingerprints on the gun, figure out the spaces and the angles. Old Mary knows what you cops do. Ask little Bobby Getchell. Ask him about his old Aunt Mary. He'll tell you Mary's not as crazy as she looks."

"*Sergeant* Getchell? You're his aunt?" Jo's ears finally started to work again, pick up the softer words, recovering from the roar of that gun.

The hall was crawling with uniforms. White nurses, light gray EMTs, blue cops, dark gray suits that might as well have been uniforms. Strobe flashes reflected down the walls, splashing out through an open door. Crime scene investigators, taking photographs. A gray suit strode past, hauling one of those aluminum-sided cases on wheels. Jo wondered how long she had been sitting in the chair.

Two metal frames waited in the lobby, tall wheeled shiny folding frames with white padded tops with dark gray plastic bags draped across them, empty, waiting. Stretchers. Body bags. Waiting to swallow Mom and Dad, waiting to hide two shattered heads behind closed zippers.

Jo felt unnaturally calm. She knew it was unnatural, but that calm settled over her and brought her heartbeat back to normal and cleared her eyes and laid the script out in glowing words in the air in front of her. She'd tell the police what happened, *exactly* what happened, and then they'd arrest her and put her on trial and punish her. Lock her up in the mental hospital with the rest of the crazy people.

She gathered strength, drawing it from the air and up from the floor beneath her, and let go of the wheelchair. She walked around Mary Thomas, around that protective bulk that seemed to have shrunk back into a short round blind old woman instead of the force of nature she'd been in the room. Jo walked up to the highest-ranking uniform she could spot and laid a hand on his arm. Her hand wasn't even shaking.

"I killed him."

"This is a crime scene, ma'am. Please stay clear." Then the officer looked up and blinked. "I'm sorry. You're the daughter, aren't you?"

"I killed him. You have to arrest me."

His brow creased into a frown. He turned to another passing uniform. "Hey, Bill. Put out another call for Dr. Schofield. We need her like ten minutes ago."

Then the officer turned back to Jo. He took her arm and gently guided her through a door, into someone's office. He left the door half-open behind them. He set her in a chair and put himself leaning against a desk where he could watch the corridor through the gap of the door but no one in the corridor could see her. He shook his head.

"We've got a psychiatrist on call, ma'am, a trauma specialist. She'll be here in a few minutes. She's had a lot of training in helping victims through the shock and grief.

You've had a terrible experience. Please just sit quietly and wait for a few minutes."

Jo blinked and sat up straighter. "You don't understand. I *killed* him. I took the gun and shot him. He hurt my mother. He hit her. He put her in that bed. Then he shot her. He had to die. Now you have to arrest me."

She felt perfectly calm and normal. That was part of the problem, part of what she'd inherited from Daddy. Casual brutality, and something more. She remembered a puppy they'd had for a week or so; she must have been six or seven. Maureen had been out of diapers, anyway.

Baby dog had messed the rug, still being paper trained. Dad went to rub the puppy's nose in it. He put his drink down on the floor, and the dog knocked it over with his wagging tail. Dad picked up the puppy and broke its neck with two hands. Tossed the dying body in a corner. Walked off to replace the drink he'd spilled. Acted as if nothing had happened. And Jo had *learned* not to scream or cry by then.

No conscience. Nothing outside him mattered.

That's what she was doing. She had to be crazy. Incongruity and blunting of effect, just like Maureen. Jo had learned the jargon, dealing with her psycho sister.

"Ma'am, I saw the room. Saw the evidence. I know you didn't do any such thing. Your father shot your mother and then shot himself. Murder and suicide. You saw them die, nearly died yourself. Now you're in shock. You need professional help, and the doctor is on her way. Please just sit here and wait."

He was very polite, very sympathetic, very much the well-trained police professional. Very wrong.

He didn't believe her. She could *make* him believe her, but she didn't dare. Using her power had caused this crap in the first place.

The policeman glanced at the door. "Please wait. She's

here." Then he slipped out through the door and pulled it nearly shut behind him. She heard mumbles, low-pitched and high-pitched voices whispering in consultation.

". . . sedative . . ."

Selective hearing. She could have heard it all, made the walls amplify the sound for her, but she'd heard the important part. They thought she was just hysterical.

Jo didn't have to stay. She stood up, formed a picture in her head, and stepped into the damp darkness of the world under the hill. The black cold coffin air laughed at her, mocking. It knew her. It knew her mind, knew where she belonged.

# fourteen

—◊◊◊—

WHERE THE HELL was Jo?

David paced the floor of their apartment, glancing at the clock, glancing out the window at the gloom of late-winter clouds over April's bleak streets, glancing at the scrap of paper lying on the kitchen counter. The scrap of green paper with the squiggly writing and those zeros in *front* of the decimal point. Advance payment for the right to turn his poems into songs.

That had happened so fast it made his head spin. A check. A contract that even a *musician* could understand. A simple, straightforward percentage on the printed retail price of each and every CD sold, nothing about net or gross or production costs or promotion, none of that backroom accounting smoke and mirrors act. It was a flaming fairy tale in itself.

*Time to celebrate, but no Jo to celebrate it with.* Last time she went missing, he'd ended up staring at a snack's-eye view of a lot of dragon teeth. Extremely *sharp* dragon's teeth. Bad precedent. They had an agreement that she'd call if she was going to be late . . .

What would he do if he lost her again? Would he have the courage—hell, the simple straightforward Anglo-Saxon *guts*—to follow her, knowing what he did now?

She'd gone storming out without lunch, thin as that might be with the bare refrigerator. Mustard sandwiches, probably, on stale rolls from the bakery thrift store. Might have gone back to the nursing home; that shouldn't take more than an hour. After all, there wasn't a damn thing she could do beyond watering the flowers and letting the nurses know that somebody was looking over their shoulders.

She'd left about eleven. He'd called Adam right after. That contract and check had knocked on the door by two. He glanced at the clock again, wondering whether he wanted the hands to move faster or slower. Four-thirty.

He couldn't help remembering that checking on Maureen at the Quick Shop that February night shouldn't have taken more than an hour, either. And Jo hadn't come back.

He shook himself. No reason to expect *that* to happen again. Besides, he had work to do.

Adam's letter had asked about new work, dangling another carrot in front of his nose. David had been gnawing at a poem, something that turned the epics on their heads. *Iliad, Odyssey, Beowulf, Chanson de Roland,* they all spoke of Heroes and Great Deeds. The good guys either won or fought their way home and kicked ass or died heroic deaths.

He'd been haunted by a memory of the sidewalk outside a grungy side-street bar, this gray-stubbled mumbling shell of a man huddled against slush-flecked bricks and begging the coins for another drink. The man had been wearing an army jacket, torn and stained but still carrying a name tag and the Combat Infantryman Badge, unit flash on the shoulder, the whole nine yards. He'd looked the right age for Vietnam.

Probably got the jacket in a thrift store or gift from the Salvation Army, but the image burned in David's memory.

*That* was the hero of the modern world's wars, home again. Maybe the flavor of Jeffers, *At the Birth of an Age,* the Volsungs meet Attila the Hun and everybody dies.

No, Jeffers drew the right images, vivid and apocalyptic, but his verse-forms wouldn't fit to music. David's image needed something formal like a chant.

*Hiawatha?*

God, *that* one would never make it into print these days—plot development glacial, no "hook," cardboard hero and villain.

But the *form* could work. Toss in a rhyme scheme for the music audience . . .

> *By the flowing Naskeag River,*
> *In the alleys deep with grime,*
> *Came the warrior fearless asking,*
> *"Buddy, can you spare a dime?"*

This would be a song for Adam, the disabled vet, chanting with that dry sandy Desert Storm voice of his, maybe even *a cappella.* Or work the background with a bodhrán at a slow march, muffled and mournful, if they *really* wanted to pile it on heavy.

David set his back-brain loose on the project, giving words the time to ferment and age before putting ink on paper. Maybe with that check they could even get a computer, join the twentieth century now that it had rolled over into the twenty-first.

*Pay the phone bill with it, numb-nuts. Then we can still connect to the* nineteenth *century.*

He glanced at the clock, at the dusk gathering outside, paced the floor. Where was Jo? Why hadn't she called? And what would he do if she didn't come back? *That* was the deeper, nastier question.

Maybe he should try a summoning spell. The aroma of coffee would pull Jo in from a block away, drag her out of the deepest sleep, smooth all but the nastiest of her morning moods. She was addicted to the stuff. He liked it well enough, but didn't need to mainline it. The phone rang while he was measuring out grounds and water. *Finally!*

He picked it up. Silence. Not Jo. Again.

"Look, dude, we've got caller ID on this line. One more harassing call and we notify the police."

Click.

That was the sixth or seventh call of the day, none of them Jo, nobody speaking. David felt that itchy crawly question again, whether the perp was checking for empty apartments to burgle or was waiting for Jo to answer. Caller ID? Pure bluff—they were lucky to have a *line* on their line. Those letters from Verizon were getting rude.

> *In the forest, by the meadows,*
> *Came the warrior and the bard,*
> *Seeking heart-songs, seeking valiant*
> *Lovers, stolen past the guard.*

*Shit.* His back-brain had other fixations. It didn't *want* to work on the anti-epic of a homeless vet abandoned by the country that had drafted him.

It wanted to work on dragons.

Horrible enough, but beautiful, too. The gleaming eyes, opalescent black scales, flowing body sinuous like a modern dancer, the mind-speech almost like poetry itself—hell, even the teeth and claws had the stark simple perfection of Danish stainless steel cutlery. If they weren't right in front of you.

The coffee machine started glugging away on the counter, spreading Jo-bait through the air. Spell of summoning, specific to one particular red-haired witch.

*Hair of fire and temper matching,*
*Passion and clear eyes well wed,*
*Witch blood drawing ever onward*
*Past the opal-armored head.*

Well, that got the opals in; never waste an image once you've laid hands on it. Sometimes parts of a poem fell into place like precut lumber. David had worked as a carpenter a few times, driving nails instead of playing gigs when the groceries ran short. One job had been a "panelized" house, with joists already sawed to length and wall panels studded and sheathed up in a shop. Trussed roof, the whole nine yards. They'd framed and closed in the entire house in one morning. Some poems went together like that. Others, well, others fought him.

No. "Past obsidian-armored head." Have to move the black opals back to where they started. The scales had been more like obsidian, sharp as hell.

Parts of *this* poem ran icy fingers down his back. He remembered Jo with her hair standing up on end when the magic took her, like static on a mountaintop in a thunderstorm. These words woke the same feeling. His palms turned slippery and his heart started racing, fear dumping an overdose of adrenaline into his blood. Words carried power—power enough that a secondhand vision of their images could pull you across the borders for a moment and form a new world in your eyes and ears.

When David worked on the images of their battle in the forest, he started to smell the torn earth and raw sap of broken trees. He started to feel the rank sweat of fear down his back. His right arm ached where he'd dislocated his elbow when the dying dragon's tail knocked him damn near into tomorrow. It seemed like something far stronger than memory, as if he could take another step, chant another stanza, and he'd be *there*.

He shivered. He stared at the coffee machine, at the hot aromatic brown liquid spilling down into the carafe underneath it, so real and bitter and mundane. The boundaries of reality *couldn't* be so fragile.

Jo had teased him that a man named Marx had no business playing in an Irish band. He loved the music, but he didn't have a drop of any Celtic blood in his veins, much less the magical "Old Blood." His family traced back to the Hanseatic League and what was now Gdansk; Danzig it was when his great-grandfather had fled the Nazis with his family. No Sidhe there. He *might* sneak in some Old Blood genes through whatever lurked in the shadowed forests and hidden valleys and dank mine-shafts of Poland, but he'd never even learned the names.

No, it was the magic of words. People talked about how a good book could transport the reader to another land, how disoriented you could feel when something pulled you out of the story into mundane life. This just threatened him with that next step beyond.

He could tell that the Summer Country fascinated Jo. She belonged there, for all the horror she'd found in their brief visit. She wasn't out of work and digging for lost change under the sofa cushions there; she didn't keep having her nose rubbed in a mother lying brain-dead in a nursing home and a father boozing and whoring the rounds of Harlot Street to keep her awake at nights.

And she didn't have to settle for a yellow-ass coward of a poet and erstwhile guitar-player for a lover. She could find somebody like Brian, tough and competent and with the power of the Old Blood in his veins. He'd seen that measuring squint in her eyes when she'd looked at the guy. Wondering how he was in bed, whether Maureen had landed the better fish.

David shook himself. He poured a cup of coffee and hauled himself over to the window, staring out at the bleak scene that Jo could leave anytime she wanted. Raining again. The thaw had uncovered a whole stack of garbage bags across the street, buried in some January storm when the snowplow came by before the trash trucks did. Now the dogs or coyotes had gotten at the well-aged windfall. Fast-food wrappers and gnawed chicken bones and brown curled grapefruit rinds and empty chili cans all over the place. Lovely, against the infamous yellow snow.

Sirens warbled in the distance, bad omen. But he could discount that. They lived about a half-mile from the hospital, had ambulances howling around day and night like banshees heralding their cargoes of woe. Had the medivac helicopters whomping over at all hours, fetching and carrying the wreckage of most of eastern Maine.

He swallowed coffee, absentmindedly wincing at the heat of it. It hadn't worked. Jo hadn't come bounding up the stairs and scratched her key into the door and homed in on the aroma like a wolf smelling fresh moose blood.

The hell with it. He turned back to the kitchen, dumped the remaining half-cup in the sink, and grabbed his hat and jacket. He needed *out*. He needed to escape from a place where Jo was supposed to be, substitute a place where her absence wasn't so noticeable. And at least the *rain* was fresh.

Fresh and clean and cold, with a wind behind it that cut right through his fog and cleared his thoughts. That poem wasn't wearing through the veil between the worlds, it was just waking up memories. Bardic magic was a pile of bull, concocted of fantasy and wishful thinking. And Jo stripping Brian with her glance was just the same as David admiring high school sex-goddesses at the mall. Aesthetic appreciation, not proof she'd be happier elsewhere.

> *Fleeing danger, legs uncaring,*
> *Dropping weapons fled the bard.*
> *Turning, weeping, no choice offered,*
> *Came again to battle hard.*

Happier elsewhere, indeed. Damned brain, still chewing on epic battles. What *would* he do if Jo disappeared? Brian had tried to warn him off, before the first time, but David hadn't really understood.

Now he *knew*, remembering how they'd leaned together against a tree, weak-kneed and drained and supporting each other, drenched in sweat and blood and pain, staring at the impossible hulk of the dead dragon only to find what stood behind it. They'd gone through all that just to be frozen helpless by a snap of Sean's fingers.

Now David knew just how many layers of danger waited, each one more vicious than the last. Sean had been little more than Fiona's shadow, and Brian said that the surviving dragon was even larger and smarter than the one they'd killed. And mad like you wouldn't believe, where the other one had merely been bound by Dougal's spell to guard the path.

That nibbled at the flavor he wanted, the unavoidable clash between two doomed characters, neither at fault. A Greek tragedy sort of thing, with the scheming gods forcing Achilles and Hector into fatal conflict.

Or whatever. David choked on the image of himself playing either role.

He'd been wandering, sloshing words around in his head like a sourdough panning sand for the rare flecks of gold. At some point the rain had stopped, and he found himself looking down the river at an orange ball peeking out from under the clouds. Naskeag was offering him a sunset, to show that all storms have an end. The ice was breaking up on the rising tide, another early sign of spring.

A flock of pigeons clattered overhead, feathered rats that infested the downtown, and they suddenly broke and scattered. A winged arrow shot through the panicked birds and knocked one spinning in a puff of feathers.

Peregrine. He'd never seen one before, but that's what it had to be. Maureen had told him that a pair nested high on a cornice of one of the bank buildings, raising brood after brood, feeding on the fat slow McBird critters. City pigeons must be peregrine heaven.

Peregrines and coyotes, skunks and raccoons and sometimes a moose or bear on Main Street, the wild world crossed into city life. Borders were often permeable things, not Berlin Walls topped with razor wire that you couldn't cross or, once crossed, you never could go back. Maybe Jo could be a city falcon.

And maybe she'd flown back to the nest by now. He turned his back on the sunset and crunched back over the melting snow. Besides, he'd left the heat on under the coffeepot.

Neither poem connected. Not yet. More accurately, both sucked. He had maybe a line here, a line there. But he knew what he wanted, and he knew how to get there. The rest was just him slogging along through a swamp of words.

No sign of Maureen's junk Toyota in the parking lot. Instead, a police car sat parked near the apartment, engine idling its exhaust fog into the cold damp air. Its cop waited behind the wheel, patient, watching. *Hey there, remember us? We haven't gone away.* Cops made him nervous, even at the best of times. *Cultural conditioning; examine your conscience whenever you see the uniform.* He almost turned the corner and walked on.

Where the hell *was* Jo?

# fifteen

—◆◆◆—

SHEN'S NEST LAY empty.

Eight nest mounds, eight hatchlings spread in a rough circle in the marsh, spaced far enough apart that Khe'sha could keep eight brainless appetites from devouring each other. They were devouring *him*, instead. The marsh had faded into a weary haze of feeding, guarding, chasing, snatching naps when enough of the hatchlings lay torpid with the night's cold or with full bellies. Each time he jolted awake in fear of what had happened while he drowsed.

He shook fatigue out of his eyes and looked again. Shen? Gone? She wasn't a rover like Po or a constant obsessed hunter like Ka. She had been the watcher of the clutch, not ill or weak or slow-witted but content to study her world with sharp eyes, missing nothing but rarely moving from the top of her mound. She would compose great songs when she grew old.

He sniffed the air and tasted the black water of the swamp. Her scent was growing stale, as if she'd swum away the moment he'd last left her. And there was another flavor in the mix . . .

Old One.

Khe'sha raised his head, slowly, slowly, slowly, and narrowed his eyes. He sniffed again. Old One, indeed. He drew the scent deep into his nose, savoring and remembering each nuance of the blend. Matching it. Drawing a picture in his mind's eye.

The Master stood there, dead though he was, and the male with the yellow hair, and the red witch, and the black. And another. And yet, the scent was only thick enough for a single thief. Deception.

Khe'sha slipped through the tangled grass and thornbush of the marsh, tracking. The trail led toward the keep. He found Shen's aroma mixed with the intruder's. He did not find Shen. If this went on much longer, he feared he would grow angry.

Blood tainted the water. He tasted it, savored it, measured the amount and the freshness of it. Old One again, a blend he did not recognize. But then, he had never tasted the yellow one. He had never tasted *any* Old One who still lived.

The amount seemed small, a large scratch or minor bite. Khe'sha slowed, sniffing to the right and to the left. Shen had come this way, but not by swimming. Her scent touched the swamp grass and hung thin in the air. The Old One's blood lay on the swamp grass, as well, and Khe'sha chuckled deep in his throat. The hatchling had teeth.

Rage built in him, and he fought it down. Seven other mounds called to him, with seven other nestlings. He must not follow this scent for long, no matter how important.

He pushed forward through the grass and reeds and water. Each stroke of his tail pushed him farther from the nestlings. He remembered Po, always searching. He remembered Ka, always hungry and sure where to find her next meal. He had not yet visited Liu and Kai on this circuit. Shen's scent pulled him forward. The others tugged him back. He thought the tension might split him in the middle.

He had searched too long. He could feel it. He raised his head and memorized the lines to the keep, to a tall tree, to the path of the sun, telling him exactly where he stopped. He stood for a moment, quivering with the tension drawing him in both directions at the same time. Then he turned.

Liu had wandered, but could be found. Kai slept on her heap of mud and reeds, fat belly to the sun. Khe'sha pushed on through his route, finally returning to Ka and Ghu. He found them safe and separate. He found Po and dumped him back into a hole in the muck and buried him almost to the water line. Let the rascal dig for a while. The work would put some muscle on his thin body.

And then he was back at Shen's mound, with no Shen and with the sun passing beyond the Crown of Heaven. He swam heedless of the brush and grass, plowing along the line the thief had followed. He found his farthest point, and slowed, and tasted the water and the air.

The traces faded and staled with the time he'd lost, as sun and wind and water fought him. He followed. Her scent remained mixed with the taint of the Old One. It swelled and ebbed, turned fresher and aged, as if he followed through eddies in the stream of time.

He found drips and smears of blood, but far less than he would wish. Small teeth could not do much damage. Once the hatchlings had minds and memories, he could teach them *where* to bite their prey and their enemies, places where even a nip could kill.

Tension grew again, pulling him forward and pulling him back. He felt as if he had two brains, one commanding the forelegs and one his rear and tail. They argued over his path. He pushed on through the swamp and neared the far shore. He touched solid ground. He had to return. He had to go forward. Shen needed him. Ka and Ghu and Po and the others needed him.

He sighted on the keep, and the large tree on a distant hill, and memorized the shape of the hard lands. He turned back. The heat built inside him and told him that he was pushing too hard, too fast. His bulk wasn't suited for a long chase. He turned and swam on, ignoring it. He had to.

Ka clung to a branch, nearly halfway to Ghu's mound. Khe'sha knew that she would rest, and swim on, and finally she would reach that tantalizing smell. She would keep trying until she did. Persistence—it was a virtue in adult dragons. It kept *him* going. However, it would be her death if he didn't stop her. He nipped her up and carried her back to her mound and buried her in the muck to slow her down. He swam on.

Ghu attacked him, always attacking anything that moved. Po had wandered. He circled the swamp, feeding, capturing, guarding his hatchlings. His brain started to buzz with the heat building inside his body. He pushed on from Shen's mound, straight to the hard lands and his last scent of her. He followed the reek of the Old Blood into forest and uphill, until it turned and headed straight for the gray keep on the horizon. He turned back.

He dove into the cold black waters of the wallow he'd dug in the center of the marsh. A spring flowed there, fresh and clean and icy, and he bathed in it to chill his body. But he couldn't stay. He soaked in the depths until his heartbeat slowed, though only to the rate he would normally call high. He drank deep from the coldest flow. He swam on.

Ka had dug herself out, a tunnel narrow and straight and perfectly aimed at Ghu's mound, barely disturbing her own. He turned and drove through the water, tail and legs pushing like the final lunge to take his prey. He followed her scent as she had followed Ghu's. He passed the shrub where she had rested. He did not find her. His head buzzed and his vision blurred, throbbing with the beat of his heart.

He found Ka. He found both of them. Ka was dead. Ghu crouched over her body, her half-eaten body, flattened his head against her torn hide, and hissed, a dragon defending his kill.

Khe'sha felt the world spin, his body's heat pounding in his head. His eyes darkened and his legs shook. He slumped forward until his chin rested on the mound.

Shen and Ka. Two females, both gone. Six remaining mounds, six remaining hatchlings. Four males and two females. Trouble, in this land where nest-mates must become life-mates because there were no other nests.

Khe'sha found his thoughts and forced them back into place. The heat had nearly killed him. Or he had nearly killed himself, pushing his body too far, too fast, too long. Humans and Old Ones could do such things. So could the hounds they trained for the chase. Their bodies allowed it, even encouraged it. They could hunt and kill by sheer endurance, wearing their prey into the ground.

Dragons could not.

The old songs told that story, as they told all things. They told of dragons pushing beyond their bodies' limits, performing great deeds that echoed down the centuries and dying in their triumph. Pan'gu had been the first.

*But I have failed. Heroes triumph and we remember them in song. Failure is forgotten. Ka is dead and eaten. Shen has gone to the stone tower. I remain.*

And the hatchlings still needed him. He rose, legs weak and dark spots whirling across his eyes. He slid down from Ghu's nest and pointed his nose along the open water that led to Po's mound. He swam, slowly, weakly, still feeling the heat flow from his body into the water.

The stone tower stood above him on its hilltop. He looked up at it from time to time in his rounds, remembering. The hatchlings would grow, their scales would harden, they would learn to think. He would be free.

He would compose the song of Sha'khe and teach it to the hatchlings. Only then could he destroy the tower and all that lived within it. That might not fit the dark witch's plan. She wanted to follow a fresher trail, heedless of the cost to others. He must wait. Even so, time swirled strangely, and he wondered if the days now passed the same for Shen as they did for him and for her nest-mates.

He would find out when he destroyed the keep. That would be *his* song.

FERGUS WIPED SWEAT from his forehead. Part of it was fading horror, a vivid waking nightmare of that panicked instant when a knife spun so close to his head that it pared a sliver from his ear and left blood trickling hot down his neck. Part of it was fever. His right biceps throbbed under its stinking bandage, reminding him of the cost of slavery to a mistress like Fiona.

She'd wanted a dragon hatchling. She'd wanted someone else to bear the risk of stealing it. And there were things she hadn't bothered to tell him when she made him steal Dougal's boots and pants and shirt and Brian's camouflage poncho to muddle the scent trail he left behind him.

He could have stolen the huntsman's leather jerkin, or even gauntlets and a shirt of chain mail, if he'd known. The scent would have been the same.

No, she'd wanted more than just the hatchling. She'd wanted a lab rat for one of her experiments.

He eased through the cool stone of the cellar wall, making use of the welcome that the masons and quarrymen had left behind when they departed, centuries ago. Human or Old One, slave or master, all men who worked and understood and loved good stone were kin.

An empty corridor waited—no deadly witches. He felt tension drain out of his shoulders and reminded himself that each breath he drew was a gift, after facing Fiona in her maze. And this deep-worked living stone was a gift. Dusty and musty, black as pitch to normal eyes, the walls glowed for him, gently giving off the Power they'd soaked up since the sun had last shone on their faces.

What did this dark maze hide from prying eyes?

He brushed his fingers over the fine-grained sandstone, feeling the magic within it. It hummed like a faceted diamond scattering fire. And yet unlike, as well, as if the light it broke and spread had been stolen from another kind of sun.

It centered on that hidden room. So did the deep and ancient pain he'd felt, and the anger. He traced his own glowing footprints back to it, puzzled again by the faint older prints that went in and came out, relieved by the smaller recent prints that *did* leave and took their deadly steel with them. He'd rather not meet that surprise again.

Good manners told him to enter by the door, not asking the stone to let him pass through unless he had no choice. He'd often wondered if others could do the things he did with stone, if they only treated it with respect and worked it the way it wanted to be worked. If they spoke to it and listened to the answers.

He scowled at the crude plane gouged into the side of the central menhir, the cruder Christian idol hung on it. They broke the shape the stone's heart had asked from ancient hands. They weakened and changed the Power and brought dissonance into the song that whispered in his ears. He brushed his fingers across the pillar and asked it if it could be made whole again, if the stone felt another shape still hidden within the five faces it showed the world.

Something woke after long dreaming. Facets glowed back at him, bedding lines in the stone's grain where hands like his could guide a chisel and redirect the Power that flowed from beneath his feet. The heart could be healed. It reached out to him, tentative with something very close to hope.

But what did it *do*? He studied the flow of energy across the floor and through the labyrinth and swirling into the quartz starburst set before the menhir; he read faint traces of Ogham runes held as memories rather than visible marks in worn old stone; he watched as phantom feet traced the pattern and left their smears on the dust and vanished between one step and the next. He shuddered as cold fingers walked like those footsteps down his spine.

Crude as it might look, the chisel-work defacing this focus had been deliberate and precise, guided by malice and a mind that read stone as clearly as Fergus ever could. Cool blue flows of energy struck the damage and scattered, sparking purple at his touch like a mountain crag that felt a coming thunderstorm. Some unknown hand had broken the magic with precise strokes of iron on stone. *No,* he thought, *bent rather than broken. Power still flows. It just no longer flows the way the original work intended.*

That unknown hand had turned the labyrinth into an eddy out of the stream. He had no way to calculate where the portal had once led, but now the way was blocked. He preferred to leave it closed until he knew what waited on the other side. He felt too much pain and anger here to act without long thought.

He knelt and studied the quartz focus. Like the paving pattern of the labyrinth, it showed the hand of a master. Milky opalescent stone formed a perfect Solomon's Seal, six-pointed and as smooth as glass, as broad from point to point as the length of his arm, yet carved from a single crystal. It fitted into the natural stone of the floor as if it had grown there. *This* work had escaped damage. And it hid something. He could feel it.

He touched the face and eased his thoughts into the crystal lattice. His hand followed, flesh moving like water through the spaces between atoms of silicon and oxygen. Cool Power flowed back along his wrist, soothing the throb and burn under his bandages.

Down, down, down into the stone he reached, drawn as much by the ease of pain as by curiosity. His wrist entered, and his forearm, and finally his elbow until he lay flat on the floor and reached the full length of his arm and knew that the quartz crystal was as deep as it was wide, pure and flawless. Only Power could form a crystal of that size and quality.

His fingers touched ice and told him it was fire. He traced facets and edges, reading them and building a picture in his head. Equilateral triangles. Obtuse facets. Icosahedron, bigger than his fist. He tried to flow into it and read its heart. His fingers slipped off, unable to grip or penetrate.

A puzzle.

And probably dangerous, of course. Most things in this land were dangerous, in one way or another. He drew his hand back, wincing as the pain returned.

He sat back on his heels and glared at the damaged menhir. It offended him. To understand stone as deeply as that unknown lout must have, and then use that understanding in such an ugly way . . .

His arm throbbed, hot and aching. Greenish pus stained the bandage into blotches edged with thin red and yellow fringes. Rot twisted his nose, and he grimaced as he unwrapped the linen strips he'd stolen from an unused bed. Fiona's experiment, indeed. The twin arcs of the bite glared at him, high on his biceps where that damned snake had twisted in his hands and clamped down like a vise, livid red ringing black dead flesh.

Dead and rotting. And it was his right arm, and him right-handed. He couldn't work out a way to cut it off. Not one that would leave him alive afterward.

But the red rings around each tooth-mark seemed narrower than before, and the stink less violent, and the throbbing less intense. Maybe the Power of the labyrinth had helped.

Or maybe he was wishing that it had. It was worth trying, anyway. He leaned forward and laid his hand on the quartz star again, letting the hot ice flow up his nerves and veins, soothing the throb and cooling the burn.

Then his eyes turned toward the door, and his legs straightened, and his feet moved without orders from his brain. Fiona was back. She had something she wanted to find out, up in the keep where that deadly witch stalked with her hand always resting on the pommel of her knife.

FIONA GAZED AT the whiteboard in her lab, seeing other things through other eyes. No, she was not *about* to let little Fergus find magic healing for his wounds. That would destroy all her data, ruin the experiment. As it was, she needed to find a human subject to provide the baseline of a different species' physiology. Maybe one of those refugees cowering in Maureen's kitchen would do.

And maybe Cáitlin, as well. One subject, or two, or even ten—not enough for a statistical sample, that was certain. Fiona wouldn't be able to publish her results in the *New England Journal of Medicine* with such a small base of experimental data. "Bacterial Ectoenzyme Reactions and Soft Tissue Necrosis in Mythical Reptilian Bite Trauma." Well, the title had enough syllables for a research paper, even if it never would see print.

Cáitlin could wait in her tree, puzzling over a leopard that refused to kill her. Fiona never destroyed a tool before it had lost all usefulness. If Cáit survived Maureen's forest long enough, she too would meet that nasty little lizard.

Fiona brought her eyes and mind back to her lab and the question of the lizard. Lab equipment hummed around her, gleaming with stainless steel and gray hammer-tone enamel, displays glowing green or red with numbers and graphs. She glanced over the readings on the mass spectrometer, ticking off compounds in her head. Nothing new. Her projection microscope displayed a tissue culture at 300X, blackened disintegration marching out from the lower left corner as one cluster of cells after another dissolved into slime.

Nasty stuff. She touched her mask with a gloved hand, then covered the filters and tested for an airtight seal. The suit ballooned around her, hissing slightly as the positive pressure air supply found its way to relief valves. No reason to take chances, even though she'd spoken nose to snout with both the dragons and lived to tell the tale.

She caressed the cold rounded enamel of the centrifuge beside her on the table. She'd used it only once since setting it up—like her neat green pastures, the lab served mostly as a stage setting for performance art, the Mad Scientist at work, Dr. Frankenstein surrounded by the crackle and ozone of high-voltage electricity.

But the equipment she *did* use gave her such solid, satisfying facts. Just because the humans had invented science didn't mean that it was useless. They'd invented these machines as well, and then politely donated them to Fiona's lab.

Well, maybe not *donated,* or at least not consciously. They were still carried on the inventory at Jackson Labs, or listed as destroyed in a bad fire they'd had a few years back. But none of the instruments had ever been signed out to the visiting postdoctoral research geneticist Fiona Fálta, Ph.D., or to her microbiologist colleague and brother, Dr. Sean Fálta. None of the machines had ever been logged to a lab where she had worked. She might want to go back there again sometime.

Fiona turned back to the cage, her belly swinging awkwardly until she felt like she was waddling along with the entire earth tucked under the front of her moon suit. Her back ached, and her ankles throbbed with the swelling. This pregnancy bit walked perilously close to bad design. She could see some powerful advantages to dumping her endoparasite in a nest and incubating it, like those dragons. For one thing, she wouldn't have to keep running to the loo.

She studied the black lizard imprisoned behind a grid of stainless steel bars. "Are mammals an evolutionary mistake?"

<Shen hungry.>

"You're *always* hungry, love. And so am I. But I'll be rid of this thing in another day or so. The stars and planets will come to their convergence and foretell the spectacular deaths of Brian and Maureen. More to the point, your father will have lunch, and I'll pick up the scraps left over."

<Shen *hungry*!>

Fiona started to bend down to the refrigerator under her lab counter, discovered for the thousandth time that her middle no longer bent, and squatted with an irritated grunt. She pulled out a chunk of beef summoned from a butcher's coldroom, grabbed the counter with her free hand, and heaved her bulk back up to standing. *That* grunt came from pain and effort.

She remembered her ongoing experiment with Fergus and checked the latch on the cage entry's inner door before releasing the outer. That midget dinosaur was *fast.* And alert, and cunning—it watched every move, and Fiona could almost *see* it memorizing the way she released the outer door. *Time to put a padlock on the latch,* she thought. *Key lock or combination?*

*Certainly something that requires fine manipulation,* she decided. *Something that requires thumbs.*

*Meat in the entry chamber, outer door closed* and *latched, double check, release the inner door.* The lizard pounced, sank its deadly needle-teeth into the meat, and dragged it back into a corner of the cage where it would be safe. Then the little beast glared at her before it started chewing.

"You don't like me, love. You don't like me even a little bit. First chance you get, you'll bite the hand that feeds you, just like in that human adage. We'll just make sure you never get that chance. Mammals *are* smarter than dinosaurs."

Or were they crocodilians? No, the hip and shoulder joints looked wrong for that group of reptiles. She'd have to run some DNA comparisons to sort out the cladistics and taxonomy, but the skeletal articulation seemed much closer to a dinosaur's. Had dinosaurs been true reptiles in the first place? The jury was still out on that one. Little Shen was due for dissection and mounting, anyway, once Fiona had finished the live experiments.

*Dissection with full biohazard precautions,* she reminded herself. She glanced up at the microscope's image projected on one wall. Death and digestion had oozed across the entire view, and again she panned the 'scope to the advancing edge of her culture.

One cell, one single cell of the bacteria that slimed the little beast's mottled yellow teeth. That was all Fiona had injected into the tissue. Let one cell past the guarding walls of your epidermis and your best bet was immediate surgery. Amputation or tissue excision, well away from the wound, followed by a massive course of broad-spectrum antibiotics.

It was such a lovely little microbe. Once she had grown a sample large enough, she'd start to teach it about penicillin—culture the survivors and go on from there. She flipped a switch and the single projected image split into four. Three of the tissue samples showed no active growth—reptile, fish, and insect. So the bacteria seemed to need warm-blooded flesh to prosper. She'd have to find out why.

Of course, she'd need a vector, too—and then she laughed, mocking herself. This was a game, no more, a way to kill time before her Powers reached their peak. The most she'd get from this research would be a new poison for the thorns that barbed her hedge.

And the antidote.

But her whim with Cáitlin and Fergus was bearing fruit, her ghosts spooking Maureen back to the bottle. Drink would weaken the red witch and further drive the wedge between her and the others.

The baby kicked her bladder with uncanny aim, and she winced. Enough! Time to evict this squatter and find a wet nurse among the slaves. But first she had to draw on its Powers to crush Maureen and Brian beneath her heel.

# sixteen

———

"TAKE IT, *STUD*. Prove that having a set of balls makes you tougher than me."

Dierdre held the long black cylinder out to him, grip first. Brian shook tears out of his eyes and tried to focus. Cattle prod. Shock stick. Phallic symbol for a dominatrix.

She poked his hand with it, forcing it into his grip. His fingers twitched and shook as commands tried to force their way past the drained synapses and connect to muscles.

She let go and the stick stayed in his hand, warm and damp from her own grip, intimate. *Interrogation is an intimate affair,* his memories played back in her voice, humming through the strange detachment of pain and delirium. *You'll get as close to your subject as to any lover. You'll develop many of the same feelings. You'll know him as deeply and as passionately. Don't try to fight this feeling. You'll succeed by becoming one with your subject, knowing his needs and fears as deeply as he does, finding out what matters to him and what does not. When he tells you what you want to know, he'll be talking to himself.*

Dierdre fogged in and out on him, a figure tall and

rawhide thin and dressed in form-fitting black now rather than the purple uniform, showing off the muscles that always came as a surprise. She'd sucker-punched him to take him out, but a straight match in a ring would have been a toss-up. He'd have weight and muscle and the ability to soak up damage and keep on coming; she'd have speed and decades more experience. Toss-up. Luck. Now she faced him alone with his hands free, behind locked doors, and sneered at him.

The cattle prod hung from his hand. She invited him to fight back. The tip wavered as his arm shook. *Alone and free and already beat to shit. Familiar with the old Chinese expression "fat chance"?* She also liked switching loaded dice into a game of craps. She didn't step back out of range, or even watch his hand. She stared straight into his eyes and dared him.

"Come *on, hombre. Do* it!"

And she'd stand there and take the shock and laugh in his face. Extremely high pain-tolerance. She'd done that in class. A class she'd taught.

As she'd taught hand-to-hand. Toughest bitch on the planet, Dierdre. Symptom of a problem. People here knew every trick he did. Fighting, intrigue, using the Power, he'd learned all of it from Them. Never taught him as much as They knew, never taught him Us would become Them, would be the enemy.

The tip of the cattle prod wavered as he brought it up. She smiled at him, waiting. He turned the stick, groping for his own head, and a crescent kick flickered past his nose and sent the tube flying to clatter into a corner of the cell. His hand stung, but she'd been careful to hit only the stick.

She could kick over his head, flat-footed. Could have taken his nose off, could have killed him. Dierdre was *always* precise and in control.

"Naughty, naughty." She stood still in front of him as if

she'd never moved. "Mother Church doesn't approve of suicide, you know. Not even under questioning."

"Told . . . you . . . truth."

She shook her head. "I taught you better than *that*."

She had, too. *Even if it doesn't matter, never tell them the truth first time off. They'll only respect it if they have to dig for it. If you want to sell a lie, bury it six or seven layers deep. Give it up in bits and pieces, always backing away from it. Lose a tooth for each word of it, make each sentence worth a pint of blood.*

And he'd told them the truth. Or most of it. After all, they were his friends and allies.

*Bad mistake. Never think you're safe, even in your own bedroom, even in the bloody loo. Tried to teach Maureen that, made her carry that damned* kukri *everywhere even though it made her remember what she did to Dougal. Forgot the rule yourself.*

Pain exploded under his ribs, and he fought for breath. More blows followed—slow, calculated, with the precision of decades of practice. Fire in his head, electric nerves flowing lava down his right arm, a late afterthought to the balls that made the rest seem like love-taps. He curled around his pain, helpless on the stone floor. The blows stopped, but the pain went on and on. The slate floor stank of old vomit and urine, as if it had been through this a hundred times before. He wondered who the others had been.

Her face hung inches from his own, blurred through sweat and tears. "Don't lie to me. 'Desperation.' 'Weak spot between the worlds.' Tell me true, tell Mother how you got here."

"Take . . . poly . . . graph."

She sat back on her haunches and looked for a moment as if she was considering his offer. "Now *there's* a thought. It's a bleedin' shame I'm the one who taught you how to beat the machine."

She grabbed his shirt and heaved him up, aiming for the

chair. Careless. He went with the flow and then overbalanced, flopping down and then adding a roll and kick that flung her hard against one wall. She bounced to her feet before he could follow up, retreating to the farthest corner and shaking dazzle out of her head.

"Good on you, ducks. Guess I didn't waste *all* that training time."

And if he *had* killed her, he would have had to sit and wake the corpse and wait for her replacement. Door locked from the outside. Surveillance camera in the corner, watching every move. And he couldn't walk between the worlds to escape. She'd let him try, right at the start of their dance, just to add to his despair. He didn't even know what world this *was*.

But killing her would have felt good, nonetheless.

His vision blurred. Her feet scalloped closer, always balanced, always ready. "Let's try another round. Let's dance the night away." He couldn't raise his eyes above her knees.

"Not up for that? Too bad. This could have been the start of a *beautiful* relationship." Pain flashed from his kneecap.

Dierdre touched the prod to her own forearm and triggered it, watching with a detached air as her muscles jerked. "Still works." She jammed it into his aching crotch and then pulled it back without discharging the capacitor through his balls. He almost pissed himself with relief.

She jabbed him again, still not triggering the shock. "Why'd you kill Liam, dearie?"

The question came out of the fog like a ten-ton lorry with no lights. She'd been on about his access to the bleeding Circle, whatever the bloody hell *that* was, and about Maureen. The Pendragons discouraged relationships that stepped outside the ranks. He'd never realized how far that "discouraging" could go.

"Attacked . . . girl."

"Did he, now?" She rocked back on her heels. "Count number one on the indictment: No proof of attack, no weapon and no threat ever demonstrated. Last seen, he was talking politely to the subject. Count number two: Subject of alleged attack was herself an Old One, capable of defending herself with high-level Powers since demonstrated to the satisfaction of the jury. Count number three: Defendant had received specific orders to stay away from Liam. Verdict: Defendant stands guilty on all counts. Take him down."

They'd been watching him watching the bastard. "Liam . . . murderer. Tortured . . . Mulvaney."

"None of your business, ducks. Policy. Policy is set by the home office, not by field ops. Tell me, what's the penalty for direct disobedience of a lawful order, under time of war?"

Shit. Dierdre was talking *death*.

He felt the prongs of the cattle prod jamming into the inside of his thigh. She glanced up at the camera again, and nodded. "Now tell me true, Arthur Brian Albion Pendragon: How did you get here? Don't expect me to believe you 'felt' a rabbit-hole and jumped down it to escape your sister. If that fairy tale were true, we'd have been up to our bums in leprechauns for the past thousand years. You're the first, which gives me cause to doubt."

He'd managed to keep the real secret in their training session, proving it by the sealed envelope he'd deposited before they took him from his room at 3:00 A.M. He'd managed to sell the cover, sell the lie. But he'd *told* the truth here, first time off. Except for Claire. So Dierdre would never believe it.

His leg jerked as she triggered the prod, and fire chased ice up and down his nerve channels. He fuzzed out and back and out and back again. His eyes blurred.

The twitching stopped, and he could focus. Dierdre was up and at the door, talking to a shadow against the hall lights.

"Nope, just getting started. You can't rush an artist. Not if you want the truth."

The shadow shook his head. His or hers. Couldn't tell. "Bring him anyway. Captain-general's orders."

Male voice, sounded like Duncan. Why were they rushing things? Reprieve? Good cop, bad cop?

They hauled him up, with a third pair of hands that materialized from the shadows. Duncan tucked himself under Brian's arm, comradely, supporting, whispering. "You're for it, lad. First Liam and now showing up in Circle territory without an engraved invitation to the ball. I think I can winkle you out, but just keep your mouth shut and let me do the talking."

His bloody legs wouldn't work right, pins and needles jostling through the veins. Stumbling down corridors and up stairs, Brian tried to memorize the turns and doors and carvings in case he ever got a chance to move. Dierdre skittered forward and back beside them like an impatient mongoose blocked from attacking a particularly juicy cobra. The unknown guard kept several paces off, fingering what looked like a Beretta SMG with suppressor screwed onto the muzzle. So that would work here? Brian filed the note away for future reference.

They passed a silver crucifix on a carved door, seemed Italian. Chapel? Work looked like Cellini, Baroque, not Brian's taste at all. He blinked and tried to shake the cobwebs out of his head.

Double doors, raised panels with men and women carved on them. Pin-cushioned by arrows, beheadings, iron grids over fires, lions out of medieval woodcut prints. Martyrs? Saint Sebastian on the upper right? Gruesome. Bugger it, omens again.

Long room, wide, flaring torches, ragged banners hanging from black hammer-beam trusses high overhead in the flickering gloom. Why couldn't they use electric lights like they had in the bloody dungeons? Bloody image games, just like Dougal and Fiona.

Great hall, probably. Long horseshoe table, with heavy chair set between the two arms, at the focus of nine black-hooded faces. Judges. Unanimous decision, or majority? Or sham? Dierdre settled him into the chair, the prisoner's dock, with a touch.

Hooded faces, but Brian could make some guesses. Central on the table facing him, obvious boss by everyone's body language, Captain-General Llewes. Left of him, long black hair showing beneath the hood and two bumps on the front of the purple uniform, that would likely be Amanda, misnamed, "Worthy To Be Loved." Reported to be vicious in the tangled head-office politics of the Pendragons. Down halfway on the right, massive signet ring on the right hand, MacDonald, head of operations and never identified any further.

Brian might come up with more names when they spoke. Or *if*. Right now, they just stared at him in silence.

His brain settled back between his ears. Duncan and Dierdre stood behind him, Duncan's hand lightly on Brian's right shoulder as either support or restraint, Brian wasn't quite sure which. The guard settled cross-legged on the floor in front of Llewes, where his line of fire didn't include any of the judges. The neat 9mm hole in the muzzle of the Beretta's flat-black sound suppressor made it look like a tenth hooded judge. Maybe it was.

The silence dragged on.

Finally, the last hood on the left pushed himself to his feet and turned toward the head of the horseshoe. He bowed. "My lord." Then he faced Brian. "Prisoner at the bar, you stand accused of deliberate and premeditated murder of an agent of the Circle, desertion, betraying secrets of the Order, and entering a forbidden area. How do you plead?"

Murder. Agent. Circle.

Those three words hit him like another kick in the balls.

Brian couldn't move, couldn't think, couldn't speak. Forbidden area? He'd expected that. Plead ignorance, plead incompetence, plead that he hadn't had any bloody choice once his bloody bitch-sister had followed him to the bloody safe-house transit room. That covered the secrets, as well. And they probably expected pillow talk with Maureen. As if he hadn't learned to avoid *that* trap long ago.

Desertion? Yeah, they might see it that way. He saw it more like resigning from an endless winless war. Like that guy in the Hemingway book.

The hood waited.

Now Dierdre's hand settled on Brian's other shoulder, right over the nerve-pinch that would drop him into writhing pain if he made any kind of move.

Murder. Agent. Circle.

Only way to make sense of it was, Liam had been a double rat, a mole. Only way to make sense of *that* was, this Circle had turned a blind eye to all the things Liam had done through the years.

Including Mulvaney. The thought made Brian sick.

Mulvaney had been a fellow Pendragon, sergeant major to Brian's captain in the SAS, old friend and solid trusted man-behind-me-back. Liam had tortured the old soldier to death, just for the pure hell of it. And Duncan had ordered Brian off the trail.

That hadn't made sense, so he'd marked it up to the garbled message, a mistake in coding or decoding, and pushed on. Killed Liam when he'd tried to take Maureen to the Summer Country.

"Let the record show that the accused stood mute." The hood sat down.

"Questioner," the signet ring spoke, with MacDonald's voice, "have you discovered how the accused reached this place?"

Dierdre stirred, her grip tightening on the nerve plexus in his shoulder. "You saw the video. Claimed he 'felt' the way and took it."

"Do you think he told the truth?"

"He beat me before, in training. The council cut my questioning short."

"Who guards the way from Joseph's Throne?"

Now Duncan stirred, his hand heavy with tension. "I do, my lord."

Silence, dragging on for a minute or more. Joseph's Throne, Joseph of Arimathea, myth tied him with Glastonbury and Arthur and the Grail. And Castle Corbin, also known as Carbonek. The signet ring lifted to form a cup under a hooded chin. "The prisoner was under your *direct* command?"

"Yes, my lord."

"You ordered him to leave Liam alone?"

"Yes, my lord."

So much for Duncan serving as barrister for the defense. Direct conflict of interest. Time to talk to the solicitor about engaging new counsel.

The one he'd guessed was Amanda stirred and turned to Llewes at the center of the horseshoe. Rumor had it that she wanted his chair. Badly enough not to mind bloodstains on it. "Is the prisoner prepared to give up his lover to stay with us?"

Llewes turned back to Brian and raised his hand, palm up, to pass the question on.

Maureen.

Time played strange games in the Summer Country. Between worlds, it was even worse. He'd been here for a few hours, a day at most. He wondered how many hours or days or weeks had passed for Maureen. Or if he'd been gone any time at all.

Most likely, though, she'd know that he had left. Left without any parting, with harsh words between them. What would she think and do?

She'd think he'd said to hell with her, packed up and left.

But she was Maureen. She'd wound herself around his heart so tightly, he couldn't cut her out and live without her. In spite of all her flaws. Funny that he should realize that *now,* when it was too late.

Llewes still waited.

Brian slowly shook his head, dazed by his thoughts and the hours just past. "No. Maureen is more important to me than the Pendragons."

Those words were probably his death warrant. But he'd sensed that this hearing wasn't about Liam, or leading Fiona to the safe house, or even about Maureen. This was about him knowing things he wasn't supposed to know. And that was beyond all help.

Dierdre's hand tightened on Brian's shoulder, silencing him and forcing him back into his chair. He accepted because he couldn't think of any way to save his ass. And he wasn't sure he *wanted* to defend himself. He might be slow, but they'd lined up enough ducks that he could finally see them make a line. Mulvaney had been Liam's price of admission, his way to prove to the Old Ones which side he was on. Duncan had known about it. Brian's stomach surged, and he swallowed bile.

*Duncan and this whole bloody inner Circle. Bastards probably ordered it. Mulvaney was old, old enough he'd known Kipling out in India. He was retiring. Get one last mission out of the old soldier and save a few quid on the pension fund, all at one go.*

And this Circle kept slaves. He'd seen them, in the castle fields and the halls when Dierdre first hauled him through that labyrinth into whatever world this was. Human slaves. No mistaking that body language. They crept around the edges of life, cringing whenever one of the Old Ones glanced their way.

Corrupt. Deep down at its heart, its hidden ruling Circle, the Pendragon order was corrupt. Brian mourned.

Amanda was speaking. ". . . Mac, you see conspiracies under every rock. Do you have any *proof* our boy wasn't acting on his own?"

The signet ring shrugged and waved in Brian's direction. "Do ye think he's smart enough? Fifty years in the British Army and nobody's ever put him in for major? Albion has his faults, but being brainy isn't one of them. He had to have help to have even found this place."

Prosecutor-hood pushed himself to his feet, bowed to the Llewes-hood again, Queen's Counsel in purple instead of black silk. "Prisoner at the bar, do you have anything to say in your defense?" He was cutting the debate short, probably on a cue from Llewes.

Brian stood, and Dierdre let him. She kept the nerve hold, though. "I came here by accident, just the way I said. No one helped me. I killed Liam because he was a murderer. I don't think love means betrayal, and if *you* think that it does, then you've betrayed your own souls." He slumped back into his chair, drained and shaking, pleased that he'd managed to string four coherent sentences together. Even if those sentences should mean his death.

QC-hood nodded to Dierdre, waiting like the unsheathed sword of justice behind Brian. "Questioner, do you think you can get him to tell us more?"

Silence behind Brian. He couldn't see her face and didn't really want to.

He felt her shake her head, through that lover's-touch on his shoulder. "I doubt that he'll change his story. You've seen his records. He beat the training test."

QC-hood nodded. He bowed to Llewes-hood and sat

down. Brian had finally tied a face to the prosecutor's voice, a thin-faced weasel named Rupert. Seemed to be somebody in the paymaster's office. Always chasing expense accounts and harassing field operatives.

"Vote." That was Llewes, barely moving the hood's fabric with his voice.

This kangaroo court rolled along on well-greased wheels as if everyone except Brian had been through it a hundred times before. That thought sickened him almost as much as Mulvaney and Liam and the slaves.

"Death." Lower right corner hood.

"Further interrogation, then death." Signet ring.

"Exile. He knows how to keep his mouth shut, and I agree with him about Liam. As you know." Third hood on the right, first time it had spoken, a voice Brian didn't recognize.

Across the head table. "Death."

Nothing from Llewes.

"Death." Amanda.

Down the left side. "Death." "Exile." "Death."

The words didn't matter to Brian. His past was dead already. He didn't want any part of this present. He couldn't see a future. He just wished he'd said goodbye to Maureen.

The hoods all turned toward Llewes, where he sat centered at the head of the horseshoe. Group dynamics told Brian that they were just advisors, and the only vote that counted was the captain-general's. And that this proceeding was marching a predetermined route.

"Death. Firing squad, in the courtyard, at dawn. Cremation with full military honors." He spread his hand flat, about six inches above the table, a king dismissing his Star Chamber court. Dismissing any further interrogation.

And that was that. Dierdre's hand told him to rise, to turn, to walk through the door. She guided him like a show horse with her eloquent touch.

He walked where she pointed him, numb to the core. He didn't even ache anymore. She hummed behind him, a tune that chased through his brain in search of words from memory. It finally connected.

"For young Roddy McCorley goes to die on the bridge of Toome today."

# seventeen

—◆◆◆—

BRIAN MOURNED.

He felt Dierdre's fingers poised over nerve holds, guiding, controlling, firm and yet just the promise of pain rather than the fact. The touch of a virtuoso, who understood that constant pressure would deaden the effect and she'd lose the threat by using it. He walked where the warning sent him, moving in a fog.

Fifty years of his life. Fifty bloody *years* he'd dedicated to the Pendragons, training and fighting and bleeding and doing ugly things in dark piss-stinking alleys, just to find out that something like Liam had been an agent of the same side. His allies were as filthy as his enemies.

Worse, even. The Old Ones made no pretense. They were what they were, right out front.

Talk about *stupid*. MacDonald was right. For all the anagrams might say, brains had never been Brian's strong point. He knew that. He made up for it with persistence. Once he started in on a task or a thought, he saw it through to the end however long it took, however much it hurt. That was how he'd finally gotten Liam.

He had just never started thinking about the Pendragons. He took them at face value. He'd been a good soldier, doing everything they told him to the best of his abilities. Sometimes they told him to do hideous things, but there'd always been a reason. There'd been a reason for Dierdre, a need he could recognize that she filled, nasty though it might be.

He'd have obeyed even that order about Liam, if the coding hadn't garbled it. And then he never would have met Maureen.

Dierdre guided him through the door and into the empty corridor. They turned back the way they'd come, the way back to the interrogation cell. Dance the night away with Dierdre, such a lovely thought. See the dawn, and die.

Well, that put a limit on the pain. He'd found out long ago, you could take almost anything if you had an end in sight. That was how he'd beaten her before. He'd known she had a week to break him, not endless minutes that blurred out into forever. Last out that week and win.

Now he just had to make it through the night. His memories would probably hurt more than whatever she had planned for him. Hints he should have read and understood, the Inner Circle's choices that hid in the shadows within shadows. Things that should have looked wrong, smelled wrong, things like that garbled message that hadn't made sense unless you changed the way you read them. He'd been using the wrong key to decode *all* the messages. Now it fell into place.

Rotten. The Pendragons were rotten at their heart and head. The foundation of his world had vanished. This was the way Maureen would feel if she found her Father Oak split open and felled by a wind that should never have troubled his topmost leaves—not just clean wood-rot but some kind of oozing stinking putrescence. This was how a priest would feel if he found out God was evil. Rot at the core of his soul.

The Pendragons were supposed to protect humans. Here at their heart, they kept human slaves. To fight the Old Ones, they'd recruited Liam.

Dierdre stopped them in the hall. "The prisoner will want to pray."

Pray for what? Absolution? No one here could offer *that*. And he'd long passed beyond hoping for eternal life. That sounded more like punishment to him. Hell was what happened after the first thousand years of heaven, when eternal bliss turned into eternal boredom. He couldn't think of *anything* he'd want to do forever, not even making love to Maureen.

They'd stopped in front of that door with the Cellini crucifix. Dierdre and Duncan flanked him, with that Beretta-toting guard at a measured distance and a clear line of fire. Brian felt anger through Dierdre's touch, tension that translated into needles where her fingers pressed his nerves.

"You think I can't handle *this* alone?" And one hand moved faster than he could think, and pain slammed into his kidney. He bounced forward, smashed his cheek against the wood carving of the door, and slid to his knees. Fingers yanked his hair back, and he stared up into Dierdre's face through blurry tears.

She shook her head, disgust wrinkling her nose. "Bleedin' British Army ain't what it used to be. *This* is the cream of the SAS?"

His head jerked forward, smashing into the lever of the latch and opening the door. He felt blood hot on his forehead as she heaved him to his feet, one-handed. Who ever said women were the weaker sex? And then he stumbled forward from another blow and the door boomed shut behind them and they were in a mysterious gloom of incense and flickering votive lights.

She let him stand, free, shaking his head to clear the daze and tears from his eyes. A chapel, yes, ancient, with carved crucifix and high altar and rood screen, with dark Gothic-arched panels that might be more carving or might show stained glass when there was light beyond them. Gallery and choir and two side boxes thrusting out between the arches overhead. Two lines of backless pews flanking a central aisle. Room to seat maybe a hundred.

She pushed him forward again, punching gently this time, almost a love-tap. "Brian, *mo croí,* you've walked one of those labyrinths before. I saw it in your face when you stepped through the wall. I'm guessing the deepest cellars of Castle Perilous, yes? So now we have a secret between us, you and I. Everyone else thinks there's just the one." Her words hit him as a colossal non sequitur.

He shook his head, still dazed. "And two can keep a secret, if one of them is dead? Is that your point?"

"No. I believe more people should know our history. Our *true* history. There are so many layers to it, just like archaeology. And so strange.

"Llewes serves admirably as a captain-general. I have to admit, though, that as a research librarian he couldn't find his bleedin' arse with both hands and a color plate from *Gray's Anatomy* as a road map. There were six of them, one for each point on that Solomon's Seal."

And with that, she dropped to one knee in front of the cross and genuflected. She had her back to him, but her words still roared in his ears and he was too stunned to move.

"Don't bother trying. You need to be able to climb stairs if we're going to pay a call on old Giuseppe." She talked the way she fought, spins and jabs and feints and always forcing him off balance, forcing him to react instead of acting.

"Six what?" His jaw ached and moved funny, and she'd loosened at least three of his teeth.

"Six gates to the city, you impious bastard. Six labyrinths, six stones connected to the one stone. Six fairy rings hiding in the forest around Corbin."

Taking her hint, he knelt and crossed himself. His head stayed straighter, closer to the ground. "And I could have told Llewes this and saved my life?"

"They'd have shot you anyway, just for the knowing. A recent scientific survey reveals that only two respondents out of nine believe that a man can know something and not use it for his gain."

She turned and grinned at him, alert and the candles glinting in her eyes. "You think I'm a sadistic bitch, don't you? Too right. But you're too much a masochist to be any fun. I'm gonna bust you out of here, see?"

Her words rocked him back on his heels. He caught his balance, lowered his head, and slogged forward. "Why the hell would you help me escape?"

"Help's help. Don't waste your time on equine dental records when the nag is free." She bounced to her feet and made a show of studying the rood screen carvings, medieval but in fine condition. She never let him out of the corner of her eye, though, and stayed balanced on the balls of her feet. He couldn't take her.

Grab her metaphor if he couldn't grab her throat. "Maybe I want to know if the horse is fit enough to get me out of town?"

"Oh, you can ride this horse clear to Glastonbury Tor on a fine spring night, *mo croi*. It's sound enough." She shrugged. "Hey, maybe I'm helping you because you and I are the only two men in this nest of deballed worms. Maybe I hate Duncan, and you're my way to knock him off the ladder and climb past his perch through the glass ceiling of our Old Boy Network. Maybe I'm as pissed and disgusted about slaves at Castle Corbin as you are." She turned and grinned an evil caprice, a face and body as expressive as any mime. "And maybe the answer is D, none of the above."

Or maybe it was E, all of the above. Brian's head spun. A lifetime of small-unit tactics left him totally unprepared for the murky long-term strategies necessary for survival in this treacherous Inner Circle. Maureen might fit in, with her convoluted chess gambits and deeply hidden goals. Or Fiona, all malice and deceit.

Dierdre sure fit.

He pushed himself to his feet, still testing muscles and bones and tendons, still regaining his balance. His creaks and groans whispered between stone arches, and he hoped that only two pairs of ears were listening to the echoes of this surreal conversation. The shadows could hide an army.

She laughed at his searching eyes, an innocent chuckle totally out of character. "Don't worry, Brian. This is the only part of the whole keep free from spy holes and secret passages for listeners. They took confession seriously when it was built, and they all had serious sins to confess. *Nobody* wanted eavesdroppers."

And she, of course, had checked that. In detail. Or she was lying, and didn't care who heard. With Dierdre, you could never tell for sure. She wouldn't offer a handhold you could grab.

"Six. Joseph's Throne, in Glastonbury, and the cellar under Dougal's keep. Any idea of where the others are?"

"Glastonbury and here are the only ones the Order admits to, on the record. Now you've told me where another lies. Llewes may know more, but he's not tellin'. I think the rest each opened into another land, four other worlds. There's no way left of checking. Old Merlinus Ambrosius made sure of that."

Brian felt a cold pit open in his stomach. "Merlin? *He* set this up?"

Dierdre's smile turned wry. "Not in building and powering the star. *That* goes back long before the Romans and the Picts, even, much less Christianity. No, our nasty little founder just buggered the heathen game. He always *was* better at destruction than creation. Glastonbury's the only door left open."

That sounded like what the Order's records said of Merlin, a much . . . darker . . . figure than White's absentminded bumbler. The old wizard had been too sure that his cause was right. If he couldn't control something, he'd break it so that no one else could use it as a weapon against him and his cause. The same went for people, too.

"Power corrupts. Absolute power corrupts absolutely." That was Dierdre all over, answering his thoughts rather than his words. No wonder she could ride the twisting winds of this Inner Circle like a hawk. "Merlin was the first utilitarian philosopher. The greatest good for the greatest number. The end justifies the means. That's the Pendragons, my little chickadee. We *are* the vision our founder dreamed."

His head spun. He couldn't keep up with the dance—the trip through strange doors to this place, finding rot in the heart of the Pendragons, finding Dierdre as an ally. *Dierdre,* for God's sake. The worst aspect of the Pendragons turned out to be the face of his only friend in this dark swamp.

She was guiding him again, that firm hold on his shoulder just caressing the nerves. He found himself wondering how she was with a lover, turning her knowledge of the body into a system of pleasure rather than pain. Or was interrogation her whole sex life? Or vice versa?

They turned aside into the gloom of the left transept, and she aimed him straight at shadow. Dead black opened at his feet; she nudged him, and his toes felt their way onto a spiral stair down into damp darkness. Down, down, around, around, cold stone beneath and to each side, steep and narrow and no handrails, he groped until he saw a flicker of yellow ahead that grew into an oil lamp in a wall niche. Some kind of crypt or catacomb opened from the stair, leading straight out from the last steps.

Catacomb or columbarium, deep niches to either side filled with musty dusty bones, air thick with the soot of oil lamps. Multiple skulls in each niche, generations and centuries of burials piled one upon another. She nudged him forward again. They passed cross-corridors and more blocks of niches, shadows and shadows and shadows between the far-spaced lamps, until they reached the end of their main corridor and a small shrine flanked by more votive candles.

The light glittered on a reliquary, silver or gold; he couldn't tell in the yellow glow. It was old work, old beyond old, none of that Cellini baroque down here. It housed a skull, shiny with much handling and streaked green with the dripped minerals of long centuries underground.

"Giuseppe Verdi," she offered, from behind him.

"*Huh?*" She was *still* keeping him off balance.

"Joe Green. Supposed to be Joseph of Arimathea, although I have my doubts. Touch him. Hold both hands on his bones, long enough to say three 'Our Fathers.' It's another of Merlin's little safeguards."

Brian did as he was told. She knew what worked here. He had to trust, untrustworthy as she seemed. The bone felt warm under his hands, almost as warm as if he touched a living head, and the surface was slightly damp. He could feel it as skin if he half tried.

And it throbbed as if he imagined a pulse.

". . . for thine is the kingdom and the power and the glory, for ever. Amen." She turned him. "It's the timing, not the words. I tried it once, by the watch. Safer to use the long form. I'm guessing our ancestors were less glib. That was after I found out that the language didn't matter. And you have to use both hands. Merlin didn't cut any slack for a one-handed knight, or even temporary injuries."

That was Dierdre, always poking, always testing limits. They strolled back past the musty dusty bones. Some of the niches showed traces of worn carving, as if they'd originally had epitaphs or at least names chiseled above the bones. Or below. He couldn't tell which level the traces labeled.

"Anyway, if you don't lay your hands on Giuseppe first, the labyrinth refuses to take you back to Glastonbury. And a bell rings, up in the chapel tower, bringing rude people with sharp blades to ask who you are and what you're doing and whether you belong. I'm one of them. Merlin didn't trust *anybody*."

They came to the bottom of the stair, barely visible in the flickering lamplight, and climbed back into shadow. "One other empirical observation: You have to go directly from here to the labyrinth. Can't clear customs with Joe and then wander around for a day and a day, stealing the crown jewels or assassinating slimy bastards like me, and then just bounce back out again. The limit is something like fifteen minutes, although it seems to vary. Once it refused me after ten."

She was giving him a mission briefing, in her own peculiar way. She really *did* mean to let him go.

That was, if she wasn't just playing with her mouse. With Dierdre, you never could be sure.

They spiraled up into the transept. Dierdre turned aside into another shadow, returned, and slapped a shadow into his right hand. His fingers recognized the weight and balance of a *kukri,* heavy and cold and familiar.

"There'll be guards in Glastonbury. One at the labyrinth and one at the tunnel entrance, and they'll not be looking for someone to come out who never should have gone in. I'm sure you'll come up with a solution."

Queasy feeling. Brian wondered if he'd know the men he'd have to kill. If he'd trained with them, served with them, bled with them, if they'd guarded his back in deadly shadows or paid for a round of drinks at his last promotion party. But if they served the Circle . . .

"And they'll be looking to kill *you,* once they hear. Before you came here, the Circle wanted to ask you a few questions.

Now you'll be 'Shoot on sight.' Every Pendragon, everywhere. Including me."

She stopped in front of the altar, back to him, and slipped something from her pocket. "This is the point where someone hits me from behind. Treachery inside Castle Corbin, the hidden hand. Brian Albion has an unknown ally. How hard is up to you."

Sweet Jesu, the woman had brass balls. Torture him, say she would be hunting him, and then give him a free shot at killing her? And with her reputation, he had to do more than just a simple knockout to make it credible.

He tucked the *kukri* into his belt, stepped forward, and scissored her neck with double knife-hand strikes. She slumped and spun away from his kick to the knee, but he followed up once, twice, three times, feet and hands and elbows, her own training that taught you never stopped until your opponent was down and out with a finisher *after* he lay still.

He checked the body twisted on the floor, blood flowing from her mouth or nose and one ear. She had a pulse. He let her keep it. The strikes he'd used, a human would be dead or in hospital for months. Between her training and the Old Blood, she'd be fit to fight again within a week.

Her hand had opened, and something glinted from the floor—a button, attached to a shred of blue cloth. He knelt close, not touching it. A metal button, probably brass, with Duncan's family crest.

He left it.

He straightened up and took a couple of limping steps. She'd *still* managed to get in a shot or two, going down. Amazing. His left leg—he'd swear she was already out cold when that kick caught him. It'd cost her a broken ankle from his own reflex trap and twist.

His hands hurt. Damned woman had a hard skull. And she hadn't told him where the labyrinth hid. She'd used up at least five of the ten minutes he could count on, to find it and walk it and escape. Just like Dierdre, to set him another test. He looked around.

Shouts echoed out in the corridor, and he heard the latch clicking. The door thumped instead of opening. Dierdre had set a bar across it. With this lot, that might hold a minute, maybe two.

# eighteen

—⁂—

KHE'SHA SNIFFED THE dark witch again. She smelled of treachery and lies. She smelled of machines and lightning, of strange unnatural liquids and acrid powders and herbs that could kill or heal. She smelled, faintly, of Shen, but she'd explained that by her scouting of the stone tower on the hill.

<I do not trust you.>

Treachery and lies made dangerous weapons, teeth sharp on both ends that sank into your own jaw when you tore your prey. You used them sparingly, and only when necessary. But this witch never told the truth unless it served her better than a lie. She probably even lied to herself, when it served her purpose.

She stood within biting range now, and he could settle that question with a quick lunge and snap of his jaws. She rested her hands on the fat bulge of her belly, standing calm under his nose, and smiled up at him. She must be defended, to act so confident.

"And I don't trust you either, love. But you need me, and

I need you, and neither of us will get what we want if we don't work together."

<I must not leave the nestlings.> Even revenge couldn't break that duty. Sha'khe lived in them. He saw his dead mate in the line of one's snout, the infant crest of another, the iridescent scale-patterns of a third. Even so fresh from the egg, Sha'khe lived in them.

The witch looked puzzled. "The tower threatens all of them. Your enemies killed your mate. They stole your hatchling. Don't you think they'll kill *you*, when it serves their purpose? Don't you think they'll use what they learn from Shen against you and against your nestlings? Why else would they steal her?"

Khe'sha couldn't remember telling the dark one of Shen's name, only of his rage at the sneak thief. But he must have mentioned her name and sex. And the witch was right. The tower threatened all his hatchlings. If they had stolen one, they could steal the rest. If they killed Sha'khe, they could kill him.

"When you attack the keep, you defend your nest." She echoed his thoughts.

But the world was hungry, with teeth and claws everywhere. He must not tell this witch too much; she would have power over him. <If I leave the nests untended for long, I will find nothing left to defend when I return.>

She cocked her head to one side, studying him. "And what besides the tower would be a danger to you? I've seen those little dragons, seen their teeth. There's nothing in this swamp would threaten them."

And then she paused, running one finger over her cheek, and smiled. "Ah. I see, love. Those teeth. And I'd wondered why you set the mounds so far apart. Ah, but they must run you ragged."

Her mind was too quick for him, and she had learned too much. Now he could tie a smell with that watching shadow in the mists. Rage flashed through him, burning hot. Khe'sha gathered his muscles for the lunge.

HE BLINKED. HE looked up. Up, into the dark witch's face. His chin pressed into cold muck at the swamp's edge. If he could read Old One expressions right, her face looked amused. Amused, and mocking.

"So Brian was right."

<?>

"Old family history, love. Brian guessed that he could stun a dragon. He was right."

Khe'sha tested one toe, stirring the muck on the swamp bottom. His foot moved—awkward and twitching, but it moved. He'd eaten a dozen Old Ones, maybe more. None had ever shown this Power. Her strength swelled with her belly, just as she had said. Between them, they *could* destroy the tower.

But this witch knew far too much. His rage still burned. He thrust against the mud and twisted his head for the killing bite.

"DON'T TRY THAT again, love. The next time, you won't wake up."

He opened one eye, bleary, and focused on the shape in front of him. She looked paler than before, and her eyes squinted as if the bright sun hurt her head. And he smelled her sweat, acrid and tinged with the hatchling in her belly.

<I . . . must . . . protect . . . nests.>

"You won't do it that way. You waste our time and my Power by even trying."

He measured the way she stood, swaying slightly, the way her hands cradled her unhatched young. He sniffed her again, finding weakness on the breeze.

<I doubt if you have the strength left to kill me.>

"Ah, but do you dare take the chance? What if my threat isn't empty? Where does that leave your little cannibals? And if I can't trust you as an ally, why should I let them live to match your strength? If I have to kill you, I promise I'll kill them."

She swiped hair out of her eyes and flipped it back, holding her head higher. Already her color had returned, and her eyes brightened. Each breath gave her more of her strength back, while his legs still tingled and he could not feel his toes. She was right. He did not dare attack again.

<I must not leave the nests unguarded.>

"Then we have a problem, love. I've counted on you as part of my attack. You'd said we have a common cause." She looked thoughtful, but he sensed that each step and word followed a plan she'd practiced.

Twisted and untrustworthy and very cunning. And strong. He'd have a better chance to eat her after she had spent herself, destroying the keep. After her hatchling breathed air. So they had to come up with a way . . .

<Can you witch the hatchlings to sleep until I return?>

She appeared to think. "Do you want that, *precisely* that? That they will sleep until you wake them?"

He grunted. He saw too many traps, too many forkings to the path. He could die attacking the tower, or she could kill him after as he intended to kill her. If he never returned to the nest mounds . . .

If they woke without him guarding, *some* would survive. The strongest, as the songs had always told.

<To sleep a night and a night.> In that time, the tower would fall and he would live and return, or die.

She ran a finger along her jaw, thinking again. Or appearing to think. "I believe I can do that, love. Remember, spells can be tricky things. They work differently on different species. Sometimes an Old One will be far stronger than the rest, barely affected by an attack that would leave others sleeping for a hundred years." She paused and smiled, as if remembering one particular savory meal.

"Even working with humans, one will wake up hours or days before another. One might not wake up at all, if the heart is weak or something else goes wrong. And I can't steal practice dragons from a lab supply warehouse. I'll have to get it right, first go. Are you prepared to risk that, or do I kill you now and change my plans?"

She was lying about something. He could smell it on her. But she wasn't lying about killing him. She'd try, if he didn't agree. He didn't dare find out whether she would succeed.

<Do you need to touch your prey?>

She laughed. "Prey, love? I don't eat lizards and snakes. I often don't eat meat at all. It's bad for working certain kinds of spells. But I'll need to be within a fathom or less, if I'm to judge my Power closely."

A small boat glided into view, empty, brown and vague against the water and the weeds, narrow and double-ended. She stepped into it, ripples spreading out across mirrored sky, picked up a leaf-shaped paddle, and settled to her knees.

"Lead on, my noble ally. And you'd best hope that none of your ravenous little terrors attack me. I'll not be held responsible for actions taken in haste."

He smelled a touch of fear in her voice. If she feared the hatchlings, she knew far too much about the ways of dragons. Perhaps Shen was *not* in that tower on the hill . . .

But the keep still hid his enemies. He must complete the song of Sha'khe, which could end only with revenge.

"I asked you to *lead*, love. I'm not letting you behind my back. Stay a length away from me and stay on the surface. I've watched how you hunt."

And she would kill the hatchlings, Ghu and Po and the rest. The threat froze his rage. Sha'khe lived in them.

He remembered the wisdom and patience of Pan'gu. A wise dragon eats his enemies one at a time. The dark witch would be weaker after fighting the tower, after her belly lay empty and flat again. He must wait.

He led. He swam at full speed, hoping the waves of his wake would distract her, even swamp the boat she'd conjured out of the mists. He reached Liu's mound and stopped abruptly, digging his claws into the deep muck, hoping the dark witch would turn careless and overrun him in her speed. Neither trick worked. Although she paddled delicately, gracefully, the boat seemed to move independent of her actions. It matched his speed, never bobbing or swerving, and stopped a dragon's length away from him.

She tilted her head, eyes and smile questioning. "I didn't reach this age by being careless. I don't sit with my back to any doors, either, and I don't trust allies just because we have a common cause. Move on, and I'll follow after dealing with your problem child."

Liu, and Po, and Ghu, and the others, he led on. The marsh grew silent behind him, the mental voices stilled from their constant whisper of hunger and curiosity. That silence chilled his heart. Treacherous as this witch was, he had no proof she was not killing them instead of spelling them to sleep. He did not know which would use less Power, and that was the real test.

She'd given him no choice.

And that was her character. She had him in her power, and she had planned each step of her attack with a cold heart and colder logic, from before their first meeting. If she wanted him dead, he would die. If she wanted the hatchlings to live, they would live. Her words meant nothing.

The red witch left him alone, the respect shown to an equal.

He'd tasted the arrows from Sha'khe's skull. Those weren't the dark witch lying to him. Those were tied to the keep, to the yellow-haired Old One and the human that had left. Those two had killed Sha'khe. But now he wondered what the true song said.

He remembered voices in the cave echoing from long years ago, old voices with moss growing on their scales and crests worn smooth by the centuries. Songs held layers of meaning, with cross-currents and eddies and changes in the flow that brought new odors to your nose as you sank deeper into the words beneath the words. Sometimes the surface of the water told you nothing of the real story, or turned it on its head.

"Forward, my dark friend. Forward only. Turn back and I *will* kill them." Her voice came from behind him, speaking to his thoughts. So he led her to the last mound, as if she could not have found it on her own, and they were done.

"And now the little dears will sleep for a night and a night, as you asked. That is, unless you do not do my bidding. We've so much trust between us that I've added my personal binding to the common spell. It ties their lives to my own. To make my meaning plainer still, if I die, they die."

She pointed to the stone tower, looming dark on the hill above them. "Remember, if I do not return from there, they will sleep until the sun dries them to powder and they wash away in the rain. You'd best see to it that we win. Shall we get on with it?"

<I hate you.>

She smiled and shook her head. "I can live with that, love. In fact, I'm rather used to it. A great many people hate me. But they can't do anything about it, and you've just joined their ranks. You're wasting time."

Each step, each stroke of his tail against the water, drove him deeper into her plot. She'd planned her moves to leave him a single path. He bowed his head into the attitude of shame.

<What do I do next?>

"I've made your role simple enough—even a dinosaur could understand. All you do is climb by the straightest way from this shore to the castle. When you reach the castle or along the way, you kill anyone you meet." She paused, smiling. "Anyone except me, but I suspect you've worked that out. The hatchlings, love, remember the hatchlings."

He growled, a long articulated note deep in his belly. Another dragon would hear that as a challenge to the death.

She cocked her head to one side. "You wish. Anyway, the forest and the land won't like your claw-marks on Maureen's soil, so you can expect some resistance."

And then she vanished between two trees. She hadn't told him what *she* planned to do. She'd mentioned other allies, other slaves more likely, but she hadn't told him who they were or what her chains bound them to do in the attack. She hadn't told him to spare their lives. That also fit her character. He had learned many things about the dark witch, but each one of them too late.

Straight to the castle? Khe'sha looked up. The way hung steep above him, near the limit a dragon could climb, tangled with old trees and heavy boulders. He had never walked this route before—when he'd guarded the keep, taking turns with Sha'khe for the Master, they'd followed a gentler path and never come close to the house of piled stone on the crest.

The red witch had killed the Master. The red witch had made no move to claim the beasts that served him. The forest and the winds spoke of falcons set free to fly, of other hunters following their own prey where they wished.

The red witch left the marsh untouched, and brought prey to Khe'sha and the other hunters, and held back the rains that could drown the hatchlings. He understood those things now, too late. But she must die. She must die, and the dark witch live, or Sha'khe would no longer live on in Ghu and Po, in Liu and Shen and Chu . . .

The red witch must become part of Sha'khe's song.

*Hair of fire and temper matching,*
*Passion and clear eyes well wed.*
*Witch blood drawing ever onward,*
*Past obsidian-armored head.*

Words grew in his head, chanting. The form matched nothing in his memories, a new song, fit for the new race of Pan'gu's children living in this new land. More would come to him, verses in the song that remembered Sha'khe through the generations.

Upward, to the tower on the hill. Khe'sha dug his claws into the hillside and felt soil gripping at them, active, aware. He shouldered his bulk between two trees and they resisted, scratching hard sharp limbs at his eyes. Dirt fell away beneath his hind legs. He dug deeper, clinging to the hillside.

The ground shook under him, gently and more local than any earthquake, and a boulder broke loose from the slope above him. He twisted away, but it swerved and rolled across his forefoot with uncanny accuracy. Sharp pain stabbed up his leg. A broken claw—broken clean off, deep in the quick with blood welling up between his scales.

". . . you can expect some resistance." The dark witch's voice echoed back to him.

The whole hillside slumped under him, a land-slip from the heavy rains and his sudden added weight. Rains that had kept to the forest, rains that had soaked deep into the soil and hadn't raised the water level of the marsh. A tree tottered on the slope over his head, and he ducked as it crashed to the ground. The outermost leaves brushed his nostrils, bitter and hostile. He slipped back toward the marsh, shaking his head, and dug his claws deeper into the soil.

Fresh stone gleamed above him, shiny with streaks of mud, a rampart twice his height where the land-slip sheared off from the slope. Dragons had many strengths, but climbing wasn't one of them. He'd have to go around, find a *new* "straightest way" to the top of the hill and the keep waiting there.

He had no choice. He turned on the slope and scouted out another route, passing the land-slip by the left, and tested each footfall as he climbed. Trees clutched at him, boulders rolled from their seats overhead, and he stalked his prey as if the earth had ears, the dead leaves underfoot had eyes. The red witch owned the soul of this forest.

> *Past the guardians of the forest,*
> *Pressing onward up the hill.*
> *Falling but to climb yet onward*
> *Proving strength is mostly will.*

He felt a resonance to the verse, as if it referred to something, someone, else, as well as his revenge. The words woke images in his head, the red witch looking up at similar barriers and surmounting them. Their fates had become bound together in some fashion he couldn't taste.

# nineteen

—w—

DAVID PLODDED ALONG, head down and leaning forward as if forcing his way into a stiff breeze, seeing just enough of the landscape to avoid stepping in front of an eighteen-wheeler on Route 186 headed out of town. Not that he had anything against semis, mind you. That would be a nice, clean, quick way to die. Nothing compared to having your brain sucked out of your head and distributed around the landscape. Still alive.

*Been there, done that. Don't want to go back for the encore.*

For that matter, his nightmares didn't have much good to say about the prospect of being served up as Purina Dragon Chow. He'd been down that road as well, and he'd still be running if he could have figured out someplace to run *to*. And Maureen had happily informed Jo that the other dragon guarded a nest and eggs out in the swamp. Maureen seemed to think it was like having pandas or some other cute cuddly endangered species in her backyard.

He shuddered at the thought. Endangering went the

other way, this time. He'd killed the one only through sheer luck goosed by desperation.

He'd been terrified. He'd pissed his pants, but Brian had been too polite to notice it. He'd pissed his pants and run away, and then had to listen to all that *Red Badge of Courage* crap about being a dragon-slaying hero.

He knew otherwise.

David roused himself enough to look both ways, then loped across the highway to another disused sidewalk. Naskeag Falls spent very little on sidewalk maintenance, on the reasonable belief that the average American citizen spent very little time walking. He was some kind of subversive, not owning a car. Part of a conspiracy of subversives. Jo didn't own one, either, and Maureen's Toyota could scarcely be called a car.

Besides, it was parked behind a chain-link fence in the evidence lot next to the police station. So Jo couldn't have driven anywhere.

He scuffed at the winter's accumulation of sand and dead leaves. *Coward. You know where Jo went. You know she needs you. You even have a clue as to how to get there. You just don't want to do it.*

Just thinking about it made his sphincter clench. That cop sergeant said she'd been in an office, he'd been talking to the psychologist just outside the door, they'd turned and opened the door, and she was gone.

Now, David could either believe that two competent professionals hadn't noticed an hysterical woman walking out that door, that nobody else in that crime-scene nursing-home riot had noticed a beautiful redheaded damsel in distress walking through the halls and out the entry and past the meat wagons, or he could believe that Jo *took* those three steps between the "real" world and the Summer Country and left the office by way of her Blood Power. No doors needed.

One other place she might have gone. He was grasping at straws, but she'd dug up Maureen's survey of the town forest out at Carlysle Woods. She'd mentioned maybe going out there to find some peace, draw on the calm Maureen had sometimes borrowed from the trees, ask some questions of the patriarch oak. Talk like that made David's skin crawl. He had too much experience with plants that were more aware than they had any right to be.

Grass heaved and split the asphalt in front of him, thin brown tendrils with the power to break stone. They didn't move, didn't search and trap and strangle, but he could swear they hadn't been there a second earlier. He kicked at the ridge, and the grass tore off and lay dead in the rotting leaves drifting across the sidewalk.

*You can't go home again.* The world had changed, and he had changed, and he did not sleep well.

Maureen had set him and Jo free from the forest. She'd threatened fire against it, and then offered it a bribe. She'd help it, heal it, balance it, protect it, but she wouldn't *control* it. She'd make the forest more dangerous than it was before.

She loved trees more than she loved people. Always had.

And that was where Jo had gone. Vanished from an office without walking out the door. Taken his heart with her.

Like the last time.

> *Bound by duty, bound by magic,*
> *Blazing ebon in sun's glow,*
> *Teeth and claws by power shackled,*
> *Set by fate against fate's foe.*

He wiped his palms on his jeans. The poem was taking on its own life. Change a word here, a line there, the sky darkened and sunbeams centered like spotlights on the actors.

And the scene froze his heart. He faced the dragon again, jerked an arrow wild into the trees again, threw away the bow and quiver and pack again, and ran.

No. He couldn't go through that . . . again.

The world formed around him, crappy mud-season Maine, and he walked on. Damn good thing Carlysle Woods sat five miles from the apartment. Damn good thing he didn't have a car. Otherwise he'd be there already, facing facts. Fact that Jo wasn't there. Fact that there was only one other place she could be. Fact that he was a coward and didn't dare follow her.

And even if he dared, he wouldn't be able to. He was human. She was an Old One. He couldn't do magic. She could. That wall always stood between them, the wall between reality and fantasy.

He only hoped that words could breach it. That he could find the words, words strong enough to substitute for the magic in her blood. Words strong enough to frame a door and open it and allow him to step through. Through to that fire-haired temptress who owned his heart.

> Hair of fire and temper matching,
> Passion and clear eyes well wed.
> Witch blood drawing ever onward,
> Past obsidian-armored head.

Shivers ran down his spine, as if he stared into that great yellow eye again. And he would, if he formed that door and passed through it. The other dragon waited, and hated, and felt no shackles around its legs.

The wind gusted sleet into his face, stinging cold. He looked up from the dirt and dangerous grass, to find clouds massing and dark on the horizon. Maine spring. Rain drove through the sleet, and fat wet snowflakes, a sudden squall as mixed up as his brain. Or schizo weather, as Maureen would say. Ask the expert. Another reason to give up, turn tail, and run back to the apartment.

He was an expert at running away. He even ran away from his own poems.

> From the terror deep and searing,
> Trembling, forcing strength to turn,
> Came again the desperate poet,
> Found his bow amidst the fern.

Did he have the guts even to work through that in words? He wiped the sweat off his palms, heartbeat racing. The crushed green bitterness of bracken filled his nose for an instant, and then cold rain washed him back into reality. Fools *died* in this kind of weather, thinking spring or summer came on the calendar.

No hat, no gloves, spring jacket. He'd better turn back. His fingertips tingled already, and icy trickles dripped down his nose and the back of his neck. Only a fool would keep on walking.

*Only a fool or a desperate man. Desperation killed the dragon, not that fool poet—desperation and the vision of Jo somewhere on the other side of all those teeth and claws.*

And Jo waited somewhere on the other side of this spring storm, somewhere on the other side of Carlysle Woods. He had to go on. He hunched his shoulders and blinked rain out of his eyes and walked forward instead of back.

And Carlysle Woods rose in front of him, the muddy parking lot and overflowing trashcans and graffiti-carved trail signs dangling sideways off their posts, rattling in the wind. An old man, fat and bald and sallow, sat in a beat-up Chevy with the radio thumping away as loud as any teenager's boom box. Must be deaf.

Snowbanks trailed off into slush and glacial moraines of stained foam coffee cups and fast-food wrappers. He skirted puddles that aspired to the status of ponds, sorting through three trailheads in his mind. Dog turds graced the yellow snow by all of them. This was Maureen's sacred grove?

The right-hand trail felt right. He climbed a rain-hardened snowbank and followed tracks between two birches and the car radio faded behind him, so fast the old man must have turned it down out of politeness. David held Maureen's map in his head, tracing the labyrinth of trails with a mental fingertip. Someone had laid out the system to give the illusion of a much larger park, with twists and turns that stretched one mile into five or six while still keeping distance between the loops. You'd think you were alone even if a hundred other people walked the path.

Trees arched overhead, breaking the wind, and the rain switched back to snowflakes as big as cotton balls. His ears and fingers warmed again, sheltered now. If you don't like the weather, wait ten minutes.

Now the place looked like a cathedral in living stone, gray columns of tree trunks rising up to an interlacing roof of branches that filtered the falling snow into grace. His feet crunched on the packed melting drifts, and chickadees flitted and chattered from branch to branch in case he stirred up something interesting. Tension leaked out of his shoulders. Quiet and calm wrapped around him, and he understood what Maureen had found here. It seemed . . . uncanny . . . so close to downtown.

<Come.>

He froze in his tracks, fists clenched so hard he could feel his fingernails biting into his palms. He remembered that voice whispering in the back of his head. There'd been an oak . . . an oak and a fox, deep in the dreams when Jo had joined him in the forest's weave; an oak and a fox had fought on Maureen's side to free him from the binding.

<My roots drink the waters of many worlds.>

David shivered. Why'd he get involved with this family

of psychos? Jo had told him some about her dad, some about her mom. A lot more about Maureen. The police sergeant had told him what had happened at the nursing home, added his conclusions on what led up to it. Cops had to learn a lot about damaged families and abused children, know how they hid and lied for safety's sake, lied even to those who might protect them. From that angle the pieces fitted better, assembling a jigsaw puzzle straight out of hell. Now that officer had seemed inclined to cut Maureen and Jo some slack. Sympathetic.

Jo had hidden it better than Maureen, built a picture of strength and freedom that she showed the world, but she was just as scarred as her sister.

Just as dangerous.

He stood in the snow, shaking. Jo had told the police that she killed her father. They didn't believe her. Wrote the confession off as psychiatric trauma. Didn't fit the facts they saw.

David believed.

He'd been afraid of Brian, when they first met. Brian was a Doberman, trained and lethal, a weapon sculpted out of flesh and guided by calculation. Totally controlled. But Maureen and Jo were something else entirely, avalanche slopes overloaded and ready to explode at the slightest sound. Forces of nature, uncontrollable.

*That's the heart of it. Way down deep, you're not afraid of the trees or the briars or even that damned dragon. You're afraid of Jo.*

No couple ever lived in perfect harmony. Ever. David knew his parents hadn't. Married thirty years now, three kids, got along okay and seemed to love each other, but they had frictions. They had fights. Words were said and left hanging overnight, never taken back.

Jo's parents. Jo had talked, late at night and sleep in her voice, bits and pieces she usually kept hidden behind her face of strength, proof of how much pain there could be in words, never mind the fists and belt.

With Jo, words could kill.

Words and determination. If she ever got *really* mad at him, he'd be dead. Nothing stood between Jo and what she wanted. No muscles to speak of, but she was the strongest person he'd ever met.

<If the will exists, a way exists.>

Tell that to a black kid in the ghetto. And yet, some of them broke free. Will *and* luck *and* the gifts of mind or body they inherited. Jo and Maureen had the gifts of the body, their Blood inherited from the Old Ones. Would his mind make a substitute, be a way?

He could feel the tree calling to him. His feet found the proper trail, clear against the falling snow.

<Come.>

If she ever got *really* mad at him, he'd be dead.

*Coward. But what if she doesn't* want *me to follow her?*

David stood on the trail, sweating as if he already walked the Summer Country instead of Maine woods in a spring snowstorm. As if he stood under that dragon's nose with nothing but words as a shield. A shield made of tissue paper. Thinner than tissue paper, thinner than thin air, against teeth and claws that would shred him in an instant.

Jo needed him. He *hoped* she needed him. He loved her.

"In the beginning was the Word." Words held power. "Workers of the world, unite." Words could shatter and kill, even without the Power of the Blood behind them. Words were the only weapon he had. The only *way* he had.

<If the will exists, a way exists.>

He stepped off the trail, sinking into the old snow under the fresh white veil. He followed blurring tracks that led straight, up over drifts and down into hollows and across gurgling water hidden deep underneath the snow, a promise of spring that even the storm couldn't kill. He felt Maureen's tree in front of him, her Father Oak, not warmth and not pressure and not music but some indescribable essence of strength and stability and protection. Even *he* could sense it. Even a human.

The tracks led to that strength. He barely noticed the cold snow packing down into his shoes and soaking his pants. Fat Christmas-card flakes hung in the air, gentle and windless, hazing the forest until a mound stood isolated in front of him and he climbed to the crest of it. The tree waited, huge and gnarled, looking as old as the hill on which it stood.

Jo wasn't there.

The tracks seemed fresh, barely melted, barely filled by the snow squall, less than a day old to his unpracticed eye, but they were empty. They came and stood and turned and led away again, and then they vanished. He'd missed her.

The tree didn't offer any words of wisdom. It just stood there, solid as the rock beneath his feet, and endured. Humans, even Old Ones, passed like ghosts through Father Oak's life. A flash of seasons, and they were gone. Dead. Even Father Oak would die, somewhere down the centuries.

David wiped his palms again. He formed Jo's face in his eyes and smiled at her.

> *Hair of fire and temper matching,*
> *Passion and clear eyes well wed.*
> *Witch blood drawing ever onward,*
> *Past obsidian-armored head.*

She sat huddled in a corner in a stone room, shivering. A half-empty goblet sat on the flagstone floor by her hand, red wine in exquisite-cut crystal. She was crying. She needed him. He had to take the chance that she also wanted him. He drew a deep breath.

*To the forest, through the shadows,*
*Came the warrior and the bard,*
*Seeking heart-songs, seeking lovers,*
*Drawn by need to face the guard.*

The veil of snow lifted, showing leaves, showing branches green with spring, showing forest duff wet from recent rain.

Showing a dragon.

Obsidian scales, yellow slitted eyes, teeth longer than the span of his hand, great charcoal gray feet with claws even longer and more evil than the teeth. Blood stained one forefoot, a stump of a missing claw. Battle was already joined.

David stared at the teeth, fascinated. He'd seen them in nightmares, seen them even in broad daylight on the mundane dirty streets of Naskeag Falls, his deepest terror. Sometimes he thought he'd seen them for years before he'd met Jo and followed her into dreams. Now he could stretch his hand out and touch them, smelled the reek of rotting flesh on them, and he didn't fear them. Calm settled over him.

<Sing, human. Sing your brief song and die.>

# twenty

—m—

MAGIC PRICKLED KHE'SHA'S tongue with a form of Power he hadn't tasted since a different sun warmed his crest. He couldn't tell if it grew from the Tree or the chanted words or the land itself, but the flavor was nothing like an Old One's guile and hidden aims. This tasted clear and sharp and pure on his tongue, waking memories of the long old songs in deep dragon-voices and the Sages weaving words into sudden truth. Pan'gu might have sung like this.

The human stood under Khe'sha's nose and sang of cowardice. The dragon would have laughed, if it would not be such an insult to the song.

Words wove images of love and life-mates and despair, of duty and compulsion, of blood and pain and terror, of fate-forced battle against great odds. Images of Sha'khe's death in courage and beauty and honor. Pale and shaking, reeking of fear-sweat, unarmed, and yet the human sang.

Cowardice?

The song ended, and the human stood in silence. He waited within reach, a single nip would end his life's song, and he did not carry the power of the Old Blood. Yet he waited for his fate. If this was a coward, Khe'sha would prefer to never face a brave man.

The song ripped Khe'sha into pieces. One part mourned for his lost Sha'khe. One part glowed in admiration of the words, and of the courage they related. One part raged to bite and slash the treachery he'd heard. And a fourth part seethed at himself, for falling prey to the dark witch's plot.

<I have been told lies.>

The human flinched but held his ground. "Thus it happened. I've told you what I saw and did. Another would have seen another story. I can't tell that one."

<I have been told lies, but you are not the teller. I can smell truth when it stands trembling under my nose.>

The song shook his world to the core. The sun had risen in the east, for ages uncounted. Now it rose in the west. This human had slain Sha'khe, but he was not evil. He had done only what his fate forced him to do.

Khe'sha had forgotten that some humans and Old Ones held honor. It was so scarce in this land that he had not weighed it in the balance. Had not even thought it possible. He had not tasted honor since Liu Chen had knotted a net of lies to trap first Sha'khe and then Khe'sha into slavery to the Master.

<You had no choice. Sha'khe had no choice. There is no blood debt between us.>

But new blood debt had been hatched. Khe'sha had lived for revenge and for the nestlings. Now Shen had vanished, stolen from her mound. The others lay frozen in sleep or death, dead by the black witch's treachery and his own errors. He'd distrusted her from the first, grown to hate and fear her, but he'd obeyed her as a means to soothe an even fiercer hate. Now that lay quenched.

Keening grief built in his belly, as he followed his memories step by step through the twisted plotting of the black witch. Lies that walked the edge of truth, truth that fogged the boundaries of lie, the central truth that this man had slain Sha'khe—without the second truth that he had followed a mate-bond as strong as any dragon's.

The greatest songs told of a battle between honorable enemies both driven by fate. Neither hero stepped aside because neither *could.*

Khe'sha lifted his nose to the sky, bellowing his grief and rage. The black witch had controlled him as perfectly as the Master ever had. She was evil. She must die.

His rage froze. She was evil, but she must *not* die. Not while there was a chance that the hatchlings merely slept. She had said that she tied their lives to hers. He doubted that she would lie in so clear a way.

As he cooled, the forest returned to him. The human lay huddled on the ground, hands pressed to his ears. A dragon's scream could deafen humans. Khe'sha blinked and lowered his head in shame. To steal hearing from a Singer, that would be a great evil in itself.

<Are you harmed?>

<We have protected him.> The voice spoke with the rustle of leaves in the wind, the slow whisper of roots sinking into stone, the murmur of water flowing clear in a forest stream. Khe'sha heard it and knew the voice of the Tree, the voice of the wildwood around him.

<The forest protects the one you call the red witch, protects all who den with her. The forest guided you to this meeting.> A small animal stepped out beside the Tree, red-furred and ears alert and much like the Master's hunting hounds in shape. <The name is "fox," I'll have you know, far superior to any dog. I'll forgive you, this one time.> Khe'sha thought that the "fox" was laughing at him.

The landslip and the falling trees, the tangled undergrowth too thick even for a dragon's strength—he'd been *herded* to this glade under the ancient oak, not guided. The dark witch fought enemies she did not know or name, enemies of great power.

<The black-furred witch has passed to her doom. She will not return. Your duty lies elsewhere.>

Khe'sha sniffed his disbelief. <The dark one is strong and weaves deep plots. She has other allies. I must help to fight her, atoning for my error.>

Dry laughter rustled through the leaves of the oak. Khe'sha felt scorn beneath his feet and deep in the rocks. This forest did not fear the dark witch. It never had, even when the Master ruled it. What made her think she could attack now, when the forest loved its guardian?

<Your duty lies elsewhere. The one you call Shen passed through these woods, caged and injured, passed beyond to the lair of the black-furred one. The dark witch brews evil there, looking beyond this day's battle. More evil than she knows. You and the Bard must end the cycle.>

Plots within plots within plots. The dark witch had confused the mercy of great strength for weakness. Mercy, or indifference. The red one knew her strength and the strength of her allies. She had tasted the strength of her enemies, and knew that. The wisdom of the Sages echoed in Khe'sha's head: "If you know yourself and know your enemy, you do not need to fear the outcome of a thousand battles."

The Bard stirred, unwinding from his knot of fear and the knives of pain in his head. He sat up, at Khe'sha's feet. "Where is Jo? Where's Maureen?"

<Your mate finds safety in the keep. The Stone has need of her power, a task of healing that may bring healing of her own. The Steward fights other battles. The Tree guides her and strengthens her.>

"Which way is the keep? I have to find Jo. She needs me." The Bard scrambled to his feet and looked around, as if seeking landmarks.

<You are needed elsewhere.>

"To hell with what *you* need. *I* need to help Jo." And the human chose a direction and started walking.

Khe'sha blinked as the forest flowed around him, the exact tree or bush he watched never moving or changing but somehow becoming part of a thicket that wasn't there a heartbeat earlier. He smelled fresh-turned earth but saw none, heard the rustle of branches and leaves even though the air was still. Now the human faced a wall of thorny green that even Khe'sha couldn't force.

The fox sat on her haunches, a sparkle of amusement in her eyes. <You will find a path, if you try the other way. It leads where the forest wishes you to go. I'd suggest you take it.>

The human ignored that advice, proving the truth of his mate-bond. Khe'sha watched as the man poked and prodded at the forest wall, shifting sideways, each time forced to move downhill as well as to the side. Nothing changed, not visibly, not where Khe'sha could see, but the forest still deflected every effort.

Khe'sha's heart warmed to him. The man did just what he would have done, separated from his mate. Khe'sha would be testing now, pushing, shifting, struggling against the tangles. Even without his mate's need driving him, he longed to find a way to that treacherous witch. But he'd already tasted the Power of this forest. He'd been forced to this place against all his strength and will. His toe ached, and he licked blood from the broken claw.

Now he understood. The red witch wanted him to live, as she wanted this Singer to live. The forest held its strength and turned its thorns aside, knowing what she wished.

He shifted his bulk downhill, toward the path that led away through the trees. He saw no point in continuing to bite stone or climb a hill of sand or swim against a current stronger than himself.

Khe'sha had walked this forest many times in many years,

sharing duty with Sha'khe. He'd never seen it so powerful and aware. The red witch had given more than freedom to the trees. He pitied anyone who came to attack the keep. A thought chilled him.

<The dark one has cast a spell on our hatchlings. If she dies, they die. Thus she binds me to her bidding. Can the red witch break this doom?>

<The Steward asks the forest to trap and hold her enemies, if that be possible, rather than to kill. Asks, rather than commands. But the dark one holds much hate and much power, and the forest has never loved her. She may die. You are needed elsewhere.>

The Singer stopped struggling with the forest and grimaced. "I guess I don't have a choice. He turned to Khe'sha and flourished an elaborate bow. "I'm David Marx. Pleased to meet you."

<And I am called Khe'sha. I am honored to meet so powerful a Singer. Although, if you will allow, I do think you need to work on that sixth stanza.>

"That and the five before it and the twenty after. I hadn't planned on a performance." Then the human shook his head and blinked. "Hey, at least half of that was improvised, revising as I went along. Dragons like *poetry*?"

<The old songs are our lives. New songs are the sun on our backs and fresh meat in our bellies. Almost you give me the will to live, knowing that Sha'khe still lives in your words.>

The Singer slumped to the ground, burying his head in his hands. Muffled words leaked past his fingers. "She was beautiful. I've never been so terrified in my life, but there was something else, something that went beyond fear. Beauty. Terror. Awe. Even a sense of mirth. She *laughed* at us. And you loved her. I weep that I had to kill her. But she wouldn't let me follow Jo."

<There is no blood debt between us.>

David looked up, face shiny with tears. "Now this damned forest won't let me go to her."

The fox edged forward, timid and skittish, and licked the human's hand. <Your mate is safe, protected by the Stone and the keep it guards. The black-furred witch battles the forest, a greater power than she knows. The evil lurking in her den is a greater threat, to your mate and to me and to all that suckle young. Destroy it. There will be great danger. Both you and the dragon are needed.> She looked up at Khe'sha and smiled her fox-smile. <There may be a song in it.>

Khe'sha bent his head down to the forest floor, beside the man. <Go the way the forest wishes, Singer. Even I could not win against such strength. Trust the forest. It protects your mate.>

David smiled, with a wry twist. "I suppose you'll tell me that the fastest way to reach Jo is by going where the forest sends me. Typical run-around."

<And on the way we can taste the phrases of your song and polish them. What is this "opal" of which you sang?>

The human groaned. He stood and wiped his face on his sleeve, stared at the thicket blocking any route uphill, and shook his head.

"Maureen's created a monster."

Khe'sha chuckled, deep in his belly. <The forest has the power to do far worse. Perhaps we should find the dark one's lair.>

"Shortest distance between two points is *never* a straight line." He shrugged his shoulders and turned, sighing. The path opened in front of them, downhill toward the east. "If Fiona's tangled up in fighting the forest, what's the danger?"

Then he paused between one step and the next, foot in midair. "Her hedge. Maureen warned us about the hedge. Probably other traps." He set his foot down and looked up at Khe'sha beside him. "I hope this forest knows what it's doing."

And they followed the path, wide enough for a dragon's bulk, smooth for human feet, formed by the wildwood for its purpose and closing off behind them. Khe'sha heard the rustling leaves and creaking branches ahead and behind, smelled the fresh earth, but everything he saw looked like an age-old forest that hadn't changed in centuries. As they walked, they spoke of the sixth stanza and the other twenty-five. Did Pan'gu revise his songs after the first singing? This Singer tasted and discarded a dozen words for every one he kept. Khe'sha marveled at his nimble mind and tongue.

A holly loomed beside the path, dark and glossy and pungent, watching. A stone wall crossed the way, dividing forest from grass, and Khe'sha felt another boundary there. This had been as far as the Master's tether let his beasts roam, the limit beyond which Khe'sha and Sha'khe could not step.

He crossed the stone and entered a new song. They walked green meadows that reeked of magic and of lies, of binding and of pain. If Khe'sha had set foot on this land even once before, he never would have listened to the black one. The land looked so perfect because each blade of grass, each stone, each rolling hillock or path-side bush, bore her touch. Nothing lived its own life or followed its natural demands. He felt the tendrils of Power that bound everything to the hedge in front of him and to the cottage that lurked behind it.

That flavor, contrasted with the taste of the forest living its own life free of the keep and its new Steward, told him much about the red witch and the black. Much that he'd learned too late. But he'd been bound by the Master first, and then by his grief, and then by the nest, and never had a chance to smell the truth.

The hedge grew tall before them, dense and unbroken. It, too, reeked of magic and control. Khe'sha and the human followed it, around and around and around, and saw the same face everywhere.

David finally stopped and scratched his head. "Maureen said there were gates. Little white wooden gates, just like an English garden. And a maze inside."

<We come to attack, so there are no gates.>

Khe'sha sniffed at the hedge, testing, amused at the thorns it presented and the way the section he approached was always denser and higher than the portions to each side. As if *he* needed to worry about thorns. Even his eyelids bore scales as hard as glass. But the smells . . .

<Shen is inside. I think that I shall bite that witch, just a little nip, and let her live. Let the poison work on her, that she should die slowly over weeks. Slowly, and in pain.>

The human backed away from him. "Your bite is *poison?*"

<It is how our small ones hunt. They can attack prey larger than themselves, dangerous prey, bite once, and escape without risking injury. Then they wait. We are a very patient race, and can go long between meals.> The human had turned pale and smelled of fear-sweat once again.

<No dragon would bite a Singer.>

"Um. Thanks. I guess. I'd better keep some poems handy, just in case."

<I smell poison in these thorns, as well. It is a sort that causes great pain to your kind. Beware what you touch.>

The dark witch did not think of *everything*. Khe'sha closed his eyes and thrust his muzzle into the hedge, biting, shearing, twisting, as if he had prey bleeding life between his teeth. Thorns scratched across his scales and prickled inside his nose and across his tongue, but he ripped out a whole mouthful of bush and heaved it over his shoulder.

Khe'sha opened his eyes and studied the hedge again, not surprised that it had filled the gap. David had retreated and stood staring at the clump of brush scattering dirt across the grass, at the dragon, at the hedge. If anything, he was paler than before.

<We will find out how much Power the black witch buried around the roots of her hedge.>

Then Khe'sha ripped out another mouthful, and another, and another, roaring his hatred, sprinkling the soil with droplets of dragon blood where the thorns scratched his nose and tongue and palate. The pale burn of the cuts and the poison just added fuel to his rage, and he gloried in the chance to match his strength against something, *anything,* after keeping his anger bottled for so long.

When he looked again, the hedge stood lower and he could see the witch's cottage over the gap. Rustles to either side told him that more thornbush and briars moved to fill the gap, but each patch of dirt sprinkled with his blood stayed bare and free of the witch's power.

He attacked once more, biting, biting, biting, clawing at the soil with both forepaws and driving forward with his strong hind legs, digging a furrow clean of roots and stumps and mixing the soil with his blood. The hedge screamed with pain, high and thin, at the edge of even a dragon's hearing, and he felt it weakening.

And then it snapped. The hedge drew back, and bare soil met his nose. He opened his eyes again. A path waited, broad as a dragon's belly, straight through the hedge and into the grass surrounding a thatched cottage. He sniffed at the brush to either side and found no taint of the black witch. He'd broken her hold.

He hoped that it had caused her pain.

He smelled pain in the hedge, as well, but something other that was strange. He'd tasted something like it in one of the moose that he'd eaten, almost gratitude at finding an end to suffering. That moose hadn't tried to flee his death. He'd stood waiting on three legs, the fourth torn and bloody and smelling of human machines.

Khe'sha flowed through the hedge and circled the cottage,

sniffing. Yes, Shen was inside. Khe'sha smelled other things as well, magic and strange herbs and machines. He smelled traps and deceptions. The doors and windows were far too small for his bulk. He could tear off the roof, flatten the walls, but that might kill Shen. Going farther required more delicate tools than a dragon's fury.

He turned back, finding the Singer just outside the gap in the hedge. <Come, my friend who was recently my enemy. This is why the forest wanted both of us.>

# twenty-one

—※—

THE TREE SHOOK under Cáitlin, as if a sudden gust ruffled its leaves. There was no wind. She would have known,
none better. Her branch shook again, and she grabbed the
trunk to keep from falling. The winds still held their silence.

Whatever shook her perch must be coming from below.
She looked down, to meet the bored gaze of the black leopard
looking up. It hadn't moved. Its *branch* hadn't moved, either.
The cat yawned at her, glanced to the ground, and followed
his glance in one flowing leap to land . . . catlike . . . on the
leaves. He really was too large to move that smoothly.

Her branch shook a third time, more violently, the leaves
thrashing. It was the only part of the tree that moved. To
make the message clearer still, the cat padded insolently to
one side and settled into a lazy crouch, tail-tip flicking to one
side and the other. Just the tip, about a hand-span's width,
with the rest of the tail perfectly still. She'd always wondered
how cats could do that.

Something wanted her to climb down. It wasn't Fiona,
because it was giving her a choice. Fiona would have just

taken over her arms and legs and let the captive brain worry about clumsiness and falls.

Well, the winds had said that Maureen worshipped trees. Apparently that regard was mutual. Cáitlin grimaced and stretched her aching body. She could take a hint.

Her hips still hurt, deep in the bone where Fiona had molded them into the semblance of a man's. Cáitlin moved slowly, awkwardly, her balance strange and muscles uncertain, swinging down one branch, then another, then a third and a drop to the ground that sent daggers stabbing up her legs and through her pelvis to her spine and the base of her skull. She staggered, grabbed the tree trunk, shook her head to clear her eyes, and checked the leopard.

He yawned again and licked his lips, showing fangs as long as daggers and gleaming nearly as bright. Not an encouraging landscape. He stretched fore and aft, kneading the dirt with huge paws. He strolled across the forest clearing, sniffed a bush here and a rock there, and then glanced back over his shoulder.

<One could nip at you like a rude dog herding sheep. Or one could be polite and let you follow. Choose.>

A cat with *manners*?

Cáitlin sniffed the winds, finding nothing that linked back to Maureen. The cat and the tree acted on their own agenda. *They* wanted her to move. Strange . . .

<One does not wish to wait all day.>

Since when did cats have *schedules*? Cáitlin shrugged. Dougal had bred and bound strange animals. Add this new witch's seasoning to the stew, and the result was going to be . . . different. She wondered if she ought to pass a message on to the Pendragons' commander, ask her winds to tell Llewes of the change brought to the Summer Country. No. He'd abandoned her to her fate, the same Old One attitude toward a broken tool that you'd expect from Fiona. Let him find out on his own, the hard way.

Cáitlin felt a kind of duality around her, as if two separate minds, two separate sets of eyes, watched and balanced and guarded this forest. One smelled of the Old Blood and one . . . was something else, and older still. The Other linked tree and leopard.

And the Old Blood seemed much more civilized.

That was a hint. She followed the cat, staggering and limping at first but balance improving and muscles warming until she could almost walk like a normal person, listening to her winds. They brought her the earthy smells of the forest, leaf and flower and rotting humus; they brought her whiffs of the sharp maleness of the cat. They brought her the musk of a fox, a vixen but with something of the Other added to the mix.

The winds also spoke of Fiona coming in rancid hate, they spoke of the surviving dragon and blood rage, they spoke of the red-haired witch hiding alone in the shadows of a stone tower. They spoke of ravens circling high in the thermals overhead and watching, impartial. Battle promised, and they remembered the dead dragon. Whatever the outcome, they knew they would feed well.

The black cat led her toward Maureen's keep. That seemed to match Fiona's wish, because Cáitlin passed her former limit and stepped into the wide meadow and saw gray stone against blue sky. The air lay still, heavy with wet grass and old burning and soaked ash, with a buzz of Power as a grace-note that tickled her nose.

<One wishes you to proceed.>

Cáitlin glanced back to where the leopard waited, a shadow under the shadows of the forest. A chill ran down her spine and back up again. She wondered if the cat was real, or a manifestation of the forest. Whichever it was, she was glad to put it behind her. That place frightened her, and few things could.

Cáitlin turned and walked slowly toward the keep,

open-handed and forcing her mind to stay calm. She wanted to make sure that the Power living there saw her and did not see a threat. A raven croaked from the direction of Fiona's cottage, and three others answered in sequence from the other corners of the sky. The call to dinner?

Soft blackness smashed her from behind, and she fell into it.

THREE CATS HERDED Fergus through hallways and up stairs. He'd tried slipping through the spaces in the stones, invoking Dougal's ghost to frighten them, and found them waiting for him on the other side of the wall. Either they knew his tricks better than he did or they knew the ways of this castle *very* well. And ghosts seemed to hold no terrors for a cat. They sat and waited for him to emerge, slowly blinked green eyes, and stood up to stretch and return to herding him.

Fergus leaned against a wall, asking it to remain solid and support him. He wiped sweat from his forehead and took a deep breath, trying to summon some of the keep's Power from the stone to cool the burning in his arm. His hand throbbed. The hallway fuzzed around him, sliding in and out of focus, and he knew that he was dying. Even Fiona knew. She'd quit ordering him around, knowing that he was a waste of time.

The cats waited for him to catch his breath. Cats, or whatever they were.

They seemed to be common house cats, an orange tom and two queens—one tiger-striped in gray and the other a blotchy scattering of gray and white. And they hadn't threatened him, just made it clear that he should walk in one direction and not another. Step wrong, and the fur would bristle and the eyes narrow. A second step, and the ears went back and he could hear a low growl in the tom's throat.

He knew enough about Power that he didn't try a third step wrong. He remembered these particular cats from Fiona's maze, and they had always been rather more than cats. Apparently they had changed allegiance.

Or they'd been freed. The thought gave him pause.

Many things held Power in the Summer Country. Most of them were bound by greater Powers. Fiona's maze was one, of course. Dougal's creatures, the dragons and the falcons and the hunting cat, even his forest. These three house cats, these things that *appeared* to be house cats. He couldn't sense a binding on them. If they were free . . .

If they were free, and still acted for Maureen, the rules had changed. Even the Stone deep in the cellars of the tower felt as if it was free to follow its own ends. Hope mixed with its ancient pain and hatred, yet it urged him upward rather than back to its dark roots. Fergus went where the keep wanted him to go.

He shivered.

<Move.>

The tom's tail bushed out again, and he edged closer to Fergus. The two queens flanked him to right and left, leaving one direction open. No domestic cats would hunt that way, like a pride of lions cooperating to set a trap for wildebeest. Fergus shivered again. But did it matter? He was dying anyway.

The tom took another step, and his ears flattened.

"You don't need to shout."

Fergus pushed himself upright, fighting through the fog and the roar in his ears. They wanted him to climb. Stone stairs spiraled up, uneven, random height and width and without a rail. He staggered, thrown off stride as the stair's makers had intended, one of many traps they'd set for trespassing assassins in the night.

He caught himself on the rough wall and pushed off again and gained another three risers before he stopped to pant and force the stairs to stop moving under him. His heartbeat throbbed from fingertip to armpit and across his skin where the red tendrils of blood-poisoning spread.

The cats waited. Fergus started to slide down the wall to sit and gain his breath. The tom hissed, his ears flat against his head and fangs gleaming between snarling lips. Fergus pushed against stone and staggered upright again.

Three more steps. Pause, breathe, bring the stone walls back to stillness around his head. Ignore the sweat soaking his hair and back, trickling down his chest. Three more steps. Steps unnumbered, leading upward without end.

A landing.

A door stood in front of him. It was locked or barred. He turned. The cats crouched behind him, tails lashing. He heard the orange tom growl, even over the roaring in his ears. They wouldn't let him pass.

Locked doors didn't matter. Not to a master of stone. He slid into the crystal structure that bound sand into stone, letting the coolness wash over him and ease his burning arm. A room opened around him, dark except for a thin shaft of light between leaves of a shuttered window, bare except for a shadow in one corner.

His eyes adjusted to the darkness. The shadow formed into a woman, the redheaded witch. The witch waited for him, waited for the cats to fetch her enemy. She sat against one wall, held a glass of wine in one hand, studied him with mild curiosity. Curiosity, nothing more. The way he'd study an ant crawling across a piece of granite in his workshop.

The scene pulsed around him, her face rushing toward him and then receding. He sighed with relief; she didn't draw and throw that knife this time, quick as lightning. She didn't seem to even carry it at her belt. She didn't expect danger. And she was right. He wasn't dangerous. Never would be dangerous again. He dropped to his knees, letting the wall become solid behind him.

She shook her head and slid away from him to the far end of a tunnel. Words came echoing down the tunnel, slurred by his fading consciousness.

"Who the hell are *you*?"

SO BOTH CÁITLIN and Fergus were as good as dead. Fiona felt mild regret—she would have preferred to get a little more service from her puppets. Now they both hung limp at the end of their strings, useless.

She stood on the woods path, letting her Power seek out the Power around her, measuring its weakness and her strength. She would have preferred to let Cáit and Fergus walk through the minefields first. Circumstances hadn't allowed that. Fiona prided herself on being practical. She would be content with what she had.

They'd told her much, her little puppets. Maureen had returned to the keep. That was wise. She had also returned to drinking, which was less wise. And she had burdened herself with a rabble of sick and wounded humans, helpless mouths to feed and a drain on the red witch's Power if she had any plans to heal and comfort them. Wise and unwise, both, because those bodies could stand between Maureen and her doom. Even humans could be dangerous, and ate Power in the killing.

Least wise of all, Maureen had loosed the bonds Dougal had held. She didn't control the forest's power or the keep's. She didn't hold the reins and direct her defense, coordinating forces and strategy.

Fiona smiled. The forest could have been formidable, a trap as strong as her own maze. And legend said that the dark keep held reserves that even Dougal hadn't known. Maureen had let both those Powers slip out of her hands. Foolish child. That would cost her.

Fiona wrapped a cloak of awareness around her, testing

the air and soil for danger. The land felt hostile, watchful, calculating. It knew her from past visits, and did not like her. She smiled again. As she had told the dragon, she was used to being hated. It made the world feel normal.

She walked. The path snaked left and right like that dragon flowing through the woods, slipping between trees and around boulders, skirting patches of wetness, whiffs of swamp and rock and cinnamon fern. The watching pressed at her, but didn't attack.

Good. Stunning the dragon twice had cost her dearly. She still needed to gather Power, drawing from the earth and the air and from the child within her. She rested one hand on her bulging belly, slowing time within her womb. The child quieted, and its heartbeat faded almost to stillness. Going into labor now would be so awkward.

But she'd underestimated Maureen once before. Fiona would never make that mistake again. She had to reach the absolute peak of her Power before she struck.

She could bear the child tomorrow, after this triumph. After binding attendants to her will. There'd likely be a wet nurse among the refugees from that rebel keep. Fiona decided that she'd have to let some of the slaves live. Pass the burden along, then, let the baby drain Power from another.

And if the dragon survived this day, she'd kill it then. It, and all the nestlings, saving only little Shen in her lab. They were too dangerous to live. Fiona shuddered, remembering how close those teeth had come, how drained she'd felt when that huge yellow eye had opened and come back into focus after the second stun-spell. She wouldn't have had the strength to run away.

No, they were too dangerous to leave alive.

She pulled her thoughts back to the trail. She'd walked Dougal's forest many times before, scouting, planning. She knew the flavor of the land, the twists of this path, the trees frowning on it, the stones and tangles flanking it. She should have reached the dragon bones by now.

The trail sloped downward from her feet. It should rise, then dip to a stream, then rise again in the final climb to Dougal's keep high on its knob of rock. And only the single trail led between her cottage and the pasture oak and the keep. No branchings, no intersections.

She sniffed the air—wet leaves, soil, a faint sharpness of fox. Water hissed close ahead, water falling from high rocks rather than the gurgle of a forest stream.

The trail had changed. She stood and felt for the sun and for the stars beyond the canopy of trees and behind the veil of daytime blue. The sky told her that her cottage lay off her left shoulder, not behind. The keep sat to her right, through a tangle of dark holly and hawthorn.

Maureen had dropped the reins that controlled this forest, but she'd made some changes first. Fiona touched her brow in ironic salute. The redhead was *not* as dumb and trusting as she seemed at first glance.

But she was still drunk and leaving her defense to others. Fiona shook her head. You *never* trusted others in this land. Alliances, yes, those could be safe—with proper safeguards, such as with that dragon. And you could buy services. But never trust. Cash in advance, and count your change, and even with bedmates count your teeth after each kiss.

She turned, setting the stars and sun right in her head and aiming straight for the keep. She drew on her Power, forcing roots and stems and branches to one side or the other, moving the trail back to follow the path it should. She walked uphill, slow against the climb and the resistance of the forest that tugged at her ankles like an icy current in a river, smooth on the surface but deceptive in its strength.

The forest offered ease, offering aside and downhill without struggle. She forced her way, and still found her footsteps curving, curving, curving, until the keep sat off her right shoulder once more and the sound of falling water came brighter and closer up ahead.

She gritted her teeth and turned once more, face to the slope and the keep. She felt the resistance stiffen, and traced the flow of Power back in her mind. There was an oak in the forest's heart, she remembered, as old and massive and deep-rooted as Wotan's world-ash Yggdrasil. Apparently it liked Maureen.

That tree would pay. Tomorrow or the next day or the next, she'd seek it out. She knew poisons that would touch even *his* roots. But she'd learned long ago to fight only one battle at a time.

Brian had taught her that. Brian, still missing in action. Her blood-tie still lay silent. What *was* that darling little boy up to now?

She settled her mind into her belly, drawing on the Power of her child. This time her touch fell less gently, and the unborn witch shuddered. Too much, and the child would weaken, even die.

But it was expendable. Fiona had Brian's sperm in storage, and her own eggs. And Maureen had succored wombs in plentitude, with those human refugees. How kind of her to provide so many surrogate mothers.

Again Fiona turned uphill, against the flow, and this time her Power killed. Leaves shriveled, limbs crumbled, vines cracked and fell apart as dust. She forced her way through tangles, leaving a trail behind her defined in brown and black. Her footprints burned the soil to sterility.

The path curved downhill, and she held the sun and stars and her cottage in their places and fought against that curving. Stone barred her way, and she drew still more Power from the unborn baby. It struggled and then stilled. Fiona wasted a second's glance, finding the heartbeat and a trace of dreaming. The girl still lived.

And she dismissed that care. Impossible snow touched her face and the flow of Power weakened further and she gained ten more paces. The forest stream crossed her path, rimmed with ice, and the trees showed black frost-nipped edges to their leaves. Her lips pulled back from her teeth into a feral smile. So summer ended? The forest's magic began to fail.

The child squirmed again, her protest a sharp rolling pain in Fiona's belly. The dark witch turned her eyes inward for an instant and smacked the brat with a stunning spell. No more distractions.

She crossed the stream and climbed the slope beyond it. She remembered the old trail and forced it into being once again. Another hundred yards and she'd reach the forest's edge, see the keep in front of her across mindless, powerless grass. Sweat tickled her brow, and she swiped her sleeve across it. Walking the forest had cost her more than she'd expected.

She drew Power from the child and climbed.

# twenty-two

—m—

THE ROAD BLURRED in front of Maureen, and an antique horse-drawn hearse formed out of wind-driven rain, long, black-lacquered, glass-sided, four-wheeled coffin box draped in black and with black plumes bobbing on the team, square in front of her hood. She slammed on the brakes, slewing sideways on wet pavement, sat for a moment, and then a chorus of blaring horns snapped her back to reality.

Hallucination. She hadn't hit anything. Nothing had hit her. Her hands shook, and the road stayed blurry. Windshield wipers didn't help. Blurs were on the *inside,* on her own goddamn eyeballs. She restarted the stalled engine and pulled over to the side of the road. Flipped on the emergency blinkers. They even worked. Hadn't tried them in years.

*Damn, damn, damn,* damn! *Mom. Dad. Brian. Jo.*

She buried her face in her hands, giving in to tears. The voices returned, whispering, accusing, sneering. *You're crazy, you know that? Still schizo, after all these years. Find a loving*

*man, what do you do? Try to claw his eyes out. Your father murders*
*your mother and then commits suicide, you just stand there dry-eyed*
*staring at the shattered corpses like they were a pair of discarded*
*mannequins lying on the dump and say, "Good riddance." Your sis-*
*ter comes to you drowning in grief and remorse, and you walk off*
*and leave her with a fucking bottle of wine for a life preserver.*

Rain spattered on the metal roof overhead, rattling into
sleet, echoing her mood. She remembered the thunderstorm
she'd drawn to the forest and the keep, and wondered if she
was responsible for *this* sudden squall or if it was just normal
shitty Maine spring weather.

Brian had left her. Out of all the shit that had happened,
she kept coming back to that. *Wrong, wrong, wrongo. He*
*didn't leave. You drove him away. You would have killed him if he*
*stayed. The man did his best. How could he live with a psycho*
*witch?*

Something tapped at the window beside her, and she
swiped tears from her eyes. A blue raincoat and plastic-
shrouded cop hat loomed through the rain-streaked glass. She
rolled down the window, heaving at the rusty groans and
stiffness of the old crank.

"Are you okay, ma'am?"

She saw a skull between the turned-up collar and the hat,
polished ivory bone and black pits for the eyes and nose and
mouth. Blue fire lit in the depths of the eye-sockets, and she
blinked. The apparition flowed and changed into a human
face, one of the cops she'd met at the station, giving her
statements. Small town, small police force. Get through this,
she'd know every one of them by name, know their wives
and their kids' batting averages and the names of their pet
dogs.

" 'M fine. Cat ran across the road, nearly hit it."

*Liar.*

The policeman shook his head and sniffed, then sniffed

again and shook his head again. "Ma'am, I should ask you to step out of the car, do a sobriety check. You've got an opened bottle of whiskey there on the seat. But you don't smell of booze, and I've heard all that you've been through. I've got fender-bender calls out the wazoo with this storm. Please just give me the bottle and drive more carefully. Go home. If you need a drink, have it there."

*Whatthehell* . . . She glanced sideways. That damned bottle of Bushmills had followed her. Her hand shook as she picked it up, splashing the contents into foam. She nearly dropped it when she handed it to the officer.

He walked over to the side of the road and emptied the bottle. She could smell that good whiskey over the rain and burned oil and acrid hot brake pads. She wanted it. God, she *wanted* it.

He tossed the empty into the trunk of his cruiser, good man, didn't add to the roadside litter. Then he climbed back into the car, flipped on the blue-blinky lights, and pulled out. The rain and sleet turned back into a snow squall, veiling the road. Ghosts drove past, walked past, crowded around her windows with accusation and threat on their faces. Dad, Mom, Dougal, Sean, Buddy Johnson. Maureen's teeth chattered. She cranked the Toyota's heater to full blast.

*That won't warm your soul a bit. Like trying to thaw a glacier with a handheld blow-dryer.*

She'd been looking for David, a set of loving arms and a familiar body to hug warmth into Jo. Couples did that, provided each other strength to lean on and a refuge against the world. But she'd driven Brian away . . .

That left Father Oak. She knew where she stood with him. Strength and stability and refuge, firm-rooted and broad-limbed and he didn't fucking *care* if his worshipers were crazy drunken murderers. *He* knew how to handle magic.

Her hands still shook. Alcohol withdrawal, she guessed.

That would explain the horse-drawn hearse, as well. Her own Freudian permutation on purple elephants or snakes and centipedes.

She wiped sweat from her palms, crunched the car back into gear, and chose a big gap in traffic before pulling back out into the spitting sleet. Maine weather, just as psychotic as she was.

Carlysle Woods, the parking lot, she jolted against a wheel-stop and sat for a moment, shaking, sweating, heart racing, still chilled. Who the hell was she staying sober *for*? Brian had left her. The forest didn't need her. Jo and David had fucking kicked her out. Mom and Dad were dead. That Bushmills would slide down real smooth right now. No, she didn't have a drinking problem. No trouble at all getting booze inside her belly.

The hazard blinkers still clicked on and off like a metronome. She'd left them running. Well, not a problem for driving slow in a storm. Besides, she *was* a hazard. Warn the world.

She shut the blinkers off, shut the engine off, listened to the rattle of sleet and the ticking of hot metal cooling. Father Oak waited, calm and strong. She could feel him already. He loaned her the strength to unlatch the sticky door and climb out, the caution to lock the car behind her, the serenity to stand and breathe deep and slow her racing heart. So Father Oak was God?

*Well, it wouldn't be a new religion. If He fulfills the basic functional requirements, 'tis enough, 'twill serve.* She was a heretic, finding God in everything. Been years since she felt the need to go to church to worship. Not to worship some remote white-bearded patriarch hiding behind Father Donovan and the Pope, accessible only through an intermediary. Her God lived in the soil beneath her feet and the air she breathed and in the heart of every rock and tree. *"The Kingdom of God is within you."*

The storm had switched to snow again, fat wet flakes like cotton balls. Wait ten minutes, and the sun would come out—New England weather. She let it settle in her hair and splotch her cheeks with cold, mingling with the streaky tears, remembering that she *could* make it miss her. For an instant she was a child again, trying to catch snowflakes on her tongue.

The snow fell around her, flakes as big as chickadees, and the chickadees dodged around the flakes and chattered and didn't care. The forest didn't care. Snow was part of life. Death was part of life. Father Oak waited, strong and serene. He'd told her a hundred times, a thousand times, that evils like Daddy or Buddy Johnson held power over her only because she'd granted it.

She turned her back on the shattered wreck of her nightmares and climbed over a snowbank to the trail. Turned her back on Naskeag Falls. Jo could have the house and whatever dust and cobwebs remained in Daddy's bank account. Maureen wasn't coming back again. That pile of sticks and mud had never been a home. Just like Dougal's castle wasn't home. Dougal and Daddy, an eye for an eye and a tooth for a tooth. Lex talionis.

*"Do unto others as you would have them do unto you."*

<Your nightmares taught you how they wished to be treated.>

That was the problem with God, both the Old Testament and New Testament versions. Implacable old bastard, judge and jury and executioner.

Father Oak never used to speak so clearly. He'd been an enigma and an oracle, a sense of strength and guide to her own thoughts. Now he was growing into another of the schizophrenic voices.

She was going mad. Madder.

She walked a trail marked by champagne buckets filled with the winter's snow, chilling France's finest vintages. She blinked and they were gone, vanished back into the labyrinth of her mind. Bottles of Bushmills and Glenmorangie cradled in the crotches of the trees around her, calling out their seductive wiles. Retsina wafted its resinous tang to mix with the perfume of spruce and fir. Just wish and they'd be real.

Her hands shook as she wiped sweat off her brow and out of her eyes. The forest spun around her, trees tilting like the masts of a harbor full of sailboats bobbing in a heavy swell.

One thing stayed firm and vertical—the power resting at the heart of her forest. Father Oak waited for her. Crazy or not, drunk or not, whether or not blood dripped from her hands and painted her face, Father Oak waited for her. He wouldn't run away from her like Brian. He wasn't afraid of her.

Warmth and strength enfolded her. Rough bark caressed the palms of her hands. The lightning scar reminded her that she could survive.

<The fox needs you to return.>

She felt courage flow into her.

<The forest needs you to return.>

She turned and squatted at the foot of Father Oak, closing her eyes and letting his strength wash over her. Her trembling died. Her breathing slowed bit by bit from the panic she'd been feeling. The fox needed her. The forest needed her. If she didn't have to go back to that damned castle . . .

<The fox knows a cave in the heart of your forest.>

*Yeah. Live in a cave, dark and dirty and cold and wet, full of an oozy smell and the ends of worms.*

She pulled her old Romanian flute out of her jacket pocket, the only thing she'd really cared to fetch from their apartment. If possessions made you a slave, God knew she was one of the freest people on earth.

She remembered that the fox had asked for the flute, as

well. She fingered the carvings that decorated the wood, touched the stop-holes on the twin tubes, and wondered again why it always felt alive. It purred to her fingers, like one of the cats melting under a scritch between the shoulder blades.

Paired notes and single notes, melodies and trills, the strange scale that had always defied her fingers now danced through the forest. *Debussy,* she thought, *that prelude, invoking fauns and nymphs and dryads. It's that kind of feel. Step into myth and magic if you want to make the flute work its own magic.*

The forest changed around her. Father Oak remained firm at her back. Snow melted into mist, and green leaves cloaked the limbs. She felt the magic of her flute wafting out and sinking into the soil, spreading, binding, weaving the fabric of balance. Balance fed back to her, welcoming. The forest needed her. It told her of the dragon, and David, and a song that broke old chains and forged new bonds freely accepted. It told her of Fiona, walking, killing, carrying rage and doubled power.

<Follow.>

The fox vixen waited, sitting on her haunches. Maureen studied her fur mask, her eyes and expressive radar ears, her tail and jaw and play of the muscles under her skin. This was a serious fox, not angry or afraid or jesting. She remembered that the fox showed her the forest's face, Father Oak's face. This was something new.

Maureen staggered to her feet, as weary as if she'd just run a marathon. Tension. Killing Demon Rum took as much out of her as killing Dougal. She followed the fox, away from Father Oak's Summer Country form and through a forest glade, past ancient lichen-crusted rocks and dense stands of dark green holly that rustled behind her as they closed the way, to a sudden ledge outcrop gnawed by rain and weather. A rowan grew there, ancient but strong, the first she'd seen within the forest. A house-rowan?

The fox looked up at Maureen and then stepped delicately sideways around an edge of stone. Maureen followed and found a hidden cave-mouth, dark and drifted with leaves. Air flowed from it, cold and damp and musty, just as she'd suspected, but it still felt more welcoming than the castle. She ought to get her flashlight from the car and come back.

<Come.>

The fox barked from the darkness, impatient. If Maureen could trust *anything* in this world, it was the fox.

Maureen shrugged her shoulders and followed, careful of her feet and head. The way seemed smooth. A minute passed, and then another, and then strangeness grew on her and she realized what was missing. The walls weren't closing in around her. She knew tons of rock hung over her head, but they didn't feel threatening. Her heart beat slowly, normally, and the palms of her hands stayed dry.

Whatever terrified her in the castle cellars, it hadn't followed her down this tunnel.

Down she went, and down, and down, in total darkness. Much of the forest stood on limestone, not the sandstone underneath the keep. Still, this seemed more like a tunnel than a natural cave. She didn't have any trouble walking, even without light, her fingers trailing along the rough walls and telling her of each twist or turn as it came up, the floor safe and smooth beneath her feet.

And then the air changed, the damp clammy graveyard flow coming in low from her right hand and the way ahead dry and . . . *warm?* It smelled clean, except for a strange musky forest tinge almost like bracken in the morning dew.

She stepped out into pale light and gasped. Green, gold, red, sheets and streams of light that showed her a cavern. Stalactites, stalagmites, curtains, rivers of smooth gleaming flowing stone—Carlsbad or Luray Caverns but scaled down into human space. She touched one wall, a curtain of stone lace or crochet work, translucent sepia jewelry, and her fingers came away glowing pale yellow. Phosphorescent algae. Her eyes had adapted in the blackness of the tunnel, and even this faint light seemed strong enough for reading.

"God. It's *beautiful*."

<It is yours. If you really want a round green door, we can make adjustments.>

Now that wise-ass dog was laughing at her, tongue hanging out. She knew what Maureen had been thinking.

A hearth sat in one corner, faint traces of soot marking the floor and wall and with a hole overhead that drew air past her reaching hand. Chimney flue. Wood waited next to the hearth, and large stoneware crocks that looked like they held food. Jugs, water or wine or oil, she didn't check.

She touched the wall again. It felt warm. Walking in a daze, she trailed her fingers along the slick smoothness until she turned a corner. A pool waited, steaming gently, hot water welling up and then overflowing into a stream that joined a cold spring and then drained away down a plate-sized hole in the floor. Indoor plumbing, just add towels and toilet paper.

Another opening, and she found a bed, tall-posted with a canopy and hangings, with hand-loomed linens and a light woolen blanket. Wardrobe with wooden hinges and latch, it looked as old as the stone beside it. A terra-cotta lamp that could be a refugee from Pompeii, filled with olive oil and wick ready for the flint and steel and tinder that lay next to it on the smooth flowstone shelf. She stared at the flint and steel—the steel had been set in a bone handle, as if whoever used it felt uncomfortable touching cold iron. Old Blood. Maureen shivered. Then she sniffed at the oil. It smelled sweet, not rancid.

"Someone lives here."

<No one has walked these stones for over a thousand years. The Tree would know. You stand beneath his roots.>

"But the food, the bed, the oil . . ."

&lt;This is a land of magic.&gt;

It felt *safe* here. She doubted if an enemy could ever find the entrance, could even get close to it through her forest. The stones enfolded her and guarded her. Unlike the keep, they welcomed her.

Home.

She'd never *had* a home, not in the sense of a safe center to her life. Damn sure the castle didn't make the grade. Father Oak came closest, but sleeping in a snowbank really sucked. That was *another* thing Daddy had stolen from her. Stolen from both her and Jo. Safety was anywhere but "home."

Maureen shivered with a sudden fierce joy, and she drank the warm musk of the cave deep into her lungs. This *was* home. It felt right. It even *smelled* right, just like Brian.

A thousand years. Maureen squinted, suddenly suspicious. "Who lived here?"

&lt;Some legends called her Nimue. Even the forest never knew her true name.&gt;

"Great. Just fucking *great.* Am I going to find Merlin sleeping off a drunk in some back pantry?" She remembered things Brian had said about Merlin, and shuddered.

&lt;The Tree says that Merlin never came here. The cave lies empty and waiting for you. It *is* safe.&gt;

Brian and safety. She remembered the reason *why* he'd been searching the cellars. "Are there other exits?"

The vixen grinned up at her. &lt;I am a fox, woman. My definition of "safe" includes at least three ways out of my den. These caves have four.&gt;

Brian.

Would the definition of "home" ever include him? The warmth faded from Maureen's stomach. She kept forgetting that he'd left her. Her brain knew it, but her heart didn't want to.

If she ever saw that man again, she'd better get some serious pair-bond work going. Damn fast. Persuade him that
staying could be a good idea. Fun, even.

<The dark witch comes. We must meet her.>

The fox turned and trotted toward another passage.

# twenty-three

—◆—

ILLUSIONS AND TRAPS.

David shook his head. A witch's cottage? That was Jo's territory, or Maureen's. They carried the Old Blood. They could use magic. Maureen had been inside Fiona's lair once already and got out alive. Rescued Brian in the process. Why the hell were they sending *him*?

Whitewashed stone, thatched roof, deep-set casement windows, it *looked* like a tourist-bureau postcard of an Irish country cottage. But Maureen had told him that Fiona lived in a labyrinth of smoke and mirrors, deadly truth hidden under layers of innocent appearance. The fields were fake, an alarm system and defenses, not real pasture. He'd seen what the hedge was like, and he was happy as hell that the swarming bees buzzed their frustration around the dragon's head, unable to sting through all that armor.

However, apparently Fiona had left some gaps in her programming. He smelled the bitter poison mingled with the sweet sap from torn roses and hawthorns, but that poison hadn't bothered Khe'sha. Wrong species. And she hadn't designed the hedge to stand forever against an animated bulldozer, either. An *angry* bulldozer, smart and persistent.

David shivered, remembering that thrashing rage and the deep booming growls of hatred. The sheer noise of it had driven him to his knees, and some of those ragged chunks of brush had flown a hundred feet and more. Fears of that rage had haunted his nightmares, ever since he'd faced and killed the dragon's mate. And now Khe'sha was his friend?

Anyway, the rage and awesome strength explained why the fox had sent Khe'sha. But what did the forest want David to do, want a *human* to do? Compose a song? That was his only talent in this land.

The forest had sent him. The forest had learned chess from Maureen, and David felt like one of its pawns in a surreal game of masters. The forest knew him, knew too damn much about him from that eternity when he *was* the forest, his soul spreading through every leaf and rootlet and sinking into the living soil and flowing in its waters. It knew his fears.

*Fear. I've lived in terror of the dragon, only to find strength and honor and friendship where I least expected them. Shouldn't that give me courage?*

It didn't. He stared at the worn green paint around the door lever, wondering if it concealed death. He stepped into the shadow of the covered porch and felt it as a chill. Sweat beaded on his brow, and his muscles tightened.

*This is Brian's job, not mine. He's the designated Hero in this Adventure. I'm the Poet, in charge of singing for our evening's beer at the Wayside Inn. I don't even own a sword.*

He touched the lever, and twisted it, and the latch clicked. He lived. His fingers didn't catch fire, or turn putrid and fall off in rotting chunks. He didn't even stick to the metal, bound forever at the whim of the Wicked Witch. The door swung in an inch and waited for him, brooding. He nudged

it farther with his toe, ready to dodge the pounce of a minia-
ture dinosaur witch-bound as a guard dog.

*It's normal to be afraid. Brian told me so. He said he was
afraid, every time he went into battle. Fear is healthy. It keeps you
alive. But I've been a hero once already. Isn't that enough?*

He stepped into a small chamber with benches on each
side, a place to sit and pull off mucky boots when you came
in from the fields. Stone flooring, looked like slate worn
smooth by centuries of feet. The granite threshold had
cracked clear through, more of Maureen's magic. He felt the
chill of her curse in the air around him.

Fiona hadn't broken it. Perhaps she hadn't cared, or
hadn't even noticed.

He studied the kitchen beyond, wall and base cabinets
painted yellow and marble countertop and a slate sink with
a hand pump. Electric refrigerator and microwave, but a
wood cook stove and hanging kerosene lamp. Herbs dried
overhead, hanging in bundles from dark roof-beams, per-
fuming the air. She'd cooked a batch of onion soup recently,
and toasted whole-wheat bread—both aromas lingered,
teasing him, and his mouth watered. He'd skipped lunch,
worrying about Jo. Could he trust the food here? He
doubted that.

But he couldn't see any teeth in the room, either literal
or figurative. No sign of the hatchling dragon.

<You *must* not let her bite you. She will try, and the
young of our kind are fast. Be *very* careful.>

Some kind of poison in the bite. He'd never thought about
how a small dragon could kill prey. With the big ones, the answer was obvious. But he'd never visualized baby dragons.
They always showed up in the fairy tale full-grown.

Gritting his teeth, he stepped into the kitchen and
started checking cupboards, opening each door as if it had
one of those coiled-up spring snakes inside, ready to pop out
at him and bite. And he kept finding just what you'd expect

to find in any kitchen, a lot of pots and pans and flour bins and china and glassware. Even cornflakes in an incongruous supermarket box.

No traps, no dragons. Khe'sha had told him Shen would be about as long as one of David's legs, a fair-sized black iguana with razor teeth, so she could be hidden almost anywhere. Smells teased his nose, garlic and onions and ginger and the herbs, and something else. Something chemical, like hospital disinfectant. It was faint and diffuse, as if it permeated the space rather than centered on a single leaking bottle.

He shook his head, and moved on. Dining room, a table and chairs and sideboard full of silver and crystal, the kind of high-rent stuff Maureen had inherited with her castle. Oriental rug, probably worth more than Jo's whole apartment, on a polished oak floor. Fireplace, with two graceful silver bud vases holding red roses on the mantel, and a cracked hearthstone.

Still no traps or dragons, though. The normalcy of it all felt doubly creepy.

A stair led up from beside the dining room, and he put that off for later. The last room was a study, old oak roll-top desk and a couple of matching four-drawer files, an oak table with a laptop computer and stacked manila folders waiting. The file drawers weren't even locked. And they didn't hold any poisonous iguanas.

*This lady doesn't expect random visitors, that's for sure. Either that, or her twisty little mind leaves obvious stuff lying around as camouflage for what she's really hiding.*

He paused and shuffled through the files lying on the table. The first held a stapled sheaf of something typed in Cyrillic; he couldn't tell if it was Russian or Serbian or whatever, with a big red rubber stamp across the top. Another, in handwritten dancing calligraphy that might be Arabic, with stamps and marginal notes in the same script. Another in Chinese or Japanese or Korean; all those ideograms looked the same to him. The constant feature seemed to be bold rubber stamps across the heads. He tried a fourth and finally struck English. And the stamp said MOST SECRET.

He was reading the first page, the "executive summary," but there wasn't any letterhead or organization given, not even an author's name. And words jumped out at him, scattered in the text, words like "anthrax" and "smallpox" and "influenza" and "plague." Discussions of vectors and virulence, morbidity and mortality, incubation periods and projected course of infection.

He shuddered. He wasn't sure why, but some kinds of mass-produced death seemed uglier than others. Why was poison gas a worse way to die than napalm? What made anthrax worse than land mines? Each could kill the unwary for generations after. Still, he wanted to wash his hands after touching the papers.

But he was looking for a baby dragon. He crossed the study off his list and climbed a twisting stair to the cottage loft. Bedroom, still prosaic, just a bed and dresser under sloping ceilings and a large mirror, mirror on the wall that offered no advice and a couple of walk-in closets with a prevailing theme of gray. Gray slacks, gray stylish suits, gray sweaters and blouses folded neatly on the shelves. The labels were worth their weight in gold, but Fiona didn't seem to give her designers much leeway on the colors. Even the damned underwear in her dresser was gray silk.

A smaller bedroom sat on the other side of the stairway, air stale, bed stripped down to mattress cover, obviously unused. He checked it anyway. No dragon. And that was that, the whole cottage.

No lab, either. Maureen said Fiona had bragged about her lab, about having Brian's sperm frozen in liquid nitrogen in her *lab.* Part of her kinky Arthurian bit of having her brother's baby. She did genetics research and biochemistry as a sideline to her trade in poisoned apples.

David froze, staring out the bedroom's dormer window at nothing. Genetics research. Lab. Those creepy papers on the study table. Stealing a baby dragon, with a bite that wasn't really poison, the way Khe'sha described it. More like *infectious,* if it took days to kill.

And the fox had warned of an evil that was dangerous to all that suckled young. To all mammals.

He twisted his way back down the winding stairs, eyes unfocused, thinking, running his fingers along the cold rough plaster to steer his body back to the kitchen. *A microwave oven, a refrigerator, a freezer out in the pantry, all of them shiny new Energy Star high-efficiency models. A few compact fluorescent lights, that laptop computer.*

He found his way out the back door, by the pantry, and studied the scene. Three long bays of photocells soaked up power from the sun. He'd been to a Show-and-Tell at the electric company's "Energy House." They ran a whole suburban family's electric toys off a *single* bank of cells that size. Fiona's shed held racks full of clear-sided lead-acid batteries, deep-cycle stuff, with an inverter that probably cost as much as a new Mercedes.

*This woman uses a lot of electricity.*

*Where?*

He pulled the main switch, and an alarm started to ring in the cottage. Apparently Fiona wanted to know if the power went out. Something out of sight needed continuous power.

"My friend, how good are you at digging?"


DRAGONS WERE *VERY* good at digging. David had watched a woodchuck remodeling its burrow once. Dirt flew in a steady cloud, loosened and thrown back by a blur of front paws. Enlarge that by a factor of ten thousand, and you had the dragon at work.

And yet that frenzy had control. Khe'sha followed the underground electric cable from the shed to the cottage's foundation without damaging it. He left it hanging along the stone wall as he burrowed deeper, leaving mounds of loam and gravel and small rocks thrown back between his hind legs.

He exposed a wall, deeper than David's height, dark with clinging dirt but apparently of the same stone masonry as the whitewashed plane that showed above the grade. Pipes entered it and drained from it in several places, twisting away underground to unknown destinations.

*There's a lot more to this simple Irish cottage than meets the eye.* But that wasn't news. Smoke and mirrors, illusions and traps.

The dragon pulled back, his bulk crushing rosebushes and knocking a sundial spinning across the grass. The hedge retreated from his tail, a really weird sight that David's eyes almost refused to pass along to his brain.

<I smell Shen beyond that wall. I hear her thoughts. It would be best if you stood back.>

David blinked and retreated. *If a dragon asks you to move, you move. Ask how far while you're already en route.*

Khe'sha cocked his head back and forth, weaving his neck like a snake. He nodded. <Her thoughts are strongest in that far corner.>

And then he struck, both forepaws with his weight and the coiled strength of his whole bulk behind them. Stones flew in a cloud of mortar dust, leaving a gap in the near corner of the foundation wall. The dragon struck again and again, blind frenzy if it hadn't been so focused. The ground shook, and a blaze of purple light blinded David. Khe'sha screamed.

David blinked the fire out of his eyes, stunned. He sat

up. Smoke rose from the corner of the cottage, black rising out of wisps of white steam that hugged the bottom of the trench. Heavy. Looked like cryogenics, the liquid oxygen boiling off while NASA fueled a rocket launch. Something brownish mixed streaks through the white, looking noxious. He shook his head again, clearing it. He couldn't hear anything.

The dragon lay still. It looked like Fiona had her own version of a TOP SECRET stamp, a trap protecting whatever hid in that cellar. A trap powerful enough to kill a dragon in an instant—David remembered the other one, thrashing and screaming and knocking him across the forest clearing and burying him in shattered trees.

But he saw a hole into darkness. Was the trap drained? He staggered to his feet. His sight blurred, tears for his fallen friend, but he owed Khe'sha. David had to try that hole, see if Shen survived.

<When this song is chanted, it will be told as a cautionary tale for hatchlings. "How Khe'sha lost his temper and two claws."> The dragon opened one great yellow eye, blinked several times as if he had to clear his head, and then lifted his right forepaw, displaying the seared gap where the title digits once had been.

David shuddered. "Thank God. I thought you were dead."

<I believe that I am larger than the enemies the witch expected. Or perhaps she dared not use a stronger spell, without destroying her whole house and whatever lairs under it.>

Khe'sha struggled to his feet, twitching and groggy. He sniffed at the vapors and the hole, and sneezed. <I smell death and poison inside. We must burn this place. Shen still lives.>

The hole was large enough for a man. The entire cellar wasn't large enough for the dragon. *Dammit, you pass one test, they just throw another one at you. I don't* want *to go in there.*

But he had no choice. That's what it always came down

to. He'd followed Jo, he'd killed the other dragon, he'd done *everything* in this insane saga because he had no choice. Just like the forest had herded him and Khe'sha to this place. The chess-master moved his pieces without asking their permission.

No choice. He couldn't retreat, so he went forward.

He climbed down into the hole. He'd expected darkness in the cellar, but pale light glowed through the vapor, and his brain started building hoodoos of lurking witchcraft or hideous bioluminescent monsters or radioactive isotopes stolen from Los Alamos. Chill dampness touched him, and he shivered. It stank, that disinfectant he'd noticed in the kitchen and a whiff of rotting meat and the sharp tang of ozone from a lot of electronics. Smoke, curls of smoke from charred beams and the fried meat of Khe'sha's paw.

Apparently his hearing was coming back, because leaking pipes hissed gently from each side. The glow firmed and focused into emergency lights, simple battery units hanging on the walls, cutting beams of yellow through the shifting murk. He sighed with relief, then coughed as the air bit his throat. Dust, or poison? *Move, dammit. You don't know* what *that vapor is.*

He found a cage, surrounded by dead electronics and lab equipment. Black fury lunged across the metal, claws and teeth screeching on stainless steel bars.

<Shen *hungry!*>

His brain fuzzed. *Even if that gas is nitrogen or $CO_2$ or Freon, it can kill you. No air. Suffocate.*

Cage, carrying cage, hatchling-sized, with guarded handles. How could he lure the dragon into it? Refrigerator. Cold steam boiling out, glass vials, nothing there. Another. Meat. Plastic-wrapped meat, still with the supermarket price labels and foam trays. Sirloin steaks, better than he'd eaten in years.

*Feed her. That will slow her down.* Was that his thought, or Khe'sha's?

He dropped the first package. Fumbled for a second, ripped it open with clumsy fingers. *Brain going. How long can you hold your breath?*

Knocked over a rolling cart, crashing glass. Baited the cage. Latched it to the larger cage. Blinked at a complicated double gate, interlocks, no *way* that little monster was going to get out by mistake.

*This lever* and *that one, arm's length apart, can't release both at once without having* everything *out of the way. Sort of like a stamping press.*

But his timing was off. Open the outside door, the inner one wouldn't budge. Try again. Inner door opened, but outer wouldn't move. Black lizard darted into the chamber and out again, faster than David could blink. Like a rattlesnake striking.

Notches in the levers, had to move just right or the metal rods wouldn't pass each other. He blinked and concentrated, made the mistake of breathing deep again, and doubled over coughing. *Get out. Clear your head. Try again.*

But the tiny dragon coughed and staggered. It would die if it stayed here, same reason.

*Hands on levers, focus, push both slowly, aim metal tab at metal slot, insert Tab A into Slot B, interlock clicks, both doors.*

*Dragon in portable cage. Lock door. Bug out. Small cage rattles, won't move. Still latched to big cage. Brain going, going, gone.*

He flipped one latch, then the other, clicks barely heard. Made sure that the door was *still* locked. Turned away. Moved toward the light. Bumped up against cold metal. Light was on the wall, overhead, glowing one-eyed headlight of a battery pack. He was lost.

He staggered against another bench, shattering glass. It held him up, and he pushed along it with his free hand, searching out another light. This one grew, developed ragged edges, turned white instead of glowing yellow. He crawled over shattered stone and clattering metal, dragging the small cage behind him as a dead weight chained to his hand. One hand, one leg, one hand, other leg, he crawled through the vapor and the murk. Light drew him. Gas hissed in his ears, and cold washed across his cheek.

He crawled across jagged edges out onto soft damp dirt. A paw as large as his own body gently dragged him out of the hole. He flopped on the grass and concentrated on breathing. The fresh air tasted like fine wine.

Fire. If Fiona had been playing around with germs and biowar, they'd better sterilize the place. He staggered to his feet, head still ringing with oxygen deficit or whatever poisons he'd been trying to breathe. He found a drum of kerosene and a fuel can in the garden shed, filled one from the other, made trips to the kitchen and the study and the bedroom, soaking everything in sight. Khe'sha pulled the barrel out and batted it into the basement hole with glugging holes from his claws. The fuel reek spread.

He searched for matches, found none, and then remembered that they wouldn't work in this land of magic anyway. But he found live coals in the stove, and blew them into flame, and touched fire to soaked curtains and rugs. Outside again, he tossed his homemade torch into the cellar lab and watched orange flame spread into darkness. Whatever the gas was, or the spell, that had tried to suffocate him, it didn't hinder fire. Something flared blue in the shadows with a *whomp* of volatility, some solvent like acetone or alcohol. A string of soft booms followed, a chain reaction marching down a lab bench.

They retreated, dragon and Bard and hatchling hissing defiance in her cage, and stared as the flames soaked into wood beams and flooring and thatch and raised black smoke to the sky. They'd done it. They'd walked into the witch's lair and walked out again, alive.

<Singer, you are bleeding.>

Something had shredded his left sleeve. Blood welled up from long scratches and short, deep punctures. Chemicals stained the cloth and the skin beneath it. He stared at his arm in stupid disbelief, until a dull ache throbbed into pain and built until it slashed him like a hot knife. The wounds were real.

It couldn't be a bite. He'd kept the hatchling safely caged. It *couldn't* be a bite. But God alone knew what he'd broken, down in that lab. God and Fiona only knew what she'd left, poisons or tissue cultures or spells, scattered across those benches and tables.

# twenty-four

—w—

A BEE LUMBERED past Fiona's nose, heavy with nectar and with its pollen baskets stuffed round and yellow. It had buzzed close enough that she felt the brush of its wings, but she was used to bees. They never bothered her. Her own hives teemed with her sentinels and spies, carrying pain in their tails. Sometimes she told them to mob intruders. They would kill, if she wished.

She froze in midstep, a chill shaking her shoulder blades. That wasn't *her* bee. Not here, not in this forest. Just like those weren't her hawthorns and briars and climbing roses.

Low humming sounded from the tree next to her, and she eased away from it. She traced the tiny bodies, in and out, in and out, a steady stream focused on a knothole above arm's reach. Now that she'd paused to notice, she could even smell the sweet-sour hive tang on the forest air. And she noticed small dots circling her, closer behind and farther in front, circling three times before moving on to the bee-tree or out to forage. A second shudder ran down her back. They knew her, watched her, waited for a command. She backed away from the tree, step by slow step, barely checking where she put each foot.

Maybe Maureen hadn't witched those bees. Maybe they were the only thing in this forest that was innocent, but somehow Fiona doubted that.

She glanced up at the sky, turned, and stopped. No. The sun shouldn't be on her right shoulder. It had been on her left. Dougal's keep was *west* of her cottage. Straight west and uphill. Now uphill lay to the east. She knew she hadn't circled the hill, couldn't be coming at it from the other side.

Fiona could swear fluently in seven languages, and she used all of them—independently and in mixed combinations. Sweat stung the scratches on her cheeks and hands and up her arms, and tufts of snagged wool destroyed the sleek curves of her sweater and slacks. Tangles and dead scraps of brush matted the elegance of her hair. She couldn't spare the Power to repair either her clothing or her own flesh.

She was lost. This was not *possible*. She'd never been lost, in all the long decades and strange lands she'd walked—always knew just where she was, where she'd been, where she was going. But the trees were wrong, the slope was wrong, the angle of the sun lied to her, even the air and the loam under her feet and the leaves she touched smelled strange.

She heard that waterfall again, off to her right. That wasn't possible. She hadn't crossed back over the stream, and there had been only one. Only one in Dougal's forest, that was. Maureen could have witched another, or even twisted these trees into a different world. Maureen had done *something* to this forest, anyway. She certainly hadn't just set it free. And Fiona couldn't believe that a novice to Power could have hidden her traps and manipulations this well. No matter how strong the Blood she bore. She had to have had help.

And it seemed like it had been hours since Fiona had last

heard news of that dragon. Either the beast was dead, or it had betrayed her. Likewise with her other allies.

She faced a dense wall of thornbush and hooked briar, opaque and interwoven like her own hedge. Dead leaves rattled against limbs in the depths of it, and she felt her own trademark turned into a blade against her. She'd killed that hawthorn once already. Killed it and the blackthorn tangled with it and forced a path to lead past it——how could it have moved ahead of her and joined a thicket and have fresh green-golden buds bursting out of dead wood and wilting leaves?

Her head spun, and she squeezed her eyes shut until the vertigo passed. Downhill lay on her right hand, not her left. She needed to climb, climb the stony knob and reach the old keep that had crowned it for time out of mind. But the damned redhead's enchantment had kept forcing her to the left, left, left, across the slope and down. Now it shone a funhouse mirror in her face and forced her to her right.

It drank Power. Each step dragged at her, cold hands clutching her feet and ankles and calves as if she waded hip-deep through the rotting mucky bottom of the dragon's marsh. She reached into the child within her belly, drawing on it to help her battle forward another step and another.

Forward, not back, a conquistador with his ships burning on the beach behind him. Fiona shivered. She'd heard feet walking her fields, across the distance and the forest, feet the grass had never known before, and the hedge had screamed terror and pain before the touch of it twanged like a broken harp-string and went silent. That had stolen her last sense of reference and direction, cast her loose from the one firm anchor in her worlds.

She was lost. She was scared. She'd never been lost or scared before, in over a century of spells and wanderings and bitter enemies. That redheaded bitch would pay for this.

The baby kicked at her again, and she hated it. Her back

ached from the swell and awkwardness hanging low in front of her, her ankles and feet hurt from the unaccustomed weight, her stomach and bladder and bowels complained of its crowding presence. It was a parasite, gnawing away inside her belly.

And it hadn't given her the strength that the legends had promised. Oh, her Power had swelled with her belly, but not enough. Not doubled. Not if this forest was any gauge.

She stared at her hand, flexing each muscle, each joint, spreading her fingers, feeling the throb of her racing heartbeat in them, a beginner's exercise in control and concentration that she hadn't needed since Brian was in diapers. She closed her eyes and followed the threads of Power flowing from those fingers, flowing to those fingers, the threads tying her to Cáitlin and Fergus and the dragon hatchlings, the threads pulling Power from the air and soil and stone around her. Cáitlin and the stupid little horrors in the swamp hung as blind lumps at the ends of her puppet strings, unconscious, while Fergus had vanished into death. She wondered why Cáitlin hadn't died yet.

The forest walled her off from Sight, squeezed the flow of Power to a trickle. It had always brimmed with magic and deception, the Enchanted Forest of a thousand legends, home to dragons and unicorns. It couldn't bar her totally from Power, but she felt its hostile guard like a dam across a river. It hated her.

She considered killing the small dragons. She could do it, simply close her fingers on the pulses of their threads and send the pressure down those lines of Power. Their hearts and lungs would stop. But that would take more Power than simply holding them. She didn't have that Power to waste.

And she was beginning to think she might need them as barter. Barter for her own life.

*Does Maureen save Cáitlin for a slave? Will she try the same with me? Stronger or not, that will never happen. She'll have to kill me. She didn't have the guts for that, the last time we met.*

*And when we're face to face this time, the brat in my belly could provide a final surprise.*

Fiona smiled quietly, her eyes narrowing as she surveyed the forest around her. This game still played on. Some things Maureen wouldn't know. Some things she wouldn't consider even if she knew. The redheaded bitch might be stronger than Fiona had believed possible, but humans and Christians always turned weak when it counted. They believed in foolish things like setting rules for war.

*Survival doesn't have rules.*

The baby kicked again, a strange feeling that began high in Fiona's belly and rippled down to her hips like a wave. Hot liquid gushed between her thighs. She bent around the cramping in her belly and stared in horror at her ruined slacks.

*I* can't *go into labor now!*

Another wave buckled her knees to the turf. *This should start slower. All the books said it should start slower, with minutes or even hours between the cramps. Labor can go on for days.*

But she'd never given birth before. Because of the hybrid curse, few witches ever quickened, and none she'd trusted with her plans. She'd studied *human* books.

And she'd rushed the pregnancy.

She wobbled to her feet, grunting with the effort. Her Power drew into itself, into the ungainly balloon lump of her belly, and ignored her. The voice of the stream called to her. It offered cool solace for her sweat and the heat flashing through her body. And the forest opened a way, passing her to stagger downhill, step by step. She paused as the next wave surged through her belly, and she moaned with the cramping pain of it.

It passed through darkness and left her head spinning.

She knelt in a clearing, in sunlight on soft grass, gathering the fragments of her thoughts together. *Grass, in Dougal's forest? I've never seen this place before. The only grass was on the crest, a clear field of fire around his walls.*

It was a trap. It *had* to be a trap. The forest had fought her for hours—for days, it seemed. It had *never* been a safe place for strangers, under Dougal's hand or for generations out of time. Now it turned gentle and offered her a soft bed for birthing?

She felt the jaws of the trap closing around her. It forced her to her feet, and she wobbled on, cradling her belly in both hands, each step a focus and an effort. Water. She needed water—cool, cleansing, reviving water. That would clear her head.

Another cramp surged through her womb, and she dropped onto all fours, hands and knees splashing into cold. The stream tugged at her, swift and wet up to her elbows and her thighs. She didn't ask how she'd come to it, just lowered her face into it and drank and ducked her head and let the soothing cool flow down her neck. She burned with a fever centered behind her navel, pulsing with the ripples of each contraction.

Power. That was Power she felt, and she sucked on it and used it, heedless of the baby, dragging her zombie-stiff body back to the stream's edge and out on thick soft moss. The cramp passed, and she flopped on her side, so limp that she felt boneless.

Cold wet wool clammy around her thighs and calves, pressure in her bowels and bladder, mindless frenzy stripping off her slacks and stockings and underwear to squat awkwardly on the moss, fouling her own legs. Instinct sent her crawling back into the stream to wash and huddle, half-naked, in the icy water as another cramp rolled from her breasts all the way down to her knees.

Soothing water flowed around her legs, her hips, easing

the cramps and washing mess away. She splashed it on her belly, up under her sweater on her damp hot aching breasts, cupped it and tossed it in her face and on her neck and soaked it into her hair. She felt it draining Power from her, from her belly and from the child there, and knew the forest's trap. It would draw her weakness in and suck the baby from her womb and drown both of them, pull their bones down into Dougal's sinkhole and the black caverns that drained the base of the waterfall.

*This brat may die, but not for someone else's purpose.*

Back to the streamside, crawling, whimpering like a beaten dog, climbing the bank suddenly steep and greasy against her, again drawing Power from the baby to sink her fingers and toes into moss and mud, reverting to an animal as each cramp stripped away more of her mind and will. She forced herself into a single core, diamond hard and diamond bright, survival at whatever price.

Strength flowed from hate and focused on Maureen. That redheaded bitch had formed a trap, lied and lured and schemed with the dragon and the forest. Must draw her to this place, draw her to gloat in triumph, turn that triumph into defeat through one last twist of Power only hinted at in legend. The bitch would never think of it, never believe and expect it even if she knew. No mother would do *that*.

A black shadow formed under the trees, sleek and flowing and deadly. Dougal's mutated leopard. Cáitlin had seen it haunting the forest. Seen it acting as Maureen's pet, a set of eyes and ears and fangs to do the forest's bidding. It sat on its haunches and watched, cool, detached, grooming one paw with a fraction of its attention.

Another pang surged through her belly, blanking all thought, and she panted against the wrenching pain. Tears and sweat stung her eyes to blurring, and when she could see again, a fox waited, ears alert, on the far side of the clearing from the leopard, looking to sneak scraps from the big cat's kill. Ravens croaked down into the clearing, rattling their feathers into place after they swooped to land in the surrounding branches. All of the predators and scavengers gathered, smelling the birth, smelling the chance of a feast with both mother and child weakened beyond fighting. They saw an easy meal.

But she kept a few surprises in reserve.

Time vanished and became eternity, and the sun moved by ratcheted jumps across the sky between one contraction and the next. And then one scream and the next. Her universe shrank to her belly and the dilating gap between her legs. With each contraction, Power swelled to the flood and then shrank away like the tides, but it ignored her and she couldn't touch it.

A wave took her squatting, screaming through clenched teeth, and she fell forward on her hands and knees again and forced her jaws open to gasp for breath. Pain ripped at her crotch. Instinct tightened her belly and the muscles in her hips, and she forced the lump down, down, down, ridding herself of the burden. Wet slimy flesh extruded between her legs and paused and extruded and paused with the troughs of the pulsing waves and then slipped free.

She collapsed on her side.

Now the leopard would attack. She didn't care. Her mind lay blank—survival and cunning and revenge wiped clear by exhaustion. A mild wave took her belly and it felt soothing by comparison, cleansing, ridding her body of tissue and blood and fluids no longer needed. And another, weaker still.

Now Maureen would come. Now, when her enemy lay in exhausted sweat, bleeding, helpless. Now she'd come and gloat and kill.

Fiona groped blindly, feeling through hot slime. She found the lump of the baby, stirring feebly, coughing in thin whines. It didn't even have the strength to cry.

She brought it to her belly, to her chest, to her face, found the cord with her teeth, bit. The blood gushed, sweet in her mouth, and she sucked it, feeling Power and strength flow back into her. Something moved in the corner of her eye, and her teeth darted to the baby's throat. Just one bite . . .

She smelled the blood, smelled the Power, hungered for it, trembled for it. The baby was too weak to live. It could still serve her, feed her emptiness. Her jaws locked, unable to close.

"You will *not* kill that child!"

The red fur of the fox morphed into red hair around blazing rage. She'd never seen a face like that, never dreamed one of her enemies could show such naked Power. Fiona cringed, holding her frozen jaws tight in the notch between the baby's chin and shoulder. She tasted skin, tasted her own blood and fluids on it, felt a thin pulse against her tongue and lips, but she couldn't bite.

Her right hand pressed the baby to her mouth. She tried to claw at the child, spilling its precious Power on her own skin if she couldn't swallow it. Maureen's fingers grabbed hers, bending, trembling, holding with muscle while Power flowed elsewhere. Fiona pulled her strength into hand and jaw and eyes, glaring rage at her enemy above the child's body. Face to face, nose to nose, sweat and smell mixing, they froze into a standoff.

Fiona glanced out of the corners of her eyes. The black cat crouched there, less than an arm's length to her right, tension in every quivering muscle, with his ears and whiskers laid back. His tail thrashed.

<One could kill you easily.>

<Move and the baby dies.> Even blocked as she was, she could kill the baby. It was still a weapon, against a sentimental weakling like Maureen.

Fiona reached out and groped with her other hand, hunting for the wet slick skin of the child's back. Press it against her, and the breathing would stop; the heart would stop.

Teeth clamped on her wrist, tight as a vise, driving pain through the skin into muscle and grating on the bone. The fox. It had to be the fox, another of Maureen's puppets.

Fiona walled the pain away and drew back into her self. She groped for the words and workings of a curse, but they wouldn't come. The birth had drained even her hatred. Cunning, though—that she still had, twisting through the fog shrouding her thoughts.

Cunning and the baby and some little dragons if it came to that.

Weapons.

That redheaded bitch would weaken soon. She was relying on sheer will, no time for spells or bindings. Commanding another Old One's muscles gulped Power the way that dragon swallowed meat. Maureen would weaken and lose control and Fiona would bite into the tender skin just touching her lips and drink the blood pulsing underneath and strike back with the Power flowing in it.

Revenge. She could taste it now, smooth and heady like the finest wine.

Like blood.

# twenty-five

—⟶⟶—

"BLESS ME, FATHER, for I have sinned." Jo stared down into the chalice in her hand, into the red wine shimmering inside cut-glass crystal. If the Church offered communion wine like *this,* damn sure they'd draw a bigger crowd for Mass. The stuff tasted like ambrosia brought down to earth.

Sinned big-time, that's for sure. Patricide would rank up there pretty far in the all-time top ten Hit Parade.

Thick-stemmed crystal goblet, cut glass and heavy but delicate, scarlet fire where she held it in the thin blade of sunlight leaking through the shutters. Scattered rainbows from the facets. Wealth and elegance. Blood.

The wine burned red like blood glowing with the inner fire of magic. Magic she'd used to murder her own father.

She'd grabbed the goblet and bottles of wine on the way up to this refuge, looking to get blind drunk. Then, between the opening and the drinking, she'd thought about Maureen. Maureen and alcohol, bane of the Pierce and O'Brian bloodlines. Thinking of that, she'd barely sipped the stuff.

Orange weight oozed between her and the wine. It settled into her lap, pin-prick of claws and warmth and fur and fish-breath. Cat. Maureen had acquired cats somewhere, three of them. Had the run of the castle, kept the mice at bay.

<You have work to do.>

Talking cats. It figured. Maureen *would* have talking cats.

<Pay attention. You are needed.>

Imperious talking cats. Jo stared into green slit-pupil eyes. They glowed in the gloom of the shuttered room. Magic.

Shivers ran across her shoulders and down her spine. Suddenly she felt cold, in spite of the wine. Cold, the cold of watching stone, waiting, calculating. Everything in this land watched, calculated, weighing advantage and Power. She felt the spiders thinking in their webs, measuring air currents and the spiral vibrations down the strands, sifting for the touch of dinner. It could drive her mad, if she weren't already there.

The eyes floated closer, closer, clear and green and glowing and hypnotic. Jo felt her own eyes crossing, trying to keep focus. Fur bumped her nose, short and bristly with static.

<You have *work* to do.>

And how the hell had a cat followed her into this room? She'd barred the door. She remembered that quite clearly, and she hadn't seen any cats. None. No leprechauns sleeping against the far wall, either. Just bare stone walls, stone floor, stone vaulted ceiling, and a lot of dust. Nobody had used this room for decades. Maybe centuries. She'd brought the wine bottles and goblet with her.

*Leprechaun?*

He lay slumped against the far wall, by the door, a small brown-skinned man in ragged clothing and bare feet.

"Who the hell are *you*?"

She set the goblet down, careful of its heavy fragile beauty,

careful of the godawful cost and labor of it and of the priceless
rotted grape juice that it carried. No need to worry about a
job in *this* place. Maureen was rich. So whyinhell did the cat
keep talking about work?

<There is pain, and you can ease it. Come.>

A paw batted her cheek, just the pad, no claws. The cat
flowed off her lap. It turned its head back over its shoulder,
*his* shoulder; she could plainly see his potent maleness, and
he stared at her and then at the huddled form slumped
against the far wall, by the door. The barred door, just as she
remembered.

Jeezum. The room spun around her, almost as if she had
chugged all that wine. This place seriously creeped her out,
people and cats that ignored locked doors. She forced herself
to hands and knees. No way she was going to try to stand
up. But hands and knees were still a reliable, four-point
stance that didn't depend on a mental gyroscope for stability. Why'd humans ever switched?

<Trading stability for thumbs. Nor are you human.>

*Right. Thanks for the reminder.*

The leprechaun stank. Not just BO and need of a bath,
unless the Little People had some strange metabolisms. He
smelled like he'd been left too long in the back of the refrigerator, rotting meat. Dead meat.

<He lives. The Stone needs him.>

Jo heard that capitalized title, loud and clear. The cat
meant something specific, not the generic stone surrounding her. Stonehenge came to mind, or one of those rough-
hewn windswept monoliths on an Irish hill. Grandfather
O'Brian used to say that people left offerings at such places—
a bowl of cereal, spring flowers, a dead rabbit, a bottle of
*uisce beatha*. Placate the old gods of the land. The offerings
disappeared, between the evening and the dawning.

The Stone wanted this scarred lump as a sacrifice?

<The Stone wishes him to live. You have the Power to make it so.>

She heard that capital as well. But she'd *tried* using her Blood to heal, and failed.

<Your mother did not wish for healing.>

In fact, she'd fought against it. Jo remembered the old Naskeag woman, speaking, soothing, calming, after all the thunder and stink and blood. Mom's spirit beating at the walls of her body like a trapped bird, longing to be free. Longing to die.

Did this little man wish to live?

She ignored the cat. It was just a figment of psychosis, anyway. She touched hot dry skin, felt the weak and racing pulse under it, felt the spreading death in blood and lymph. Her fingers traced scars old and new, followed rivers of pain, felt weakening lines of Power, slipped into feverish dreams of a labyrinthine pattern etched in fire. A core of stone waited, deep inside, not cold stone or ash but living brilliance of rainbow gems in the sun. Yes, this man still wished to live. Did he deserve healing?

He wasn't evil. She could feel that, as well. He didn't love people, didn't care whether most people lived or died, but he did love stone. He loved this pile of stone around her. He loved its heart and . . . grieved for it?

Yes. Grief. Grief and rage at some scar or vandalism and a way of healing twisted through his fever dreams. But his heart felt nothing like her father's, nothing like Sean's. Calculation, but no malice.

Green threads bound him, draining Power beyond the poisons in his blood. Vines, twisting evil vines of magic that sucked at his life and thoughts and fed them back to another. Jo shuddered. Her loathing burned the tether, cutting the small man loose and leaving the orphaned vines to shrivel into dust.

His scars faded, but the livid infection still raged through his body. It would kill him, kill him soon. His own Power couldn't touch it.

Sweat dripped down Jo's forehead and stung her eyes. His fever burned in *her* veins, devouring the wine. Even the heat could kill. She reached to one side and found the goblet and drained it, ignoring the creepy feeling that it had followed her across the floor on magic feet. She let the alcohol flow straight through her body and the touch of her hand on his arm and turn its fire into cooling evaporation. He shuddered under her hands, relaxing as the binding died.

Bandages wrapped his arm, hiding the source of the infection. She tore them, her fingernails sharp as knives, and found black oozing sores underneath, and curved rows of pits down through his flesh. She gagged on the stench. Gangrene. A vision touched her, the black dragon she'd faced in the forest shrunk small and mindless, twisting claws and teeth and sudden pain and blood. Those tooth-marks would fit the curve of such a jaw.

Jo's shoulder muscles burned with strain. She reached back in her mind, seeking the Power, and the Stone responded. Power flowed from the heart of the keep, and she sent it pulsing through the man's blood and bone and nerve.

He writhed under her hand, slick now with sweat, the Power eating poisons and microbes, and he screamed. More wine foamed into the goblet, and she stared into it and willed the water in it *elsewhere* and transmuted wine into brandy. Alcohol splashed the arm, killing, sterilizing; alcohol flowed into the man's veins at a concentration that would kill *him* if she didn't guard his brain and guts and healthy tissue, but she didn't have the time to summon penicillin or other modern magic. She didn't have the time for them to work.

Complex poisons tainted his blood, and she lacked understanding of how they worked. *Fuck this,* and she broke the chains of molecules as she'd broken the binding vines. The molecules no longer killed. Her power swept the tattered remnants into his liver and left them there for cleansing. Brandy oozed from his pores, undigested alcohol cooling her patient's fever as it evaporated.

He shuddered and lay still.

Jo rocked back on her heels, exhausted, head spinning. Dead flesh peeled from the wounds as she watched, dry, falling as black flakes and harmless dust. They left deep pits behind, shiny with scar tissue. She didn't know if he'd ever use that arm again, with so much muscle damage. Call in the rehab therapists. Different specialty.

<He will live. He will work again. The Stone embraces you and protects you.>

The cat licked her fingers, wet cold rasping tongue soothing the burn where Power had flowed stronger than her flesh could bear. It had left her limp, the same wrung-out dishrag feeling she remembered from her killing rage, but this time a man lived because of her.

This time she felt clean. She'd *healed* someone.

She couldn't make sense of what she'd done. By all she knew, that concentration of alcohol should have killed the man. Embalmed him. Instead, it had cured him. Maybe it had been metaphor, her brain turning the magic into forms it could understand. But the tower reeked of brandy, and all the wine bottles lay empty on the floor. Still sealed.

<Do not try to fit magic into the framework of human medicine. Results matter, not methodology.>

Five-syllable words from a *cat*? But the message rang clear, whether it came from her own subconscious or the broad flat head of an orange tomcat or from the stones around her and the glowing heart she'd sensed in that pattern of fire buried in the man's fevered dreams. Results mattered.

She remembered the old Naskeag's words about magic. "Nothing to be ashamed of, child. Nothing bad. Just how you use it, that's all that matters."

Jo *could* use her Power to heal.

Ease flowed into her. Killing Sean, killing Daddy, those had been a form of healing. Those men had been pathogens, just as much as the bacteria she'd banished from this patient sleeping under her hand. Daddy had been an overgrown form of the AIDS bug, killing his family slowly across decades. Look what he'd done to Mom and Maureen.

*Look what he did to you, for Chrissakes, thirty-two years old and just groping your way into your first healthy relationship with a man. You think what you did with Buddy and all the others was any less sick than Maureen's fear?*

Jo shivered. David was the first lover she'd ever had, *lover* as opposed to sex toy. She gritted her teeth as pieces fell into place and the puzzle formed a picture. Most of the others had been modeled on Daddy, one way or another, starting out with Buddy. She'd only met David because Maureen had brought him home . . .

Her heart froze. Jesus Christ and all the angels, *David*. She'd been so busy running away from herself, she'd left David behind. And he couldn't come here by himself. She had to go back.

<The Tree has spoken to the Stone. There are other paths between the worlds. Your mate comes.>

Relief flooded through her. If she was going to fuck up that badly, she was sure as hell glad to have a safety net she could trust. "The Tree" must be Maureen's Father Oak. She felt his strong rough bark again, smelled his bitter tannin and damp moss. His Power touched her for an instant, instantly familiar.

<Few understand the Power hidden within trust. You and your blood bring a new thing to this world. Believe in it. Trust defends you now.>

She couldn't decide whether that was Father Oak speaking, or the Stone, or the cat warm in her lap. Or all of them combined.

<Come.>

The orange tom flowed off her lap again and stretched from end to end and marched to the door, tail up. He sat down and stared up at the bar. Apparently he wasn't going to walk through the wall while anyone was watching.

"I thought I was done. You said this man would live."

<Others suffer.>

She staggered to her feet, woozy from the flow of Power and exhaustion. Her shirt stuck to her shoulder blades and she stank of sweat. Didn't Maureen have a hot-tub somewhere in this pile of rocks? A good long soak, waiting for David to show up . . .

<You have work to do.>

Insistent little bastard. Persistent. Whatever. Words tangled up in her head, a symptom of exhaustion. Or maybe all that alcohol hadn't burned away. She unbarred the door and stepped out into the stairwell, to face two more cats. They wanted her to go down. She followed them, hand on the wall and careful of her footing, fingertips drawing strength and clarity from the rough stone as she went. By the time they reached the bottom, she felt almost human. Or whatever.

The cats led her into the great hall and the stink of sickness. A compound of vomit, piss, shit, rot, rancid fever-sweat, all the sickroom stench they'd kept under control at the nursing home—it roared in her nose and wiped questions of her own need for a bath off the slate. Dozens of bodies lay swathed on the floor, thrashing in pain and fever or lying ominously still. Drifts of straw padded the floor and soaked up the worst of the fluids, but the scene looked more like a pigsty than a hospital. At least she was wearing boots . . .

Maureen had mentioned some refugees, humans fleeing an attack. She hadn't mentioned *this*. God above, even the stones felt the pain and mourning.

Or maybe Jo just hadn't heard. She hadn't been exactly . . . rational . . . when she arrived.

The nearest form lay still, eyes open and empty, staring at the ceiling. Jo thought the woman was dead, until she saw the slight rise and fall of her chest. She knelt on a dry patch of straw and laid her palm on the woman's forehead. Cold. Empty. Deep inside, she felt the same deep-locked vault of pain and fear she'd found in her mother's head. And inside *that,* she found freeze-frame images of flame and blood and butchered children, and a brutal rapist who looked a lot like Daddy. Or maybe Jo painted her own memories into the picture.

Her hand jerked back, and she shivered. The Power reached out again, using her hand, and the images grew again, but as each one reached clarity, it crumbled into ash. Fire—gone. Blood—gone. Children—gone. And the rape, oh, yes, the leering drooling rape, wiped into blankness that left no memory of the last days of the sacked and ravaged keep, the burned village.

That was all she could do: Leave a gap in the woman's life where horror had passed through. Maybe the poor wretch could live with what was left.

Her head hurt. Jo wasn't sure whether it was her own head, or the woman's. She staggered to her feet and moved to the next makeshift bed. She knelt and touched skin again, reading pain. This one was fever, second- and third-degree burns, an infection. At least the leprechaun up in the tower had trained her for those. She pulled more Power out of the stone beneath her feet.

She stood up. She staggered, groping for the wall to hold her up, and her head hurt.

"Is there any coffee in this shithole?"

A man appeared at her elbow, steaming mug in his hand. She swallowed two gulps, savored the heat and bitterness of it, and let her eyes come into focus. That was *good* coffee, just like the wine had been good wine. And her head eased. Caffeine withdrawal, not a hangover.

The man studied her eyes for a moment and then blinked. He seemed to relax. "You're not Maureen." He was tall and thin-ish, with long blond hair pulled back into a ponytail. Her nose told her he was human. She was having trouble getting used to this species thing.

"I'm Padric. If you need anything, just ask."

*Padric?* Maureen's jailer, and she'd let him *live?* That girl was turning into a Christian in her old age.

The next one was dying, no question, shock and blood loss and infection and he didn't want to live after what he'd seen and lost. But he seemed to feel her near and opened his eyes. They focused on her crucifix, and his fingers stirred. Jo pulled the chain over her head and set Grandfather O'Brian's gift in the man's hands and closed his fingers around it. He smiled gently. She granted him grace as best she could remember and waited a minute while he died. Then she reclaimed the crucifix and moved on, numb, to another bleeding, sweat-soaked body.

And another. And another. She moved through a daze, no longer noticing the stench, dead to the pain, sustained by Power drawn from the keep and the solid stone on which it sat.

And then she came to one who lived in terror, a broken leg and bruises but nothing that threatened his life. She sank into his thoughts, seeking the fear, bringing oblivion to wipe out the horror once again. She touched memories, and recoiled. They'd promised safety and wealth . . .

"He was a spy."

She staggered to her feet, retreating, suddenly frantic for fresh air and sunshine. She heard mutterings spread across the room behind her, stirrings of the whole among the broken, and she didn't want to see what happened next.

Padric held her elbow, guiding her from the hall. She ached all over, every inch of her body where one or another of the wrecked bodies suffered. Images of fire and blood and destruction fogged the stone around her. Her knees wobbled, and she slumped against the wall.

&lt;Go to the gate. Hatred approaches.&gt;

That wasn't the cat. The stone walls spoke to her, voices of delirium, warning of danger. And she could barely walk.

# twenty-six

—◆◆◆—

I𝚏 THE LE𝚏T transept hid a stair down to the crypt, what about the right? Brian remembered that Gothic builders didn't insist on symmetry, but he didn't have time for random searching. The door thumped again, prodding him.

A shadow opened in the floor at the mirror point, another blind black stair, and he felt his way downward and around and around and downward, favoring the ache in his leg, to another flickering lamp and another corridor and more bones. The Pendragons had buried a lot of dead, down through the centuries. He wondered if the two crypts joined, if there was a direct route between the relic and the labyrinth. Dierdre had wanted to be found at the altar, so there'd be no clue that she'd been the one to show Brian the way out.

Complicated plot, but that was her specialty.

The air smelled different, less dust, more dirt, more moisture, more greasy tang from oil smoke. The end of the corridor opened out into a small room with lamps all around, square, with another buried menhir in the center. This one lacked the carved niche for a cross. A familiar pattern traced across the floor.

He hoped it led back to Maureen.

Brian took three deep breaths, calming and centering himself. Dierdre had bloody well told him he'd have to kill someone the instant he walked this pattern. Probably someone he knew. She knew he hated jumping into combat blind.

And then she'd proceeded to half cripple him, just to add to the fun. What the hell was Dierdre up to? Things she'd said and done indicated that she respected him, even if they cordially hated each other. That wasn't enough reason to let him go. She had a sense of duty, a sense of allegiance owed and the need to do ugly things when necessary. God above, she was good at that. And she'd never let small questions of guilt or innocence bother her before.

He flexed his left leg, wincing at the deep muscle pain from her kick, twisted his torso, and asked it if she had truly broken those ribs in their intimate tango of interrogation or had only bruised them. But he couldn't waste time on healing. He had to walk the labyrinth before Merlin's magic counted down its heartbeats and blocked him from the passage. Before someone broke that door open and found Dierdre lying battered and unconscious at the altar.

Maybe she felt she had a duty to Mulvaney and his betrayed honor? More likely this was Machiavellian office politics, a way to tie Brian and Duncan together and destroy an enemy blocking her path. Duncan she didn't even respect, and the hate she'd shown in flashes down the years had nothing cordial to it.

Dim shouting echoed down from above. They were in.

He shook his head and cleared it. He couldn't waste time on thinking, either. He wiped the sweat from his hands and focused on the stone pattern set into the floor, remembering the Way he'd walked that other hidden pattern, dropping his mind into the Zen archer. He placed his right foot squarely on the line, and walked. As he walked, he drew the *kukri* from his belt and carried the bare steel balanced in his hand. Its calm weight was a comfort. Steel was always calm.

Again the room fell away from his concentration, from his meditation, as he became the stepping of his feet and then the clockwise inward spiral of the line they were stepping on. He visualized the arrow touching the tip of his nose and turned his head aside and closed his eyes, letting the target grow in his mind, draw nearer, swell until it filled the world.

He was the archer and the bow and the arrow and the target all in one, and the target loosed him to fly free. Power warmed him and drew him and he sank into the heart of it. He felt it flooding to a peak, this time, and beyond where the other Way was blocked. He couldn't miss.

"Halt! Who goes there?"

The words echoed in a hollow space, even though they had been spoken into dead silence rather than shouted, and they carried the feel of boredom. Brian had spent his time on sentry-go and knew the flavor well.

"Brian Albion."

"Huh?" And the man shook his head from the shadows. "Anzac."

Sign and countersign. Reflex answered, "Gallipoli."

"Advance and be recognized."

Brian stepped across the lines of the labyrinth, shielding his knife in the gloom. *Have to talk to the head of security about predictable passwords, traditions be damned. But that would be Dierdre, of course. At least she's told you that today is April twenty-fifth, somewhere under Glastonbury.*

*If she wasn't lying about where the pattern took you.*

The sentry stood in shadow, peering at a list and clutching a submachine gun in his other hand, pointed at the ceiling. Brian gritted his teeth and then forced himself to relax.

He concentrated on walking casually, the pace of a man who belonged. Body language could lie as persuasively as words . . .

Or broadcast the truth. The guard's fingers tightened on his SMG, and the *kukri* flew before Brian realized his hand had moved. Time did its battlefield trick where he swore he could see bullets in flight, and the muzzle of the 9mm swung down toward him and the *kukri* spun glinting through the air and orange sparks lit the bore and both he and the guard grunted surprise and impact and pain.

Spent shell casings tinkled across stone. Brian sank to his knees, swaying gently. The guard collapsed with a faint gurgle, one hand clutching the hilt of the *kukri* where it protruded above his left clavicle. Strange target, but Brian hadn't chosen it. The knife and his eyes and arm and fifty years of combat had made the decision for him, judging the bulk of the uniform as body armor and changing his aim in midswing.

He waited a moment, wondering why he could hear such things as the shell casings and the rustle of cloth as the man fell. He should be damn near deaf, with a 9mm fired in a tight space walled with stone. Suppressor. What the Yanks would call a silencer. So maybe the other guard wouldn't be here in seconds, or wasn't already taking aim from distant shadows.

He explored his left arm, finding blood hot and oily on the sleeve. The guard hadn't quite traversed far enough before he'd fired. Maybe had his weapon set for a three-shot burst rather than full auto, so he didn't keep firing as he fell and his fingers jerked in dying reflex. Forearm wound, a glancing furrow, Brian's fingers told him that the bone remained whole and major blood vessels intact. He'd had far worse before.

But his left side was another matter.

Brian sighed, gently, gently, his breath limited by stabs

of pain. *That* one felt nasty. Descending colon, his body told him, perforation and leakage. Classic gut wound. Prognosis— massive infection, ugly lingering death without immediate surgery and antibiotics.

For a human.

His abdominal muscles writhed, he curled around the fire blazing through his gut, and a hard lump slithered down inside his shirt. Just one slug. He gritted his teeth as the flames spread out from his side, his body ripping pathogens into shreds and knitting tissue across the ravages of the wound. He reached out for Power, felt it slipping away from him, couldn't grasp it. Merlin again, blocking, controlling, even after centuries. The old bastard wouldn't allow competing magic in this space.

He blinked swirling dots from his eyes and staggered to his feet, mopping sweat from his forehead with his sleeve. His ears buzzed. Cumulative effect, the wounds and Dierdre's multiple gifts and the shock of finding something slimy crawling out from behind the Pendragons' crest. Plus, he hadn't had anything to eat or drink since leaving Naskeag Falls. Damn good thing he'd kept in training . . .

And now he had to find out who he'd killed.

He nerved himself and stumbled the distance the knife had flashed in a second and stared down at the corpse. He'd killed before, more times than he could count, mostly strangers in the wrong clothing who'd been trying to kill him. Sometimes men or women he'd known and loathed with a consuming passion, like Liam. Never anyone who had been a friend or ally.

Healing tissues blazed again as he knelt by the body, avoiding the really excessive splash of blood you get when you cut the carotid artery, and turned the face to the flickering light of oil lamps. Young, but all the Old Blood looked young for a century or more. Straw blond, dark eyes frozen wide with pain and the surprise that death was real.

Nobody he knew.

Brian grunted with the effort of jerking his knife out of bone. He wiped it on the loose uniform, another of those stupid purple Renaissance things the Pendragons seemed to affect for their secret Inner Circle. He felt the hardness under it, some kind of flak jacket of plates laminated with Kevlar fabric. Hand and eyes had read it right. He carved long strips of velvet from the outer sleeve and wrapped them as a pressure bandage around his forearm. He couldn't waste Power on healing minor problems. The major ones needed far more than he had.

The SMG *did* have a suppressor screwed to the muzzle. He studied the weapon for a moment. Standard Pendragon issue, which meant it had been keyed to the sentry's hand. Wouldn't do Brian any good until he found half an hour and some tools to bugger the mechanism, and the blood on it might serve as a beacon to any tracker. He left it where it lay.

*Now to get the hell out of here.* He groaned to his feet, fixed the pasture oak in his head, not taking chances, and forced the three steps necessary to move from one world to the next. Then he shook his head. The gloomy labyrinth and grotto still walled him in. Merlin again, with his layers upon layers of defense. The man must have been a certifiable paranoid.

So Brian would have to do it the hard way. He tested his body again, gently twisting, bending, swinging his right arm and grimacing at the effect that had on his left side. Those muscles tied into everything. Then he took a deep breath, nearly collapsed as that stabbed him in the gut, forced himself upright, and strolled up the corridor beyond the corpse, again doing his best to counterfeit the air of someone who belonged. In spite of all the blood staining his arm and side.

Flickering oil lamps glowed from niches in the walls, barely lighting the way, looking like they'd been put there by the Romans or by the Picts and Scots before them. Black soot shone with a greasy glaze on the walls, centuries of oil vapor condensed on the cold damp stone. The flagged stone floor had been worn smooth by millennia of feet. *Just keep putting one bloody foot in front of the other. Sooner or later, this buggering ramp has to end.* His rubbery legs told him otherwise, told him the climb stretched for miles.

He concentrated on the *kukri* in his hand, heavy, strong, calm. Deadly, like the men who carried its brothers. The touch raised shouts of *"Ayo Gorkhali"* in his ears, wars long ago and far away and a mental salute from the Gurkhas he'd led into battle. They marched indomitable across his memories, lending him strength and will from a cooling spring that had seemed endless. Like Maureen's strength and will.

The corridor spiraled up and outward, a long corkscrew widdershins in the climb, deasil on the descent, like a snail shell or the labyrinth itself.

And then a shape formed out of the gloom, a man, the back of a man standing at a formal "parade rest" and watching closed-circuit TV monitors mounted on the ceiling. Brian crept along doing his best imitation of a ghost. He could try to disable, or he could kill.

The second guard kept watching outward like a dutiful soldier because his mate was guarding his back. Brian lifted his knife, fire blazed through his wounded side, and breath hissed between his teeth. The sentry started to turn, weapon rising, and the *kukri* took his head off with a single stroke.

The head fell to one side, body still standing and pumping blood like a fountain for seconds afterward. Then it collapsed all in a heap. Brian almost followed it down; the effort of swinging his arm and the knife left him swaying. He stared down at the weapon, another Pendragon-issue submachine gun. Forget it. Then he knelt and checked the head, even though he wondered if he'd be able to get back up again. He had to find out . . .

Her head. Dark gleaming hair cut short, startled eyes still moving and focusing. Her lips tried to form a word and failed. Claire. Bugger. His gut spasmed, a red-hot iron, and he swallowed sour vomit.

It had to be *Claire*. His eyes blurred for a moment, and he felt his heartbeat stagger. Out of all the possible combinations and permutations of Pendragons, it had to be Claire standing between him and Maureen.

Not exactly a friend, not exactly a lover. You didn't really have friends or lovers inside the Pendragons. But Claire was someone he'd trusted more than once to guard his back. He remembered her long white body in bed, hard and angular and as big as most men's but emphatically female. She'd been bisexual, sometimes had it off with Dierdre. He wondered if *she'd* known who was on duty when she cut her prisoner loose. Her position, she must have.

Bitch.

Plots within plots within plots. Dierdre was beat to shit, broken bones and all, and Brian had killed one of her known lovers. Clues that Dierdre had been a victim of the plot and not its authoress.

And the bitch had a nasty habit of adding two and two and ending up with five or six. He hadn't told her about Claire, about that stumbling gasping run and the words in twos and threes that told him where to find a further refuge. He'd kept the secret. But the evidence said that she knew. This served as punishment for both of them.

He knelt there and cursed and wept, silently in case of any other guards. He'd trusted the Pendragons. He'd bloody well *believed* in them. This was where they'd led him. Killing a friend, a former lover. From behind. Assassination. Murder.

He had to keep moving. He could almost hear the hounds baying on his scent. Brian cleaned his blade again and forced himself to his feet, swaying, leg and arm and side throbbing. Blackness washed across his eyes, and he found himself leaning against the cold stone of the wall. He reached out for Power, hoping, and it came to him grudgingly. Merlin's spells waned with distance. The thin flow let Brian stiffen his knees and clear his sight and dull the flames of half-healed flesh. He could walk again. Slowly.

His head still spun with the convoluted politics this hidden "Circle" had revealed to him. Claire had known about them, been one of them. Each layer he peeled off the onion, the stench got worse.

Dierdre had said there were two sentries. Be just like her if there were actually three or four and he got his ass shot off this close to safety. That might serve her purpose, whatever her purpose was. Brian resumed his jungle stalk, limping and slow, a wounded tiger slipping through the shadows and the tall grass, trusting nothing. And then the corridor ended in a door in stone masonry, a simple blank metal door with a crash bar like any fire exit in any building worldwide.

He tensed, relaxed, balanced the *kukri* in his hand, and nudged the crash bar with his hip. The door swung open, no closer or springs, hit a stop, and bounced back halfway. The room beyond lay empty, a small cell with two doors. The outer one was wood, old, worn, with iron and brass hardware from several centuries ago. He'd seen it in one of the monitors back where Claire had watched . . .

Again he swallowed bile. Dierdre had known exactly what her plot would mean.

The inner door had a modern keypad lock, a high-grade model that Brian had seen in military security. The outer door was set up for a heavy oaken bar that stood waiting on a pivot. No fiddling around, one swipe of your hand and it would thump into place. Even so, that door opened out as a further bulwark against battering rams. Pounding on it would just make it tighter. Generations of paranoia, carved out of oak planks.

It opened into a narrow alley, little more than shoulder-wide and dark under stars, no place to set your battering ram without first taking down the next building. And the alley opened into a dark one-lane street, high brick walls and shuttered windows and blank doors, no eyes on whoever came and went.

He felt the air loosen around him as he staggered to the end of the alley, as if his skin relaxed over his muscles. That must mark the edge of the warding set by Uther's favorite war-wizard. Was it still Merlin's original spell, or had Pendragon mages renewed it through the generations? Bugger-all difference it made, really.

But Power seethed around him, stronger than he'd ever felt in the "real" world, as if it piled up in waves against the dam that held it out of a place where it wanted to go. He gulped it like air to a drowning man. His eyes cleared and the fire of his wounds died back to a glow. He felt his hands shaking and knew he'd pay the price for this tomorrow, but he didn't have a choice. Not if he wished to reach tomorrow.

He found a street sign, memorized it in case he needed to find this place again, and then glanced up and down the sidewalk, fixing the buildings in his mind as well as making sure no one saw him vanish between one step and the next. Not that they'd believe their eyes . . .

But where was he going? Where would Maureen be? More to the point, *when* was he going? How had time been flowing behind his back, with the different streams of the Summer Country and the mist lands and the Pendragons' secret lair and the so-called "real" world?

Then he realized that he *knew* where Maureen was. He'd never heard or read of this before, but he could set her face in his mind and go to *her,* rather than a place. He could go to her, twisting time to her urgent need, and she needed him *now.*

And he needed Maureen, needed the Power of her healing,

needed the clean smell of her to wash foulness from his nose, needed trees around him and sky above instead of old blood-soaked stones that reeked of treachery.

He saw her face in his mind, felt her hand, smelled her heady fragrance, and stepped through darkness to the image. She crouched on grass in a forest clearing, part of a tableau of statuary that included Dougal's black leopard and a fox. And Fiona, naked from the waist down with her face buried in the throat of a newborn baby.

With one hand, Maureen tugged at Fiona's grip on the child. Maureen's other hand clamped the baby's cord. None of it made sense, but instinct told him old Alexander had the right idea. Sometimes you just cut the bloody rope instead of trying to untie it.

Especially if Fiona was involved. He stumbled across the grass and yanked his sister's head back by her sweat-soaked hair, knocking the baby to the grass. Then he had his knife at her throat, shaking, his muscles replaced by Power and will.

She glared up at him, rage and cunning on her face. "If you kill me, the baby dragons die."

That froze his hand. She squirmed away from the sagging blade, eyes frantic and hunting for the baby, screaming as she saw the fox take it gently by one leg and drag it away across the grass.

Maureen shook her head and slumped, squatting back on her haunches. She looked drained. "You . . . dumb . . . *shit*!"

<One trusts that the dog is showing care.> That seemed to be the leopard.

<Call me a dog again and I'll nip your tomcat balls off while you're sleeping.>

"Cut the crap, you guys." Maureen shook her head again, as if flies deviled her. Her face looked pale and hollow, much like he felt, exhausted by fierce magic. She glanced from the cat to the fox. The baby now squirmed feebly on the grass, between the vixen's legs, nosing around for milk.

Then a twist of her head and eyes motioned Brian's knife away from his sister's throat. Maureen's hand flashed out and slapped Fiona hard like a cracking whip.

Brian stared from his sister's flaming cheek to Maureen rubbing her hand. The redhead blew on her palm, cooling the smart of it. "You really *are* a stupid bitch. I ought to let Shadow eat you."

<Is it fit to eat? It smells like carrion. One prefers one's meat fresh and clean. Feed it to the dog.>

<*Dog . . .*>

"Can it, okay?" Maureen wiggled her fingers and spoke to them. "I could get used to this sadist bit. Sometimes giving pain is fun." Her eyes focused back on Fiona. "Other people just don't matter to you, do they? Even your own baby? A true antisocial personality, clinical case. What they used to call a psychopath. Brian tried to warn me, but I didn't take him seriously."

Fiona sneered. "Don't bother with the diagnosis, love. You're no holy gems yourselves, a drunken killer matched to a dumb thug with the smell of death blood on him. How'd you sober up so fast? Must be a useful spell, living the way you do."

Maureen just shook her head again, apparently amused. "That's where the fucking stupid part comes in, *love.* Your spies weren't watching *me.* That was Jo. You were so focused on your hate, you forgot that there are two of us. All your plots and plans, and your big boogeyman isn't even fucking home when you attack. And you weren't fighting *either* of us. You were fighting the forest. It doesn't like you."

<The forest is not alone in that.>

The mental speech boomed, deep and resonant like a cave given voice. Brian turned and reflex moved him back two steps as a bloody huge dragon limped into the clearing, favoring one forepaw. But it glared at Fiona, not him, and David walked unscathed by its side. Brian willed his shoulders to relax.

<But the dark one did not lie. Not this time. It has bound the hatchlings to its own life, and I would ask you to spare it long enough to break the binding.>

"Kill me, kill the hatchlings." Fiona's eyes turned sly and dangerous. "Safe passage to go home, and I'll release them."

*Fiona and Dierdre, sisters under the skin. Always another plot beneath the one you're seeing, and another still beneath the second.* Brian stared at a column of smoke rising beyond the trees, beyond David and the dragon. He measured the angle of the sun and turned it into a compass. "I don't think you'll be going home again, dear sister. Not *this* time."

She twisted to see what he was seeing, paled, and slumped back on the grass. "Gone. My home, my work . . ." She shook her head, biting back other words. Brian wondered just what they'd destroyed.

But she rallied. Fiona *always* rallied. "Safe passage, or I kill the little dragons."

Maureen had picked up the baby and cradled it against her chest. The child stirred weakly and seemed tiny, arms and legs thin even for a newborn. Understanding flashed through Brian's head—that was his child, Fiona's child, rushed to birth as a weapon. He wondered if it could live.

Black rage swallowed those thoughts. For an instant, he could understand Merlin and the Pendragons. Something like Fiona almost justified Dierdre.

Almost.

His rage cleared, and Maureen was speaking. Blood stained her fingers and her lips, Fiona's blood from the birthing, source of a Power that sent shivers down his back.

". . . and you'll never bear another child. May your womb and ovaries shrivel into wood and your womanhood pass from you with the afterbirth. May food and drink taste of ashes in your mouth. May the sun refuse to warm you and the dark deny you rest and the waters never cleanse you of your guilt." Maureen paused and an evil smile crossed her face. "And may all your clothing fit you like a camel draped in a shit-stained ragged tent woven from goat hair."

Ouch. That last one was nasty! Brian grinned in spite of himself. Then he dropped to his knees as the world turned fuzzy.

# twenty-seven

—∾—

<WALK TO THE sun.>

Jo went where the voices told her. First the cats, then the deep green fragrant grass and rough ledge outcrops under her feet, then the ancient trees gray-bearded with moss—they whispered in her ears and told her where she was needed. This land lived and thought. It understood her, understood what she could do that needed doing.

She just hoped she had enough strength left for it. Right now, she was having a hard time walking straight.

She'd never been *needed* before, not in any sense of life-or-death. It felt . . . strange, deeper and more powerful and sustained than sex.

That was the thing about sex, she saw with a sudden wince. It felt good, yes, but there was this ugly secret hiding deeper down: She needed to feel needed. Sex made her feel valuable, at least for a little while. It was an easy way to make men *need* her, Power with the capital "P." Her own form of insanity.

But this wasn't schizophrenia or any other kind of

madness. This was magic, and like most of life, it gave back what you brought to it. Daddy had brought hatred and domination and cruelty to the magic, and it gave back death.

The land had shown her that, and once she understood, Jo felt the guilt start to loosen in her chest. Maybe she'd killed him, but blaming her would be like blaming the ground for a plane crash.

Maureen brought a love of trees and wild things and solitude to the magic, and those things loved her and protected her and gave her balance in return. The magic gave back what she brought to it.

And Jo brought a wish to heal and soothe and nurture and protect. She'd seen enough fucking *pain* in her life—now she could do something about it. Damned if she knew or cared where the Power came from, but those people in the castle . . . their need for healing and safety bordered on ferocity. And she could help them.

She had to stay.

David *must* have some kind of place in this land. But would he want her back? Would he want to come here? She'd hurt him. On purpose. And scared the shit out of him, too; she'd seen it in his face. Jo felt tears running hot down her cheeks, and she wiped the blur out of her eyes.

A body lay in front of her, sprawled facedown near the edge of the forest. The slim build and dark hair reminded her of Sean, but surface and detail and edge seemed vague as if seen through a shimmer of mirage. The land showed her more than her eyes could see. *Illusions.*

She knelt by the figure and touched her fingers to the back of its neck, wondering if this was a refugee who'd died before reaching the castle. Jo let her senses sink into the skin, finding a woman, alive, skin warm and pulse beating strong, felled by a blow to the back of the head. No permanent damage. Nothing here of the images of terror and fire and blood she'd found in the refugees. Instead, she found the same twisting coils of magic that had bound the man she'd healed in the tower.

Jo growled deep in her throat, feral rage at what she found and felt. *Fucking bastards . . .*

The Old Ones kept slaves. People, trees and grass, the dragons and the cats, even the stones of the castle on the hill—slaves bound to the wills of the Old Ones. Like Daddy had bound his family.

She had the Power to stop that shit.

Jo gathered the strands of binding in her hands, tearing them loose from the woman and ripping them into shreds with her anger. She tugged on the magic cord that had connected them and found the way it led, downhill and into the forest. A quick jerk brought fear and deep exhaustion pulsing back, and she followed them. Strength flowed into Jo, welling up from the soil beneath her feet.

The forest had changed since she walked it last. Now it welcomed her and supported her, offering a soft smooth trail underfoot and a clean smell of leaves and soil and water. The hate and fear and sense of danger had vanished. This was the other face of the Enchanted Forest, enchantment as love and joy.

Now this felt like Maureen's forest—Maureen climbing high in a limber sapling birch and swinging it down like the boy in Frost's poem. Maureen turning over rocks in the stream and squealing with delight as she captured a tail-snapping crawfish for inspection. Maureen flat on her belly peering into a chipmunk's hollow log and reaching in and pulling out a handful of beechnuts and cracking one to eat but putting the rest back because the furball needed a good stash to survive the winter.

<You are indeed our sister.>

A red fox stretched sphinx-like on the trail, pink tongue lolling out of open jaws as if the animal was laughing. So the Land of Faery had a lighter face?

<Faery, like magic, can resemble what you bring to it.>

The fox stood by halves, rear and front, and stretched like a cat and then turned, trotting daintily along the trail ahead of her with the bushy tail and white fur tip as a beacon whispering for Jo to come that way. Maureen loved foxes. If her forest offered one as a guide, it was safe to follow.

The vixen froze in midstride, cocking her ears. She bounced sideways, stiff-legged, and then snapped at something between her paws. Jo heard bones crunching. The fox swallowed, shook herself, and then trotted along the trail as if nothing had happened.

Jo shivered. No, the forest was not safe. This *land* was not safe. Death lurked behind that rock over there, a grin on his skull and scythe at the ready, waiting for her to make a mistake. But somehow, knowing that made her feel more alive than ever. Her skin tingled.

Golden light outlined the leaves, and she heard voices in the breeze rustling overhead. Maureen's trees guarded Jo, guarded this trail. And a truck could have splattered her any time she crossed a street in Naskeag Falls. *Life* was dangerous. Invariably fatal.

Jo glanced back over her shoulder. The trail vanished behind her as she walked, turning back into tangled wilderness. She knew that was the face the forest would show to a stranger or an enemy. Which face would David see?

<The Singer opens his own path.>

*Yeah. But does that path come anywhere close to me?*

And that thought brought her into a clearing, grass leading down to a brook that laughed of trout and otters. Maureen and Brian stood over a woman crouching on the near bank, and a dragon bulked huge on the far edge of the woods. Next to the dragon . . .

"David!"

They met halfway, the sun glowing exactly warm enough and the air sweet, details like him setting down a heavy cage and her leaping from stone to stone across the brook tossed off by bodies running on autopilot while the brains focused on more important things. She drank in the smell of him and the lean hardness of his body enfolding hers, the fire of his lips. Had she been downplaying sex? Damnfool thought.

But this place was a little too public for her taste. Wouldn't want to shock the dragon. She pulled back and stared into his eyes.

"I'm sorry." There, she'd said it, blanket statement covering a multitude of sins. Next step was *acting* on it.

Then she saw his pain. He winced and slackened his hold, favoring his left arm. The Healer inside her saw the ripped sleeve, the dark blood clotting there, the aura of infection, and grabbed hold of her.

Slashed wounds and punctures, livid skin spreading from them and blackness starting to fringe the cut lips. Her fingers traced the edges, listening to his body. *Infection, yes, and a nasty one.* She remembered the buzz and reek of it, killing that small strange man in the tower. The same germs, the same kind of wounds, bite or claw slash or cut. But this had barely started. She almost smiled.

Her hands ran up his arm, inside the torn sleeve, and ripped it like tissue paper all the way to his armpit and then circled his shoulder, tracing the skin, feeling the heat of the germs warring with the antibodies in his blood, finding the end of them. Fingertip to fingertip, thumb to thumb, her hands ringed his arm and squeezed gently. *Toothpaste in a tube,* she thought, *run the fingers down the tube and bring all the paste to the end and squeeze it out.*

His arm trembled under her touch, and she felt his muscles bunching from the pain, but he didn't pull back. He trusted her.

He needed her. *Her,* not just her body.

Her hands reached his fingers, followed each out to the tip and nail, and then retraced the path to the slashed wounds on his forearm. Foul yellow-green slime dripped from the raw meat there, and she tore the wrecked sleeve into pads to mop it up. Her touch left shiny scar tissue behind, purple with new-grown skin but clean and cool and pure.

The healing dragged strength out of her and left a strange calm ecstasy behind, Zen satori or Sufi trance or some other kind of mystical exhaustion. God flowed through her hands.

She laid her palms on either side of his forearm, feeling her way deep into the muscles and tendons, asking them about lurking death or hidden damage. All seemed well.

White ringed his eyes and his lips, but he smiled. He shook his hand, gently at first, and then flexed his fingers into a fist to remind him of what his forearm *should* feel like. He captured her hands and kissed them, and Jo felt the thrill up her arms and down into her belly.

And then her knees gave up on her and she thumped down on her butt in the soft grass. The forest pulsed around her, in and out as if she saw the clearing through a zoom lens hunting for the proper framing of a picture. David knelt beside her, tender hands cradling her cheeks, fear replacing the wonder that had replaced the pain on his face.

She waved the fear away. "Long day. 'M okay. Just tired. Done a lot."

"Jo . . . your father . . ."

"Had to happen. Should have happened years ago. Rabid dog."

She closed her eyes and sank against his chest, letting the warmth and strength of him enfold her. Support her. *That's* what this pairing thing was all about. Not just sex. David made her stronger. If they worked right, pairs grew rather than shrank. Not like Daddy's vampire act, sucking life from Mom to fill his own emptiness.

<I smell you.>

That voice in her head . . . Jo cringed and broke loose from David's warmth and the soft kitten-purr of her own comfort, staring up at razor-edged obsidian scales and a huge yellow slit-pupil eye staring back. They plunged her back into the terror of the *other* dragon. This had to be the mate, freed from its master's power and seeking blood . . .

David's arms tightened around her, calming and protecting. "That's a formal greeting, not a threat. Jo, this is the poet Khe'sha. He's decided to add our song to the dragon-sagas, rather than feed us to his brood."

<I hear your name, Cynthia Josephine Pierce. No dragon would eat a Healer. Most certainly, no dragon would eat a Singer or his mate.>

"Pleased to meet you." Jo tried hard not to stare at the long serrated teeth within arm's-reach. She tried hard not to gag, as well. *This* dragon had halitosis thick enough to wilt the grass for ten yards around. But she was sure that puking would be seen as bad manners, even in draconic society.

*Poet? Dinosaurs were poets?*

<Our songs are our lives. The Singer gave me your songs and showed why blood came between us. Where there is no choice, there is no guilt.>

The huge head swung away from her, to stare at Brian and Maureen and the woman crouched between them. <Guilt comes from choosing evil. I would eat that one, instead. But it still holds my young in danger.>

Maureen cocked her head. "*Does* it now?" she drawled, with a hard edge to her voice. "And I thought we had a bargain." She stared down at the woman at her feet, drew back her foot, and kicked. Her toes stopped a scant inch from the woman's belly.

Jo shuddered. Maureen had always had that edge of suppressed rage, but this seemed a little too calm and calculated. Sadistic. Then Jo listened to the forest around them, and it approved. It knew more about the scene than she did. It hated that woman. It would have done far worse.

The woman squirmed on the ground, curled around her

stomach as if protecting a wound. Maureen tilted her head to the other side and drew her foot back again, aiming. "Release those hatchlings, or *die! Now!*"

The woman fought for breath. "Your word. Your word . . . that I can . . . leave . . . the forest."

"If the dragons live, you live. If they die, you die. Release them!"

"Your . . . word."

Maureen barked a harsh laugh. "You lie as easily as you breathe, and just as often. You want my word of honor? Okay, *love,* you've got it. If you release those dragons and they are alive, you have *my* word that the forest will let you live. It doesn't want to, but it will."

The woman slumped limp on the grass, mumbled a few words, and shook her head as if that movement took all the strength she had left. "They're free. Still asleep, but alive and free. If they die before I leave the forest, it isn't any fault of mine."

Brian looked skeptical. He knelt, that heavy knife of his ready in one hand, and touched his other to the woman's forehead. He squinted, concentrating, the moment stretching into a minute or more, and then nodded.

"They're free. She doesn't hold anything now, dragons or trees or fields or people."

Jo tested the thread of binding that she'd followed. It sat limp in her hand, dissolving even as she tested it.

<I go.>

And the dragon slipped between the trees, a black streak glittering in the scattered shafts of sun. Jo blinked and it was gone. How could something that large move that silently and fast? Newfound friend or not, it sent shivers down her spine.

Something odd in the scene . . . she'd spotted David, zeroed in on him, and the rest had vanished from her thoughts. Jo gasped as her brain finally analyzed the impossible thing her eyes had been telling her all along. The fox now lay curled around a newborn baby, protecting it and suckling it, giving the magic of the wildwood as milk.

But the fox was the spirit of Maureen's forest . . . *Maureen's* baby? Had time slipped a cog again? Jo had become an aunt while her back was turned? Nine months lost at right angles to her life?

Maureen seemed to read her thoughts, or at least the sudden focus of her eyes. "It's Fiona's, Fiona's and Brian's. She wanted a weapon, not a baby. She was going to kill it for the Power in its blood. She'll never touch this child again, or have another."

Well, *that* explained the rage and the kick. The woman . . . Fiona, *Sean's* twin . . . stirred and glared up at Maureen. Jo winced at the hatred on that face, and suddenly realized that the woman was naked from the waist down, lying in blood and mess. She'd just given birth. No wonder the baby seemed so small and . . . well, *ugly.* Wrinkled, purple, scrawny, head still squashed out of shape—a face only a mother could love.

Fiona spat at Maureen's feet. "Let it suck your Power, then. Ask your dragon poet about the curse of children. That thing will weaken you for years."

Maureen shook her head. "And that's a problem? You haven't learned *anything.* Power scares me. I've got too fucking much of it for safety."

This was a Maureen that Jo had never seen before, calm, self-confident, strong. And sober, even though the sister Jo knew would have had to be stone drunk to stand there like she owned the world and feared no part of it.

*Something* had changed, Jo was certain. Maureen must have exorcised a major demon. They needed to have a sisterly giggle-fest and late-night whisper, like she remembered when they were girls sharing a bedroom.

Have to find out what Brian had been up to, as well. He sported a black eye and bandages on *his* arm, blood soaked his side, and he seemed to be favoring one leg. He was still standing, but knight-errantry looked like a rough trade. As far as she was concerned, David should stick to poetry.

Maureen turned back to the woman on the grass. "Okay. Playtime's over. Grab your pants and move your sorry ass. You've got your life. I never promised freedom. I place the forest as a guard on you, an endless maze like your own hedge. You'll find food, and drink, and a dry place to sleep if your dreams let you, but you'll never leave. The trees will kill you if you try. I gave you *my* word, not theirs, and they are doing me a favor. They don't fucking *like* you. Don't push it."

Fiona crawled over to a pile of cloth, dragged it to the stream, and rinsed it and wrung the water out before pulling it on. She staggered to her feet, moaning and clutching at her stomach.

Jo's sister frowned and shook her head. "Cut the crap. We know you're stronger than that. These days, even *human* mothers get kicked out of the hospital the same day they give birth. *Walk!* The forest will show you where it wants you to go, and Shadow's going to be following you. I think he's hungry."

<One still questions whether this is fit to eat.>

A huge black cat, Jo thought it was a jaguar or something similar, formed out of the shadow of a tree. It stood and stretched lazily before strolling across the clearing.

The dark witch straightened up, glared at each of the others in turn, and gritted her teeth as if she was biting back a curse only because she lacked the Power to make it stick. She turned and walked away, limping but steady, seeming to gain a trace of strength with each step. Her head lifted, defiance stiffening her spine and shoulders.

Maureen watched until Fiona reached the edge of the meadow. "And if you think you can escape by walking between the worlds, the forest knows how to trap stronger Blood than yours. Remember the legends of Nimue and Merlin."

Fiona's shoulders slumped, and she turned halfway back. Then she shuddered and walked on. The woman and the cat vanished under the trees.

Maureen stared after her, shrugged, and shook her head, as if wondering if she'd made a mistake by honoring her word. Then she turned to Brian.

"You came back."

"I didn't mean to leave in the first place."

"Yeah. Well, you could have left a goddamn *note*." She bit back words and swallowed.

Then her face softened. "Sorry. I think we need to have a long talk with Father Oak. *Both* of us need to make some changes in our lives. You're a family man now, with responsibilities."

He winced. Then Maureen smiled at him slowly, seductively. "And I haven't had a fucking drink in"—she checked her watch—"at least forty hours, and I really could use a little positive reinforcement." She tugged on Brian's arm, the one *without* the bandage, and they limped off into the woods with the baby.

Jo blinked. It looked like Maureen had finally figured out why men existed. Speaking of which . . .

Warm sun, soft grass, a man, an empty clearing. Jo lay back in the grass, tugging David down beside her. He lifted one eyebrow but didn't put up much resistance.

"We need to talk about a bunch of stuff."

"Later." She ran her fingertips up and down his left arm, the closest bit she could get her hands on.

"Maureen wants us to take over the castle, as soon as they figure out how to break some kind of curse on it. She hates the place. Wants to live in the forest." He sounded positive, as if he'd found his own kind of balance with this land of magic.

"We've got more important things to discuss than castles." She closed his lips with her own and rolled over on top of him, sinking into the kiss.

<We'll tell the cats not to wait up.>

Jo blinked her eyes open. The clearing wasn't *quite* empty. The fox seemed to be laughing again. It winked at her, turned, and trotted off into the forest.

Celtic myth and magic from
critically-acclaimed author
# James A. Hetley

# *Summer Country*

0-441-01220-5

Maureen discovers that her lineage goes
back to the sorcerers of Camelot—and now she
must travel through the Summer Country to
claim her birthright.

"Like an old Irish whiskey—dark and smoky,
abounding in flavor and detail...all the things
a good novel should be."
—Charles de Lint

"Hetley combines Celtic legend with
modern-day psychological suspense to produce
a hybrid fantasy reminiscent of
Charles de Lint and Tanya Huff."
—*Library Journal*

Now in Paperback

# Coming December 2005 from Ace

## The King Imperiled
by Deborah Chester
0-441-01353-8

The saga that began with the acclaimed *The Sword, The Ring, and The Chalice* trilogy continues with a new story of King Faldain and his warrior queen.

## Age of Conan: The Venom of Luxur
by J. Steven York
0-441-01345-7

The exciting conclusion of the *Age of Conan, Anok, Heretic of Stygia* trilogy.

## Beyond Singularity
edited by Jack Dann and Gardner Dozois
0-441-01363-5

Fourteen original visions of a future where man is an endangered species.

## Coyote Rising
by Allen Steele
0-441-01251-5

The epic of Earth's first space colonists continues.

## The Decoy Princess
by Dawn Cook
0-441-01355-4

A princess discovers she's not really royalty, but just a decoy in the first in an all-new series.